# VISIONS V

## Books from Lillicat Publishers

### Visions Series
Visions: Leaving Earth (2014)
Visions II: Moons of Saturn (2015)
Visions III: Inside the Kuiper Belt (2015)
Visions IV: Space Between Stars (May 2016)
Visions V: Milky Way (August 2016)
Visions VI: Galaxies (November 2016)

The Future Is Short: Science Fiction in a Flash (2014)

Sunshine & Shadow: Memories from a Long Life (2014)

# VISIONS V

## MILKY WAY

EDITED BY

## CARROL FIX

LILLICAT PUBLISHERS
USA

# VISIONS V
## MILKY WAY

Milky Way Galaxy
Credit: NASA/ESA

# Contents

STEPPING STONES TO ETERNITY.............................XI
INTRODUCTION...................................................1
SHIPS IN THE NIGHT...........................................5
    *JAY WERKHEISER*
END AROUND.....................................................19
    *E. J. SHUMAK*
UNWANTED GIFTS...............................................37
    *S.M. KRAFTCHAK*
WHERE THE LAST TRAMZ STOPS........................57
    *SAM BELLOTTO JR.*
CLAIM JUMPERS.................................................81
    *DOUG C. SOUZA*
BLACK HEARTS AND BLUE SKINS.........................109
    *TIMOTHY PAUL*
GREATCLOAK.....................................................129
    *JONATHAN SHIPLEY*
THE DEVICE......................................................149
    *TARA CAMPBELL*
EIGHTEEN WINTERS...........................................175
    *D. A. COUTURIER*
YELLOW STAR...................................................197
    *JOHN MORALEE*
THE SHADOW OF A DEAD GOD.............................223
    *LEIGH KIMMEL*
WELCOME TO YOUR DREAM HOUSE.....................239
    *STEVE BATES*
PAN AD ASTER.................................................255
    *BRUCE C. DAVIS*
RACHEL'S FALL.................................................265
    *TERESA HOWARD*
WHEN UNKNOWN GODS LEAVE.............................279
    *MARGARET KARMAZIN*
FIRST SUNRISE.................................................293
    *MARIE MICHAELS*
DROPWORLD.....................................................309
    *FREDRICK OBERMEYER*
BRIGHT HORIZON...............................................327
    *TOM OLBERT*
THE MIRROR DIALOGUES.....................................355
    *RICHARD ZWICKER*
THE DRIVE.......................................................373
    *W. A. FIX*
ABOUT THE EDITOR...........................................405

# STEPPING STONES TO ETERNITY

The *Visions* series tells the story of how humanity must ultimately venture outward from our tiny home and explore the Universe.

*Visions: Leaving Earth,* the first volume, describes our first faltering steps to rise from Earth's surface and build homes in space.

*Visions II: Moons of Saturn* confirms that humankind has left the Earth and is at home in the other planetary systems of our solar system.

*Visions III: Inside the Kuiper Belt* proclaims humankind's domination of all that dwells within the solar system—from our Sun to the outermost reaches of the Kuiper Belt.

*Visions IV: Space Between Stars* astounds us with the infinite possibilities of adventure and danger far from any suns or planets—in the cold, dark regions of deepest space.

*Visions V: Milky Way* leads us to explore our own galaxy. Although vast and unreachable with current technology, the Milky Way is but a tiny point in the Universe. We must first learn about our own home galaxy before we can go even further outward to other galaxies.

Beyond these volumes, we will explore other *Galaxies* and the *Universe.*

Our vision is limitless.

# Introduction

*Visions V* stories take place somewhere—anywhere—in the Milky Way Galaxy. Planets, stars, and aliens, with no limitations, form the subject and action taking place outside our Solar System and within the Milky Way.

Humankind has forded the immense stream of space between stars and reached our nearest solar neighbors. What will we discover on hospitable planets circling those new stars? Will we find almost familiar moons, asteroids, planetary rings? Or, could there be never before seen astronomical formations? The sky is no longer the limit for our soaring imaginations, because somewhere out there is a potential haven for the remnants of our beleaguered civilization.

Global catastrophe is a constant threat for our war-torn and dysfunctional human race. No one can foresee the future, but we have lived on the brink of extinction since the invention of the atomic bomb and, more recently, with germ warfare and genetic manipulation.

Astrophysicist Professor Stephen Hawking has said, "I believe that the long term future of the human race must be space and that it represents an important life insurance for our future survival, as it could prevent the disappearance of humanity by colonizing other planets."

The vast Milky Way Galaxy may allow the seeds of our future to be widely distributed, past the danger of a final extinction.

*Visions V: Milky Way* brings together a collection of fascinating and entertaining stories by award-winning science fiction authors.

*The Editor honors differences in international writing styles by leaving most spellings and conventions as the author prefers. No matter where you are reading this, please keep in mind that typos and misspellings could be variations in regional interpretations of the English language.*

Carrol Fix
Editor
Lillicat Publishers
June 20, 2016

*Isolated communities on a frontier long for news from elsewhere. When that frontier is space, elsewhere can be awfully far away in space and time, and the tales told by traveling strangers may have a grander scope than anyone suspects.*

# SHIPS IN THE NIGHT

### By

### *Jay Werkheiser*

"Whatcho drinkin', offworlder?"

Well, the guy sure ended the awkward silence stage quickly. Conversations stifled by my arrival resumed in hushed voices. He appraised me with his eyes and apparently found me wanting. I put on my (hopefully) disarming grin and asked, "What do you guys brew around here?"

"White ale."

"What's it made from?"

"The hell do I look like, a botanist?"

"Calm down, Zhake." The bartender stared him down, then turned his attention to me. "It's fermented from a gen-modded rice hybrid."

I nodded to the bartender. "I'll try it."

"Aincho never been on Nouvelle Terre before?"

"It's been a few generations in your frame. Most of the population was still living in orbital habs."

Zhake grunted. "Last ship came by, I was just a boy. Wasn't yours, then."

"Nope. Mine does a high-c circuit, long trips and heavy time dilation."

5

The bartender plunked a glass in front of me. The nearly colorless liquid foamed like beer and had a similar aroma. I took a long draught, savoring the flavor and texture. I nodded. "It's good." I swallowed another gulp and put the half full glass on the bar.

Zhake cracked a grin. "Yer all right, for an offworlder."

"This is the best part," I said. "Sampling what new worlds have to offer. New cultures, new sights, new tastes."

"Yeah?"

"Like on New Hope, where they make a minty liqueur distilled from the blood of some sort of mushroom-shaped trees."

"Uh, blood?"

"It's complicated." I glanced around and noticed a handful of nearby patrons had turned their attention to us. I downed the remainder of my drink and pounded the glass onto the bar just a bit too loudly. A moment's eye-lock with the bartender sent him scurrying for another.

"Where else you been?"

"Anyplace that has a high-c particle cannon. Like Haven, where they use meat with reversed proteins. Has the sweetest aftertaste, but you can't eat much, and you need to take an enzyme pill with it."

"So it's true, then. You spacers live your whole lives wandering the stars, never putting down roots." He brushed the idea away with his hand. "That ain't no kind of life."

"The colony worlds are like the city states of ancient times, separated by vast tracts of wilderness. Travelers and traders are what held them together, made them a civilization."

"Helluva wilderness to cross."

I held my newly-filled glass aloft. "This is what makes the long trips worthwhile."

Zhake squinted at me. "Must be boring."

"Usually is. But there was this one time—" I took another long pull from the glass.

"What happened?"

I looked at the growing crowd sheepishly. "Ah, nothing. I shouldn't say anything."

"What? An engine malf? Pinged by a pebble at high-c?"

"Nah, nothing like that. It was a pretty normal flight; it was just luck we noticed it at all."

"Noticed what?"

"Well, I do in-flight nav, which is pretty boring because the particle beam does all the aiming, and we can't really steer much at high-c." I noticed that the conversations had again quieted and every eye was on me. "I mostly take parallax measurements of nearby stars to make sure we're on course."

"What did you see?"

I took another gulp of the fizzy drink, savoring its light, dry flavor. "This particular run took us past two red dwarf systems, within a couple light years of each. UV Ceti and Lacaille something or other."

"Nothing special about red dwarfs. No colonies at any of 'em."

"Actually, old Earth only ever sent unmanned probes to a few of them. Theory is, planets would have to be too close to the star to get enough warmth. That close, you'd get problems like tidal locking and radiation from flares."

His face slacked as he tried to follow me. "No sense wasting probes, then."

I nodded. "These two were just as dull as you'd expect. The first of them was a binary, redshifting to the rear right on schedule by my math. I reached for my tab to log the spec data, and I must have bumped the spectroscope with my elbow. I didn't know it at the time, but I

7

jostled it off target by an arcsec or two. My apprentice Dar found it on the next shift."

I filled my bulb from the coffee tap and settled into an empty seat. Most of the crew slept during 4-shift, so the lounge was quiet. I unrolled my tab, ready to do a little reading, when it buzzed. I tapped the comm app and said, "What's up, Dar?"

"I've got a heavy blueshift on the spec." Her voice warbled with insecurity. "What should I do?"

"Damn it, kid," I said, "you're aimed at the wrong star. If you've been drinking on shift again—"

"I'm clean, Brad. Honest. I got UV Ceti centered in the sighting scope."

"It's a close binary. Did you subtract out the orbital Doppler?"

"This isn't my first trip, you know."

"Second. You're still a newb."

"Well, whatever this is, it's blueshifted hot. Like point six c. In our frame."

"Jeez. That can't be right." I let out a long breath. "Okay, I'll be up."

The instrument blister was attached to the cargo ring, which doesn't rotate like the hab ring. It was a short trip up the access tube to the hub, then back out the cargo tube to the blister. Dar was floating next to the spec mount, looking sheepish.

"This better be good," I said.

"Take a look, Brad."

I peered at the spec screen. "Jeez, Dar, those are ionized helium-4 lines. You're not even aimed at UV Ceti."

"That's just it, Brad. What the hell *am* I looking at?"

I didn't have an answer for that. I looked through the sighting scope. There was UV Ceti, right in the middle where it belonged. I zoomed tighter, and again. "Hello there. What are you?"

"What is it, Brad?"

"I don't know." I unrolled my tab and tapped the captain. "Hey Mehgen, I got something you should see."

She came on, voice only, her words slow and groggy. "Better be important."

"I got something strange near UV Ceti."

"Who gives a rat's ass?"

"It's a tiny point of light, hot and fast, coming toward us."

"Flare?"

"Not at high relativistic speed. Can you turn the big scope on it?"

"Let me check with Kam. Meet me in the lounge in an hour."

I rolled my tab and turned my attention to Dar. "Keep your eyes on it."

I headed back to the lounge and tried to focus on the novel I'd picked up on Haven. I stared at the same few paragraphs until the captain arrived. She opened a screen on the table in front of me without a word.

"What am I looking at?"

"Your annoying little spark. Look closely." She slid her fingers across the screen, zooming on an intense white smudge. "See that dark spot in the middle?"

"Yeah."

"It's a ship."

"Wait a minute." Zhake's eyes narrowed. "Who the hell would go to a red dwarf? Ain't nothin' there."

I let my lips curl into a small grin. "We didn't know at first." I took another long drink. "What do you think it was?"

He rubbed his chin for a long moment. "Some idiot lost his way looking for one of the colony worlds?"

"Nah, their courses are plotted by the particle beamers." The voice came from behind Zhake, in the crowd that had gathered around us.

I nodded. "Now there's another clue. They weren't flying by particle beam. They were using fusion."

"Right, the helium spec."

"Maybe one of those old robot probes," Zhake said. "They used some kind of fusion thrusters back in those days."

Another voice from the crowd said, "But they couldn't get close to high-c."

"Ghost ship." I spun my head to stare at the bartender, who stood, arms folded, defending his statement with stoic silence.

I emptied my glass, giving the crowd time to think about it. "What makes you say that?"

"Old guy worked here years back used to tell stories he'd heard from spacers in his day. Stories from before we had the high-c particle beams, about explorers setting out from old Earth in fusion ships. About a lost expedition, never heard from, maybe wandering the stars to this day."

I stared at my empty glass for a moment. "We thought about that too. But here's the kicker. After a couple dozen shifts, we had enough info to plot their course."

Zhake spoke up, his voice hushed. "They were coming after you?"

"Nah. They were heading for Lacaille what's-its-number."

"From one red dwarf to another? Nobody does that."

"No human," I said.

"Aliens?" Mehgen stared me in the eye. "You're telling me it's an alien ship?"

"You have a better guess? One that explains their flight path? The fusion signature no human ship has ever used? The high-c speed no recorded fusion ship has ever reached?"

"Why didn't anyone ever see them before? We're not even carrying any real scientific instruments."

"No one's ever looked," I said. "No one cares about stars without colonies. It was just dumb luck our spec was aimed at the wrong place at the right time."

She blew out a long breath. "Okay, say I buy into your theory. What do you suggest we do?"

"Contact them, of course!"

"How?"

I met her steely eyes and realized that she knew I hadn't thought it through. I got up to refill my coffee bulb to buy time. The empty light flashed. "Damn it." The damned thing mocked me, blinking on and off. Blinking.

*Aha!*

"We can aim the signal laser across their path. Modulate the beam in, I don't know, prime numbers or whatever they do in alien invasion vids."

Her eyebrows arched just a bit. "Not a bad idea. We should be able to project their position, assuming they maintain a constant acceleration. Might be easier to aim while their proper motion is still relatively small. Closer they get—" Her gaze went distant.

I knew better than to disturb her, so I set about refilling the coffee. When I finished, I found that she had left the lounge.

Things happen slowly on a high-c transit. Calibrating and aiming the laser, deciding what to transmit, waiting for the signal to get there and back, and before you know it, nearly a year had passed. Light can seem very slow sometimes.

Shipboard routine drifted back to its equilibrium state. I finally finished that novel, and the shifts melted away. I was putting in my treadmill time during a 5-shift when Mehgen tapped me. "Get up to the instrument blister."

"Dar's on duty."

"Your aliens got the message."

"How do you . . . never mind, I'll be right up."

I was up the nearest access tube and out to the cargo ring before I even had time to process the information. *First contact!*

"What's going on?"

"Good, you're here." Mehgen pointed to the sighting scope. "Take a look."

UV Ceti had long since faded to the rear, so the alien ship was an intense spark against the dark background. Except now it was a streak rather than a dot.

"What happened?"

"They turned," Mehgen said.

"They're changing course mid-flight?"

"Pics from the big scope should be coming in soon but yeah, we're pretty sure they're moving closer to us."

"How close?"

"It'll take a while to track their new course."

"Wait, they were coming right atcha?"

"Nah. It's not easy to change direction at high-c. They did more than we could, a few degrees deflection, but the best they could manage was a quarter light year at closest approach."

"How close is that?"

"Maybe fifteen, twenty kilo-AU."

"That doesn't help."

"Let's just say we still needed the scope."

The bartender slid a plate onto the bar in front of me. "It's a sampler. Thought you'd like to try some of the foods we have around here."

"Thanks." I picked up a deep fried strip of something starchy and bit into it, savoring the complex flavors.

"What I'm wondering," the bartender said with a suspicious squint, "is how they got up to high-c using fusion."

I met his gaze. "We figured it was a fusion ramjet."

He nodded. "Heard of them. Old Earth never could get them to work right."

"Looks like these beings did."

"So what happened?" Zhake asked.

"Like I said, things happen slow on the high-c circuits. It was another few dozen shifts before we knew there was a problem."

"What kinda problem?"

"Well, they'd been taking themselves off course to come check us out. Sooner or later they had to head back toward Lacaille."

"What, they turned around too soon? Never got close?"

I sampled a tiny pastry filled with some sort of ground meat. "Too late, as it turned out."

"How was that a problem for you?"

"They were using fusion engines, remember?"

"Ah," the bartender said. "You were in their exhaust plume."

"I don't see why it's a problem," Dar said. "Our shielding can handle cosmic radiation at high-c. Can't be worse than that."

I slammed my coffee bulb onto the table. "Most of our shielding comes from the plume of ions from the particle cannon. That's in front of us. The alien's exhaust is coming in from the side."

"Yeah, but we have magnetospheric shielding, too."

"Sure. And what happens when all those exhaust particles get dumped into the plasma at once?"

"Uh . . . it heats up?"

"You did manage to learn something."

"So the captain is worried about the ship overheating?"

I blew out a sigh. "No, no, no. Plasma leaks away too quickly at higher temp, and we don't have enough gas on hand to replace it."

"That's why the captain has been bitchy lately."

"What do you mean lately?" I gave her a mischievous grin.

"How can you joke around? We're going to die."

"Or at least glow in the dark."

She huffed.

"Don't get your pressure seals undone. We'll come up with something."

Something is a rather vague thing, though, in the face of the very concrete mortal danger looming. Before long, nerves frayed and tempers flared. I found my playful jabs at Dar becoming less and less playful. Then one particular 3-shift, Dar interrupted me in the instrument blister.

"Hey Brad, I have an idea."

"Dammit kid, can't I just serve my duty shift in peace for once?"

"Just listen." She swung her arm in anger, setting herself into a slow rotation.

I laughed.

"Don't be an ass."

"All right, what's your big idea?"

"Their ramjet uses a giant electromagnetic field, right? So why don't we use our magnetosphere to push on it? Plasma produces a magnetic—"

"Won't work. They're not nearly close enough for that."

"But you said their ramjet field had to be huge."

"Not that big." I laughed again. "What made you think . . . wait, are you crying?"

She swatted at her eyes. "No. I'm fine."

"Look, I'm sorry. I know I've been—"

"Aren't you terrified?"

"Hell yeah. Believe me, I would have been thrilled if you were right."

"I can't handle just sitting and waiting. I want to do something, even if I have to throw ions at them by hand."

My back went rigid. "Throw ions. That's brilliant!"

"What?"

"The ion beam that's pushing us. From the particle cannon back on Haven. If we can deflect it, we can send all those ions into their magnetic field. That should push them away.

Hope flashed on her face for the first time in far too long. "Will that work?"

"We won't change their path much, but we only need a couple of arcsecs."

"Tap the captain right away!"


"So that's it?" Zhake's eyes narrowed suspiciously.

"The actual doing of it wasn't interesting. An engineer did a few calculations, a programmer wrote a quick app, Mehgen pushed a few buttons."

"But you didn't get to talk to them?"

"Who, the aliens? We didn't even get a good look at the ship. They passed too fast, too far away."

"So you never found out why they did it? Why they threatened you?"

"Threatened? We just assumed that they didn't know we were in danger."

"How could they not know?"

"They didn't use a particle beam to reach high-c, so they didn't have an ion plume to protect them from cosmic rays. Maybe they didn't need it. Maybe they figured we didn't either."

"Humph. That's a lot of supposin'."

"I suppose so. I'd rather believe that than the alternative."

The bartender spoke up. "That there's aliens out there who would rather kill than talk."

I nodded, looking down into my mug. "Lander'll be launching soon." I downed the last of my brew and stood. "Thanks for the hospitality."

I took my time walking back to the lander. The ale had put a bit of a wobble in my step. I absorbed the scenery, mostly gen-modded Earth life and prefab habs. My last view of a living world for a couple years.

Yes, it was like an ancient village on old Earth, isolated, self-sufficient, and surrounded by a vast wilderness. Only this wilderness was vaster and more barren than the ancients could have imagined. Isolated civilizations stagnate.

The lander's cargo bay doors were still open, and a familiar form tinkered at the entrance.

"Hey, Daria," I said. "You ever heard of fusion ramjets?"

"I'm not a newb."

"You think you could deflect one with ions from the particle beam?"

"Ha. Particle density's way too low. Even if you could, recoil would push you out from behind your shielding ion plume. Whatever gave you that idea?"

"Just talking with the locals."

"That's all you ever do."

"We're modern day minstrels, Daria, wandering from community to—"

"Yeah, yeah. Planting the seeds. Curiosity and exploration."

"Go ahead, scoff. We'll be gone for centuries subjective. These people, their descendents will explore beyond the few meager colonized star systems. If not them, the people of Haven, or New Hope, or—"

"Get aboard and help with the preflight checks."

I sighed. "Sure thing."

Who knows what they might find out there?

Generations flash by in but a few years subjective on the circuit, but those years will peel away shift by interminable shift. Sometimes high-c travel feels slow.

*Jay Werkheiser teaches chemistry and physics to high school students, where he often finds inspiration for stories in classroom discussions. Not surprisingly, his stories often deal with alien biochemistry, weird physics, and their effects on the people who interact with them. Many of his stories have appeared in* Analog Science Fiction and Fact, *with others scattered among several other science fiction magazines and anthologies. You can follow him on twitter @JayWerkheiser or read his (much neglected) blog at http://jaywerkheiser.blogspot.com/.*

*"Ships in the Night" was previously published in the June 2015 issue of* Analog Science Fiction and Fact.

Bersim only wanted to raise her kits in peace. They lost her husband, forcing her return to active duty but in the company of the same alien species that had her husband.

# END AROUND

## By

### *E. J. Shumak*

The setting moons matched the yellow glory of the new pride, spilled out like honey among the purple grass. One of the kits lying close by their mother nipped an ear a bit too playfully. Cuffed hard, she tumbled across the grassland. Righting herself, she shook her head violently and looked back at Mother, offended.

"You bite your sire like that and you'll have claw tips to pluck from your cheek," said Bersim.

"Mom, I was just playin', you never mind Mohlan bitin' you."

"He is male and must be allowed his aggressions. You are a huntress and must learn restraint. Mohlan need not learn restraint, he will have his size."

The lecture cut short by the roar of a surface flitter, as it landed near the den. The kits leaped up, their feet churning wildly before their claws could gain purchase in the soft grass.

"Daddy, Daddy," they screamed, running to the landing pad, but this was not their sire's flitter. A black and gold Pride Authority craft, with two stern looking females aboard, landed smoothly. The kits froze halfway to the flitter, then skittered into the den. Bersim stalked by, ears at half-mast and teeth bared in what could never be described as a smile. This flitter would land here for only one reason: something happened to Togar, her mate.

The flitter settled and the combination hatch and ramp-way snapped open. A large female pride council adjutant, in combat black uniform, stood at the corner of the landing pad waiting for Bersim.

"State your business, Adjutant," ordered Bersim.

"I have pride authority information to pass, with supporting documentation. You are requested to accompany us once this message is delivered. I have a keeper for the kits."

"You may approach," said Bersim, "I will judge your sincerity."

The adjutant approached Bersim and, unsheathing her claws, placed her hands on Bersim's shoulders. Facing her, Bersim did the same.

"As our ancestors judged truth pass between them, let it be so now as I speak. Bersim, your mate is dead. You are needed to identify the body and speak for his spirit. He died fighting alongside fifty-three other brothers and sisters at the Heshnes port. A rogue Vorlatin ship came in and the port is half destroyed."

Blood swelled beneath the adjutant's tunic as Bersim squeezed the adjutant's shoulders and let out a pain-filled rowl. The adjutant's ears went flat, as blood slowly splattered onto the tarmac of the landing pad.

"Truth sister, I feel it," said Bersim as she disengaged her claws from the adjutant's shoulder. "I'll accompany you, but first I must speak to the keeper and Togar's kits."

Bersim, motioning for the keeper to follow, walked into the den great room. It appeared empty—the kits hidden safely in shelter pockets.

"Kits, come forward," ordered Bersim. Suddenly, as if from nowhere, four golden speckled kits appeared in the center of the great room, ears back and heads bent to the side, exposing their throats to their mother.

"Kits, your sire is dead. Togar is no more. This is your keeper. You will address her by no other name as she is of our pride. She will have full authority over you, as I must be gone for a period of time. I know not how long. Understand this authority is not limited and includes her sending you to join your sire, if required. Yes, kits, your sire is dead. I go now to work on substantiation and you go now to his honor mourning. The keeper will lead you on the proper trail to honor your father."

Bersim spun and disappeared, before the kits could absorb what had happened. Bersim would not risk the kits seeing her tears.

The flitter rose with a roar and Bersim turned to the adjutant, "I've served twenty years on a patrol ship. I take one lousy year to have kits and you couldn't let me keep my mate with me, could you? But you come running to take over my life when you manage to get him killed," Bersim's ears flattened against her head fur. The adjutant remained silent with her eyes focused forward. "I better get more information, once we get to Heshnes."

"Truly sister, it is all I am authorized to convey. I am but repeating a message I would prefer never to have heard."

The rest of the short flight to the space port remained silent. They covered over two hundred miles at nearly eight hundred miles per hour. The flitter swung about as they left the atmosphere. The port came into sight, giving Bersim her first view of the damage. Her indrawn hiss made her sentiment evident.

Whole sections of the huge station remained exposed to the vacuum of space, and merchant ships, alongside military cruisers, sat decimated. They made no effort to discriminate between military and civilian targets. Avoiding pieces of ships, mixed with dock sections and bodies, made the landing difficult and dangerous.

"They actually landed, sister. Storm troopers swarmed over the docks for half an hour. The egg-eaters used projectile and laser weapons!"

Bersim unbuckled her harness and watched as the open landing bay came even with their flitter. The flitter settled on the pad inside and the bay doors closed behind them. Bersim could no longer hold back her tears. As they waited for the dock to pressurize with the bay, the adjutant turned to her.

"Sister, I feel for your loss. Though I have no mate, I lost three sub-pride group members in this attack. May the path open before you."

Bersim unlatched the flitter's dome when the pressurization light switched to blue. She hopped down from the unit. "We will meet again under other circumstances, sister. Your concern will not be forgotten."

Just on the other side of the dock airlock, Bersim noted another pride adjutant, this one a large, seasoned male. His ears went three quarters back in greeting and he nodded slightly.

"Bersim, I am Eslor. I will accompany you to the temporary station offices."

Bersim followed Eslor. Her claws clicked on the decking as they walked—she could not keep them sheathed. They went past the old station offices and Bersim saw only a new dock seal, blocking off what now apparently opened to the vacuum of space.

They came to the blue residential area; emptied of residents, it now served station duties. A large cooler in a restaurant now became a morgue, the smell of death overpowering. Bersim and Eslor flattened their ears and tried to maintain their peripheral vision, as hunter vision narrowed their field of view.

"This is Dr. Ekrod. He will show you the body," said Eslor.

"This way, please," said the doctor and led Bersim still further into the maze of body filled carts.

They stopped at the back corner of the converted cooler and the doctor pulled back an orange sheet, exposing the head and shoulders of a large-maned male.

Bersim hissed, "This is not Togar. He works for you, gives his life for you to squander as you please, and you don't even know who he is. Where is my mate?"

The doctor looked away, shaking his head, "This possibility concerned us, but the importance of indisputable evidence required it. Eslor will show you to pride council headquarters for a briefing."

The doctor spun and left, before Bersim could even reach out and grab him. "I will eat of your newborn! You will learn respect for my mate, you egg sucker!"

Eslor came up behind her, "Bersim, please, I will show you the way. Things are not as last you served here."

She glared at him, but followed. He escorted her to a hatchway marked with a very familiar crest, the pride council seal, with five claws ripping through it. She returned to Pride Defense Administration.

Surprised, Eslor followed her in, she wondered what prey he held in this. They sat down and waited to be seen by the director. Some things never change. The inner door opened and Bersim found herself greeted by Tolshon, the pride defense director, and her previous boss.

"Come in, come in, commanders. I have been waiting for you."

"I am no longer addressed as commander," said Bersim, her back arching in irritation.

"Ah, yes, I suppose no one bothered to tell you. You have been reactivated, Bersim, and you will be working with commander Eslor here. Togar is missing. Assigned to work on the docks, he observed smugglers and similar crimes. Then the Vorlatin ship hit. We suspect he and three others, all non-defense administration, were taken captive. Your response to the body confirms this. You leave in three hours to get them back."

The room spun as Bersim took this all in. "You possessed no right to lose him in the first place! He at least held honor rights to die! You have taken him from his kits and sentenced him to torture and dishonor?"

"We will get him back. Bersim, you know that less would be unthinkable. Whatever the costs, he will be returned, or he and those assisting him will die trying. Do you think we could do less for him?"

Bersim slumped into the corner seating pad. "You have some idea how we're going to do this?"

"We have information Sun clan is involved and FaLac is the most likely location for the prisoner's interrogation. We have obtained a Vorlatin lynx class military scout vessel. The alleged 'Rogue' ship with no clan markings, but we believe it to be the EtTur. You and Eslor will run out to FaLac."

"So, how are we supposed to get in?"

"We have another surprise for you Bersim. We have been very busy while you bore kits. Eslor, show adjutant EsMarn in."

Eslor walked to the side panel and activated the hatch release. As the bulkhead parted, a Vorlatin trooper entered. The sight of the eight-foot-tall, furred beast, in full armor, overwhelmed her. Bersim lunged and rolled left, her shoulder a pivot point as she came into a crouch, but Eslor blocked her. She fell to the floor hard, his massive body crushing the breath out of her.

"Commander, restrain yourself!" said Tolshon. "He is with us and the source of our new Vorlatin Lynx class scout ship."

Bersim's body went limp and Eslor loosed his grip on her.

Tolshon continued, "This is EsMarn. The Marn clan is no more, being completely absorbed by Sun clan. Es here lost his entire sub-clan group, as they did not accept the takeover. Es then agreed to serve his new masters, but later managed to overpower the two Sun clan troopers assigned to work with him. He escaped and brought the EtRas here to us. Those Sun clan troopers with him are no more, by EsMarn's own hand. He has joined us for retribution on those who have wronged him. He has nowhere else to go. He is ours. I will allow him to explain himself."

The eight hundred pound Vorlatin spoke Manifest Standard quite well, "What has been said is true. I must add, I'm not interested in a suicide mission. I wish to bring dishonor and disrepute upon the Sun Clan and to right the destruction of my clan. If we can show all

Vorlatins what Sun clan became, and show all clans the danger, then perhaps Marn clan can be rebuilt from those of us remaining."

"What's the status on the mission?" asked Bersim.

"We are stripping the EtRas down now. All unnecessary equipment is being removed and the weapons collar and controls are being ripped out. This has given us the perfect opportunity to flight test the new drive. Although the work is done on it, it has never been tested long range," said Tolshon.

"How are we supposed to protect ourselves?" asked Bersim.

"You can't. Your only chance is to outrun them. The modifications we are making with the new drive will give you thirty percent more speed and forty percent more range. With any luck, enough to allow you to either outrun or over-jump anything coming after you."

"Eslor, have you seen the EtRas?"

"Yes, Bersim, but before they finished with her. I don't think we'll have any trouble handling her; she looks to be a good ship. There won't be any use for your weapons comp abilities, though you're well known navigational skills will be imperative. We will need to look and act like a Vorlatin ship. You have more experience than anyone in tailing them. We hoped your skill would translate into an ability to mask us on their own trail."

"You act as if you know me. I am at a loss."

"I have only heard of you," replied Eslor, "You see, we are both picked for this mission for more than one reason. I worked under your husband for the three years in the void and not station-side. He spoke often of you and felt extremely proud of your work. He admitted inferiority to no one but you. He believed you the best navigator who ever lived."

"I certainly hope you avoided convincing by such rubbish," replied Bersim, once again holding back tears at Togar's memory.

"Oh, but I am convinced. I not only believe in your abilities, I am betting my life on them, as you will be wagering your life upon my piloting skills, skills you are totally unfamiliar with. I think it to be a fair bargain—I at least know of you."

"All right," interjected Tolshon. "I want the three of you on board the EtRas, familiarizing yourselves. Eslor can explain the changes implemented and EsMarn will tell you both all he can of the ship's original operating characteristics, as well as what will be expected of such a scout ship. Eslor will be in command. He is junior but will be the pilot and is most familiar with the mission plan. Once on station at FaLac, Bersim will take command with command reverting back to Eslor when back in the void. Is this understood and accepted?" asked the director.

"Hunter, your wisdom is unquestioned," answered Eslor.

"Accepted, hunter," answered Bersim.

They needed to walk on either side of the Vorlatin; even so, they twice fended off attacks before they made it to the EtRas. Once inside, EsMarns' relief seemed palpable. He pulled off the armor and stowed it in a locker near the weapons comp station.

"There is only marginal equipment on board. We have the weapons and tools thought needed for the escape and there is plenty of food and fuel. We really don't know how long we'll be out, but there is only the station seating for sleep, along with the four extra stations for our passengers on the way back. We won't have quarters or sleeping shelves this trip," explained Es'Marn.

Bersim looked around and felt quite impressed, as well as just a little worried. Though never before aboard any Vorlatin vessel, she observed plenty of Lynx craft vessels manufactured by her own species, and knew enough to recognize a ship totally stripped.

"You really think this will stand up to full g stresses during acceleration and maneuvering?"

"Oh, she'll take it all right. You just punch the right numbers into comp and this baby'll do the rest," replied Eslor.

"I must admit, I, too, felt concerned. However, your tech people seem sure of themselves on this. So much so, the only thing left being the self-destruct sequence. We can't afford more than forty minutes getting your people out, or we won't have a ship," added EsMarn.

Bersim looked hard at Eslor and he responded.

"We couldn't, and can't, risk the Vorlatins getting this technology. Go ahead and punch up the nav-comp. I think the numbers will surprise you."

Bersim sat at the Vorlatin-sized seat and punched up the computer. What she saw took her breath away.

"If these numbers are right, we are in the fastest and longest range ship that has ever flown in Manifest space. This thing might even be faster than a Garretin Ship!" exclaimed Bersim.

"We believe it is. It's not evident from the exterior, but those panels back there are a little thicker than normal, because it's got dual inline panels. So far, they have worked. If our mission is successful, we will bring back not only Togar and three other of our people, but we will bring back a new speed technology for our entire species."

"Well, I'd have to agree with the director on this one. We really don't need weapons if this ship is as fast as the navcomp says it is, and if it isn't, we're all dead."

The bridge remained quiet for the next hour while they went over their respective duties, both preflight and mission critical. There remained just enough time for a preflight feed and, as if by some unheard signal, they all got up and headed for the ward room.

Bersim pulled a htasi quarter from the dispenser, pulled the warming tab on the tray and grabbed a cup of fet from the sideboard. Already seated, Eslor and EsMarn fed as Bersim sat down. She glanced over at the Vorlatin.

"My sire in his tomb! It is true, you are herbivores!"

EsMarn looked at his tray, "Granted, there is vegetable material here, but it is splattered with a raw meat not unlike the htasi you find so tasty over there.

We find a mixture of what mother life has given us serves us best."

Eslor and Bersim fed quietly, tossing their trays into the disposal when finished. Neither felt the stomach for seconds and neither wanted to discuss their partner's eating habits. Within a half hour, all three returned to their stations on the bridge.

"We're all plotted in, course fully laid out. I still won't believe we can make Fa'Lac in two jumps until we survive the next few hours subjective," offered Bersim.

"EsMarn, you're going to sit out for a while and I'm going to have Bersim handle comm until we make first jump. I don't think our neighbors would take kindly to a Vorlatin face right now."

"Understood."

"Once we're out, and then until we get ready to redock, you will handle all communications."

"Also understood."

"Okay, Bersim, let station know we're pulling out. EsMarn cut us loose from grapples and station lines."

"Working, hunter," replied Bersim as she turned to the communications console.

"We're loose, captain," replied EsMarn.

"Station gives us clearance to jump point, all other traffic held or given priority behind us. We're sure getting the royal treatment," said Bersim.

"Out and spinning, captain, controls to your board," said EsMarn.

Bersim's stomach churned as station gravity let go, momentarily weightless until ships revolution pulled her back down into her seat. She cleared the comm board and looked over her navigation figures, just one more time.

"Prepare for acceleration," said Eslor.

Bersim felt her chest heave in on itself and she could neither breathe nor open her muzzle. The ship screamed as if being torn apart, but the system telltales stayed green, it seemed to be holding together, even if it didn't sound like it.

Eslor cut back the acceleration and spoke. "We have experienced three quarters only. We'll have trouble retaining consciousness at full emergency acceleration. You'll need to have nav-comp computed and laid in before each drop. We may have to make the return run on auto-nav."

"If everything goes as it's supposed to, everything is already laid in and computed," replied Bersim. "We are seven minutes from jump point."

They reached jump and everything disappeared. No one really knew what happened when the jump panels cycled, putting them into hyperspace. Somehow, they lost half a month in a few short moments. It took, seemingly, a half day for Bersim to reach the retros as they came screaming through FaTep.

FaTep existed as simply a jump point in Vorlatin space, named after the star located there. A star with no inhabited planets and no space station, only a navigation beacon and a few sensors. Just a star with enough gravity pull to get them back into real-space.

EtRas output her Vorlatin ID transmissions. EsMarn recorded them at FaLac, a strictly illegal action, and against several provisions of the Manifest. Then again, the way they planned to blow through this system violated a lot more than mere provisions of the Manifest. It violated things like common sense and the idea of having some care for personal safety.

The bridge came alive with a flurry of activity. Alarms went off, telling them what they attempted violated sanity, and the navigation beacon instructed their navigation computer to slow down. Everyone stayed busy resetting overrides and manual controls, to prevent the navigation system from obeying normal navigational procedures.

Bersim, first to speak, said, "Eslor, we're right in the hole, center of the window. We can jump again in three minutes at present acceleration."

"Excellent. EsMarn, we got any visitors?"

"Nothing within scan range and no trails. The place is cold, captain."

"OK, Bersim, hold course and jump at will."

"We're goin' back in," replied Bersim.

Suddenly, Bersim remained unsure if they just went through FaTep, or remained en route. Then, just as suddenly, they came out of hyperspace again, dropping back down into reality. Now a full month after they left Heshnes, yet, at many times light speed, she lost only a few moments. Except for the trip through FaTep, the flight seemed nearly instantaneous.

"Dump speed, Bersim. We don't want to look too fast, not yet anyway. EsMarn, we got any traffic?"

"All quiet right now, it will be a few minutes before we're challenged. I just hope the codes are still good."

"You're not the only one. Stand by for velocity dump. We're gonna' have to hit the retros hard to keep from flying into their laps."

Speech became impossible once more, as the ship dumped speed from eighty-five per-cent light to a more manageable, and maneuverable, in-system speed. They would brake hard for nearly twelve minutes before they could approach the station at FaLac, and they would continue to break for several hours before they could dock. This would be the longest portion of the flight, and they needed to be the most alert during it.

EsMarn took a set of shackles from the equipment locker closest to his station. He held them out to Bersim.

"Look, you're a nice Vorlatin and all, but you sure aren't puttin' them on me," said Bersim.

"Allow me to explain. Instead of a remote infrared control, these are manual, though they look exactly like the others. One inserts a claw tip here," pointing to a recess on each side of the shackle, "and the unit is locked. In this way it is a fail-safe design. Should you fall or be injured, the claw-tip comes out and the shackle is released. The only requirment to free oneself is to no longer keep pressure on the contact holding the unit together. They have been used in both our species' enforcement agencies for decades."

"Here, I'll put 'em on," said Eslor as he grabbed the shackles from the Vorlatin, "You keep him honest, Bersim."

He placed the shackles around his wrists and inserted a claw-tip into the right side slot. The shackles hummed and closed loosely around his wrists.

"We'll, they aren't uncomfortable, let's see if they release right."

He relaxed the pressure on the slot and the shackles fell noisily to the deck. A Vorlatin voice interrupted the training session. Bersim and Eslor would have to trust their partner the rest of the way in. They could understand little of the Vorlatin communications, as they spoke very little of the language. Manifest Standard wouldn't cut it anymore. The rest of the trip passed slowly with sporadic voice traffic with station. They docked without incident and EsMarn led Bersim and Eslor out the air lock, shackled and with six weapons concealed between them.

Joined by two armored storm troopers, all fell in beside EsMarn, yet remained silent. They walked greasy dockside corridors that would make the stationmaster at Heshnes sick. The place made the whole Sun clan look desperate. Bersim just hoped they behaved as sloppily as they looked.

Bersim wouldn't have believed it, if she hadn't seen it for herself, but the military sections remained in even worse disrepair than the docks. As they came into the prison hallway, a blind corner concealed them from view. EsMarn spun and backhanded the Vorlatin on the left, dropping him in one motion. Before Bersim could react Eslor grabbed the other guard by the throat and rendered him unconscious.

"Just why is it you two brought me along?" asked Bersim as she took the shoulder weapon from the guard EsMarn took out. He went around the corner alone to deal with the next guard and to get the grates open. Bersim and Eslor never knew exactly how, but EsMarn pitch hummed and they came around the corner to an open grate and dead guard. Beyond the grate, they

31

could see Togar and three other large pride members chained to the wall.

"I have come for you my mate, father of my kits. Those holding you are now dead," Bersim spoke softly, barely audible. She did not hold back her tears, not this time.

"I'm again indebted to you. More than any mate should be in one lifetime. You truly must live forever, if I'm to repay you."

Eslor and Bersim went to work with the hand lasers cutting their people loose, while EsMarn kept watch and scent marked the cell. They would know Marn clan returned here.

Within twelve minutes of the time they walked into the holding compound, they assembled back at the entrance ready to leave, with six armed pride members and one redeemed Vorlatin.

"Now comes the hard part," said Bersim. "We have no choice but to run for it. We can't convince them EsMarn has us all prisoner."

"I die now with a light heart. My clan is honored and Sun clan has been defiled by a lone Marn clan member, assisted only by animals! I am free!"

The run for the ship went smoothly, until they made it within fifty yards of the EtRas. Then everything broke loose. A Vorlatin patrol came around the curve of the dock to see the EtRas' crew running for their ship. The patrol though confused, didn't stop to ask questions, their projectile weapons spoke for them. EsMarn, Eslor, and Bersim spun left while Togar and the other ex-captives spun right, effectively confusing the Vorlatin patrol. They hesitated to shoot in the direction of EsMarn when the group became split, and Togar's group remained behind a docking collar abandoned on the deck.

Bersim saw what needed to be done. Dropping the shoulder weapon, she ran roaring towards the Vorlatin patrol. The Vorlatins, seeing her unarmed, and assumedly insane, came out from cover and opened fire. Togar stayed ready, and the four Vorlatins had no chance once distracted by Bersim. Togar slid across the deck and threw a disrupter into the middle of the Vorlatin patrol. Bersim lay in a spreading pool of blood.

Togar, first to reach her and without even slowing, swept her up at a full speed, headed for the EtRas' ramp. By the time Togar got her there, both their golden pelts ran red from Bersim's left side, torn open, with only half her left arm remaining. Togar bit down on her arm and, crushing bone, flesh and fur together, slowed the flow of blood from Bersim's arm.

One of the ex-prisoners, Taser, grabbed the medic kit and sat down next to the crash couch Togar just put his mate in, finally tying off the arm so Togar could release his grip.

"Get us outta here!" yelled Togar, just before he felt the tearing of metal as the EtRas pulled loose of the moorings.

"Get in the station couches, we're going to full acceleration!" yelled Eslor, just as Taser got the seal-tape set to Bersim's left side.

Togar jumped up on top of the crash couch, wrapping himself around Bersim and the couch, with his claws sunk three inches into the back cushions. Within fifteen seconds they all lost consciousness.

The rest of the trip home depended upon the preset calculations of a bleeding, unconscious, mother of four, held in her crash couch not by the safety webbing, but by her mate. None of them would fully regain consciousness until about twelve hours out from home. But how they made it home didn't matter anymore. Togar and Bersim were heading home to the kits, this time for good.

*EJ Shumak, C.P.A., Ph.D., lives in metro Chicago, Illinois, and has spent most of his life in northern Illinois and southern Wisconsin. He has been many things: police officer (disabled), large cat sanctuary operator, C.P.A. and on again-off again writer . . . lately on again. He has held active membership in S.F.W.A. since 1992, and has sold four books, three fantasy novels and one non-fiction, along with several dozen short*

*science fiction pieces and non-fiction articles. Some of his current work is available at amazon.com/author/ejshumak*
*ejshumak@sbcglobal.net*

When Taryn, a thirty-year-old medical assistant, reluctantly agrees to meet her ex-fiancé for old time's sake, he brings a birthday gift from her estranged father, a man she despises for abandoning her in slaver's territory sixteen years earlier. Nothing could have prepared her for the truth of her abandonment and her father's final . . . unwanted . . . gift.

# UNWANTED GIFTS

### By

### *S.M. Kraftchak*

Taryn stared across the star port and clenched her jaw, fortifying her resolve not to run. The Tin Cantina, a dive in the Perseus Arm of the Milky Way, held a lifetime of good memories and one bad one that still made her heart ache. Her fingers instinctively found the ever-present knot at the base of her neck as she blew out loudly. She was content in her new life and was willing to face him to prove it.

The familiar stench of rancid grease, overcooked imitation meat product, and rich Andromedan coffee welcomed her like an old friend. A few less lights than normal didn't diminish the garish carnival appearance, when compared to the darkness beyond the edge of the star port. There were very few customers which made it easy to spot his black hair in their usual booth. His back was to the door and as she approached, his one hand nervously tapped a four-inch square box that sat next to a paper envelope.

"Hey, Freat."

The middle-aged man popped out of the booth, went to hug her, but stepped back and captured her with his crystal blue eyes instead, as he offered her a hand.

"Taryn, I'm glad you came. I got you a drink . . . Slow Nova gin and ginger?"

"I was sure you'd have forgotten by now," Taryn said and slid into the booth.

"I also remember it's your birthday," he said easing the paper envelope across the table.

In one motion, Taryn pushed a strand of red hair out of her face and slid her hand onto her neck as the corners of her mouth turned down. "Please let's not go there."

"No, oh no, it's not from . . . it's from . . . well, just read."

Her fingers caressed the rare paper envelope and then slid under the flap. Taryn carefully removed a single sheet of vellum and bit her upper lip as she read. When she reached the bottom, Taryn lowered her arms onto the table. "I can't do this."

"Why not? You've always wanted to know why and what happened."

Taryn shook her head. "That was years ago. He left. I don't need him. I'm doing fine without him."

"But he's your—"

"I know who he is supposed to be, but a father doesn't leave his fourteen-year-old daughter to fend for herself on a maintenance orb in the middle of the Trader routes."

"I'm sure he had a good reason?"

"No, chasing a painted-on spacesuit while on a drunken binge—"

"Maybe it's not what it appeared to be."

"Oh, yes, let's get noble and say he was trying to replace my mother who died tragically. I didn't want or need a replacement mother. I wanted to be with my father, but he couldn't stand to look at me because I'm the spitting image of my mother!" Taryn's eyes filled with tears as her gaze bore into the top of Freat's head. She watched his fingers tap the small, gray box, knowing how in the past he would have wrapped her in his arms to comfort her. She was surprised to find part of her missed that.

"Then you probably don't want this." Freat started to put the box in his pocket.

Taryn knew his ploy, but fell for it anyway. "Don't want what?"

His fingers lingered on the box as he pushed it to the middle of the table. "I got a delivery from Pnum 5. It had two notes and this box. Your father asked me to give you this," Freat said and pushed it the rest of the way.

Taryn eyed the box and then looked at Freat. "What is it?"

With a shrug and a tip of his head, he said, "I don't know."

"I don't want anything from my father."

"Could you at least try it on so, when I have to return it, I can say I tried?"

"So you *do* know what it is."

"It's something simple. Just open the box, try it on, and be done with it. Don't make me a liar."

With an expansive sigh, Taryn opened the box. Her eyes widened and her lips pressed into a thin line as she pulled a thick, gold, oval bracelet from the velvet lined box. She ran her fingers over the smooth, shining surface, marred only by an imbedded hinge and the scroll engraving, 'To my dearest, with love'. She startled when the latch popped open. Taryn looked at Freat, who raised his eyebrows and bobbed his head, and then she slipped it on.

The moment the gold band snapped shut, it shrank to snuggly fit her wrist and grew warm. She clawed at the bracelet, in vain. "What the hell is this? My hand is tingling and it's running up my arm."

"It won't hurt you. He promised."

"What have you done to me? This isn't from my father, is it?"

"Yes, it is." Nodding Freat slid from the booth with an apologetic expression. "He knew you'd never come if he just asked. It's travel nanites. They'll compel you to travel to their programmed destination. When you arrive, the bracelet will loosen and the nanites will deactivate. There'll be no lasting effects."

"And where the hell is that, your bedroom?"

Freat shook his head. "It is a birthday present from your father. I was the only one, other than you, he was allowed to contact and he said he had to beg them for that."

"I don't want this and I don't want to see him. Take it off!" Taryn thrust her wrist at Freat like a right jab.

"I can't. It won't come off until you reach the nanite's programmed destination. Your father said he needed to see you one more time before he dies."

"He died to me sixteen years ago."

"I'm sorry, it has to be this way, but he says it's not just for him." Freat turned and rushed to the door, paused and then shouted across the cantina, "I really hope things work out. I hope you know I still love you . . . and always will," and then left.

Taryn slammed the bracelet on the table and even tried to pry it off with the edge of the table, but the band remained in place. The tingling had quickly engulfed her body and then ceased. "I don't care what he wants, I'll be damned if I'm going to give that man even one more minute of my time," she said stalking out of the Cantina. Facing the empty star port, she burst into tears.

She wandered in the darkness where her anguish stayed hidden, safe, like the last time she had left the Cantina, only this time it was her father that brought her to misery. She grabbed at the base of her neck with both her hands, digging deep into the burning knot. Why would her father choose now to invade her life after he had disappeared so many years ago? She never knew if he was alive or dead, during those two weeks of hiding out in the darkness of the storage facility. Beating off rats with a pipe flange, licking condensation from the walls for water, and the constant knot in her stomach, were the best of her memories. She had prayed ceaselessly for her father to return and no slavers to find her, until one day she simply walked out of the darkness and never looked back. She remembered staring into the surprised eyes of the bespectacled old man at the scheduler's office when she identified herself and demanded transport off that God-forsaken tin ball.

"Where do you want to go?" his voice was squeaky and small.

Taryn startled, and then gaped at a young man with frameless purple-lensed glasses. His raised eyebrows looked like caterpillars perched atop his lenses as he waited expectantly. Confused, she turned to find she was in the starport transit terminal, not the maintenance orb; damn nanites.

"Ehem," the young man said.

"What?" Taryn turned to stare at him.

"You said you wanted off this tin ball, but where do you want to go?"

Taryn blinked, and looked around again. "Um, I'm not sure."

"I can't help you if you don't know, unless of course you'd like to meet me in," he glanced to the side, "half an hour at the Tin Cantina. We can have a few drinks, a few laughs, and then—"

"When does the next available transport leave?" Taryn blurted out. She thought the young man looked part alien with the green hue from his data screen reflecting on his face.

"There's one leaving in ten minutes."

"Good, I'll take one ticket, please."

"Will that be one way or . . ."

"One way."

"There are no accommodations on—"

"I don't care, just give me the pass."

"Are you taking any luggage?"

Taryn scowled at the young man as if he were speaking a different language.

"Lug-gage?"

"N . . . no, I've sent it ahead."

"That would be quite a trick since you don't—"

"Just give me my damn pass before I miss my flight."

The man puckered his face at Taryn while his fingers tap-danced on the screen in front of him. He suddenly held up one finger and smiled sarcastically. "Place your thumb on the pad for identification and payment, please."

Taryn pressed her thumb onto the fingerprint-payment terminal, and waited for it to beep.

As soon as it beeped the man's finger dropped onto the screen in front of him. "Your reservation has been confirmed, Ms. Cardif, and your flight departs in seven minutes from gate twenty-one at the far end of the platform. If you run, you might make it. If not, I'd still be happy to meet you—" He grinned and fluttered his caterpillars.

Taryn didn't let the man finish. She ran out to the gallery line, dodged several other travelers, spotted the sign "Platforms 11-21" pointing to the right and began to run. She avoided the three or four people sauntering along, passed a dozen gantry pods, several disembarking passengers and some with service carts nearby. When her chest felt like it would burst in the low O2, she kept running. She had to get on that flight. Something told her she'd die if she stayed there, so she pushed her legs faster, stumbled, but kept her feet and continued running. With only six more gantry pods to go, she could see the last one loading and called out. "Wait! Please, wait!" came out like a squalling baby, but she spotted one of the attendants look in her direction and then point. Taryn's feet slapped the deck as she slowed. She leaned on her knees gasping for breath in front of gate twenty-one.

"Are you all right, Miss? You know you really shouldn't run in low atmo. Can I get you a mask?"

Taryn bobbed her head.

"Do you have a pass?" a female attendant asked as she held a rectangular device with a small square screen and an abbreviated alpha-numeric pad in front of Taryn's face.

Taryn straightened up, still panting, gave the woman a scowl and then pressed her thumb on the square screen.

The attendant studied her readout. "Very well, Ms. Cardif, If you will please step into the gantry pod, we'll give you a mask and board you. We're set for departure in two minutes and we wouldn't want to be late, now would we, hmm?"

Twenty minutes later, Taryn relaxed in her seat and pulled the O2 mask from her face. She thought back through the last hour and cursed Freat. She had heard of nanites and their effect on the human body, but had always believed they were exaggerated; not anymore. Damn him to hell, and damn her father too. As soon as she got wherever *there* was, she'd give him a piece of her mind, spit in his eye, and walk away. After he had abandoned her and she had stepped out to live life on her own, there was nothing she wanted or needed from him, ever.

"Good evening, this is Captain Jenks, your pilot. We have jumped to light speed and will be arriving on Pnum 5 in three hours. Time of arrival will be 1600 local. Please remember that Pnum 5 has no accommodations and is merely a transfer point for the TRAPPIST-17 penal colony, the Larenian Refuge, and other planetary facilities in orbit around the ultracool dwarf star, a very dim sun. For your convenience, Pnum 5 maintains a Terra Prime artificial atmosphere and standardized light. If you need assistance with your transfer, please speak to an attendant, and thank you for traveling on Transgalactic Transport."

Taryn whispered to herself, "Well, that would be great if I knew where I was going."

As if she had heard, the cabin attendant appeared in front of Taryn with her handheld device. "Ms. Cardif, I noticed that in your haste to make the flight, you neglected to book your transfer. Please allow me to help you with that. I'm guessing since you don't appear to be Larenian, and travel to the other planets in the

TRAPPIST-17 system require pre-authorization, you will be traveling to the penal colony?"

Taryn didn't like the woman's condescending, know-it-all attitude, even though she was pretty sure that's where she'd find her father. "Actually, I'm meeting my father on Pnum 5. He has my transfer authorization."

"Oh," she said with wide eyes, taking a step back, "I hope you enjoy your flight," and then quickly walked away.

Confused by the surprised and suddenly guarded attitude, Taryn shook her head and began to mull through what she would say to her father. She had years of vehemence to spew at him. She could almost understand his drinking binges after Mother died. They had been ridiculously in love. But after Grandpa died, Father had become irreconcilable. He spent every waking hour searching for women, all of them in some way reminded her of her mother. He had refused to talk to her or allow her to console him. He always got that pained look on his face and said, "You are so much like your mother," and then walked away. She would tell him how thoughtless he had been; how she'd come close to being caught by slavers, not once but twice, just because he was a drunken, selfish, bastard who cared more about himself than his own daughter.

Taryn suddenly buried her face in her hands and sobbed as quietly as she could. After several minutes, she gained a modicum of control by reasoning tears didn't help her and he didn't deserve them. When the knot at the base of her neck suddenly spiked pain up into her brain and then down her back arching her painfully backward, she clenched her fingers around the back of her neck, folded onto her knees, and sobbed herself to sleep.

Aware of a gentle hand on her shoulder, Taryn sat up and pushed her hair back from her face. She rubbed her eyes, quickly swiped at her nose, and then looked up into the sympathetic face of the cabin attendant. "Ms. Cardif, would you like a wet cloth? We've landed and will be disembarking momentarily," she said in a kind voice while holding out a white washcloth. "I'm sure you'll want to look presentable for your father."

"Thank you," Taryn said and smiled at the lady, surprised by her change in attitude.

After mopping her face and taking several deep breaths through the warm, lightly bleach-scented cloth, Taryn departed the transport.

She raised one hand to shield her eyes as she entered the circular transit area. Living in the dim light of the star port for so many years made Terra Prime lighting quite bright. Pnum 5 was sparser than the star port, and much cleaner. She counted five gates: the one she'd come through labeled System Arrivals; one labeled Larenian Refugees in both English and the circular letters unique to their language; one labeled Penal Colony; and two others labeled RESTRICTED ACCESS 1 & 2 respectively. Just outside the last gate, a man in a black jumpsuit stood surveying the passengers. He stood with his feet shoulder-width apart and his arms folded across his chest. The moment his eyes met hers, his stoic expression cracked with relief and then returned as he strode toward her. Taryn clenched her jaw and her hand went to the back of her neck.

"Ms. Cardif?"

"Yes?" There was no sense trying to deny it. Since the bracelet hadn't loosened, the nanites were still active and she'd wind up where they wanted her to be.

"Will you come with me?"

"Where?"

"I'm not at liberty to say?"

"Where is my father?"

"He couldn't be here so he asked me to meet you."

"How do I know this isn't some elaborate scheme to kidnap me?"

"Come with me now, or come with me next cycle, but the nanites will take you where you need to be, and you'll find it more comfortable to come now than to suffer their torture while you wait for next cycle," he said pointing Taryn's gold bracelet.

"Is my father in trouble?"

The man tossed his head back, gave a great big "Ha", and then smiled before resuming his stoic expression. "He is not in trouble, but we need to go. Are you feeling well? You look pale?"

"This whole . . . thing . . . has been a little stressful," Taryn said offering her best smile.

The man nodded. "I can only imagine. My name is Rin. Let's go." With a hand on her upper back, he gently guided Taryn toward the RESTRICTED ACCESS 2 gate.

"Wait, I thought," Taryn pointed to the penal colony gate, "he was . . ."

Rin shook his head and kept walking. As soon as they passed the entrance to the gate, a klaxon actuated and a clear dome descended, surrounding them. Rin's hand tightened on Taryn's elbow, pulling her close. "It's okay," he said near her ear.

"Identify," a female voice reverberated through them off the cylinder.

"Agent Darinctolevason escorting visitor for Dr. Authur Cardif."

"Doctor? Oh, no, that's not my father."

"Yes, it is. He's saved a lot of lives since you last saw him sixteen years ago."

The female voice lowered to a conversational level and a blue circle of light appeared on the cylinder. "Visitor, place your palm in the blue circle and state your name and occupation."

Taryn looked at Rin, who nodded, before she obeyed. "Taryn Cardif, medical assistant."

"Identity confirmed. Welcome, home Taryn Cardif. You may proceed. A shuttle is waiting."

"Welcome home? What's going on? What does she mean?" Taryn yanked her elbow away from Rin and fell against the thick glass when the dome and floor suddenly began descending as one, creating a large capsule. "I'm not staying here. I'm just going to satisfy some delusion of a man who claims to be my father and then leave once this damn thing is off." Taryn waved her gold bracelet. "This isn't my home. If I have to stay, I don't want to see him. Let me out of here now! Please!"

Taryn grabbed the back of her neck with both hands, squeezed her eyes shut, pressed her elbows together, and began to cry.

Rin gently supported her by her upper arms and helped her to her feet. "Calm down. No harm will come to you. If after you've seen your father, you decide you want to leave, you don't have to stay. That was just an AI who assumes Dr. Cardif's daughter would want to remain with her father."

"I don't even know who my father is any more. He abandoned me when I was fourteen."

"I know. I was the one who rescued your father."

Taryn pressed her back to the tube, and peered at Rin past her elbows. "Rescued him?"

"There's a lot you don't know, and so much more you need to know, but it isn't my place to tell you. I know we just met, but please accept my assurances that you will *not* be held against your will after you meet with you father." Rin pressed his hand to the middle of his chest.

Taryn stared into Rin's eyes for a full minute before she said, "Okay," and then gasped when the capsule slipped into space outside Pnum 5. Pale light illuminated them from the floor while Taryn survey the unfamiliar solar system."

"It's okay. The shuttle is below us."

"Will it take long to get . . . wherever we're going?" Taryn asked.

"Only another sixty minutes once we're on board. How frequent are the headaches?" Rin's face was pinched with concern.

Taryn turned to Rin, still holding her neck. "A lot less frequent before the stress of this whole escapade. Why?" Her brow suddenly furrowed. "And how do you know I've been having headaches?"

"Your father said they would have started. I can give you something for it once we're on board."

Taryn stepped to the other side of the tube. "If it will make this pain stop and the trip shorter, I'll take anything."

Rin leaned close to Taryn's ear. "Ms. Cardif, we're at the facility. If you would like to rest some more or get cleaned up, I can take you to your quarters."

Taryn sat up immediately, passed a hand over her neck, and then stood and faced Rin. "You said I didn't have to stay."

"You don't. All visitors are assigned quarters, regardless of the length of their stay, as a courtesy."

"No, I want to get this over with. Take me to my father."

"Very well, please follow me."

Taryn followed Rin at a leisurely pace for nearly ten minutes before he stopped outside a door identical to the hundred others they had passed. He waved his hand in front of a square on the wall and the door slid into the wall, exposing a very dimly lit room.

"Is he asleep?" Taryn whispered. "Is he unwell?"

"I am not asleep, Taryn. Please, come make peace with your father."

Taryn stepped into the threshold of the room. A sudden chill rushed through her. She wasn't sure if it was hearing her father's voice for the first time in sixteen years or the nanites releasing their influence on her body as her bracelet fell loose on her wrist.

"Please come in. It's been far too long and there's much to say . . . and little time to say it in. Come in and let the door close. My eyes don't take well to the bright lights of the corridors."

Once Taryn cleared the threshold, the door closed behind her and she was plunged into near darkness. Slowly her eyes adjusted and she spotted a silhouette on the far side of the large room. She wasn't waiting to hear any of his excuses. "Seems you've done pretty well for yourself. Was it a rich, painted-on spacesuit, or are you really entombed here in an insane asylum that caters to your delusions of being a doctor who is saving hundreds of lives?"

"You're bitter. I'm sorry for leaving you on that maintenance orb in the middle of nowhere," her father said.

"Not half as sorry as I was."

"I was desperate to find—"

"You know, it really doesn't matter now, what you were doing." Taryn stabbed the air between them with her finger.

"But it does! If you will just let me—"

"Explain? There's no excuse that could justify—"

"Would trying to save your life be good enough?"

Taryn laughed and tossed her hands in the air. "You've either perfected your sense of the dramatic, or are downright delusional. Abandoning me in slaver territory hardly qualifies as trying to save my life. Let's just stop this now. I came, not that I had a choice," she slipped the gold bracelet off and threw it in the direction of the silhouette. "But now you can see I'm alive. Your duty, if you ever thought you had one, is done. Good-bye." She turned and stepped to the door which didn't open.

"Taryn, you're dying."

"Nice try," she called over her shoulder. "Now how do I get out of here?"

"How often are the headaches coming, once or twice a week?"

Taryn turned back to the silhouette. "How do you know about them?"

"I got them just before my thirtieth year, too."

"I'm sure everyone gets headaches."

"Not like ours. How frequent are they?"

"Does it matter?"

"Yes," he said angrily, and then more softly, "It does."

"I'm getting them daily, now. I'm a medical assistant and have access to the best care in the Milky Way. They have found nothing. They say I'm just wound too tight."

"Daily?" Taryn's father's voice cracked.

"It doesn't matter. Let me out of here. I don't need some fraud giving me his quack diagnosis."

"Has the pain started shooting down your back?"

"Being practically kidnapped doesn't exactly help my stress level, you know."

"It has? Taryn, you only have days left if you don't go through the ceremony."

Taryn banged on the door and shouted. "Let me out of here."

"Taryn . . ." Her father's voice was strained, but controlled.

"Let me out! Rin you promised!"

"Taryn . . . your mother . . ."

Taryn spun and took two steps into the room. Her voice was low and filled with menace. "Don't you *dare*, speak about my mother. If you hadn't been so absorbed in your work, she might still be alive."

"Taryn, I loved your mother more than my own life and would have gladly given mine for hers, but . . . there was nothing that could be done. It wasn't my fault."

"I wish you had died instead of her!" Taryn sobbed.

"That would have served you better," Taryn's father said softly.

Taryn saw his silhouetted head bow and heard the pain in his voice. It pierced her anger and pain, silencing her.

After a long minute, her father spoke. "Taryn, please . . . I beg you. I can't lose you too. You *need* to listen to me. Nothing I have to say will be easy to hear, and would have come much easier from your mother and me on the celebration of your fifteenth year. You know that special chair we bought that fit the three of us so snuggly to watch vintage TV shows? That's where we were going to tell you the truth about your birth; help you understand that you aren't just any normal girl. You're a Purian."

Taking another step toward her father, Taryn spoke softly, "I can't be. I don't look like them and they are now just myths. No one has seen a Purian for hundreds of years after they were all harvested by zealots fighting the Sagittarius Wars."

"Very carefully seeded myths. We learned to change our appearance and disappeared into the human race, but sometimes—" Taryn's father stepped forward under one of the dim overhead lights and revealed his sage-green, leathery Purian face. "Our young are born with human appearance, like you, but only our carefully guarded ceremonies have kept our line alive. On the anniversary of their birth in their thirtieth, year, each Purian receives part of their parent's Tarneal gland. To human medicine, it looks and acts like the pineal gland in humans, but ours does much more. It gives us our ability to heal. Usually a mother gives to her daughter and a father to his son. If a daughter can't receive from her mother, a gift from the father will work, if he has already received the gift from his father."

"You were two months from your thirtieth when your father died," Taryn said. "So you hadn't received the gift, and with Mother gone—"

Her father continued. "You would have no gift, and would be slowly revealed as Purian before you died in agony by your thirty-first birth." He held his hand out to Taryn, who slowly placed her human looking hand in his leathery, claw-like fingers. She remained silent as she considered her father's words and allowed her father to guide her to a chair.

"We cannot heal ourselves, but can assist most others," Taryn said, still looking at the floor. Now she knew why she was so good at what she did.

"Exactly. I began the change days before my thirtieth year began. I carefully fabricated a drinking binge to hide my symptoms and the medication I took for their relief, but was also seeking out any other unknown female Purians to see if they could pass the gift to you."

"Your chasing painted-on—"

"Yes."

Taryn suddenly looked up at her father's leathery face. "Do you still suffer the pain? How are you still alive? You are nearly forty-six?"

"Rin recognized my symptoms and brought me here."

"Rin is Purian?"

Her father nodded. "We are a small colony of Purians and human healers who specialize in the most difficult maladies and procedures. They were able to find me a compatible gift to allow me to live, but not to return my human appearance, and that is why I could never return for you or ever claim you as my daughter, without risking your life."

"So if you cannot give me the gift and mother did not, is my future the same as yours?"

"No," her father offered a hideous smile and but then grew serious again. "There's something more I should tell you before I tell you the rest." He sandwiched his daughter's hand between his own and held tight. "Your mother didn't die that night."

Taryn's lungs refused to fill. Tears streamed down her cheeks. She swallowed hard several times before she croaked, "She's alive?"

"She was, but her body passed nearly a month ago. Unknown to me at the time, there was a Purian at the med platform she was taken to after she was attacked. When she was declared clinically dead."

"But we saw her go. We were there when they turned off the machines!"

"No, that was a bandaged simulacrum. Her body has been kept alive, here."

"So then, you will give me her gift?"

"Sadly, no. It was after her clinical death that they realized why she had been so brutally attacked. Someone had harvested her."

"No!" Taryn launched into her father's arms and sobbed. "How could anyone do that to someone so good and kind? How could they have known?"

"Sh, sh, sh, ssshh. She didn't feel any pain in the end. She went peacefully." Taryn's father rocked her until her sobs subsided.

"So if there is no help for me, why did you bring me here?" Taryn said into the nap of his high white collar.

"There is hope, but you will like it even less than what I have already told you."

Taryn eased off her father's shoulder, back into the chair and sat studying her father's hands. "I can handle anything now that I have you back."

"But you won't for much longer."

"Wha—?" She looked up into her father's tear-filled eyes.

"Before your mother's body finally failed, they found that a tiny piece of her Tarneal gland had somehow regenerated over the years. I had them implant it in me in hopes that it would continue to re-grow and be useful to you when your time came." He gave her a bitter sweet quivering smile.

"It worked?"

Father nodded. "But after all I've been through, when they harvest your mother's gift from me, I will die."

"No . . ." Taryn breathed. "Then I don't want it."

Easing onto his knees in front of his daughter, he said, "You must accept it or die; all your mother and I have suffered for will mean nothing. Taryn, with your mother's unique gift, the Council here believes you may become the strongest Purian ever to live. Never has a Purian Tarneal gland regenerated. You will hold the hope of a new generation. You cannot betray our race or yourself. I beg you, don't discard all the good you will be able to do."

"But without you and mother, who will I depend on?"

"You learned to be strong for years without us. Besides, there is someone else who already accepts you for who you are."

Taryn looked into her father's sapphire eyes. "Freat. He knows?"

Her father nodded.

Taryn stood outside the RESTRICTED ACCESS 2 gate on Pnum 5, patiently checking each face of the passengers when they disembarked the latest transport and stepped into the circular transit lounge. There had been fifteen Larenian and a handful of humans, but none of them was the face she'd hoped to see. She fiddled with the well healed scar at the base of her neck and felt her heart jump when Freat emerged from the gantry pod. He stood squinting around the lounge until he spotted Taryn. She saw his face break into a wide smile a moment before he sprang into an open-armed run toward her.

*S. M. Kraftchak*
*Whether voyaging the universe, or journeying in a fantasy world of my own making, I'm passionate about discovering all kinds of characters and relentlessly tracing their heartfelt stories so I can relate them to you. I love sunrise on the beach, sunset in the mountains and portraying Elizabeth Tudor. I have one dog who thinks she's a footrest, another who almost catches a Frisbee, and a cat who rents me my desk for open-window-time. I have three awesome daughters, and a husband who is my best friend, my harshest critic, and my most fervent supporter.*

Does reality have a place in a society where everything is artificial? Today we can have our bodies re-sculpted. Much of the food we eat is prepared in a laboratory. Even "reality" TV is fabricated. What will the world be like in the future?

# WHERE THE LAST TRAMZ STOPS

By

*Sam Bellotto Jr.*

1136 UTC.

So which legs was he going to wear today?

His reliable everyday Walkers were out for inspection and wouldn't be back from the shop until later this evening. He shouldn't have worn them for that jog around the flesh tanks yesterday, but for Gloriosus sake it was only a run in the meadow! How'd he know the groundskeeper would miss a couple of pock holes? His trusted Walkers blew a hydraulic and had to be inspected all over again after the tech work, meaning no Walkers, and he didn't own a spare pair. Most people owned at least two Walkers, but he couldn't resist the awesome black Mountaineers which were on sale. So the Mountaineers it would have to be. He'd look like a damn troll humping around on those things, but his Diplomats wouldn't hold up under everyday use.

A person could function quite admirably with raw leg stumps, "provolone cheeses," if you didn't mind waddling around like a geriatric penguin. Even with pants on, the massive musculature of Mountaineers was evident, the bold stride, the weighty boots that came with them. Not so the Diplomats which were indiscernible with clothes on. But Diplomats were designed for gentle, catered affairs involving lots of standing and even more sitting at tables, daises, and auditoriums. They absolutely wouldn't hold up under everyday use.

Bobbob Sixty-seven was a newsmaker. He'd been a newsmaker for the past five years; an honest profession; he had to go to school for training and immersion in the history and application thereof. Which made him a second tier citizen. And how proud he was of that designation; and being a newsmaker. Everyday use for a newsmaker meant lots of legwork. Therefore, the Diplomats were out.

Last week's airplane crash in northeastern New Jersey was entirely his story. It was a remarkably inventive piece of writing that he had to carefully research. Hours of arduous shuttling through the netosphere to figure out the best way for an airplane to fail, ultimately eschewing mech failure in favor of terrorism. That was a stroke of brilliance. It forked into two distinctly separate stories—the airplane crash itself, and subsequent roundup of a terrorist cell squirreled away in the back of a kosher meat market in Miami. The public loves a good terrorist story.

Bobbob prepped himself in front of the wall-sized mirror app. He was clean. His skin was nice and taut, the color of old paper, not a crack or fold anywhere. Glabrous was the word. From the top of his squarish head to the bottom of his leg junctions he was glabrous. He liked the word glabrous. That's because he was a writer. So descriptive. He hadn't applied any hairpieces yet. He'd coupled a pair of standard male arms (with hands) over his natural arms, what was left of them, anyway. (He had cosmetic surgery done when he was a kid to remove most of his natural arms; natural arms were extremely limited in function; replacing them is a routine augmentative procedure nowadays.) He needed arms to prep; he wasn't wealthy enough to afford a valet. So putting on arms was usually the first thing he did after rolling out of the sack in the morning.

Now which of his wigs to screw on?

The blue Medit cut hair would do. Blue Monday. Blue hair. A double thump on his temples and he could have blue eyes. But Bobbob loved to be the nonconformist. Three thumps. Green, blue, indigo. Indigo eyes. Now where did he put those Mountaineers?

1315 UTC.

The sixpack to the office was comfortable and not at capacity. There were only two other riders this morning, aside from Bobbob. The conveyance was nicknamed a sixpack because it coincidentally resembled one of those antique six packs of beverage containers, the kind that existed when people *had* to drink to obtain enough liquid water. Thanks to dietary supplement science, drinking was a recreational pastime now, mostly for experiencing different flavors and temperatures. As for drinking to get drunk, well, there are better ways to do that, today, too. The modern sixpack was significantly larger than its namesake—each cylindrical "container" was for holding a whole person instead of a half-liter. Bobbob boarded. One of the empty cylinders cracked, exhaled, and divided for Bobbob to climb onto the platform, then closed back up, sealing him in. Bobbob stood. No reason to sit down because later model prosthetic legs never got tired, so no seats were provided on the sixpack. On the clear windshield in front of him, Bobbob selected Events from the menu which would bring in the feed from a variety of reality sources, including his own news outlet. He smiled. There was the link to his own piece about the airplane crash. They were still called airplanes; no reason to change that designation; it was descriptive and remained accurate. Of course, airplanes didn't "crash" anymore, but near disasters and subsequent rescue operations made for exciting reading. The fact that airplanes didn't "crash" anymore helped newsmakers cover their stories. The first rule of good newsmaking: report nothing that can be irrefutably verified, unless it can be irrefutably verified.

The Law of Irrefutable Verification (IR, in news jargon) may sound like a tautology but it is relatively easy to understand. First described by Prof. Ericowen

One-thirty-three in his watershed *Elements of Modern Newsmaking*, the concept meant that a proper news story had to read (or sound) like it could actually have happened, but not reveal enough to independently prove if it did actually happen, unless it actually happened. A violation of IR would be a serious breach of the newsmakers' oath because it would lend credence to the widely rumored charge that nothing much ever happened and most news was manufactured. Which it was. Because nothing much ever happened. Unless something really did happen. Which was exceedingly rare. Pretty simple, really.

The news crawl announced that Bobbob's latest story was hitting the feed. Already? Bobbob punched it up. The article panned in from the right, in a lovely twelve-point Moderno Medium.

### TIME JUMP KILLS NOTED SCIENTIST
*Location of secret lab remains under wraps.*
*By Bobbob Sixty-seven*

*Dr. Seththomas Nine-forty-six, noted physicist and three-time finalist for the coveted Wattazir Prize in Theoretical Physics, was killed yesterday in a freak accident. According to investigators, Dr. Nine-forty-six had been attempting to create an artificial bunghole through time and space in his West Bendover laboratory when an anomalous infinite loop in the secondary time stream was generated, drawing everything within the laboratory, including Dr. Nine-forty-six himself, into another dimension. The location of this other dimension is undetermined. Remote surveillance feeds, which escaped absorption through the temporary time flux, captured the accident in ultra-def holographic video.*

*Dr. Nine-forty-six was claimed by many to be the foremost temporal paleontologist in his field, and his work has been the subject of much controversy as well as praise. For the past several years, however, he has devoted himself to creating a bunghole through the fabric of time-space that would enable him, like pulling a rabbit out of a hat, to reach in and retrieve specimens from eras long gone by. Only a month ago his*

*experiments met with limited success when he opened a
bunghole to the previous decade that lasted 45 seconds.
Short-lived as it was, Dr. Nine-forty-six was able to
retrieve a maxillary denture; but to whom it belonged
remains a mystery.*

*From the data on the video, the following is clear,
say investigators. At 1823 UTC in the afternoon, Dr.
Nine-forty-six successfully opened a bunghole, about
the size of an office chair, easily big enough for a grown
man to step through. The image from the holocam, even
at wide range, distinctly revealed a sunny field at the
opposite end of the bunghole, and something moving
across the field. Dr. Nine-forty-six reached in and
struggled to pull out what appeared to be a massive
reptilian head, closely resembling a large iguana.
Investigators suggest that the animal could have been
an immature Dimetrodon, or a Sphenacodon. Hard to
say. The animal was not around for very long.*

*It has been speculated that the struggling reptile
may have been responsible for the subsequent and
tragic destabilizing of the time stream. Investigators
added that the hole buckled, then snapped closed on
Dr. Nine-forty-six's arms. He attempted to yank free. In
reaction, the bunghole closed tighter and, like the intake
manifold on an industrial vacuumbot, sucked up
everything within a ten-meter radius, Dr. Nine-forty-six
included. Then the bunghole popped out of existence. A
shard of ceiling tile fell to the floor.*

*Dr. Nine-forty-six was sixty-two years old. He lived
alone and had no family. At the time of his demise he
was on sabbatical from his post at the Liverspots
Institute, a private brain trust where he often gave
lectures to graduate students from around the world on
a number of time-related topics. The case remains under
an official government inquiry and the laboratory is in
an undisclosed location.*

1355 UTC.

The sixpack decelerated to a stop in front of the
Central Information Academy, a single-story building of
alabaster poured stone, polygon-shaped, that took up
the full city block and then some. Bobbob's container

divided in order to let him out and closed back up with a sigh. The sixpack moved on.

Bobbob's strides were the ambulatory equivalent of Lowell Thomas' ancient radio broadcasts. He was certain he was going to take a ribbing because of the Mountaineers. And he was right.

Barely a meter down the hallway to his office: "Morning, Sixty-seven! Planning on climbing Mt. Obamayama today?" gibed Laurajen Ten, another newsmaker, quite a bit his senior. You'd hardly know it, however. She'd had so many plastic surgeries and body part replacements she looked thirty-five; the best shape money could buy.

"My Walkers are in 'spection," he groused.

"Oh, yeah, one pair of Walkers. Living dangerously."

He snorted.

"Nice job on the time geek accident, by the way."

"You read it?"

Laurajen adjusted her left ear. "Num. Liked the rabbit out of the hat bit. Reminded me of something old I saw on the vidstream the other day."

Most apartment buildings were skinned, meaning that the interior surfaces were coated with a media transmitting polymer that could display the full spectrum of popular video and audio feeds, anywhere, formatted and sized to taste. In the bathroom, a person could monitor live webcasts from the Deep Dish Array on the walls and ceiling and take a meteor shower; in the bedroom a person could log into the Mariana Trench Cam and sleep with the luminescent fishes.

"And?"

"Hah! Bunghole through time-space. Dinosaurs. Secret labs. Clever. Real clever, but you take too damn many risks." Laurajen shook her head. "You knit a story *that* intricate," she warned, putting more distance between her and Bobbob, "and you're bound to drop a stitch."

"I do like living dangerously."

"Hah!"

Bobbob forged ahead in the other direction, to the office that he shared with Irageorge Two-oh-two, a stocky fellow fond of the chiseled male look and chocolate skin tones, and Amycarolyn Seventy, short blond hair, wispy, a devotee of Mode Mannequin. The office was nicknamed Cell Block D; it said so on the front door; they'd put the plaque there in jest a long time ago and the name stuck. The office was also skinned, with a large puffy sofa centrally located, a washroom, and several vending machines full of non-calorie flavored Stix of every shape, texture and color imaginable. Each newsmaker had a personal recliner.

Into this scene, Bobbob strode on formidable legs.

"Hey, what's up, Bobbob?"

"Nothing much."

It was the old newsmakers' in-joke. Of course nothing much happened. That's why they were newsmakers. If anything ever did happen, they would have to become news reporters. They all laughed, nonetheless.

The laughter was interrupted.

Amidst a fanfare of trumpets and whistles, a video of the Pope imaged onto the nearest wall. He was, in fact, the boss, but everybody called him the Pope. About seventy. He was obese—corpulent in the extreme—with a large nose, jowls, thick lips, pig eyes, a high forehead, and a salt-and-pepper topknot. His skin was pink, where it wasn't yellow. He was always saying he'd go in for a standard lard-o-suction, paint job, and bodysculpt, but always forgot to. The surprising thing was that after all these years he was still alive. Maintenance drugs can work wonders.

"Bobbob. Please come to my office. We got a problem."He wheezed. He sighed, He fidgeted. He mopped at his cheeks with a hand towel he always carried around with him. The video closed.

"Uh-oh," remarked Irageorge.

"The Pope requests an audience," Amycarolyn observed.

"Better not keep him waiting," Bobbob muttered on his way out.

The sign on the boss's door said Walterlewis Ninety-two, Editorial Director. The door slid open with a gasp as if it expected Bobbob, which it did, allowed the newsmaker to trudge in, and slid shut behind him.

"Boss?"

Boss Walterlewis was cradled in a body-fitting scooter chair behind his desk, his back to Bobbob, staring at the wall which now displayed Bobbob's latest article on the time jump tragedy in large type. In a moment he swiveled around to face Bobbob. He planted both hands on the desktop with his palms raised off the surface a few centimeters by his fingertips, like five-legged spiders.

"Dr. Seththomas Nine-forty-six isn't dead," he stated reservedly as if announcing that, under normal circumstances, somebody important had died.

"Of course he's dead. I wrote that he's dead," corrected Bobbob.

"No. He's alive," explained Walterlewis. "Alive! He really exists. You didn't just make him up."

"Nonsense. I verified the namelogs."

There was a long pause during which Walterlewis blinked and Bobbob blinked back. How could Dr. Seththomas Nine-forty-six not be dead? He was never alive.

"There was a glitch," said Walterlewis.

"In the namelogs?"

Impossible.

Families hardly existed anymore, which coincided neatly with the age-old and much touted concept of the "rugged individualist." Most people were about as independent or "ruggedly individualistic" as a blade of grass is from the rest of the lawn, but that was entirely beside the point. Perception is everything; if a person thought of themselves as being a lone wolf, although the last sighting of a gray wolf in North America had long since faded from everyone's memory, it was all that mattered. The sizzle sold the social order.

Population was controlled for a variety of reasons, some good, some not entirely that bad. The overpopulation crises of the last century nearly wiped out the human species. Food shortages resulted in hostilities, cannibalism, and raids on all-nite mini-marts. Living spaces too often became dying spaces. Besides, women got damned tired of sacrificing their girlish figures and adventurous sex lives to what was largely unessential procreation. Men were enthusiastically on board with that ultimatum, too, it must be pointed out lest the womb-bearing half of the population get all the blame, credit, whatever the politics of the moment.

So when new people were needed they were created by artificial means. Nothing that hadn't been tried before. In vitro fertilization worked the best: babies in a bottle. Routine sexualization associated enhancement and augmentation procedures provided enough human germplasm to populate an entire solar system with warm bodies; maintaining a stable demographic wasn't even a challenge. The task now solely rested with the monolithic Central Birthing department. ("Ready whenever you are, CB!" went the slogan.)

Names got tricky, though. ID numbers fared poorly in polls. Here's how the system of human nomenclature finally worked out, in a nutshell:

Take chromosomal girls, for example. A list was made of every known female name, in alphabetical order. Less acceptable nicknames like Lardbutt or Sunflower were eliminated. The finalized list was coupled with a duplicate of itself, side by side. Every female got a name from each list, mashed together; the first name on the first list butted with each name on the second list, top to bottom, for as many individual names as the entries on the list. The last name was always One. Then the second name on the first list butted with each name on the second list, top to bottom. The last name was still always One. Repeat until all names on the first list have been used up, then repeat *with Two as the last name.* Ad infinitum. Dominus vobiscum. Who's your Daddy? The first female to get a "novaname" this way was Alicealice One, for the sake of explanation. The second female was called Alicebetty One. Down to Alicezelda One. Then back to Bettyalice One. After Zeldazelda One is assigned, the entire process repeats with Alicealice Two. Understand? As with any government program, the minute details enumerated enough to fill entire memory banks, in this case the *Ordinances for Population Nomenclature v.3.5*, but this simplified explanation will do.

The same system was used for chromosomal boys.

That's how Bobbob Sixty-seven got his name.

It worked.

Very well.

Until it didn't work.

Today.

"Jeez . . . How? I ran the namelogs at CB. Twice." Bobbob was partly confused, mostly frustrated.

"Apparently there was a glitch on their end, doncha know."

The entire framework of the newsmaking industry balanced precariously on the single commandment: it did not make any mistakes. Ever. Not even a typo. The implications of a falsification were, if not earth shattering, then at least dire. On a mere confusion of fact, the entire news organization could collapse, dissolving peoples' perceptions of the world around them in a steaming miasma of doubt, putting millions out of work, raising worldwide stress and taxes. If you couldn't trust the news, what could you trust? At least this was the party line. There were rumors. There were always rumors.

The name of Seththomas Nine-forty-six came up as unassigned. Seththomas Nine-forty-six did not exist. Bobbob used his newsmaker authorization to assign the name to his fictional character; thus Seththomas Nine-forty-six did exist. Except that Seththomas Nine-forty-six already existed; the assignment records had gotten inadvertently purged.

"Damn bureaucrats," Bobbob complained. "Maybe nobody will ever notice? Not like this other Seththomas Nine-forty-six is a wrock star. He isn't, is he?"

"Don't matter," the boss insisted, "we can't take any chances."

"So what do we do? Murder the poor skin sack?"

The boss did not even smile, or smirk, or twinkle. He uttered in a businesslike monotone, "We have the authorization."

"Wha—?"

Murder was a little-known protocol granted the newsmaking community for implementation in unforeseen screw-ups just like this one, in order to keep society happily rolling along like a well-oiled conveyor belt. Small sacrifices . . .

"Fortunately for us, the old guy's a bit of a recluse. Lives way outside of town, by himself. Rarely goes anywhere. Has few friends. He won't be missed."

"Goody for us," grumbled Bobbob.

The boss drummed at a spot on his desktop that turned into a tile that slid aside uncovering a small chamber out of which levitated an instrument of silver and glass and devilish purpose. "Take it," he offered. By accepting the weapon, Bobbob's epithelials would merge with the SensoGrip and legally register the device.

"I can't go blow somebody's head off like placing a bet on the lottery!" protested Bobbob.

"You took an oath as a newsmaker to protect the infallibility of the profession," said the boss. Bobbob did. All of them did.

"But . . . You do it. You're the boss."

Walterlewis scooted back half a meter from his desk to reveal his massive bulk, his walrus-like physique, his doughy hands that could barely hold a weapon let alone fire one with any accuracy. He didn't need to say anything. Besides, the boss didn't write the story. The oath was quite specific about responsibility.

"You're going to die if you don't get to a body shop soon," observed Bobbob.

"Not this week," answered the boss.

Back to the point. "There's gotta be repercussions," added Bobbob.

"You're a newsmaker, for Gloriosus sake." The boss was getting exasperated. "Handle the repercussions!"

Bobbob snorted. His mind kept batting around the notion that there had to be a better way, an alternative to becoming an undercover hit man for Organized Newsmaking. Nothing dawned at the moment. But something would, he was certain. He needed time to think about it, a commodity that he did not have at the present moment. Furiously, he snatched the weapon and heard the tinny weapon voice declare "Registration of Bobbob Sixty-seven accepted, have a nice day." He pivoted, then thundered from the office in great muscular strides.

"And requisition a normal pair of Walkers from Operations if you have to!" the boss called out as Bobbob departed.

1825 UTC.

*I will practice my profession conscientiously and with exacting research.*

*The tranquility and trust of society will be my only considerations.*

*I will guard the secrets which are confided in me.*

*I will protect to the death, by all the means granted to me, the integrity and the truthfulness of the newsmaking profession.*

It was that last paragraph from the Newsmakers Oath that got Bobbob into his current inextricable dilemma.

Forty years ago, give or take a summer, legendary newsmaker Gaillinda Eighteen was returning from her nephew's *Ball Mister*, working off a few too many Stix and Stonz, when the perfect story hit her plumb in the face. She thought it was a perfect story, so she ducked into the nearest net parlor and filed it.

The story which made the newsfeeds within hours related that a Hazelamy Forty-four and an Ernieed One-thirty-three lived on a nondescript 40-acre soybean and oat farm somewhere in the middle of the midwest where the air smelled of cow manure and locusts. You couldn't find the place on a map with a magnifying glass, even if you wanted to go there, which nobody did. But it seems that multiple times over the year, the couple *had* been visited by an Interstellar Garden Club. Planters from Outer Space. The Club had heard tales about the legendary farmlands of Earth and at last had the opportunity to dig their spades into it. Nobody knew why, except that following each visit Hazelamy and Ernieed were given thank-you gifts: golden jars of green jelly and a large blue marble. The jelly was delicious but the purpose and composition of the marble was never fully understood. It may have been an alien representation of Earth, for a charm bracelet. It weighed half a kilogram, though.

The alien farmers, described by Hazelamy and Ernieed, were short, round, albino, with shoulder length copper-colored hair, and had saucer-shaped ice-pink eyes. They wore what looked like denim with red-checkered neckerchiefs. They were gentle, however, not menacing in any way. They spoke perfect English (with a Jamaican accent); sang it actually, and the music was enormously comforting. It put the couple to sleep and that is why they had no memories of what happened during most of the growing season.

Exciting, absorbing, and perfect, Gaillinda concluded.

Except it was quickly discovered that a flesh-and-blood Hazelamy Forty-four and Ernieed One-thirty-three really did exist. Hazelamy taught crafts and political science at the local senior center. Ernieed was a gambler and part-time bookie. They didn't know each other before the story was published. After it ran on the newsfeeds, they knew each other all too well.

They had colluded, conspired, gotten together with each other at a nearby stimulant cafe and plotted to defraud. The flesh-and-blood Hazelamy and Ernieed sought to capitalize on their mistaken identities by claiming it was them in the newsfeeds. They had sold their spread, or something along those lines, they explained. They were now offering media rights to the highest bidder. They expected the real Hazelamy and Ernieed might eventually show up but as the real (fake) couple lived on a remote farm, it would take a while. So they had to act fast. They were, of course, unaware that there was no real (fake) Hazelamy and Ernieed, living on a farm or otherwise. The newsmaking community, however, couldn't take any chances. It obviously couldn't be revealed that the real Hazelamy and Ernieed were, in fact, frauds, because they weren't. The fraudulent Hazelamy and Ernieed were the frauds. It might have gotten complicated. But fate and the gods of newsmaking stepped in to save the day. The real Hazelamy and Ernieed, in their greed, unwittingly presented the CIA with the solution to this dilemma.

The solution was simple. Because the real (fake) Hazelamy and Ernieed were not in fact real, it could be reported that they chose to go live with their alien sod-busting buddies and subsequently departed the planet with them, forever to sow their oats on extraterrestrial acres, generating hours, even days, of speculation, and selling plenty of additional newsfeed subscriptions. Meanwhile, the inconveniently real Hazelamy and Ernieed were lured to an undisclosed location with a generous offer for exclusive media rights and summarily whisked away in a large black FreightLev never to be seen or heard from again. After all, had they not departed for galaxies unknown with their benevolent visitors from the stars?

Case solved. Squeaky clean. Except somewhere along the line the fact had been overlooked that the CIA didn't have the right to eliminate people to protect the integrity of their stories. It was an outrage. Not having that right. A law was subsequently passed, in chambers, called the Newsmaking Source Protection Act, which established that right.

And that is how that last paragraph from the Newsmakers Oath got Bobbob into his current inextricable dilemma.

2105 UTC.

The house that Seththomas Nine-forty-six lived in was about 20 kilometers outside of town, down the first left turn past the last tramz depot another couple of kilometers, and behind a stand of scrubby pine trees. The single-story house was nearly ancient, made of wood and bricks, materials hardly ever used anymore. That it was still standing was a wonder. It hadn't been condemned; no reason considering the location.

Bobbob settled the plastic green with silver trim company shooe just to the side of the trees where the path to the house began. Bobbob wasn't sure what he was going to do on his way out here and he wasn't sure what he was going to do now that he'd arrived. His nose for news sensed something; sensed something that warranted forging ahead full bore and letting the moment dictate the consequences. *Trees? Grass? A cowpath? A cottage? Made of gingerbread? Should he be skipping?* Bobbob was out of his element.

It got weirder.

As he approached, he saw a panel on the side of the house that he presumed was the door. It didn't have a hand plate. It had a ball attached to it. He passed his hand over the ball, but nothing happened. He touched the ball. No response. He knocked on the ball.

"Open," he commanded, hesitantly. "Door, open. C'mon door, open!"

It did, finally. The door didn't slide open. It swung open like a flap. Bobbob couldn't help but stare at the odd mechanism; he'd read about them; he'd even seen one in a museum; this was for real. Elegant in its simplicity, absent the barely imperceptible hum of modern sliding doors; manually operated.

"Then you haven't come to kill me and I can put this thing away?" asked the man who had opened the door with one hand, holding an obsolete but still very effective Sig Sauer P290 in the other hand.

Bobbob was too absorbed in the primitive portal technology to pay any attention.

"I imagine not or we'd be in a heated gun battle right now," the man decided. "That's good. I don't want to kill you either and I sure the hell don't want you to kill me. Are you coming in?"

"Kill?" Bobbob replied the best he could, distracted as he was. He stepped indoors.

There were things on the walls. Not images. The walls weren't skinned. Real items hung from them: pictures, mostly; a small, older wall-unit TV monitor; lighting sources; the head of an antlered ruminant; clothing. Curiously absent were any appliances—no legs, arms, implants, hairpieces. Against the far wall stood a large white enameled box with bits of rust like scabs. It could have been a personal shooe, but it didn't have any windows. "What's that?"

"Pleased to meet you, too. That's a refrigerator. It holds food."

"Eating food? You eat food?"

"All the time. It's tasty stuff. You should try some. Your gut's not entirely atrophied. Believe me, I know. And you are . . .?"

At last shaken from his reverie, Bobbob excused himself, flushed, reached out a palm, "Sorry, I'm Bobbob Sixty-seven."

"Dr. Seththomas Nine-forty-six. But you know that already." The old man introduced himself. He was very old and it was disconcerting to see a man so old lacking any ordinary replacements, upgrades, longevity enhancements, simple surgeries, or nutritional additives to retard spoilage. He was probably close to 90, the way nonagenarians used to look before geriatric medicine and biomechanics extended the average lifespan to 150, while at the same time stabilizing the aging process to around 55. His head looked like the skin had been stingily spray-painted on over the skull, covered with a thinning pelt of limp white hair that you could see through. His long face and jaw bore a scruffy coating of unshaven beard. His teeth, yellowed, were large, a few of them missing. He had skinny arms, the hide itself the color and toughness of beef jerky, with knobby protruding elbows. He was wearing a retro black tee-shirt and pants. The pants seemed stylish, although dirty. He had on sandals. He was tanned. Country tanned. Farmer tanned. Not like the cosmopolitan beige of Bobbob's own dermal pride.

"Do you drink? Can I get you anything to drink?" Seththomas inquired. "I don't have any Stix. Never touch the stuff."

Bobbob declined with a gesture. "You said you are a doctor, too? That's a coincidence."

"Yeah. Animal doctor. Dog doctor. Cat doctor. Fish doctor. Long time ago. Gave all that up with the rest of the fakery. Mostly. But I'm not entirely unenhanced, you know. My left ear's bioelectronic. I've taken a few nano injections. I'm actually 120. What can I say? I'm not a hypocrite, though. I never pretended to be a purist. I got sick and tired of living in a big screen version of reality and came out here to . . . well . . . live real."

Bobbob nodded. He could sort of understand.

"Sure I can't get you anything? A ham sandwich? Got some fresh-made veggie cheese. Fruit is abundant out here. It's like the stuff grows on trees!"

"Ham?" Bobbob was taken aback. "That's meat, isn't it?"

"Yes, it is. You plastic people are completely unaware of what's an hour or so beyond your techno-bubbles, aren't you?" Seththomas grinned, showing off his big teeth. "All kinds of wild game, fish, birds, fruits, nuts, berries. Trapped me a turkey last month. A turkey. Imagine that. Big old hen. Dee-licious."

"C'mon," scoffed Bobbob, "*Wildman Willy. Lives off the land. Squirrel skins for boots. He eats what he can.*" He recited a popular nursery rhyme.

"Now who's exaggerating?" Seththomas retorted. "I said I was a veterinarian. A damn fine one, too! I got quite a bankroll stashed away. And with some careful investments, I'm probably wealthier than you are. Good Internet connection here. Satellite feeds. The last tramz stops up the road."

"Sex?"

"Never the marryin' sort. Last tramz stops up the road."

Bobbob had mixed feelings. Every now and again the thought of chucking the whole assembly line and cutting for a dreamy utopia had often crossed his viewscreen. But he quickly realized the folly of the fantasy with his very next craving for a flavorful Stix or intoxicating touch of a fleshy male or female. He was wedded to city life. The bright lights served his passions and he served the bright lights. As an elite newsmaker, he had the power to affect peoples' lives, generally for the good. Yeah, it was mostly entertainment. What wasn't these days? He was creative. He had authority. He had prestige. He had influence.

There *was* a price. The demands were enormous, often with long hours. The responsibility would weigh on lesser shoulders like balancing a tub of poured stone while slogging through an eternity of sand. Fortunately for Bobbob, his shoulders were the latest model, physically and figuratively. He not only slogged, he pranced. He could understand what drove some people to seek a simpler existence on the fringes of the modern world; let them go, as long as it wasn't too many of them. For him, making food, obtaining nutritional requirements the old-fashioned way by eating, and the subsequent bodily functions that entailed, sent a queasy wave through his own scrupulously clean gastrointestinal plumbing. One could even hire sex workers who were also licensed to process bodily fluids. A prehistoric custom. Charming, perhaps, to ancestors long dead, but too damned messy for Bobbob!

There was still that pressing matter he had come out all this way to address.

"Rectifying your fake news article with my name in it," flatly declared Seththomas. Then he gradually smiled as if to reveal a long held secret. "That's right. I knew it was phony the second it came across the newsfeeds. But not just 'cause of my name. I've always known you folks made all that stuff up. I suspected there'd be repercussions."

"What?" Bobbob's fingers tensed around his own weapon. "How?"

Seththomas reacted. "Is that what it's going to be, then? Draw, pardner." He chuckled. "You don't seem like the shooter type to me."

"I'm not," Bobbob relaxed.

"Me neither." Seththomas paused. He changed the subject. "It isn't that difficult to figure out, you know, that most of the news is entertainment. Manufactured. Like nearly everything else in this life. It all got too tawdry for me. Told you I wanted to get away from it all. That's why I'm out here. The moment I saw my name in that article, I knew you guys would be after me, though. Dammit."

"I'm not a murderer," Bobbob confessed.

"Me neither," Seththomas repeated.

"Bit of a pickle."

"You want one?" offered Seththomas. "Fresh made. Let me get you one out of the fridge. Crispy cold. You'll love it."

Bobbob hadn't eaten anything of real substance in a long time. One small pickle couldn't hurt, although he'd probably still need to run into the Jiffy Purge tomorrow. "Okay. Thanks."

All pickles aside—and it was good, refreshing, tart, crunchy—Bobbob was knee deep in a quandary and sinking further by the minute. Kill or be killed was not exactly what he signed on for with this job. *We all take the oath, never imagining in our wildest fantasies it would come down to this.* He chewed. He fretted. "Got another pickle?"

"Two pickles? You are reckless."

It was a two pickle problem.

There had always been rumors that more people than the official estimates suspected the news wasn't news, but played along for a number of reasons: no desire to upset a comfortable existence; conformity; it was such rollicking great entertainment. Mostly the latter. Kind of made one wonder if the newsmakers' oath was necessary in the first place. The question of which rattled loosely round in Bobbob's brain at the moment. He squelched it fast. *Heresy!*

"So shoot the moose," suggested Seththomas.

Bobbob looked up.

"The moose. On the wall. Shoot it."

"Why?"

"You can't go back empty-handed, so to speak. You'd be unceremoniously drummed out of the newswriting . . . newsmaking . . . corps, whatever. Forced to become a sixpack driver or worse, for parts. Shoot the moose. I know how those laser weapons work. They register discharges. Double tap the moose and you've got a record to show for it."

"That'd be dishonest." Bobbob protested. The irony was palpable.

"You lie all the time, for chrissakes! Handle the repercussions." That sounded familiar. "Fabricate some idiot story about a nuclear gas leak, right here, right where I'm standing. Hot gases. Lots of radioactivity. Half-life of decades, maybe centuries."

"You'd have to move."

Seththomas almost wanted to shoot himself. "It's not *real!* You'd be off the hook. Nobody'd come out here . . . forever. Except maybe the people who know it's not real. I already mentioned them. But the people who think it is real, or want to think it is real, which it isn't, they'd be convinced. End of story. Your integrity remains intact."

"It might work," muttered Bobbob.

"Shoot the moose."

A night owl in flight over the little house that evening would have seen the flash of light from the laser weapon spill through the cracks and seams. Several times. But heard no sound. Laser weapons are silent. Bobbob was, after all, a seasoned newsmaker and devoted to his craft.

0232 UTC.

Registered eroticist Mollymaya Twenty-three was waiting in front of Bobbob's apartment when he arrived home. He'd almost forgotten that he'd made the appointment. Mollymaya was pleasantly meaty, with a round face, large features, and the best figure money could buy. Today she was female, wearing a wig of short jet-black hair and heavy plastic eyeglasses. She didn't need the glasses, of course; they were purely for decoration. As was everything else. Her sheer red dress revealed a good amount of cleavage, as well as her bare legs from above the knees down. She smelled like cinnamon with a musky base foundation of pheromones.

"Hi!"

Bobbob reacted with a pleasant rush. His midsection bulged. He couldn't take his eyes off her. In the mood for a female, he had chosen well. Distracted, he forgot to pass his hand over the doorplate and it wouldn't open at first.

"Sorry."

"No prob."

Finally, the door slid open. He walked in. She waltzed in. The door slid closed. The room was sparsely furnished; a jumbo sofa near the far wall, a few faux-glass tables, some shelves.

"What would you like?" asked Bobbob.

"On the walls?" she inquired.

"No, no. Can't."

Mollymaya held her breath. It was apparent that the skinning had been removed from the walls. Instead hung a gallery of two-dimensional pictures, framed. Although Mollymaya hardly recognized any of the images, there was the Mona Lisa, a Warhol, a Tubifex Worm, and a triptych of unspecified origins.

"You ain't a wingnut?" Mollymaya asked apprehensively.

"No, of course not," Bobbob assured, "just a little bored with the pop culture scene. Figured a spot of retro for a change of pace. Get back to one's roots. Live real."

"I need a Stix," was all that Mollymaya said.

"Got something better."

Bobbob walked over to a strange metal-like cabinet that made a hiss when he struggled open the heavy door. He reached inside, clanged against something, and brought out a large, clear container. The door shut loudly by itself.

"Pickles!" Bobbob announced. "You must try a pickle."

*Sam Bellotto Jr. is a retired magazine editor with almost 40 years of experience piloting a wide variety of magazines from automobiles to xylophones. Currently, he is editor of* Perihelion Science Fiction, *an online magazine that he actually launched back in the late '60s as a print publication. He also occasionally writes stories. His work has appeared in the* Twisted Tails *anthologies,* Bewildering Stories, Every Day Fiction, *and elsewhere.*

Two con men learn the "barren" planet they're selling to a cold-blooded Mafioso may actually be inhabited. To make matters worse, something very odd is happening inside the underground chambers.

# CLAIM JUMPERS

### By

### *Doug C. Souza*

Stupid hatch.

Bulky and cumbersome, like it belonged on some ancient submarine. Instead, it sat smack-dab on the barren surface of New Hygiea. Pockmarked and barren, the onyx terrain screamed, "Free property for those who get here first!"

Prime to be seized, had it not been for that stupid ugly hatch.

You see . . . hatch meant inhabited.

"Definitely man-made." Ronnie's smarmy tone had me wondering if his enviro-suit could absorb a stomach punch. The high-end enviro-suits the Fat Man, our mark, had lent us. Ahem—excuse me—our investor Mr. Ruffinego.

"Lighten up," he jostled my shoulder. "We'll still close the deal."

I brushed him off, "We *did* close the deal and were nearly gone before you let the Fat Man pull us back."

He seemed about to reply, but then thought better of it.

The microgravity on New Hygiea only added to my aggravation. The weak pull required walking-sticks that pierced the granite type surface. Our boots were also spiked, but far too weak for anything other than slight tread.

Ronnie and I had plodded along, like two centenarians, piercing the ground with the seven-inch lance. The feeling had been something akin to mountain climbing—except we would have drifted *upward* to our death.

I went to rub my temples, but my hands bounced off the faceplate. I settled for a hard wince and sigh.

Ronnie shrugged and kicked the side of the hatch.

"You didn't think to check the shuttle for overrides?" I asked accusingly. We were a quarter of the way home when The Fat Man remotely accessed our shuttle and summoned us back.

"No, 'cause I didn't think we'd get called back while in range. Usually takes a day or two before the mark wises up."

"Too busy counting the money." I turned away to stare at the myriad crescents overhead. New Hygiea's skyscape was speckled with billions and billions of asteroids. Rocks the size of freighters glittered like small moons.

"No." Ronnie jabbed his data-pad in my face. "I've been busting my hump finalizing the transfer. Also, I've done a complete info-dump of all facts New Hygiea. *I'll* find out who was brain boiled enough to come here, you keep the run going with the Fat Man. Remember, this is a two-man job. We'd be looking at nothing if I hadn't—"

"Get your game face on," I interrupted. "Here he comes."

We watched the magnificent space-yacht *Tyrannis* pivot above us as a schooner exited its docking bay. I glanced over at our own shuttle parked a few meters back. The Fat Man had merrily lent it to us when everything had been copasetic, just over an hour ago. Not only had he paid us a handsome finder's fee, he had lent us the schooner: an Elite-class shuttle we didn't plan on returning.

All scans had run nice and happy until— WHAMMY—that prehistoric hatch appeared on some viewscreen in the *Tyrannis*, blemishing the otherwise desolate planet of New Hygiea. The hatch wasn't exactly prehistoric, but definitely pre-Solar Expansionism, or whatever they're calling the Space Rush nowadays.

The Fat Man did not look happy. He didn't use the cumbersome walking-sticks and boots. Instead, he had a small mini-jet at each wrist. His gut bounced furiously as he maneuvered toward us. How he made it jiggle in New Hygiea's microgravity was beyond me. Obviously he was no veteran when it came to operating mini-jets in low-g. Vivincia, his Amazonian bodyguard, sailed in after him. Her graceful glide was much easier on the eyes.

Heavy, choppy exhales sounded in my earpiece as they came within range.

Through the enviro-suit's faceplate I saw that the Fat Man's salt-and-pepper hair hung down in strands. He had prepped in a hurry. Not a good sign.

He shoved past us with a small burst from his mini-jets. He knelt at the hatch and slapped his hand against it several times. It took me a moment to realize he was trying to knock.

*Don't you think it would have opened from the inside already if we were a welcomed sight?*

"Open it," he ordered and stepped away. Vivincia landed gracefully as an egret. She examined the hatch while pulling a small satchel of tools from a pouch.

Still no "Hello" for Ronnie or me. Another bad sign.

I fumbled for the all-talk switch on my wrist console. The safety bracelet attached to my walking-stick hindered my movements. "Mr. Ruffinego,"—you didn't call him Fat Man to his face— "that may not be safe," I said, using my most cautious, scientist-type voice, "There may be micro-contaminants—"

"See that suit of mine you're wearing," he pinched my sleeve, "it may be skintight, but it ain't weak. It's what's keeping you from popping like a zit out 'ere. I ain't worried about catching a cold."

Dribbles of spittle collected on the inside of his faceplate as he talked. A horizontal line dropped down and whipped the moisture away.

I nodded and returned my attention to the beauty working the hatch. As Vivincia bent down to lift the hatch, she gave us a view of her glorious backside.

Skintight indeed.

The hatch budged a mere few centimeters. We watched for any response from inside.

Nothing. Finally, a good sign.

She rearranged her hand on the rung, utilizing the thrust from the mini-jets at her wrists.

"Ahach-ck!" Ronnie coughed.

The Fat Man didn't flinch.

"AHACK-HAK!" he coughed more loudly.

The Fat Man remained transfixed on Vivincia's progress.

I switched off the all-talk. "We still got the private channel," I confirmed as I looked away to conceal my face. I had a feeling the Fat Man wouldn't appreciate our conducting private conversations behind his back. "Don't get lazy, always check your 'all-talk' switch." My partner was too much of a professional to allow such an error, but I chastised him anyway. Taking him down a peg or two felt good.

Ronnie shot me a hurt look and then said, "That's some view, tell her to give it a little shake, eh Fatty?"

No response to Ronnie's comment.

Instead, "Give her a hand," the Fat Man growled.

I made a face showing I didn't appreciate being ordered around. He returned my look with a glare saying, "I'd love to take you back to my yacht and have you jettisoned somewhere near the outer rim." I knelt down to help. I anchored my feet and shoved.

G-pull on New Hygiea was about 0.008 of Original Earth. The hatch must have been gummed up because it barely budged as we toiled.

While the buffed beauty and I worked, Ronnie wormed a different approach to our run with the Fat Man.

"Mr. Ruffinego, according to the most recent addendum, primary appropriators can still attain mining claims on discovered territories as long as any pre-existing territories are sufficiently abandoned," Ronnie said as he tapped his data-pad meticulously. It was amazing how seconds ago he sounded like some garish juvenile and now he carried the cadence of a pompous, finely threaded suit.

"Sufficiently abandoned," the Fat Man muttered. You could practically hear the wheels cranking to life in his head.

I wanted to grin. Such strokes of genius were why I brought Ronnie. He may underestimate the complexity and dangers to the job, but he could fabricate legal jargon like no other. He had planted a properly evil seed for the Fat Man to cultivate.

Remove pestering habitants = ownership of planet. Not a difficult job for a capo in the Stellar-Mafia.

With new vigor, the Fat Man knelt down and helped us open the hatch the rest of the way.

We peered down into the dark emptiness.

"Throw your light," the Fat Man told Ronnie.

"Uh . . . what?"

Vivincia reached over, tore open a pouch at Ronnie's thigh, and yanked out a compact lantern.

She flicked it on and tossed it down the hole.

It drifted, slowly spinning.

No ladder. Not a surprise, ladders weren't common in microgravity.

Finally, the light settled, maybe ten meters down. Smidges of shadow revealed footholds and a grab-rail along the interior of the walls down the shaft.

"You first."

Dammit, he had pointed at me.

I flicked a button and the walking sticks retracted with a quick snap. I sheathed them at my side. A subtle magnetic drag started on the soles of my boots as I entered the hatch. I maneuvered two footholds at a time, not needing the grab-rail, and it wasn't long before I was on the floor picking up the compact lantern.

"Well?" the Fat Man asked from above.

"Nothing, idiot," is what I wanted to say, but instead I answered, "It is difficult to discern with the limited illumination, however, it is clear the structure is abandoned."

"Done and done," Ronnie cheered in our private channel.

"Go down," the Fat Man said. I waited to see who joined us. If it were Ronnie coming down, the hatch closing us in would be the last thing we saw. That meant the Fat Man had discovered Ronnie and I weren't legit. These moments in the run got my blood going, part of the thrill and addiction.

I pointed the light upward and was greeted with Vivincia's wonderful behind. Did I mention the skintight enviro-suits?

Ronnie soon followed. We listened to every grunt and groan as the Fat Man made his arduous shuffle down the shaft. "Turn off your all-talk switch," I willed. No go.

I stomped my feet to get the blood flowing. It was a sparse g-pull, about a tenth normal.

I handed Ronnie back his compact lantern and pulled out mine. The design made it difficult to hold. I fiddled with it, trying to get a decent grip with the cumbersome enviro-suit gloves. Two seconds later I saw Vivincia snap it into place just under her palm. I copied, pretending I knew how to all along.

We scanned our surroundings. Besides the steel flooring, footholds, and vertical railing, the rocky walls were practically empty. Thin striations creased the interior. Some metal struts lined the inside, but very few. I searched for any symbols or letters on the steel plating, but found it covered with grimy mucus. I ran my gloved finger to clear some away, but doing so scraped bits of the metal with it.

I examined my glove, but the substance dried instantly and dissipated into nothingness. I checked the steel-plate and discovered that the trail was gone. I peered closer. It was as if I had never touched the plate.

"There." The Fat Man pointed his lantern toward a single door hidden inside a grotto. The door appeared similar in bulk and design to the hatch.

Vivincia started working the door. From the drag of her feet it was clear she also had magnetic soles. I assisted of my own accord, depriving the Fat Man the satisfaction of issuing more orders. Using the lantern, I checked to see if the door was welded shut because it wasn't budging. The same grime covered the handle, making a solid grip difficult.

"I think it's paired with the hatch," Ronnie said in our private channel. I sneaked a glance up to see he was correct. A drop-pin had locked the hinges. Had I been in a more helpful mood, I would have commented on this and even suggested we use the walking-sticks to increase leverage. Since no one had come to greet us, I gambled, hoping the Fat Man would send us on our way.

*It's locked, might as well go home,* I thought.

Vivincia turned to the Fat Man shaking her head. Wisps of dust floated around us. It grew thicker each time we displaced more grime.

He shined his lantern across to the door. Then above it. Then following the lever connecting the pin to the hinges. Then he eyeballed the hatchway.

*Dammit.*

"An airlock. Shut the hatch," he ordered Ronnie. My partner nodded exorbitantly, playing the kiss-ass lawyer to perfection. He even fumbled a bit with the footholds and grab-rail.

*Okay, don't overdo it.*

We watched as the locking drop-pin lifted when the hatch above us closed. I waited for the telltale signs of an airlock being accessed, but no torrents of air gushed inside. Searching the walls, I found the vents, but they remained still.

Nothing changed as Vivincia pulled open the door. It revealed a narrow corridor, similar to those in old seafaring battleships. A maze of pipes, arranged in some brilliant engineering feat to save space, decorated the walls. It made for a tight squeeze.

"Mr. Ruffinego, it appears our work is done here," Ronnie held up his data-pad, taking pictures. After a few snapshots, he showed the Fat Man the evidence that the structure was clearly abandoned.

He ignored Ronnie.

"Go," he ordered Vivincia, then pointed to me, "You next, then you," to Ronnie. Single-file, we started down the passageway, the Fat Man bringing up the rear. I switched off the power to my magnetic soles and drifted at a cautious swim down the passage way. "U" handholds appeared every other meter,

It didn't make sense. The Fat Man should be ecstatic. Not only had he *supposedly* just laid claim on a highly sought-after planet, but he would *supposedly* gain rights to this structure. Why not let us go? I wasn't worried about a double-cross because, as far as the Fat Man knew, Ronnie and I were the only ones who could draw up the legal papers for procuring this planet.

"How did we miss this during preseason?" I asked Ronnie privately.

"Easily, I've been covertly pouring over file after file and anything with New Hygiea comes up nil."

"Yep," I muttered sarcastically, "no one's ever been to New Hygiea or settled it."

Something changed the deeper in we went. The walls of the corridor shimmered. Small bits of lettering appeared, but had grown indecipherable, overrun with filth. I ran a hand along a wall and discovered it was wet. Not heavy moisture, but a thin film. Again, it dried and disappeared from my hand.

"What's that?" the Fat Man asked, peering past Ronnie's shoulder.

Clueless, I rubbed my thumb and forefinger together. Not much difference from my other hand.

"I do not have adequate tools to conduct a conclusive test, however—" I tried.

"What?" the Fat Man grabbed my hand to get a closer look.

"Water," I said with confidence, but had no idea what it was.

He flung my hand away. It was then I noticed the pipes along the wall were splotched with mold, but I kept it to myself. The last thing I wanted to do was pique the Fat Man's curiosity.

We came to a threshold. The door was open and we had to descend a gangway to get inside.

A medical bay. Or what appeared to be. It was hard to discern in the roaming beams of our four compact lanterns. Rows and rows of steel beds bolted to the smooth rocky floor. A spongy lining topped the bed. I pressed my hand into the material. It broke away at the slightest touch.

"Decontamination chamber," I adlibbed, "used to check for contaminants."

"No kidding, genius," the Fat Man said.

*Yeah, like he knew.*

"Abandoned," I reminded him. "Long ago."

"You still taking pictures?" the Fat Man asked Ronnie.

Ronnie held the data-pad up, "Yes sir."

"Stop," he said heading back to the door, "and delete the ones you got."

"Yes, sir," Ronnie answered. You could hear the delight in his voice.

"Get a burn crew down here," the Fat Man told Vivincia, "use no more than three guys, guys who can keep their mouths tight." He slowed, making sure Ronnie and I comprehended, "Guys that realize speaking *one* word about this place will be a horrible mistake, 'cause they don't know what they saw."

I fought every cell in my body trying not to pirouette gleefully in the low-g. Instead, I struck a stoic pose, and feigned hesitation. A true scientist would want to explore. Ronnie holstered his data-pad and turned to hurry out. A lawyer would just want to leave.

"You drop that schooner at Deimos Port as planned," the Fat Man put a hand up, stopping Ronnie, "I've got markers to set planet-side. You'll get the rest of your money once the deed clears."

"Since we've got absolutely no property licenses to put the fix on you anyway," Ronnie started on the private channel, "how about we just keep the shuttle, the 15% down, get lost on a beach Earth-side and you go to—"

The Fat Man's head snapped around, his eyes fiery.

Ronnie gulped, sharing my thought: he had been boasting over the all-talk.

But it was Vivincia. She hadn't moved.

"Mr. Ruffinego, over there." It was the first time I had heard her voice. She must have been calling him during Ronnie's playful rant.

Our lanterns joined Vivincia's lone beam and centered in on the intruder.

Someone stood stock-still in a vintage spacesuit. Bulgy, cylindrical arms and legs connected to an unwieldy torso that held a bubble-shaped helmet. It looked puffy and almost comically out of place. The convex face plate reflected a gold tint in the beam of our lanterns.

"Run that through your search," I told Ronnie.

"Already am."

Something was off about the posture. The head cocked to the side, as if examining us, but the rest of the body stood hunched forward, unnaturally still. Like a marionette doll, waiting to have its strings tugged. Awaiting directions.

He moved.

His arm drifted upward like a leaf on a breeze. Wisps of dust swirled throughout the room.

"Must be remnants of an air circulation system," I tried, but even as it left my lips it didn't sound convincing. The entire time we had been in the med-bay I hadn't felt the slightest drag of an air current.

"Or could be gyrostatically moving within New Hygiea's orbital pull," Ronnie piped in.

That made more sense.

"No." Vivincia wasn't sold. I noticed she had a weapon drawn and pointed squarely at the intruder. Her doubt troubled the Fat Man. We kept our lanterns fixed on the person in the old spacesuit as the arms lifted only inches.

The movement wasn't random. The guy *did* stand slightly hunched, but his arms twitched with a purpose. Not sign language. Too slow, and hardly noticeable at first glance. A pattern to the movement became clearer.

As if underwater, his arms dangled upward, stopping just below chest level, and the thick fingers of the gloves opened and retracted. The same movements over and over. Like he was completing some private task.

Vivincia stepped closer, drawing us with her. Each of us kept our lanterns trained on the lethargic intruder.

"Hey!" the Fat Man yelled.

No response and I didn't feel like explaining that sound-waves were practically nonexistent down here.

"That guy's gonna mess everything up," Ronnie said.

"Yep. Start thinking of something."

"And what the hell's he doing?"

Vivincia kept her shooter locked on the target and waved her free hand in a large arc. She stepped up to the body.

Somehow, I knew she didn't need the shooter. The guy moved too drunkenly to be a threat. His arms just drifted in front of him, slow-mo typing on some invisible keyboard. A cloud of dust-bunnies drifted away and disappeared.

Using the tip of the lantern, Vivincia prodded the guy's hand. And then his arm.

His whole body turned and scarcely lifted off the ground, but dropped back down and stood. Vivincia took a step back, keeping her shooter pointed at the guy.

He leaned against the wall. His back turned, but his hands and fingers continued to open and close in that same pattern. The helmet turned subtly and then back.

Vivincia gave a rougher poke and the body fell completely to the ground.

*So some grav-pull on him, but not much.*

His arms and hands still grasped errantly, like a kid wanting his teddy. For a long moment Vivincia knelt next to the guy, her lantern running up and down the length of the archaic spacesuit.

The Fat Man waited patiently near one of the old medical beds, arms crossed.

I snuck Ronnie a "What do you think?" look. He shook his head.

"Mr. Ruffinego," Vivincia said, her lantern fixed on a spot near the guy's tinted faceplate.

The Fat Man swung his bulk forward, shined his own light and quietly asked, "How can that—"

His voice wavered, absent of that machismo drawl.

The Fat Man stared at the guy in the spacesuit while waving us over. His gesture was fast and pleading: no yelling, no belittling.

Ronnie trailed and drifted next to me as we realized what had spooked the Fat Man.

At first I didn't know what I was supposed to be looking for. The guy's arms and hands continued their slow movement.

Vivincia knocked her lantern on the faceplate. Up close, the beam of light penetrated the reflective tint. I squinted to make sure I saw it right.

Just the inside of an empty helmet.

Empty.

I jumped back, jostling the body with a kick as I stood. I spin-tumbled in the low gravity.

A hand grabbed my shoulder, righting me.

It was Ronnie. "Easy," he said on our private channel followed by, "What is it?" over the all-talk.

"There's no one in there," I said.

I watched the spacesuit slowly spin upward after my kick. The hands still moving of their own accord.

"Some automated system?" Ronnie asked over the all-talk. "This would sound better coming from a scientist," he reminded me privately.

I blinked hard, "Uhm, yeah, probably old protocols from a wayward algorithm, simple program still running."

Mumbo-jumbo. That suit was controlled by something else. I hit my hand on the faceplate of my enviro-suit as I tried unsuccessfully to wipe my brow. I blinked away sweat that had trickled into my eyes. Sensing the moisture build-up, my internal wiper squeegeed the inside of my faceplate. The auto-feature nearly had me yelping. I reinstated the magnetic pull on my boots.

Vivincia reached up and dangled the suit before the Fat Man. He looked closely, yanking the hands.

"Weird," he said, followed by "Burn the suit first."

Vivincia grunted, tossed the old spacesuit into the air, and shot it. A percussion wave tore a hole through the stomach. The perimeter of the hole sparkled bluish and silver embers as the spacesuit disappeared into the darkness of the med-bay.

We turned to leave.

I walked in a daze, wondering how it was possible. The old suits didn't have anything automated except for the bare essentials like air exchange, catheters, temp control. It wasn't until recently that spacesuits had incorporated typical EVA controls into sleeves and leggings. But that suit was far older.

Too caught up in my own thoughts I accidentally bumped the Fat Man. I hit him pretty hard and awaited the inevitable scolding. Instead, he said nothing, but fired his mini-jets frantically, falling back and nearly trampling me. Again, I stumbled in the low-g.

*What the hell?*

I rose, looked past him, and immediately understood.

The way we had entered was blocked. Numerous spacesuits stood hunched. Some in the doorway, but most in the corridor outside.

Ronnie reached around me, pointing out something to my left.

It was another spacesuit, but not near the doorway. This one stood near a medical bed. Just like the first spacesuit, it moved its arms in a practiced motion. As if meticulously working on some unseen patient.

The four of us waited back to back, lanterns sweeping across the med-bay. Each beam of light revealed spacesuits that hadn't been there moments ago. Vivincia stood closest to the bodies at the door, pointing her shooter.

"Take 'em out," the Fat Man said evenly.

Just as before, a percussion wave ripped through the ancient material, but this time it continued through more than one suit. The bodies toppled backward. Shiny dust sparkled and exploded like fireworks. Instead of fading, however, the flickering dust brightened and then coalesced into a cloud.

The suits behind the fallen plodded forward. They didn't step over the bodies, but came in a slow wave. They jammed the doorway.

The Fat Man's heavy breathing sounded in my earpiece.

Vivincia took another shot immediately followed by a second, and a third. More dust collected into the nimbus, which became a thick milky blue. Then radiant layers of light trickled out and rippled across bits of dust.

More bodies pushed through, the torn spacesuits drifted upward.

Vivincia shouldered her way into the crowd, her mini-jets at full-throttle. For a moment it looked like she was going to make it through. Ronnie jumped after her.

And stopped short as I grabbed his leg, yanking him back.

"No," I said. "Not yet."

He surveyed the med-bay wondering why I stopped him. We watched Vivincia go deeper into the sea of bodies. Ronnie thrashed, trying to break free. I freed one of my walking-sticks, anchored it and reeled him in.

Vivincia seemed okay, yet my gut told me to holdfast. The bodies ignored her as something flickered. I held my walking-stick with one hand and righted Ronnie with the other so he stood at my side.

"What're you doing? We have to get outta here," he yelled.

I nodded toward Vivincia.

The crowd of bodies was no longer ignoring her, but they weren't exactly bothered by her either. They simply moved to face her. Instead of continuing past the doorway, toward all of us, they focused on her. The blue nebula faded into the crowd of spacesuits.

"Oomph," she gasped over the headset.

Phosphorescence wisps darted from suit to suit, spiraling in on Vivincia, now dead-center in the crowd. Our lanterns were no longer needed in the pulsing glow. She continued to club the empty suits away, but there were too many.

"Get her out of there!" the Fat Man glared at us.

The bodies had fully converged on her. A fine blue light hovered around them, the apex remained locked on Vivincia. Her arms stopped flailing. Her voice quieted of any protest. An eerie resignation that had me wanting to yank out my earpiece. Of course, I couldn't, not with the enviro-suit. The blue nebula drifted into her suit. She dropped.

"This way," I said releasing the walking-stick and hoisting myself along the med-bay beds as I pulled Ronnie in tow. I called after the Fat Man, ordering him to follow. I glanced back and saw Vivincia slouching listlessly, the crowd of bodies turned away from her and toward us. The blue nebula returned and sparkled above the crowd of suits. I led us into the darkest corners of the med-bay. Illuminated beams from our lanterns swung intermittently, searching for a way out.

"There!" Ronnie shouted.

Only a few bodies littered the narrow passageway. The Fat Man pointed his shooter.

"No!" I yelled. "Don't touch the suits, don't shoot the suits. Try not to rip them." I demonstrated how to make our way through by letting myself drift over, under, and around the small crowd. The intact spacesuits made no attempt to stop us.

The walls in this corridor shone brighter; glimmering in the glow of the lanterns. I did a horizontal mad-dash grabbing any handholds and pipes within my reach. The Fat Man bounced around from behind, his mini-jets dangerously sporadic. I watched for any hint of blue behind us as I rounded each corner. It grew fainter.

"Up there!" I pointed to an open doorway. I clutched the doorframe and yanked myself to a stop. Ronnie and the Fat Man tumbled past, but eventually joined me. Seeing no spacesuits, I signaled the all-clear. No one budged, so I went first. After signaling *another* all-clear I ushered the others in, lanterns leading the way into more darkness.

We stepped into a room of no discernable purpose. Empty racks bedecked the walls. Massive girders outlined the ceiling in serried rows. Puddles riddled the floor.

*Puddles?* That jarred me.

Ronnie tried to shut the door, but it wouldn't latch shut.

"Ghosts?" the Fat Man asked absently.

I anchored my pole and sat behind it with my back to the nearest wall. Damned spirits? Possessed spacesuits? Space-station poltergeist? It surprised me the Fat Man wasn't hounding us about leaving Vivincia.

Ronnie and I did a quick inventory, checking the pouches on our enviro-suits. We didn't find much: a couple aerosol containers (probably for emergency thrusting), some folding pliers, back-up battery packs for the suit. I flicked off my lantern, as did Ronnie.

"What're you two on about?" the Fat Man asked, shining his lantern in my face.

I didn't know what a man of science would say in this situation. At that point, I didn't care.

"Those aren't ghosts," I said.

"The hell they ain't! I never seen a ghost, but those things pretty much act like what I think a ghost would act like," he stood over me. I had half a mind to kick his shins and drop him.

"Whatever they are, turn your damned light off! I don't want them following us." I stood to face him. I wasn't so worried about the spacesuits anymore, but the blue glow that emitted from them once ruptured.

Ronnie came forward, "Mr. Ruffinego, couldn't you just call the ship and have some of your crew come down and clear us a path."

"Tried that," he waved him off, "too weak a signal under this much rock."

"Can you boost it?" Ronnie asked.

The Fat Man dug a finger into Ronnie's chest, "I don't got the power for that, didn't bring amp-runners. Wasn't planning on staying down here that long."

"Can you get through at all?" I asked, gesturing toward the spare battery packs.

"Near the hatch, in the airlock probably, that's what Vivincia was trying."

A soft humming sounded over my earpiece. The melody was unfamiliar and the voice sounded dazed, as if trying to remember a tune. Then it was gone.

"That was her," the Fat Man said, then added hazily: "I think." He turned off his lantern.

No one commented further on the humming creeping into our earpieces. It may have been her voice, but it wasn't her.

The walls suddenly shimmered to life, almost metallic silver. The glow was similar to what I had seen since our trek deeper into the station, but more pronounced. The Fat Man pulled his shooter.

"No!" I blurted out and grabbed his arm. "This is different." I understood the Fat Man's apprehension. The glow wasn't natural. However, I didn't know what a percussion shot would do in such cramped quarters.

The Fat Man must have considered this as well because he holstered the shooter, albeit hesitantly, as we observed the glistening walls. It was clearly unlike anything we had ever seen, yet it was different than the blue glow. The dancing lights on the walls flashed airily and didn't bear any substance.

Ronnie handed me his data-pad. He had the backlight on the lowest setting. I cupped a hand over the display to shield the light coming from the glowing walls.

"Neural-networking?" I asked.

"What's that, what're you doing?" the Fat Man demanded, pulling the data-pad from my hand. "What is this?"

I rose and grabbed it back, scanning it quickly, "Has to do with merging thought patterns . . . mapping neural pathways . . . shadowing consciousness. Some practice made illegal before it was fully tested."

"So?" the Fat Man asked.

Admittedly, I had the same question.

"I don't know," Ronnie answered, taking the data-pad back and bringing up a different screen. "All I did was take a pic of that blue glowing stuff when it first gathered from the ruptured suits, hit 'find' and it brought up this article."

"You got some kind of satellite access out here?" the Fat Man asked.

"No, of course not. I did an info-dump on all information pertaining to New Hygiea before we left the shuttle."

"What's New Hygiea got to do with neural-netting?" I asked.

"Neural-networking." Ronnie corrected me and then continued scrolling through the pages. "And I don't know. I thought maybe it would bring up schematics or some type of map of this place."

A distant voice sounded in my earpiece again saying, "Columns three through eleven, omit five and find the standard deviation, carry over to next sheet—"

The Fat Man looked more shaken than before. It was Vivincia's voice again, but absent of any life.

"Here!" Ronnie yelled as he read from the data-pad. "Dr. Craig Deushane, forefather of artificially assisted neural-networking, nearly a trillionaire back when a trillion meant buying your own country. Had enough clout to legalize neural-networking for a brief period, a method by which computers shadow the neurotransmitters responsible for conscious thought."

"Shadow?" I asked.

"Yes, says paired with biochemical impulses, shadowing tiny portions of synaptic plasticity proved to be more effective than mapping. Created a sort of real-time database, but could only run a fraction of what a person was thinking. By linking several individuals, they could collectively problem solve. At least, that was the goal."

"What's that got to do with this base?" the Fat Man asked and I had to admit, I too didn't see the connection.

"Dr. Deushane, frustrated with regulations opted to leave and work independently, free of restrictions."

"He was one of the first to leave Sol System 1?" I asked, the doubt clear in my voice.

"Yes, with many followers. Most scientists agreed that overbearing governments hindered true progress."

"But they didn't have the means."

Ronnie shrugged, "Says here that Deushane convinced them space travel of that magnitude was possible if it were a *one-way* trip."

"Sounds more like a cult than a research team," I muttered.

The Fat Man caught up, "You're saying this guy settled New Hygiea."

"About two centuries ago," Ronnie confirmed.

"Those suits were empty," I pointed out. "Whatever neural-net's going on . . . with empty spacesuits."

"And possessing Vivincia," the Fat Man commented.

Ronnie scrolled through several pages, found something, and then added, "That's the reason the practice was ended on Original Earth. People started linking up beyond their control. The algorithm modified itself by the millisecond and the shadowed thought patterns repeated aimlessly. Random thoughts reprocessed endlessly, via Deushane's program, drove users mad. Dr. Deushane was certain he could make viable adjustments should he be able to continue his research."

"It's that blue glow," the Fat Man mumbled.

"Probably," Ronnie said. "Nimbus-Wave Plasma-tech eliminated the need for external hubs."

"No," the Fat Man whispered, "I mean . . . door."

We turned to see a faint blue light blossoming just outside the doorframe.

"Crap." I gulped as the blue nebula filled the entire doorframe, barricading us in. The faint glow on the walls disappeared.

The three of us backed away to the farthest corner of the room, only to see wavy fronds stretch out to seek us.

One hit me.

A bombardment of thoughts ripped into me. Each violently disconnected, beyond comprehension. I felt my consciousness ebbing away, as if my mind was handing over the controls.

Madness . . . blissful madness. I felt my body and arms moving of their own accord. A deep slumber swallowed me.

Restful.

A turbulent wave erupted to my right. The Fat Man writhed as he covered a gaping hole at his stomach. His legs kicked spasmodically. The blue glow backed away and then spiraled out of the room.

I clicked on the lantern at my wrist as I tried to shake the Jupiter size headache.

Reality returned.

Ronnie sat across the room.

I dashed over to him.

"You're back," Ronnie glanced up, "How'd you do it?"

"Do what?"

"You were one of them, like Vivincia, and then you came back." He murmured.

I shrugged, not remembering anything but the disarray. He held the shooter.

"What the hell happened?" I asked, my head throbbing from the invasion.

"The haze thing got you," he whispered.

I rapped his faceplate, "Ronnie, snap out of it. What happened?" I kept glancing behind me, afraid the deadly nebula would return.

Ronnie stared ahead, unperturbed.

"Ronald Benjamin, report!" I ordered.

He blinked hard, but still seemed lost, "Mr. Ruffinego freaked out, shot at the haze, and then tried to shoot you. I kicked my spikes up at him. Knocked his arm up just in time. Percussion bolt nearly took my head off."

"Self-defense then?"

"Suppose so."

"And the blue nebula?" My head hurt just thinking of it.

"That misty stuff? Yeah, it got you and then took off after you woke up."

*It took off?*

"Okay then," I didn't have time to work out why we were left alone, just that we had a window of opportunity I didn't want to pass up. "Let's get out of here."

I peeked around the corner of the doorframe. The blue nebula was nowhere to be seen. *Perhaps a large window of opportunity.*

The Fat Man's hands remained locked over his giant gut, but it was obvious his wound penetrated clear through.

Ronnie showed me the shooter, "We wrestled, I shot him."

"Yep."

I stared at the Fat Man, realizing this was far from how the run was supposed to play out. Poor Ronnie. I promised him long ago this sort of thing wouldn't happen. He wouldn't have taken the shot unless forced,

"Sorry Mr. Ruffinego," I said as I undid the clasps for the mini-jets at his forearms. He didn't resist.

"Both of you are dead," he coughed through grunts.

I handed a mini-jet to Ronnie, but he just stared at the empty doorframe.

Finally, he pulled up his data-pad. "You drive and I'll map us a way out."

"Sounds good." I strapped on both mini-jets.

"Well, let's get before the ole blue nebula of death returns," he forced a chuckle. Ronnie was acting weird, his mind obviously somewhere else,

Keeping sharp during overtime is what separates the pros from the amateurs. This con had gone terribly bad, but after getting my brain invaded and manhandled, I was determined to get off New Hygiea. Sure, an ethereal entity hungered for us in a closed area *and* I had panicked the first time, taking us farther away from the hatch. Not only did I have the challenge of trying to recall the layout of this primitive base from Hell, I would have to keep an eye out for the faintest hint of blue down any corridor. Having to explain a dead Mafioso was also something I wasn't looking forward to.

I hoisted Ronnie in a half-hug under my shoulder, set the mini-jets on low, and started down the corridor. It was nearly impossible to navigate and carry Ronnie, but I managed.

"Ew, gross!" he cried out. "I think I know what happened to the people."

"What?" I asked and turned to scan the passageway to see what had grabbed his attention.

Nothing but darkness.

Ronnie continued, "They *were* in the suits when we got here."

"Uh, no they weren't." I continued forward, realizing Ronnie was researching instead of mapping a route. Since he had nearly gone comatose earlier, I held back any chiding.

"What was left of them. Dr. Deushane required organic material to create the hubs for his neural-networking."

"So."

"So, what do you think happened to the people in those suits if they stood around talking about spreadsheets all day?"

"Yep, that's gross."

Long minutes ticked by as Ronnie continued bombarding me with theories. Not once did he offer any input on which direction to take.

"Ronnie."

"Yeah?"

"Was I the only one it went after back there?"

He waited and then said, "Yeah, you were."

"From what it looks like, it's a proximity thing," he explained. "Get close enough and the thing snags you."

I don't know why I had asked. Maybe part of me was stuck wondering why Ronnie was busy theorizing instead of helping me map a way out.

*What are you up to Ronnie?*

Finally, I had us back in the corridor that led to the med-bay. I cranked the mini-jets and flew past torn and lifeless spacesuits that bobbed in the low-g.

A thick cloud of dust shot out, blocking the entrance to the med-bay. It coalesced so profusely our lanterns couldn't penetrate.

I refused to panic. The dusty mist was darker than the blue nebula and that seemed foreboding in itself; *and*, it moved as though it were alive. Whatever.

No blue = good.

"What's this crap?" Ronnie asked as he pushed past me toward the dark nebula.

"Relax," I grabbed his ankle and pulled him back. "I think it's from the grime. I scraped some away earlier. It was wet, but dried and drifted off. Don't go jumping into it though."

"Yeah, don't know what I was thinking."

The dust suddenly shifted and disappeared all the way into the med-bay, clearing our way.

Ronnie voiced exactly what I was thinking. "Someone's opened the hatch."

We flew into the med-bay.

A troop of standing spacesuits blocked our only way out. The blue nebula sparkling fiercely above. Old spacesuits. Not a rescue party.

"Get yourself outta here," Ronnie said, forced me back roughly, and lunged toward the blue nebula. My reach for his ankle fell short.

*Suddenly, he's coherent?* Ah dammit, Ronnie had pulled the old Shell Game. Making me think he was in some state of shock while planning to make some heroic atonement.

*Self-sacrificing idiot!*

Luminescent tendrils snaked out and pierced his faceplate. I finally reached him and pulled, but it was too late.

Ronnie's breathing got heavier.

The nebula's intensity increased as Ronnie went limp. I realized this must have been what Ronnie saw when I was attacked earlier. Add that to whatever he had learned off his data-pad and he knew something about this blue nebula taking over one host at a time. Watching it, I could easily surmise that was exactly what was happening. The thing basically ignored me.

For a second I was tempted to bolt past the thing and to the hatch. But only for a second,

Instead, I did the only thing I could think of; I grabbed my walking-stick, set the tip to pierce, and stabbed Ronnie's dangling ankle.

"AAAGHH!" he cried out and cradled his leg.

The blue tendrils recoiled and the nebula darted back.

"Son-of-a—. Holy lordy, that hurts. Why?" His eyes pleaded. "It's leaking air, you moron." He hunched over and grasped his boot, "I've gotta hold it to keep from losing air so I can breathe. It hurts so bad."

I pointed the lance at my own foot, should the blue nebula come any closer.

It didn't.

The blue nebula hovered and circled us, but wouldn't approach. I stood and braced Ronnie under my shoulder. He panted and clasped his boot tight. I hit the mini-jets and flew over the spacesuits and steel-beds.

"So not fair," he sobbed.

"Remember that, next time you set up a run on the side!"

I got through the doorway, cleared the med-bay, and my lantern revealed hundreds of spacesuits littering the gangway.

Whole spacesuits. Not torn by a percussion shot.

They stayed where they were as we exited. I felt like I was at some crowded party, almost saying, "Excuse me, pardon me, coming through," as I gingerly made my way past. A quick glance behind revealed a trailing blue nebula.

The bodies thinned as we neared the airlock. I knocked a couple a little hard in my haste. The blue nebula remained a few feet behind us the entire time.

Ronnie's sobs quieted.

I barked at him to *not* pass out.

We passed a blank-eyed Vivincia. I stabbed her in the foot, but to no avail. For a second I thought she might have been the one who opened the airlock, but she was too far gone. A stream of air spewed from the hole I had made in her enviro-suit boot.

"We . . ." Ronnie muttered.

"What?"

"We . . ." he coughed a spooky laugh, "We should bring her with us."

"She's a vegetable." I said.

"Yeah," he cheesed a rueful grin.

"Do not. Pass out." I ordered.

"Hey, the boot's sealed over my wound." His hands drifted loose from my grip and he stared at his own fingers with wonder. He smiled as he continued explaining, "I was too busy holding the rupture to notice. Imagine that."

Ronnie going into shock would shut off his pain receptors and bring the nebula. At least, that was my working theory. I readjusted my grip and double-timed it down the corridor to the airlock.

"Life without bodies," Ronnie muttered as I climbed into the airlock, the blue nebula still trailing. It seemed closer. I shoved the heavy door shut behind us.

"The mad doctor's dream was consciousness without physical form. But his little neural-plasma-net thing ended up eating their hosts." He chuckled and then sighed heavily.

I grabbed his head and examined his face. He had a sheepish smirk which he quickly tried to replace with a stern glare.

"What?" he asked.

"Do not pass out."

Shutting the airlock door did little to stop the blue nebula. It simply crept in through the vents. It was closing in fast. The blue tendrils reached toward us.

Ronnie slumped, his arms dangled loosely. I kicked his wound.

The blue nebula hesitated.

He coughed something unintelligible.

I kicked again, higher up his leg, as I drove the spike into his shin.

"Aaaagh!" he cried. Again. "I hate you." But he was alert.

The blue nebula darted away, but remained just inches from us in the airlock. The wispy arms reached again.

I grabbed Ronnie, ignited the mini-jets, and flew upward to open the hatch. The lantern snapped off as I worked the hatch lever.

"The plasma in their brains had nowhere else to go after death," Ronnie continued, as if he hadn't nearly passed out just seconds ago. I cranked open the hatch and jetted us to the surface. "Combined with that neural-networking crap, it evolved into a separate consciousness."

"Stop freakin' talking!"

"It hurts, okay!"

I accidentally overshot our exit from the hatch and had us drifting away from New Hygiea. The abyss of space was a welcomed sight. Anything but blue.

I maneuvered the mini-jets and made a beeline for our shuttle.

Four crewmen inspecting the Fat Man's schooner eyed us as we sped away. They had their shooters drawn.

"Your boss has been calling you for hours and he's pissed!" I yelled on the open channel.

The blue nebula emerged from the hatch for a moment and then changed course toward the crewmen.

Finally, at the shuttle, I leapt in, set Ronnie on a table, and tossed him a first aid kit. Besides possibly going into shock, he'd be okay. He screamed as he cauterized his wound.

No demands came from the Fat Man's crew, nor did I feel any percussion shots raking the shuttle as I started a rapid preflight procedure.

The shuttle lurched to life, but too slow for my liking. I was in a damned hurry.

A soft chuckle sounded in my earpiece.

"Ronnie?" I asked.

"Those goons are so screwed," he said, staring out the porthole. I watched through the starboard viewer as the blue nebula attached to one of the crewmen while the others shot at it.

I didn't find it as funny, but then again, I wasn't soaking up morphine.

Glancing back at that lonely hatch on New Hygiea's surface, I wondered how I'd ever tell the authorities what the hell just happened. Not that I cared for the fate of some mob crew—I didn't want any future prospectors stumbling across that soul-sucking death cloud.

*Doug C. Souza has always had a love for the art of storytelling. His favorite genres are science fiction and fantasy, but he enjoys a good yarn of any variety. His story "Mountain Screamers" was published in "Asimov's Science Fiction" magazine August 2014. Other works have appeared in numerous anthologies and ezines. As a member of the local writers' Meetup group, he helps aspiring writers find their voice (and possibly a paycheck) for their work. Doug C. Souza teaches fourth grade in Modesto, California where he lives with his wonderful wife (and main reader/editor) Nicole. You can find him at dougcsouza.com.*

On the run from human politzia, Martin Silverman is desperate to find his kidnapped daughter, when a mysterious, tight-lipped band of Jeroxians takes control of his quest. What evils will the human race carry to distant worlds?

# BLACK HEARTS AND BLUE SKINS

### By

### *Timothy Paul*

"I'm home," Martin announced, as he pushed through the soft enviro-shield of their front door. Somewhere in the back of his mind a memory flashed. He'd once seen an ancient photograph of a door to an ancestor's house. In place of a gravi-metric shield to keep insects, leaves, and other environmental particles from seeping into the living quarters, those long-removed relatives on planet Earth had used a second door panel. Flimsy things. Narrow wooden frames covered with something called screens, they looked like flat rectangles of diffusion fabric.

"'Li'ah," he called out. "I stopped at the store on the way home." Years of playing the corporate game and kissing up to management had finally paid off and he was eager to celebrate an impending promotion with his Jeroxian wife. Mixed marriages were unheard of when he'd proposed. A natural-born mediator, Martin excelled in public relations, but he'd always considered his courtship of Jelli'ah to be the pinnacle of his accomplishments.

With the steady arrival of humans from a distant star, the legislative branch of Jerok-Two, the home world to nearly twelve billion inhabitants, initiated a calculated migration to the outer planets. Primarily a defensive strategy, the unified government sought to control the pace of human integration. Orlanik, the seventh planet in the Jerok system, now boasted a large number of mixed couples. Yet even after eleven years, certain things about Jelli'ah mystified him.

Colleagues, both human and Jeroxian, often complained about arguments with their spouses. Most centered around miscommunication. Somehow, despite coming from very different cultures and having to master new languages, he and Li'ah rarely fought. Martin couldn't remember a single time they had bickered over a misunderstanding. Passing the foyer, he turned the corner into their bedroom and froze at the gruesome sight in front of him. Slipping from his hand, the bottle of wine struck the wooden floor and shattered.

Spread out on her back, naked, his wife lay across their bed in a massive pool of blood. Her natural, royal blue skin was a faded pastel, a clear indication she was already dead. The man beside her had half his Jeroxian skull torn away. An iron prybar lay on the floor beside him.

Martin fell back against the frame of the bedroom door and slid slowly down into a sitting position as strength drained from his legs. *Who is that man?* thought Martin. *And how could she? Jeroxian women don't do this.*

Minutes passed as he tried to grasp all the implications and the implausibility of the scene in front of him. When the initial shock passed, another began. *Sam'etha.*

Rolling off his haunches, Martin put a hand on the floor and pushed himself up quickly, slicing his palm on the broken wine bottle. Dashing down the hall to his eight-year-old daughter's room he called out, "Sam'etha!" A quick visual brought a brief moment of relief. Nothing was out of place in the child's pristine sanctuary. No blood anywhere and no body. And then relief turned to a new terror. No Sam'etha.

A knock at the door barely registered in his mind. Nor did the voice of someone calling his name. He needed to link the politzia. Turning back down the hallway he pulled out a phone to call for help, then tucked it back into his pocket. An officer was standing at his bedroom door, looking over the scene inside. Kurt Planktin was the ranking local authority with a reputation as a hard-nosed sheriff. Frequently featured in news reports, his face was well-known by everyone on the outer planet's oldest human colony.

"Sheriff," Martin said. "I was just going to call you."

Sheriff Planktin turned to Martin. "What happened here, Silverman?" he asked. "You catch 'em together? Or did ya finally get tired of blue skins?"

The implications of the sheriff's questions stole the air from Martin's lungs. He saw the officer's judgmental expression and his eyes moved slowly down to his bloody hand. *A man in my wife's bed. Jeroxian, like her. Both dead. Blood on my hand.* He didn't need a background in law-enforcement to see what was on Sheriff Planktin's mind. Jelli'ah was dead. No one could help her. But Sam'etha was missing and Martin was about to be detained, if not arrested. Reflex more than thought made him bolt out their side door.

Dashing across the back yard, Martin reached the woodland grove without any sound of pursuit behind him. Not daring to look back, he scrambled further into the ever-thickening forest, oblivious to the thorns tearing at his skin and clothes or the poisonous silkspins and slythers waiting for fresh prey.

When he reached a rough clearing of moss-covered ground, Martin stopped to catch his breath. Minutes passed and he breathed easier as he became certain the sheriff hadn't followed him. Long shadows told him the sun would soon disappear over the horizon. Wiping his bloody hand across the moss, he saw the wound was long and deep. He needed medical attention for his hand, not to mention shock. The hospital was close. He'd have to pass through another thicket, then cross half a kilometer of open commercial property. By now, most of the shops would be closed for the night. If he could make the clearing before the sun went down, he'd have a good chance of reaching the hospital unseen.

Thick, wooden branches posed more of an obstacle than he anticipated. The trees on this side of the woodland were stiff and the low branches thick. Night had fallen by the time he crawled over the heavy, rough bark of a flawtheil branch. Weak from his ordeal, he staggered forward a step and glanced down. A large arachnid was climbing up his shirt. With a swift wave of his hand, he brushed it to the ground and stomped as hard as he could. Taking a moment to assess, he felt no sting or pain on his chest. Whether it had been a poisonous variety or not, it hadn't bitten him.

When he reached the admitting desk to the hospital, he was barely able to give his name before the room began to spin. He fell backward, but strong arms caught him and helped him to a hover-chair.

Orderlies escorted him to a curtained room and washed his wounded hand. A Jeroxian nurse brought him a hot drink and he sipped at it as the man took his vitals. Two more Jeroxians came into the room wearing shimmery camouflage cloaks, the sort of attire urban legend might associate with secretive, government agencies. Their demeanor was authoritative and urgent. A verbal exchange, in a native dialect Martin had never mastered, made him shift uncomfortably in his seat. That was the moment he realized, the Sheriff had probably issued a man-hunt by now.

Martin paid special attention to the nurse's activity and noted that he made no eye contact with the two observers. After treating his wound, the nurse left and one of the two Jeroxians followed. On the way out he closed the door and locked it. Martin glanced up into the most lifeless expression he'd ever seen on a face, Jeroxian or human. *He'd make a good politician,* he thought. *Or a used shuttle salesman.*

"I can't stay here. I have to go," Martin said.

The man's rigid posture assured him that leaving was not an option.

"We'll take you to another room soon."

"I have things to do. Things that can't wait."

"Understand something. The local politzia are hunting you. You either come with us now, or you'll be in prison by morning and executed in a week."

"I don't understand. Why would you be hiding me from the politzia?"

Instead of answering his question, the man asked, "Did you know the Jerox-man who was laid in bed beside your mate?"

The image of two naked bodies on his bed exploded in his mind's eye. Martin gripped the handles beside his chair as his hands quivered with rage. *I know her better than that.* "She wouldn't have been with that man by choice."

"Your answer clarifies nothing," the mysterious official said. "Did you know him?"

"Who are you?"

"Call me Klosh. Did you know the man?"

Martin identified the name Klosh with a fearsome beast in a Jeroxian fairy tale. Seemed like just last year he'd read it to his daughter. He didn't want to cooperate with the man, but he needed to leave. Needed a way to find Sam'etha. His stomach churned as he remembered the blood, the body, and finally the face of the pale blue corpse that didn't belong in his bed, Martin took a deep breath, then shook his head, no.

"Did you take note of his half human features?"

*What kind of question was that?* "One hour ago I went into my home and found two dead bodies in my bed. One was my wife."

A tap on the door drew Klosh's attention. Martin was on the alert for any opportunity to slip past his guard, who stood just outside the door conferring with his partner. Two more Jeroxians joined them, a man and a woman. They all wore the same ankle-length, black cloaks.

Klosh gestured to him to follow them. Martin looked around the room, weighed his options and grudgingly accepted the reality that he had none.

Outside the room, he saw another man—a human—wearing the same suit as Martin, with his hand bandaged in the same manner. One of the Jeroxians nodded and the man darted toward the nearest exit. At the end of the hall, he pushed through one of the magnetic, swinging doors. Martin heard a voice shout, "There." The man bolted. Before the magna-door swung closed, a Jeroxian in a familiar law-enforcement uniform hustled off in pursuit.

"This way," Martin's escort said. The two newcomers took hold of Martin's elbows and hustled him down the hall toward a utility lift. "Who are you?" he asked.

"Stay quiet and keep walking."

Other questions filled his mind and new fears arose. And underneath it all was the one burning question. *Where was Sam'etha?*

At the second tier of underground transport cubicles, Martin was packed in the middle seat of a nondescript ground vehicle. Klosh sat at the navigation console and tapped in a destination. Sliding up a ramp and out onto the local thoroughfare, the vehicle merged into traffic. Martin twisted his wedding ring back and forth, finally centering the emerald filigree in an upright position. Numb from shock, he watched the landscape speeding past. The maze of streets, thoroughfares and personal transport cubes testified to the human influence on the pastiche of disparate civilizations. His gaze eventually turned to Klosh. "So you're not law enforcement?"

No one answered.

"Planning to kill me then?"

"If your death was our intent," said the woman beside him. "We'd leave you to the sheriff's net."

"Who are you?" Martin asked again.

"You can call me Gretel and my partner Hansel."

"You read human fairy tales?"

"We've studied your culture."

Martin's fingers drummed anxiously on his thighs. He had no idea where they were going, but the compact transit cube picked up speed as it moved farther away from his home. Farther from Sam'etha.

"Why are you detaining me?"

No answer.

"I need to find my daughter."

Gretel put a hand on his shoulder. "Trust and be still."

Klosh added, "Sam'etha's future is in your hands."

A chill ran through his nervous system and by reflex, Martin pushed back into the soft padding of his seat. Klosh had used her name. These people knew things they shouldn't. He thought back on the questions they'd asked him. *"Did you know the Jerox-man who was laid in bed beside your mate?"* He'd missed the significance at first. But their reverence for language was more than a half-assed attempt at poetry. Jeroxians were precise. The passive voice in the sentence meant that someone had put the man's body there. Probably after both were dead.

Lashing out in frustration he said, "If you're not going to kill me, either answer my questions or let me out of here."

Three blue faces turned to him for only a moment. No one spoke, and the vehicle slowed slightly, then banked sharply for a quick turn. Another block and they turned again, heading back in the direction they'd just come.

"Pursuit?" asked Hansel.

"Uncertain," Klosh answered. "Human law enforcement west, Jeroxian east."

Tense silence ensued as course adjustments sent their vehicle zig-zagging deeper into the heart of the city.

"Listen to be precise," said Klosh. "Your daughter will soon pass outside our ability to help. If you wish her to have a life worth speaking of, you must take these steps."

"What the hell is—"

"You're wasting time. Listen close. I'm going to tell you where you need to go from here."

Desperation clawed at Martin's gut as he tried to focus on the man's quick instructions. Without warning, the vehicle pulled to the side of the thoroughfare. Stepping out, Gretel took Martin's hand, pulled him out, then climbed back in without a word as they sped off.

With his heart pounding, Martin took in a breath of the oxygen-heavy atmosphere and scanned the pedestrian crossing. Footbridges crossed over the slightly depressed roadways. On the opposite side, argon lights outlined a corner market. As instructed, he went into the store. *"Buy something,"* they'd told him. *But what?* All he could think about was his daughter and his poor, dead wife. Did she suffer? Was it quick? A sense of aloneness swept over him like vertigo. Thoughts of his daughter allowed him to push aside the mental paralysis.

"May I, sir, offer some assistance for you?" a Jeroxian woman asked.

Martin shook his head slightly; suddenly aware he was standing in front of a check-out counter. *What to buy?* He should be hungry. "I was just contemplating an energy bar," he said. Stepping up to the display he picked out a sugary pastry and had just set it on the counter when he noticed the news monitor behind the clerk. His face filled the image and a crawl underneath read: *Politzia Are Searching For Martin Silverman, Prime Suspect In A Kidnapping And Double Homicide.*

"Would you care for anything more?" asked the clerk in that sing-songy Jerox-speak.

"Um," he said. He turned his head back and forth surveying the display, hoping to distract the clerk until the news clip passed. "I'll have one of theeese as well," he said. "And maybeee." His face vanished from the monitor. "How about this." He slapped a pack of nuts on the counter and stepped up to the retina scanner to complete the transaction.

Instead of the instant approval he normally received at checkout counters, the scanner hummed slightly and nothing happened. He took in a breath. Had his accounts been frozen because of the manhunt?

"Our apologies, Mr. Silverman," said the clerk. "Our connection to the financial net has been slow all day."

When the scanner display read APPROVED IN FULL, he forced a smile and thanked the clerk before moving quickly out the door.

"Wait! Come back!" the clerk shouted.

*Shit. My picture must have come back up.* He turned to the north as he'd been instructed and took off at a run. A block further he slowed to a walk, cursing himself for not exercising. He'd never have a chance in a full-on pursuit. Glancing back, he saw no one was following. None of the people on the street seemed to notice him. Flashing lights on the roadway caught his attention. Five politzia chase cars had surrounded one transport. It was the same one he'd been riding in. Standing on the passage, Klosh stood arguing with the politzia. There was no sign of Hansel or Gretel, but he imagined they might be in custody. Martin noted Klosh no longer wore his shimmery cloak. Who were these people? He didn't know if he could trust them, but right now, they were his only hope for finding Sam'etha.

Grasping for the com-pad in his pocket, Martin punched the link for his daughter. *Why hadn't he done this sooner?* Sam'etha didn't answer. In place of her voice mail, the link went dead. He glanced at his pad and saw a message: IDENTIFICATION CONFIRMED. LOCATION VERIFIED.

*Shit, shit, shit.* Martin dropped the device in a public trash bin, turned west, and walked briskly away from his designated path knowing law enforcement would be there any minute.

When he finally drew close to the appointed destination, he recognized the building Klosh had described. Sitting at the edge of the city limits, the forest encroached on three sides of a refueling port equipped for everything from personal vehicles to cargo transports. Inside he knew he would find a small convenience store that offered a few essentials at inflated prices. Shelves would be filled with inferior products, compared to the bustling Jeroxian market he'd run from an hour earlier. Yet, narrow-minded humans who would have nothing to do with mixed cultures kept these places in business.

Down the road, flashing lights of a law-enforcement patrol moved toward him. Stepping off the path, Martin ducked into a patch of unkempt shrubs and waited. He watched the politzia cube pass and waited to be sure it didn't turn back.

A large-framed man in ragged coveralls staggered out of the convenience store door. He zig-zagged across the lot and stopped in front of Martin's hiding place. Unzipping his pants, the man began to urinate on the bushes, barely missing Martin's shoes. Then, in a quiet yet clear, sober voice the man said, "You're wasting time. Politzia will be back any minute. Get into the shop quick. And understand something. The clerk is no friend of yours, but he's no friend of the local law either."

Martin hesitated.

"Go now," the man muttered through clenched teeth.

Martin darted across to the entrance, glancing back at the *drunk* who weaved his way through the bushes he'd just watered and disappeared into a thicket of trees. Inside, a man wearing a sweat-covered T-shirt and a black vest, stood behind the counter, leaning on the flat surface of the checkout stand. He eyed Martin over a pair of thick-rimmed sun glasses without moving his head, then turned his attention back to a monitor.

"I'm supposed to meet someone here," Martin said.

Tapping a command on the counter, the man stood upright, which may have added two or three inches to his height. What he lacked in size was offset by attitude. Purple and green tats of korntapests adorned his arms in amazingly precise three-dimensional art. If they'd been living rodents, no one who came into the store would ever walk out. The man pulled off his glasses revealing a narrow, weather-worn face and an unnerving frown.

"I can just wait." Martin's head turned as a flashing orange light speared through the small, glass window next to the door.

Looking down at his monitor, the clerk shoved the glasses back on his nose, pointed to a wall in back, then stabbed a finger into something under the counter.

Martin heard a sharp click, turned and saw that a piece of the back wall had opened slightly. He barely managed to step behind it before another gesture from the clerk slammed the hidden doorway shut again. His hiding place was void of light so he had no way of knowing how large the room might be. Pushing his ear against the edge of the door, he strained to hear the conversation, but could only make out muffled voices. Time passed and Martin's frayed nerves grew more anxious with each minute. Wiping his sweaty palms on the sides of his slacks, a new fear grabbed hold of him. Someone was in the darkened closet with him.

First it was just the faint odor of pinoura, reminding him of a fresh-cut lawn. Now he recognized the cologne as well as the sharp tang of a Jeroxian woman. Hansel and Gretel were here. "I know you're here," he whispered.

"Stay silent," a whisper commanded.

Time passed. Martin breathed. Quietly. When the wall in front of him finally clicked and a crack of light filtered through, Hansel pushed the door open and led him out.

Approaching the clerk, Gretel asked, "Why, Mr. Graves, have you deigned to exhaust our time in such a way?"

Without so much as glancing up, the clerk answered, "You didn't want the politzia to see you. I made sure they didn't."

"Those men left twenty minutes past."

"Had to make sure they were gone. Hope you weren't too uncomfortable in there."

Before anyone could say another word the door flew open and Klosh stepped inside. He waved them all back into the transport. Martin sat between Hansel and

Gretel once again and in a short time they wove back into the heart of the city. The transport cube made a final turn onto a hidden ramp, spiraling downward at a dizzying pace. When they came to a stop, they stepped out of the vehicle and walked briskly along a brightly lit hallway.

A tall man with a short-sleeved shirt, accentuating the largest biceps Martin had ever seen on a Jeroxian, was waiting for them at the far end.

"I'll take him from here."

With a slightly exaggerated bow, Martin's three captors disappeared, each going in a different direction.

"Where am I and what am I doing here?" Martin demanded.

"For now, avoiding a quick and fatal prosecution."

"And who are you?"

"You can call me Agent Facina," the man said, as they turned a corner and looked out into a wide room full of desks and computers. A large, oval logo on the floor, in gold filigree, with the letters JSF finally told Martin who he was dealing with.

"Jeroxian Security Force?" Martin stammered. "You deal in interplanetary matters. What do you have to do with my wife's murder?"

"While I offer my condolences on your loss, your wife is not our concern. She was killed early this morning. Maybe half an hour after you left for work. Mnangtiel was killed later."

"Mnangtiel? That was the Jeroxian in my bed?"

Facina nodded.

"So my wife wasn't . . . with . . . him?"

"No."

"Why was he there? What happened? And who would want to kill my wife?"

"Mnangtiel is a sex trafficker. He specializes in targeting young girls. Especially runaways, orphans, and kids from large, lower-class families. He'll watch a mark for weeks, recording their habits and their timetables. Once he has a list of twenty or thirty suitable girls, he calls his team together, charters two or three mass transit cubes, then sends his minions out on a coordinated route to pick them up. The kids have no warning and no chance to escape. Once they're aboard the transit, they're drugged and carried to a departure bay at the shuttle port to the first moon. He's meticulous and calculating. Or was. By the time anyone knows they're missing, his victims are already off planet."

Martin's hands and arms began to shake. "Did he take Sam'etha?"

"His team went out to pick up the assigned targets, but they added someone to the list. Mnangtiel disagreed with their action and paid the ultimate price."

"So his people betrayed him, killed him, and took my daughter."

Facina nodded. "Nearly as we've been able to piece together, her abductor showed up at your house minutes after you left for work. Something must have distracted your wife. When she turned her back, he pulled a knife and she died without a struggle."

"Why would she ever let a strange man into the house?"

"Because he wore a uniform."

Uniform? Martin shook his head back and forth, unbelieving. "Politzia?"

"Sheriff Planktin, to be specific. He wanted to take control of Mnangtiel's operation."

"And he took Sam'etha?"

"Yes. He killed Mnangtiel, took the body to your home, stripped both corpses and laid them out beside each other. Would have been a good frame if we hadn't been waiting for Mnangtiel's next shipment. With all the attention focused on you, Sam'etha would have simply disappeared."

"Why didn't your men tell me who they were?"

Facina frowned. "First of all, we didn't know much about you. We're secretive by nature–or by habit. And we still don't know for certain how many other politzia are involved. Most of all, we are struggling to understand the motive."

A security door opened beside them. "Agent Facina," a young man said. "Krefield is approaching the house."

Facina, nodded, then motioned Martin toward the open door. "Step inside Mr. Silverman."

A wide room, unadorned by furniture, with half a dozen Jeroxians standing at stations along the walls, housed an impressive bit of technology. He guessed the holographic house and surrounding landscape must have been on a scale of roughly one thirty-second. And the detail was astounding. Even more incredible, a Jeroxian woman of the same scale was walking toward the house. "What is this?" he asked.

"Your daughter is inside this house. Along with twenty-three other children. But before I can authorize an action that could get her out of there, I need to understand why this human sheriff wanted her when she doesn't match the profile established by Mnangtiel."

Martin shrugged. "I don't really know Planktin. Just his reputation. He's hard-nosed, but I never dreamed he was a killer."

"You're something of an earth historian, is that right?"

"Not really. It's more of a hobby than anything."

"Do the letters KKK mean anything to you?"

"The Ku Klux Klan was a white supremacist mob back on ancient Earth. They hated, feared, murdered, people of other races. But that was centuries ago, on a world many light years from here. Are you telling me they still exist? And they've come here?"

"Seven of Mnangtiel's team have those three letters tattooed on their chests."

Martin's eyes widened in horror. "That's why they took Sam'etha. The KKK was passionate for ethnic cleansing. They were especially brutal to people of mixed race." Feeling faint, Martin looked around for a chair, but there were none. Facina caught his arm as he started to go down.

Martin looked up into the agent's eyes. "If there's something you can do. Anything. Please."

Facina lowered Martin to the floor and looked into the hologram. The woman, Krefield, was at the door talking with someone inside. "Green light. All forces, move in."

Seated on the floor, Martin had an eye level view of the hologram. Through a dizzy haze he watched Krefield grab the man inside the house, throw him to the ground and, in a single move, clasped restraints on his hands and feet. At the same time, the woods around the house came to life with armed Jeroxians in shimmering cloaks. They poured out from behind trees and rushed through the open door like a horde of Earth ants fleeing from a flooded nest. That was all he saw before he lost consciousness.

Martin woke in a something resembling a hospital bed. Facina and Klosh stood at his door conversing quietly. Calling to them he asked, "Sam'etha?"

Facina answered, "She was unharmed in the raid, but Planktin had her pumped full of narcotics. Would have killed either a human or Jeroxian but something about her mixed parentage saved her life."

Still shaken, Martin ran his fingers along an intravenous tube attached to his arm. "What about the others?"

"They only had mild sedatives in their systems and most have left the hospital," Facina said. "Planktin still intended to traffic the lot of them."

"Where's Sam'etha?"

"She's resting comfortably. They've flushed the toxins from her system. You've got some tough decisions ahead."

"I don't understand."

"Sam'etha's half Jeroxian. She'll have some of your wife's empathic senses. Going back home isn't an option for her. Even stepping inside the house will likely bring about a severe anxiety attack."

"So I need to look for a new home."

Facina sighed and looked back at Klosh. "You want to handle this one?"

Jeroxian facial expressions were sometimes hard for humans to discern, but Martin had no trouble reading trepidation on Klosh's face. "Apparently you were the last piece of Sheriff Planktin's plan. He worked hard to set up a perfect frame. Thanks to the evidence we've turned over to prosecutors, you've been cleared of any wrongdoing and the politzia involved have all been arrested. But the mass coverage surrounding your manhunt has destroyed your reputation. Working for a PR firm, I doubt your employer will take you back regardless of what the court says."

"But it's all I know. How will we survive?" Martin's stomach began churning as the anxiety of last night's hell returned. "Where can I find a new home without an income?"

"We are able to offer you an option, but you would have little time to pack and all your legal affairs would have to be handled by a third party long distance."

Martin flinched. "You mean I could join a convoy back toward Earth. Live out our lives in travel between the stars."

"Not quite as grim as that," Facina said.

"We've negotiated with the high council of our home world," Klosh said. "You've been invited to take a position at Tringkiet University on Jerox Three."

"But that's just one planet out from your home world. The treaty won't allow it."

"Exceptions can be made to any treaty," Facina replied.

Martin nearly yanked the tube from his arm as he shrugged. "What would I teach?"

"Earth history and culture," said Klosh.

A human doctor stepped into the room and motioned to Facina. As they spoke, Klosh pressed Martin. "I'm afraid your alternatives are limited. But you should understand, this is a tremendous honor and a huge leap of faith from the Council."

Facina turned back to Martin. "Your daughter can be discharged at any time, Mr. Silverman. It's your choice, of course, but don't underestimate the long-term impact of being the first human to see the inner ring."

Monitors on the wall told him his blood pressure had nearly returned to normal, though his heart rate was still elevated. He sighed. "There are humans, and probably a number of Jeroxians, who would call that choice a defection. Might even label me a traitor."

"As I said, consider the long-term impact. If you choose to accept our offer, your transport can be ready in an hour."

Sam'etha wrapped her lanky arms around Martin's neck. Jeroxian tear ducts produced several times those of humans and the back of his shirt was soon saturated. He began to think she would never let go and he'd have to leave the hospital with a teenaged daughter plastered across his chest. Her strength must have given out, as her arms eventually loosened and her long fingers held his face still, just inches from her own. Her eyes pleading, but for what?

"Your mother's—"

"I know."

Of course she knew. She was there. "The Jeroxian Council has—"

"I know."

"What do you want, sweetie? It would mean leaving your friends behind." Sam'etha's eyes widened and she cocked her head slightly. Taking Martin's hand, she led him to a chair. Puzzled, he sat, obediently.

"You never saw it," she said. "Mom did. You should know, I don't have friends here. I'm mixed blood. The first. I don't know if a school full of Jeroxian kids will be kinder than here, but they sure won't be any worse."

Martin had lost count of how many times his heart had broken in the past twelve hours. He pressed a button at the side of his chair and said, "Tell Mr. Facina, we will take his offer."

*Timothy Paul. Tell me a story that makes the impossible seem plausible or show me a truth wrapped up in a lie. Stage a conflict and I'll side with the underdog. Make me think in ways that lead to coffee shop debates. Lay out a mystery and you'll capture my attention. Take me into the Twilight Zone where I can devour moral ironies or expand my finite comprehension of creation and beyond. From sci-fi thrillers to the woes of hobbits, werewolves, aliens, and leprechauns, I am drawn to well-crafted dilemmas clothed in dreams.*

*Gene Roddenberry gave us a "Wagon Train to the stars," then used his vessel to mirror human flaws disguised in the skins of alien worlds. If and when our fallen race crosses the great expanse to find new civilizations, will we carry with us the moral purity of Starship Enterprise, or will the darkness of our souls pollute the cultures we find? Blue Skins and Black Hearts shows the good, bad, and ugly side of the human race.*

*At timothypaulbooks.com my tagline states:* **In stubborn pursuit of traditional publication.** *I've been privileged to contribute to each volume of Lillicat Publisher's Visions series and continue to weave new tales of both novel and short story length. Spectacular scenery, elaborate architecture, comic books, and travel are just a few of my favorite things. Topping my list is Saturday morning writing time with my beautiful author wife and soul mate, D.A. Couturier.*

The moment when apprenticeship ends and independence begins always carries stress, For Rissa, Excellenza-in-training of the Imperium, the moment is rendered even more stressful by being a very public interplanetary conference. Yet all that pales before the news that the Emperor himself will be attending the conference arrayed in his warcloak of immense destructive power, All for reasons unknown.

And Rissa is expected to cope.

# GREATCLOAK

### By

### *Jonathan Shipley*

The chatter in the command center seemed deafening, not because of volume, but because it was all directed towards her: *How shall we organize this? When should that happen? What is our policy on this?* Rissa tried to keep her face pleasant as the barrage continued, but it pounded at her head like a drill. She ran a hand through her short, dark hair and tried to calm herself. These routine questions of protocols and policies shouldn't even be necessary.

"Please, if I could just have your attention one moment," she said. Her voice barely carried over the din of her staff. Gods, her people had taken on a life of their own in the organization of this conference, but it wasn't necessarily the direction she wanted to go. This was *her* training test, not theirs, and she wanted more than anything to pass and be that much closer to becoming a full Excellenza.

She glanced down for reassurance at the glittering silver uniform she was wearing for the first time.

Imperial Silver carried powerful connotations throughout Imperial Space. Then she tried again to impose her will and her voice on the room, but control skittered away. Abruptly the din of voices abated as eyes shifted to the doorway behind her. Rissa turned, expecting all the pomp of the Archconsul of Datar, who was hosting this regional conference for selected worlds of the Spiral Arm. Instead there was a lone woman—tall, youngish, blond, pale by Imperial standards—dressed casually in an old-style riding habit of embroidered tunic and split-skirt over boots. Rissa wasn't fooled for one moment. The lack of uniform in no way diminished the sense of presence the woman exuded. Staff, however, seemed unsure, sensing something, but not recognizing who this was.

Then the woman started forward and there was no longer a question in anyone's mind. She had The Walk. Call it the command walk or walk of power, it was the trademark of the Excellenzi. She was a full Excellenza; moreover, she was First Cadre and very senior.

"A moment of privacy, please," Ydaire announced as she crossed the room. The balance of Rissa's staffers who hadn't followed The Walk glanced up at the tone of her voice, recognizing that the woman before them was one of the Emperor's long-lived and preternaturally powerful Excellenzi. They glanced, they recognized, and instantly evacuated.

"That is how you give an order," the woman said quietly. "Courteous, but direct with no equivocation. There should never be any doubt who is in command." It seemed mild enough, ostensibly directed at no one, but Rissa tensed. She knew a reprimand when she heard one, no matter how mild the tone.

"Ydaire." Rissa managed a thin, forced smile. "I had thought this conference was to be a solo operation."

"It is. But as this is your first time, you should be relieved to have a more experienced eye look over your plans."

"Relief competes with apprehension," Rissa, attempting a lightness of tone. "As it is my first regional conference and the details are overwhelming, assistance is most assuredly welcome. But First Cadre is still First Cadre and never to be taken lightly."

"A pragmatic assessment," Ydaire nodded, turning her attention to the data fountain in the middle of the room. "So Joseph Sutherland is co-chairing the Terran delegation. He's not a trouble-maker, but he also resists Terra falling into the Empire's orbit. If you notice a curious lack of support from him, that's why."

Rissa quickly blinked the filter in her eye to pull out delegate info from the mass of data cascading up from the base. She hadn't known it was possible to differentiate data without a filter, but First Cadre Excellenzi were said to have a number of amazing talents. She recalled that Ydaire was a native of Terra, which made Rissa wonder if that was the reason for monitoring this regional conference. But how to ask that? She didn't know if it was a point of sensitivity that Ydaire hailed from a near-barbarian homeworld. Perhaps an oblique approach.

"It's seldom that an Excellenza has the privilege of opening up her own homeworld to the larger galaxy, as you did with Terra last decade. You must be proud of the steps your people have taken since."

Ydaire gave her a cool look. "My people have taken no noteworthy steps in the interim. They've been keeping a very low profile, in fact. What is it you're actually saying, Rissa?"

With a sigh, Rissa gave up the oblique tactic. "I am wondering if Terra's presence at this conference is the reason you're the one serving as backup."

"Terra is still adjusting culturally to the shock of discovering they're a backwater world in the hinterlands. I expect nothing interesting in Terran diplomacy for another half-century. But it happens I know the Spiral Arm better than most, having Intervened here in recent history. That's why I am here."

Rissa nodded automatically, a little off-balanced by the casual reference to Intervention. It was the highest level of political force an Excellenz could enact, usually involving bringing down old governments and creating new ones. That was currently above her pay grade and the mechanism by which a single individual could achieve that result was still mysterious.

"Be careful how you position the Streggi," Ydaire continued. "The Border Wars are decades in the past, but there is still old hostility. Use your Datish hosts as buffers as much as possible. They are one of the few local cultures that Streggos did not attack. And are the Xcathi actually presencing themselves, or merely sending intermediaries? The data seems incomplete at that point."

Rissa readjusted her filter to follow. "I didn't expressly ask. Is it significant?"

"Logistically, yes. A fully grown Xcathi is a huge personage. It would have a profound impact on seating arrangements at the conference table. Any difficulties with the Archconsul as host?"

"No, he's been very supportive so far. Should I expect difficulties?"

"Expect a subtle jockeying for status. Always remember that though the Datish are hosting this conference, you are the one running it. Those are the only concerns I spot at a glance."

"Duly noted," Rissa answered, relieved to have gotten off lightly. In point of fact, Ydaire had pre-diffused three potential time-bombs.

"You have plenty of detail work to fill these last two weeks before the delegates arrive," Ydaire continued. "And I have three conferences of my own, plus a war to mediate. I'll see you in two weeks."

As Ydaire strode from the command center, Rissa stole an envious glance at the retreating form. To be so supremely confident of one's own competence—she wished someone would tell her how to achieve that.

Rissa reined in her staff. Now that she had Ydaire's voice in memory, she could reproduce some of the commanding tone. It was enough. Staff was talented, but only human. She needed to remember that she was a step beyond them, just as Ydaire was a step beyond her. An Excellenza in training was still an Excellenza in the eyes of the world.

The two weeks continued to dwindle. Three days before the delegates were scheduled to appear, Rissa was revising the agenda yet again when an adjutant scurried over. "Excellenza, the data fountain," he murmured uneasily.

She looked toward the center of the room and saw that all data display had ceased. She tensed, knowing this meant high-level communiqué from Throneworld, then realized everyone was waiting for her to act. "A moment of privacy, please," she told her staff, using both Ydaire's tone and exact words.

When the room was clear, she approached the empty data display. "I am the Excellenza Rissa. Is there a message?"

The display resolved itself into a face with the carefully neutral expression of professional staff. Her eyes widened as she took in the gold-on-gold uniform he wore. This was the staff of the All-Highest himself.

"Greetings, Excellenza," the staffer said. "I am instructed to inform you that the All-Highest will attend the regional conference you are organizing. Expect him for the opening and revise your ceremony accordingly. No agenda. Throneworld, out."

For long minutes after the face disappeared and the data flow started again, Rissa stood paralyzed by the fountain. The All-Highest was coming. After the first adrenaline rush of those words, her emotions veered toward all-out panic. She had no idea how to apply protocol at that high a level; she could barely cope with the protocols she was currently working with. And to fail in any way before the Presence would be the last of her career.

Eventually Rissa realized she was still standing alone in the room with staffers exiled to the outer hallway. There were only three days left. She had only one course of action.

"Ydaire," she told fountain and waited for the supremely confident face with the vivid green eyes to appear before her.

"The Excellenza Ydaire is currently in high-level negotiations and cannot be reached at this time," a dispassionate, disembodied voice told her. "Your communication will be relayed when she becomes available."

Another surge of panic. Then Rissa took a deep breath, squelched her own chaos, and summoned staff back into the command center. They entered quickly but tentatively, sensing something of magnitude had just transpired.

"Gentlehoms," she began, forcing her voice to remain steady. "We are to be honored at the opening ceremony with the Presence of the All-Highest."

It was like watching her own wave of reactions played out on the faces of her staffers: surprise, inspiration, then dismay and out-and-out panic as the logistical reality sank in. Her staff was no more certified for protocols at that level than she was. And they were all looking to her.

"This will be a stretch on short notice, but here's the plan," she said, trying to exude a quiet confidence. "First Priority: divide up the list and personally contact every head of delegation and present this as a sudden honor that underscores the importance of the conference agenda. Stress that this is a change in ceremony, not of substance. All discussion topics will proceed as planned. In the course of your conversations, ascertain the emotional reaction of the delegations. There may be some participants whose anxiety at standing before the Presence precludes their coming. That's acceptable— much better than an unfortunate scene. We shall arrange an alternate schedule for them to arrive after the opening ceremony. Go. I'll carry the news to the Archconsul in person."

As she started down the long hallway that connected the conference wing of the Archconsular palace with the more personal reception areas, Rissa wondered what she would do if her Datish hosts panicked. Well, that simply couldn't happen. She would have to present the news in such a way that it wouldn't happen.

A prickle against her temple told her she had incoming com. "Rissa," a calm, precise voice said. "Has something happened?"

Rissa stopped, blinked on the eye filter to accept visual transmission, and found herself looking at the interior of a Shuttle of State with Ydaire at the controls. "Thank you for your quick response," she said, trying to mimic Ydaire's calm tone. "Throneworld has just informed me that the All-Highest will be attending my opening ceremony."

Ydaire's cocked an eyebrow. "Why?"

"No idea."

"Who relayed the message?"

"A Gold-on-Gold staffer."

"What did he say about agenda?"

Rissa thought back. "He said no agenda."

"Ah." Ydaire sat back with an intense expression.

"Should I"—*or you*—"contact Throneworld to ask for details?"

"No. Gold-on-Gold has no idea what's going on."

Rissa frowned. "How can that be if they're the personal staff of—"

"The All-Highest can be singularly uncommunicative," Ydaire interjected. "He doesn't explain; he just does. Gold-on-Gold spends an inordinate amount of time trying to explain his movements to the rest of the Empire, movements that they themselves don't always understand. No, only the All-Highest knows why he is coming to your conference, but be assured it has nothing to do with you or with the conference itself."

"I'm sure that makes sense on some level, but not to me."

Ydaire quirked a quick smile. "On this topic you now know as much as the rest of us. I'll be there as soon as I can. I still have an interstellar war to deal with, but I'll press for quick resolution. Welcome to the High Protocols, Rissa."

As the image faded, Rissa allowed herself a very unprofessional shudder. This shouldn't be happening— even Ydaire implied as much. And it was all very well for First Cadre to be mystified about the motivations of the All-Highest when they were accustomed to the Presence. Rissa, on the other hand, had no more experience with the Presence than the average bureaucrat. She hadn't reached those levels of training that brought her into personal contact with the Highest.

Non-Imperials never quite understood what that moment of contact meant to a child of the Empire. They always mistook it for the fear they themselves felt at the Presence. But the All-Highest, more than being Emperor, was an immortal god, the last of a race of gods of immense power. Rissa had grown up in adoration of the All-Highest. To be with him, to speak with him carried so many emotional overtones that she feared she would be too rattled to moderate the conference. And then she would fail her mission. Before the Presence, she would fail. That very thought sent a frisson of terror up her spine. Perhaps she wasn't Excellenza material after all.

Then the moment passed, and Rissa realized she had no excuse to panic, not yet. Failure, if that was to be her fate, would come later. Until then, she still had a myriad of details to attend to.

The next two days went surprisingly smoothly. Her staff, fueled by adrenaline, shifted into a hyper-efficient mode. No major problems arose within the delegations from the addition of the Presence at the conference. Rissa was actually proud of her status when Ydaire walked into the command center mere hours before the delegates were due to arrive. This time there was no hint of casualness in the senior Excellenza. She was Imperial Silver dress uniform all the way.

"Rissa," she said in greeting. "Walk with me."

They started down the long reception hall, their boot heels clicking in perfect sync with one another. The local

Datish functionaries gave their very official-looking conversation wide berth.

"I repeat," Ydaire said, "this isn't about you. The Imperial Presence complicates things considerably. This conference can no longer be a solo operation and certainly not a solo by an Excellenza in training. We'll divide responsibilities as follows: You will continue to oversee all matters regarding the agenda and the delegations; I will attend all matters that touch upon the All-Highest. With luck, he will be satisfied with one appearance at the opening reception."

"And if the All-Highest decides to stay and participate in the negotiations?" Rissa asked.

Ydaire lifted an eyebrow. "Then both of us will be working very hard to compensate." At Rissa's shocked expression, she added, "The All-Highest seldom involves himself in actual terms-and-treaties negotiations because he dictates rather than negotiates and core conflicts are never resolved. He knows this better than anyone. That's why he has Excellenzi. But his very Presence complicates interaction between participants. It creates a peculiar situation where the interests of Emperor and Empire are not the same. That's why it will take two of us. What reaction from the delegations?"

Rissa actually felt a slight lessening of tension. This question she was prepared for. "The Datish Archconsul was been most accommodating—pleased even."

"Accommodation is what the Datish do best," Ydaire commented under her breath.

Rissa assumed a back-story but didn't stop to ask. "Twenty-three delegations are expected from throughout the Spiral Arm—no change there. Some tensions will be present, specifically between the Terrans and the Streggi, who have not had normal diplomatic relations since their border wars two decades ago. Can I assume the Presence will reduce outward display of those tensions?"

"No, interactions may well become volatile because the stakes have been raised for everyone. The All-Highest brings a sense of history with him."

"But I don't believe there are any races in the mix with historical interaction with the All-Highest, either positive or negative," Rissa pointed out.

"My point exactly," Ydaire responded. "These are all rising, young cultures with no history of interaction. With a *nouveau puissance* mentality, they become more likely to do or say the wrong thing. This conference couldn't be more wrong for the Presence. I am told that the Archconsul has placed his best guest suite at the disposal of the All-Highest. I'll inspect the quarters and the route between the suite and the reception hall. We want no offensive artwork within view this time around."

"The All-Highest is offended by art?" Rissa asked with a frown.

"Not at all, but many works depict historical events, which creates the possibility of an attitude counter to his. Not that displaying these attitudes is intentional, of course. To the current owners of limited lifespan, these are most often just pieces of art. But it can be awkward. Meanwhile, prepare for early arrivals."

"First scheduled arrival is the aKee delegation three hours from now," Rissa reported.

"Those arrival schedules never mean anything. Especially with young cultures, there is a perceived advantage in being first on the scene. Expect early arrivals and expect them to try to buttonhole you, which you want to avoid. Your role as neutral moderator precludes unplanned private conferences. Internalize that and you will save yourself a great deal of grief in your—"

"Ydaire . . . Excellenza!"

The male voice calling them was unfamiliar, certainly not any of the staffers assigned to this mission. Turning, Rissa saw a tall, young man hurrying to catch up with them. Dark hair, nicely sculpted face, and too pale to be anything but Terran Caucaze. So true to Ydaire's warning, the Terran delegation was here five hours ahead of schedule.

The young Terran approached, huffing a little. "Talk about fast on your feet . . . you two move like a small whirlwind. I've been chasing you for ten minutes."

Young and chatty and oddly intimate with Imperial Officers of Rank. Rissa assumed this was someone of Ydaire's acquaintance, though that really didn't excuse the chattiness. Perhaps this was the first example of *nouveau puissance*.

But Ydaire's reaction was oddly non-reactive. "How do I know you?" the Excellenza asked after a moment.

A strange question. With eidetic memories, Excellenzi literally never forgot a face. Ydaire would know if she knew this Terran or not . . . yet she seemed unsure.

The young man's face fell. "You said you wouldn't forget me," he muttered.

Ydaire gave a start. "Eric?"

That put a smile back on his face. "Yes!"

Ydaire caught Rissa's eye. "He was nine years old when I last saw him on Terra, eleven years ago," she said in explanation.

Rissa gave a nod of understanding. Reconciling a nine-year-old boy with a twenty-year-old man would challenge the best memory. From the perspective of the long-lived, aging always made identification of acquaintances a little tricky, especially with the growth spurt of adolescence added in.

"Why are you at this conference, Eric?" Ydaire asked. "You can't be part of the Terran delegation."

"I'm personal staff of the Legate," he answered. "Dad arranged it. He didn't really want me to come, but I finally wore him down at the last minute. I'm no debater, but I'm dogged."

"I remember that trait," Ydaire nodded. "And why did you insist on being here?"

Eric shifted uneasily. "I have one favor to ask . . . it's about my . . . condition. The seizures have been getting worse for years. I've been to every specialist on Terra, who all say the same thing—it's a psi thing, not a physical thing. That was the main reason Dad didn't want me to come. I'm supposed to stay near the door and get out of public sight whenever I feel a seizure coming on. It's inevitable that one or two will hit during the conference."

A delegate with psi seizures. Rissa closed her eyes a moment, trying to assimilate that into an already complicated mix. She fervently hoped that personal history made this young Terran Ydaire's responsibility, not hers.

"So what's the favor?" Ydaire asked sharply, her tone paralleling the things Rissa was feeling.

Eric hesitated a second, then plunged in. "They say your Emperor has immense psi ability and can kill or cure with a thought. Would you ask him to cure me?"

*Powers of Night!* Rissa thought, trying to keep her reaction off her face. Only a non-Imperial could conceive such an insult to the Presence. She couldn't wait to hear Ydaire's answer.

"Eric," Ydaire said with surprising calm, "one doesn't approach the All-Highest Emperor as a medical service. One doesn't even ask."

"But you're one of his Excellenzi. He'd do it if you ask him to—I know he would." The desperation in his voice was wrenching.

"I'll try to explain, but we have to resume the whirlwind. With so much last minute prep, I have to be in three places at once. Walk with me, Eric."

As the two of them set off down the corridor, Rissa felt a profound relief not to be part of that conversation. One didn't assault the All-Highest with trivial requests. The Excellenzi knew this better than anyone. As a group, they were the buffer between the day-to-day workings of Empire and the unpredictability of a god. And quite frankly, the psi seizures of a random Terran would be of no interest to the Highest. Then she looked down the corridor and quickly tabled that whole disturbing topic. Two more delegations had just arrived.

Rissa slowed her breathing to control her pounding heart as the update trickled into her ear. He was here.

The All-Highest was here. A moment for the honor guard to form around him, then he would enter the reception hall where she waited with the twenty-three delegations. Her eye went to Ydaire who was standing unobtrusively at the edge of the crowd. Ydaire returned a slight nod of support.

The entrance of the All-Highest was expected to be a spectacle. As the great doors were flung open for the procession of honor guard and brightly uniformed attendants, Rissa assured herself it had the right look. It was all improvisation, of course. Producing a true honor guard this far away from Throneworld was impossible on short notice. She had substituted staff and crew from her diplomatic cruiser.

A fanfare of trumpets, then the All-Highest himself, a radiant image of golden hair, golden eyes, and trailing golden cloak that roiled around him like a living creature—

Rissa stiffened. The Greatcloak? Why had no one informed her that this was to be a Greatcloak event? It wasn't just a change in protocol, it was also a matter of security.

"Ydaire," she subvocalized into her com implant. "Why is this a Greatcloak event?"

"No idea," came the terse reply. "We'll deal with it."

Rissa fought to replace the impending panic attack she felt with the studied calm she ought to be projecting. But she had no idea how to deal with this. The Greatcloak was as much lethal weapon as ceremonial garb. The Highest could—and did—burn detractors with the flick of that cloak. And the substitute honor guard was now woefully insufficient. Only Stedren warriors knew how to position themselves as buffer between a crowd and an angry cloak. These temps did not. Any sudden mood swing in the Highest could be disastrous.

She shunted her fears aside as the ceremony began in earnest, requiring her active participation. All the dignitaries remained standing, indeed all chairs had been removed from the hall. Since the Highest seldom sat and by protocol no one else sat in the Presence, there was no need of seating. But her mind kept cycling back to one question: Why was the Highest wearing the powerful Greatcloak to a small regional conference? Being what he was, his perceptions often ran in prophetic directions. Did he know something was about to happen?

The ceremony dragged on. Rissa knew it was proceeding exactly on schedule, but with herself in hyper mode, every minute seemed a small eternity. She kept glancing back at Ydaire, a restless guardian in Imperial Silver prowling the edge of the crowd. She strongly suspected that Ydaire's pacing meant an event of some sort was coming.

Beyond Ydaire, at the very back of the room by the service door, a tall, dark-haired figure stood apart from everyone else. Why was he—ah, it was the Terran ex-boy hanging back in case he felt a seizure coming on. She saw Ydaire give him a nod as she passed by to prowl the other side of the hall.

Rissa snapped her attention back to the ceremony just in time to introduce the next head of delegation to the All-Highest. This presentation ritual accomplished nothing of substance, but seemed to be of immense importance to the delegates themselves. An introduction and a few words of conversation, and they were happy.

She looked for Ydaire again and saw that something had changed. The senior Excellenza had stopped cold and was staring back at the Terran by the door. Rissa strained to think, as she was thinking, *Greatcloak ... incident ... seizure.* That was it, the pattern of events.

Ydaire was on the move again, directly toward the Terran, but she was too late. He spasmed and began to fall. Sprinting the last few steps, she reached him before he hit the floor and was able to cushion the fall.

"Rissa," Ydaire's voice murmured through the com. She began pulling the inert form toward the door, though he outmassed her considerably. "Small incident. I'm removing Eric from the hall and will be out of circulation for—"

Rissa felt the sudden surge of heat a second before chaos erupted.

Her head snapped up in time to see the Highest turn abruptly, Greatcloak whipping a fiery arc around him. Psychic seizure . . . psychic attack. That's what it must have felt like to him. She flipped channels. "Guards. All-Highest in motion. Form up perimeter lines—"

Too little, too late. The guards had no idea what to do as the Highest set sail across the room. Pandemonium as delegates scrambled to get out of his way, some screaming as the cloak lashed past them. It was Rissa's nightmare scenario.

As she stared, unmoving, her mind began pumping out plans of action seemingly of its own volition. Whatever was occurring between the All-Highest and Eric was now Ydaire's to handle. The rest of the room was Rissa's.

Over Eric's prone form, the Highest descended to a squat, his golden cloak flowing outward in all directions, charring the marble floor like a molten river. Across the room, the better-heeled dignitaries squatted as well, to keep themselves from being higher than the Highest. Others just stared. This was a disaster for protocol, for the ceremony, and most likely for the overall conference. Unless someone could clean up the mess.

From the front of the room, Rissa saw what seemed to be argument between the All-Highest and Ydaire . . . but that was unthinkable . . . how could even a senior Excellenza dare such? Yet an argument was what it appeared to be. A moment later, she saw Ydaire enfold Eric's upper body in a lockhold as the Highest reached out to touch his forehead. When the touch came, the Terran screamed and spasmed. *Disaster*, Rissa thought with a shudder. The All-Highest burning delegates and torturing a fallen guest. Not exactly the image the Empire wanted to imprint on the emerging Spiral Arm nations.

But what she also saw quite clearly was the Highest *not* destroying the screaming Terran. In fact, if destruction were the purpose, the Highest wouldn't be sitting on the floor with his intended victim.

The screaming stopped. Another intense exchange of words followed between the Highest and Ydaire. Then he rose and was gone in a flash of golden light. Gone from the hall, from the palace, from Datar, and most probably from the Spiral Arm.

"Dead?" Rissa subvocalized through the com.

"Cured," Ydaire answered. "Get the room under control."

Rissa turned her head to survey the shambles of the opening ceremony. Diplomats were recovering, some getting blustery now that Highest and Greatcloak were gone.

"Your attention, please, gentlehoms and sentients." Rissa's voice was amplified to ring across the room. "Apologies for the confusion, but we have just witnessed a medical emergency in our midst. A member of the Terran Legation suffered a life-threatening seizure, and the All-Highest was moved to take immediate action on his behalf. Again, all apologies for any inconveniences suffered, but the All-Highest is not one to trifle with, even at his most merciful."

Ydaire's voice tickled her ear. "Mercy underscored with an unstated threat—not at all a bad spin. Keep going."

"After such a momentous occurrence, we would do well to adjourn for the rest of the evening," Rissa continued to the delegates. "Tomorrow we shall resume in the conference hall as outlined on the official agenda. May you all have a restorative night and return refreshed for the work ahead."

And amazingly, her words seemed to have the intended effect. The delegates broke into smaller groups and shuffled off to their quarters with no displays of negativity.

In the stillness of the night, Rissa stood in the vacant command center, filtering the data fountain for any mention of the disastrous ceremony or the seizure. There was nothing.

"You're wasting your time, Rissa," Ydaire said from the doorway. "The Highest does not post reports. When he's displeased, we hear about it much more directly."

That sounded grim . . . probably *was* grim. "Are you implying that he's *not* displeased with my disaster of an opening ceremony?"

"As I said before, his being here had nothing to do with you or the conference. He had his own agenda."

"Which was?"

"What can you infer?"

Rissa thought back to that intense moment when Ydaire seemed to be arguing with the All-Highest. "Something about your Terran and his seizure . . . he presents a broad-based danger of some sort."

"Good," Ydaire nodded. "This evening confirmed what the Highest had sensed from afar—Eric has immense psychic potential that broadcasts disruption across a wide spectrum when he seizes. The Highest alleviated the most immediate symptoms, but the rest is up to Eric."

"So you persuaded the Highest to spare him."

Ydaire gave a snort. "Swayed, but not persuaded. I bought some time for Eric. Either he learns to control his psychic gifts, or eventually he'll have to be dealt with."

Rissa grimaced. That euphemism was all too clear. He had almost been dealt with tonight, which would have put the conference well beyond her abilities to salvage. But the situation hadn't descended into that abyss. Thankfully, First Cadre had been there to sway, if not persuade. And now First Cadre would evaluate. She waited silently for Ydaire's assessment of the not-quite-abysmal evening.

"And from the perspective of a neutral observer, how did your first public function go?" Ydaire asked.

Rissa frowned. She hadn't been expecting self-assessment. Calling up the training technique of stepping outside oneself to achieve objectivity, she focused, then said, "It was chaotic. No amount of training could have prepared me for all the factors I had to deal with. By the end, I was operating on sheer gut instinct."

"And how were your instincts?"

Rissa focused again. "Better than I would have guessed. I think I salvaged the conference without disgracing the Empire. And I believe I avoided disgracing myself before the Presence." She thought a moment more. "All things considered, not a bad outcome . . . but, perhaps, you disagree."

Ydaire quirked a smile. "That's no longer relevant. You have proved yourself under fire and should listen to your own voice. Welcome to the Cadre."

*Jonathan Shipley, a member of Science Fiction Writers of America, writes short stories and novels in a vast story arc ranging from Nazi occultism to vampires to futuristic space opera, He was one of eight finalists for the 2014 Washington Science Fiction Association's Small Press Award with a whimsical story about Hell, and also in 2014, the After Death anthology where he was a contributing author won the Bram Stoker Award. His list of publications has topped five dozen with several additional stories still pending release. A list of his publications can be found at www.shipleyscifi.com.*

Madame X suspects her daughter-in-law of hiding something. When the girl returns from her studies on Earth, Madame is intent on finding out the secret and how it might hurt her son. What she learns forces her to confront her own long-hidden secrets.

# THE DEVICE

### By

### *Tara Campbell*

The girl was hiding something.

Madame X watched her daughter-in-law lift a saucer to her mouth. The young female's sleek, grey paws curved expertly around the delicate bone cup. Her eyes flashed briefly at Madame X across the breakfast table before she stuck her tiny pink tongue into the bowl and lapped daintily at her drink.

Madame X curled the tip of her tail around the leg of her chair, the better to keep it still. She leaned over her own saucer, grumbling at the girl's affectation. This scholarship to Earth may be creating an expert in Humanology, but it was also allowing a perfectly healthy linnean to put off having young—and was that really what Council had intended?

She watched the girl set down her saucer and look around for one of those silly little eating cloths she'd brought back with her—*napkins*, she called them. Why she expected anyone to use them, Madame didn't know. Regardless, the girl would make a show of looking for a *napkin*, and then pointedly not ask for one, as if to imply old Madame couldn't possibly be enlightened enough to appreciate another planet's peculiar customs.

Now, however, the girl cut her little act short, licking her whiskers with circumspect, almost embarrassed quickness. Perhaps she was finally learning a little humility toward her elders.

Or, more likely, she was hiding something.

Madame X ran her tongue slowly across her own whiskers. She licked her paws for good measure, watching the girl's almond-shaped eyes narrow. Madame X closed her eyes and purred, lengthening the strokes of her tonguebath to encompass her whole front leg. Her tail unwound itself from the chair leg and flicked languidly on the floor.

She shouldn't really try to antagonize her daughter-in-law like this, but the girl had become insufferable at the table: scooping food into her mouth with a tiny bowl on the end of a stick, impaling her meat with that little four-pronged staff, dabbing at her whiskers with *napkins*, like she didn't have a tongue or teeth of her own.

"Bett's getting off work early today," said the girl.

Madame X's eyes snapped open and she glared at her daughter-in-law. Of course she knew her own son's work schedule.

"We're meeting some friends for dinner," the girl continued. "Will you be all right here? Shall I make you something before I leave?"

"No, that is kind of you, but I'll be fine." Madame didn't know what the girl was saying; she didn't "make" anything. All she knew how to do was press a button and fill a bowl with kibble. Breakfast for dinner. This generation; no conception of hunting.

"All right," said the girl. She lifted her coffeepot and poured, but only a trickle came out.

"Give me your saucer," said Madame X, resting a paw on the self-warming decanter she'd had installed next to the table. She was quite proud of it, actually, and had to admit she enjoyed showing off a bit for her guests, refilling their saucers with the touch of a lever.

"Thank you, but I'm drinking decaf."

"Still?"

The girl swirled the liquid in her cup. "I'm re-conditioning."

Madame said nothing. It was the girl's own fault. She'd gone off coffee as soon as the link between caffeine and increased fertility had been discovered. And what did that get her, now that all young linneans were required to drink it. Behind, that's what it got her. Behind.

A shy smile crept across the girl's muzzle. "So, did Bett tell you I got to visit an Earth coffee plantation? I brought some home for you."

"That's very kind, but really not necessary. Our engineers have figured all that out."

"Well, yes, we can grow the beans, but our fields aren't the same. The conditions there are completely different. When you drink it, you can almost taste their sun, their soil, their air." She swallowed the last sip from her cup and purred.

Madame shrugged. "It's all coffee."

The girl's smile faded. She picked up her cup and pot and left the table.

*Well, decaf's better than nothing*, Madame grumbled to herself.

While her daughter-in-law messed with a coffee grinder behind her, Madame simply pushed her saucer over to the decanter and pressed the lever. A bit of coffee sloshed onto the table as she pulled her saucer back toward her. Madame darted forward to lap the hot, brown liquid off the table, then settled back on her chair and sniffed at the steam curling up from her cup. She had to admit, she did rather look forward to those packets of beans the girl brought back on her breaks. She'd even tried holding a saucer in her paws once— more than once—in private, but wound up having to lick most of the coffee out of her thick, white fur.

Her daughter-in-law approached the table again, saucer and pot in paw. "Thank you for breakfast, Mother."

Madame's right ear twitched at the last word.

The girl remained for a moment, uncertain. "Well, I'll be upstairs."

She nodded and watched the girl leave. Her step was quick—nervous. But why?

Madame lapped at her coffee and batted distractedly at a stray piece of kibble underneath the decanter. The tip of her tail swatted the floor, and she dipped her tongue into her saucer. Her coffee was cold. She pushed the saucer away, the silence in the room magnifying the scrape of the cup over the table.

"Call Bett at work," said Madame, and the communicator patched the call through.

"Hello Mother." Bett's fluffy, broad face appeared on the wall in front of her. Behind him, coworkers crawled through segments of clear piping, pulling tools out of holsters and checking connections.

"Bett, darling, is this a good time?"

"Yes, Mother, how are you?" He leaned closer and twitched his whiskers. "How are things going?"

Madame X smoothed her fur. "We just finished breakfast and she's gone upstairs. I thought I'd take this chance to tell you, dear, I don't think she's terribly happy."

"What happened?" He curled his tail around his haunches and settled in, as if waiting for an entertaining story.

*Dear Bett; will you ever start taking life seriously?* "Nothing's happened *here*," she replied. "What I mean is, I think your wife isn't happy on Earth. Think about it: she's started this whole research program, with a generous grant from Council, when what she wants more than anything is to be at home with you."

"I don't know, Mother. Earth is her passion."

Madame X's nose twitched. This was, indeed, the whole problem with the girl. Well, that, and she was a shorthair. Poor Bett had always had a weakness for shorthairs, but Madame didn't trust them. "I understand. And where would we be without bold adventurers like her to chart wild, unknown civilizations? I just wonder at what cost."

"Well, so does Council, apparently," he said. "They're threatening to cut the exploration budget next year."

"But that's next year, and you're ready to start a family now."

Bett let out a quick, soft growl. They both knew she was right. They'd talked about it more than once.

"You know," she purred, "Geera likes you, and she's ready to have young too."

"Mother—"

"None of the other grantees' spouses are waiting."

"How do you know?" he asked, flicking his tail.

"You forget where I work." Working at B&Y, the Birthing and Young Complex, meant she didn't miss much of who was breeding with whom. "Now, I know you like Geera, and our families get along so well—"

Bett held up a paw to stop her. "Please, can we talk about this when I get home?" He turned toward a commotion to the side and nodded before looking back at her. "Look, I've got to go. One of my colleagues on litter leave is visiting with her young."

"Well, by all means, go see them," purred Madame. "Maybe it'll give you some ideas." She smiled, licked her paw and held it toward the wall. He returned her paw-lick and ended the call.

Dear, sweet Bett, content to wait on his little explorer, impatient with his mother for pushing. He'd never qualify for a promotion if things kept on like this. As one of only five siblings, he should know better. Hadn't he watched her toil in menial positions while larger families around them advanced? His brothers and sisters had learned the lesson; they'd already had multiple litters of their own and were now enjoying the rewards of high breeders.

"Madame X," intoned the feeding room wall. It was the voice of her supervisor at B&Y.

"Connect," she responded.

Her supervisor's face appeared on the wall. "Madame X, we need you for an extra shift this afternoon."

"Yes, Madame H."

"Report for the second feeding. I'll set your alert."

"Yes, Madame H."

Only when Madame H disappeared from the screen did Madame X voice an annoyed little chirrup. This was supposed to be her day away from the tumult of noise at the Nursery of Defense. Her division housed the most aggressive newborns, specially selected to be raised away from their families and groomed as warriors—she'd need more rest before facing them. She pushed her chair away from the table and padded out of the feeding room on soft paws, then climbed a carpeted ramp toward her sleeping space.

The large, open area of the second floor was empty. The coffeepot and Madame's good bone saucer lay on the floor, unattended. Her ears flattened in annoyance. A murmur drifted down the third level and, piqued, Madame climbed the upholstered post to the next story. Huffing at the top (she normally didn't take the post so quickly), she swiveled her ears to track the muffled voice. It was her daughter-in-law in a one-sided conversation, apparently using her communicator in privacy mode.

She'd known the girl was hiding something.

Madame's fur rose and she instinctually pressed herself to the ground. The girl's voice emanated from a separate room with a round opening in the front wall: Bett's sleeping space, which he shared with the girl when she was home from her field work on Earth. Despite the indignity of creeping around her own home on all fours, she crept across the floor toward the cube-like room. She stood up on her rear legs close to the opening, holding herself against the wall and straining to hear the girl's whispers.

Madame tingled with curiosity—or were those her muscles protesting the impromptu hunt in her own house? She vowed to get back into her stretches.

The girl was saying something unintelligible, something harsh and clipped. Could it be she was speaking to one of those *people* on Earth? As though she didn't already spend enough time there, leaving her husband behind at home. Throwing away her

scholarship on a backwater planet like that was bad
enough, but putting off her son's plans for family was—
  The girl purred.
  Madame didn't like the sound of that purr. It was—
coquettish.
  "Disconnect," the girl commanded.
  Madame leapt away from the cube-like room and let
herself silently down the post to the second story. She
hurried across the spacious room, resisting the urge to
gather up the abandoned coffee items, and crept down
the ramp to the main level. At a thump from upstairs,
she ran to the breakfast table and sat down. Clumsy in
her quickness, she knocked her bone saucer off the
table. Her eyes squeezed shut at the *crack*, and she
reluctantly reopened them to the sight of cold coffee
leaking onto the floor.
  Her daughter-in-law entered, holding a coffeepot
and unharmed saucer. She was wearing one of her
Earth shawls, a pretension which Madame had learned
to read as her intent to leave the house. The girl gasped
at the mess on the floor and rushed to grab a towel, but
tiny cleaning mites had already emerged from the wall to
ingest the brown liquid and pieces of bone.
  "Don't worry," said the girl, twisting the useless rag
in her paws. "It happens to everyone at first."
  Madame X stared.
  "Mother, I can teach you how to hold it, if you like."
  Madame's ears flattened before she could stop them.
  The girl quickly excused herself and vanished on
some vague errand. As the cleaning mites finished their
task and scurried back into the walls, Madame
contemplated following her. Would she have enough
time before work? As she debated whether or not to go,
her window of opportunity passed. The girl would be too
far to track now.
  Madame X circled the room twice before sinking into
a pile of pillows in the corner. She closed her eyes, just
for a moment. She never slept well when her daughter-
in-law was in the house.

A pleasing cascade of tones pealed from speakers behind the walls, telling her she'd have to leave for work soon. She licked her whiskers and smoothed her fur. Why hadn't she followed the girl? It wouldn't be dignified, but then how dignified was it to sit by while her daughter-in-law came and went as she pleased without producing any young?

A second, less pleasing set of tones rang through the house. Madame yawned and rolled to the floor for a bracing stretch on all fours, then stood and quickly checked the pantry on her way out—she'd have to do some light hunting on the way home.

She waved to a couple of neighbors along the winding path to B&Y, but didn't stop. The last thing she wanted was idle chatter on her way into the cacophony of the next few hours. Madame turned to the left to take the long way, wishing the faster route didn't run so close to the city wall. The shortcut would be quieter, and it was a pretty path through a forest of tall, purple ferns, but she hadn't set foot on it since that morning she'd heard the sounds from the Plains.

The ferns had been rimmed with frost that day, and the tips of her ears were cold. The whoosh of transport and the yowling of street vendors had carried through crisp, clear air into the forest. But that clear air had carried sounds from outside the city wall as well. Someone—or something—out in the Plains screeched and clawed at the wall. She'd heard a snarl, then a great, barrel-chested roar, then a scream. Then nothing.

Bett laughed at her now, insisting the perimeter had been secured since then, but she still didn't care to get that close to the wall. She quickened her pace. She should feel fortunate about her position at the Nursery, her second chance to stay and contribute to the community after producing an underwhelming number of young.

As she reached the B&Y grounds, she noticed a familiar figure ducking out the front door of the complex. The skittish-looking girl held a bundle of some sort. Madame squinted. It couldn't be . . .

It was her daughter-in-law!

The girl turned right and walked briskly along the edge of the building. Madame rushed across an expanse of blue-green moss to get closer. As she neared the complex, she wondered if inertia would draw her through the front doors and to her post. No, not inertia: cowardice. One didn't miss work. But on the other hand, one didn't just let one's daughter-in-law exit B&Y without investigating further.

Madame slipped behind a pregnant female who happened to be going the same direction. Every few steps, she craned her neck to make sure she could still see her daughter-in-law's back. The girl's posture was stiff, her gait quick. And she wasn't wearing her precious Earth shawl anymore. That must be the odd bundle she was carrying.

Madame X tensed when she recognized Madame Q, a coworker, heading toward her on the path. Madame Q's face blossomed with recognition as she approached. "Why Madame—"

Madame X raised a paw to her mouth. Q froze, confused, and Madame X watched her daughter-in-law disappear around a corner.

"Madame X?" asked her colleague. "Is something wrong?"

"Yes. I mean, no, nothing's wrong." She grabbed Madame Q's shoulders, looking past her at the empty spot the young girl had occupied. "Are you heading to the Nursery now? If anyone asks, tell them I'm on my way." She let Q go and hurried after her daughter-in-law. She tried not to think about being late. If she could be quick, she might not be noticed. She'd just have to think up an excuse for not having signed in right away.

Madame peeked around the corner, hoping the girl wouldn't choose just that moment to look back. The path ahead was empty. The girl had instead chosen to walk across a mossfield toward a thicket of ferns.

Why would she head that way? There was nothing beyond the ferns—except the city wall. She had no cover in the mossfield, so Madame could only watch from a distance and wait to see where the girl went.

Why would she have been at the clinic, Madame asked herself, unless—could she be pregnant? If so, she'd just arrived back home, making the sad but obvious question, "By whom?" Or, given her current post, "By what?"

A low rumble of disgust filled Madame's throat. Breeding was, of course, impossible with a Human. But then who was on Earth with her? And if Bett was waiting for her—which he by no means was required to, but since he'd decided to—wouldn't the decent thing be for her to wait for him?

The girl disappeared into the tall, purple ferns. Not even her head was visible, but Madame could pick out the trail of plants that had curled up at her touch. Madame's pulse quickened. She abandoned her hiding spot and crept on all fours across the blue-green mossfield toward the ferns.

She shouldn't be surprised that Bett chose to wait. She and Fen had planned on monogamy, so she couldn't really be angry with her son for feeing the same way. But that was all the more reason he had to find a suitable mate and start a family now—his own family, not someone else's.

She stopped at the edge of the thicket and tried to look through the mass of purple fronds. The leaflets that had rolled up at the girl's touch were unwinding themselves again. The trail would disappear soon. Madame pushed forward, fronds shrinking away from her as she passed.

The ferns thinned out, and Madame slowed her pace. She ducked and watched as her daughter-in-law exited the thicket and wandered to the middle of another mossfield. The girl stopped and hung her head. After a few moments she sat down—not carefully in the least, Madame noticed. She must not be very far along.

Madame held still amid the ferns, watching the girl, until the fronds surrounding her began to relax and unfurl themselves. She held her breath, trying not to think about how close they were to the city wall. As much as she dreaded hearing them, she couldn't help but listen for noises from the Plains. Was that a yelp far off? A howl? She was inexcusably late for work now; was sure to be written up, and with that on her record—

She began, very carefully, to back away. The girl started and twisted to face her.

"Mother?"

Madame closed her eyes, opening them only at the rustle of the girl's paws over moss.

The girl stood before her, holding the bundled-up shawl discreetly under her front leg. "Mother, what are you—I thought you had today off."

Madame X stood up straight and strode out of the ferns. "I was supposed to, but they called me in. I should be there right now, except I saw you on my way in."

The girl's expression shifted from surprise to suspicion. "So you followed me?"

"You looked distressed. Is something troubling you?" She glanced in the direction of the city wall. "Should you be out here by yourself?"

"I can take care of myself."

"Can you, Daughter?" asked Madame, as tenderly as she could.

The pride in the girl's face wavered and she looked, for the first time, vulnerable.

"Is everything all right?"

The girl nodded.

Madame knew better. "You were with a physician."

"It was just a check-up," she shot back.

"I see." Madame looked down at the bundle. "Daughter, is there anything—"

"I'm fine," said the girl. "I just wanted a little quiet." She straightened her spine and shifted the bundle.

Madame regretted overusing "Daughter." That had been too much closeness, too soon. "Well, I've got to get to work," she said, changing tack. "I'm rather late now."

She was gratified to see a hint of guilt in the girl's eye, and took advantage of it to guide her back through the purple ferns toward the B&Y complex. "Come with me and take a peek at the newborns," she commanded. "They're quiet, and they always make one feel better." She knew the girl would relax and open up after seeing them. They seemed to have that effect on everyone.

Madame's mood sank with every step toward B&Y. It occurred to her that she hadn't heard from her supervisor. She checked her communicator, prepared for condemnation from her boss. Instead she saw a message from Madame Q: "Signed you in, be discreet—and quick."

Madame almost dissolved with relief. She didn't know why Q had done it, but there would be time to worry about that later. She tugged on the girl's paw, then pushed her through the front door and shooed her up to the newborn viewing area. She signed her guest in and hurried upstairs to her station. Madame Q was indeed discreet, smoothly handing her a cage holding two plump rodents as soon as she entered.

"Here," said Q, "take these over to that corner. You've got six little ones to feed, so I gave you two Pladsratten."

"I can't thank you enough, Madame Q—"

"Don't thank me. Just don't get yourself into trouble; we need all the help we can get here."

Madame looked around, shaking her head. The Nursery's feeding room was crowded with workers like her, stalking and pouncing, training hordes of young to hunt.

Q leaned closer. "It's no illusion, X. Everyone knows there's been an increase in production, but nobody wants to talk about why."

Madame X's hair threatened to stand up. She smoothed it with a paw. "Perhaps I should just go feed the—"

"Wait, listen: I heard something in the—" Madame Q went silent when another coworker walked by to fetch a cage of Pladsratten. Q grabbed a cage for herself and whispered to Madame X before walking away, "Meet me after shift. I need to talk to you."

Madame stood with her cage of snuffling rodents for a moment, until the sounds of hunting and squealing snapped her to attention. Madame gathered her charges into a corner and released their lunch one by one, holding the meal down while the little ones practiced pouncing and killing. While they ate, she wondered if she really wanted to hear what Madame Q had to tell her. Q had a tendency to speak her mind, which was unwise. And Madame X already had her own problems to worry about.

After all the young had been fed, she slipped down to the lower ward to check on her daughter-in-law. The girl was, thankfully, still there, holding her bundled up shawl and staring through the glass. Knots of tiny, fluffy newborns slept together on cushions, sucked at wet-nurses or batted at toys. Madame stepped next to the girl and uttered the usual words: "They're beautiful, aren't they?"

"Yes." Her voice was flat and low.

Madame's whiskers twitched. No gushing, no cooing? "Tell me about your studies," she coaxed. "Tell me about Earth." Any way to get her talking.

"The whole Earth?" The girl swished her tail derisively.

Madame maintained her air of patience. "Well, no. Tell me about the part of it you study. The Humans."

"Even that is a huge subject," she said, staring at the newborns. "Just like here on Miala, Earth has many regional variations, customs, different languages—although one can get by in most instances with Mandarenglish or Italian."

Madame wondered which of the two she'd heard her speaking that morning.

"I mean, biologically they're similar to us," the girl explained. "I couldn't go there otherwise. They breathe air, although I have to take oxygen pills to supplement. They drink water, which tastes horrible—we sometimes joke that's why they invented coffee."

*Who's we?* Madame wondered. Fellow student? Professor? The father of her future young?

"Like us," the girl went on, "Humans eat plants and other animals. It's funny, though, most of them don't like seeing things killed. I mean, it's this weird disconnect; intellectually they know that's what happens, but they don't want to think about it, so they don't want to see it."

"Dear, these Humans sound a little unstable. Surely they don't send you over there *all by yourself.*"

The girl shrugged. "We have a group orientation before leaving home, but it's pretty worthless because we're all going to such different places. I mean, what can you tell me about Earth that will be useful to someone going to Yeno or Vhan'thu? All they can really do is offer general interstellar travel tips and warn us to remain objective and not break any local laws."

The girl continued, still staring at the newborns. "We're there to study them, that's all. We're not there to get involved in their lives or make any changes, even when it would really help them. We simply observe. We talk to them about their customs and their societies, compare our observations to their self-assessments, and do all this without getting involved. Without, Flick forbid, forming any kind of real connection."

So, Madame thought, she had no study partners on Earth. If she's expecting, then, that would mean . . . But that simply couldn't be possible with a Human. Perhaps someone during transport, then; a crewmember.

"Their newborns are actually not that strange-looking next to ours," the girl said softly. "I mean, their adults are—well, I'm not supposed to assign any subjective qualitative descriptors to them, but they look so weak and defenseless. I mean, imagine a full-grown, adult creature only covered with a few patches of fur." She shook her head. "They seem so backward at first, but once you gain their trust and really talk to them, you start to understand their customs. And when you look at one of their *infants*—that's what they call their newborns—you can actually see some potential, you know, if you could feed it right and raise it with more advantages."

Madame caught her mouth hanging open and closed it. Could the girl actually be . . .? Was she trying to talk herself into actually carrying half-human young?

"Humans are as fond of their young as we are of ours," the girl said. "Different hormones, same effect, I suppose. But . . . well, we don't actually know why, but Humans seem to have a more—a different—approach to reproduction." She dropped her tone to little more than a whisper. "They have the same biological urge to reproduce, but as a society they seem to have additional goals. Goals unrelated to growing the population." A sharp edge entered her voice. "Goals that wouldn't make sense in our world."

Madame looked warily at the girl. "Let's discuss this further at home."

"Even though they only bear one *child*—that's what they call young—at a time, in some places they actually try to manage the number of *children* they bear." The girl turned to her. "I mean, manage *downward*. In many of their societies, a Human can mean something even if they don't—"

"Quiet, girl!" hissed Madame. Now she had no idea what the girl was getting at. She only knew that it would lead to trouble.

The girl stared at her, eyes wide. "Thank you, Mother, for bringing me here," she stammered. "I really must go." Madame didn't know what to do but watch her daughter-in-law hurry out the door.

Madame returned to the Nursery, where she spent the rest of the afternoon in a distracted haze. She couldn't shake the feeling that her colleagues' eyes were on her, as though her daughter-in-law's scandalous talk of limiting childbirth had covered Madame herself in an aura of discord and—disobedience? Her stomach pinched. Disobedience. Such an ugly word, with its implications of force and subjugation.

She'd never been forced, not really. She'd wanted to have young with Fen, but when he hadn't been able to produce them, trying with someone else was simply the right thing to do. No one ordered her to, but everyone knew that expansion with order was what would keep them from reverting into the ragged, vulnerable pack their ancestors had been. Civilization meant cooperation and renewal, and those who couldn't live by those tenets were better out on the Plains anyway. There were supposed to be safe enclaves out there, enough to give someone a chance, should they choose not to help provide linnean society's needs.

Even for those like Fen, from whom nature had taken the choice, there was another option. He'd been offered the opportunity to guard the northern perimeter. He might still be there, as far as she knew.

A lilting chime pealed throughout the Nursery. Madame's shift was over. Madame Q appeared at her side, and they descended the levels of B&Y together. Madame contemplated an imaginary errand on the way home, one that would take her in a different direction from Madame Q. She didn't think she could listen to Q's secrets today. They were usually unsettling—and they often turned out to be true.

Madame X hesitated as they stepped outside, but when Madame Q cocked her ear and flicked her tail, Madame X felt obliged to fall in alongside her friend. Q *had* signed her in, after all. They padded away from the B&Y together.

Madame X's heart beat a little faster when they neared the turn to the shortcut, which she knew Q preferred.

"I know what you're thinking," said Madame Q. "I don't like the shortcut anymore either, but we need some privacy."

Madame X chirruped inquisitively as Q led them into the forest. Purple ferns loomed over their heads as they walked in silence.

Finally, Madame Q told her: "I heard something out in the Plains."

Madame X froze.

"Screaming. Screeching," said Q. "Just like you heard."

Madame X shivered. "When? Where?"

"The other night, here, on the shortcut." She nudged Madame X and they started moving again. "Those—*things* are getting too close to the wall again. Council keeps telling us the area's secure, but too many linneans have heard otherwise. Council can't ignore it anymore. But because they never admit to any problems, they never tell us how they're going to solve them."

Q stopped suddenly and her ears swiveled. She started walking again, faster, and Madame followed. Q continued: "I've heard Council's long-term plan is to generate more citizens for both Defense *and Construction.* There's talk of building a new wall, a vanguard wall, farther out into the Plains. But they have a short-term plan too." She stopped Madame X and looked her head-on. "They're reassigning everyone they can get to perimeter security—those who aren't fulfilling their duties elsewhere."

Madame put a paw to her chest. "I can't fight at my age! I was just a little late—"

"I'm not talking about you."

Madame's whiskers trembled. "Not . . . Bett?"

Madame Q put out a paw to steady her. "Don't panic. You'll just attract their attention. Nothing's official yet; they're not going to start rounding up linneans tomorrow. But you need to talk to him."

Madame's heart pounded. Her muscles felt like wound-up springs, cocked to propel her straight to her son. But Q was right: failure to retain her composure would invite scrutiny. Madame Q urged her to come for a quick hunt at the grocery fields to keep up appearances, but Madame X couldn't think about food. She thanked her friend Q and hurried home as unobtrusively as she could.

Of course, she'd forgotten that Bett would be at dinner by the time she got home. She'd have to speak with him first thing tomorrow morning about mating with Geera. Madame circled through her house, drafting speeches in her head. There was no more time for monogamy. They simply couldn't rely on his space-trotting wife anymore. But he wouldn't be easy to convince. He was just as stubborn as she'd been at his age. Back then, Fen had been the only one who could convince her to let him go.

She exhausted herself stalking the house and planning her appeal to Bett. Finally, there was nothing to do but head to her sleeping enclosure on the second floor. As soon as she curled up on her cushion and closed her eyes, her body tensed, sensing the memories waiting to slip through her consciousness. Only on occasion would she let the latch slip and allow herself to think about Fen. She could still conjure up the memory of his scent, the way he nuzzled her and whispered her name. Her chest constricted with regret. She should have gone with him. The device would have allowed it.

They'd both thought Fen could stay and help raise her family, even if the young weren't his own. That was until Council started conscripting neuters to guard the northern perimeter. The outpost was no place for a family—but then, no one else knew she was pregnant.

They could make this work, she'd told him. She would decelerate her reproductive cycle. She'd already made all the arrangements to get the device from the shadow market. She'd use it to halt gestation and go with him until the government changed its mind and let them come back home.

It was Fen who had exposed the flaw in her plan. If her fertility came into question again, he'd warned her, she might be required to undergo more testing. They would find the suspended embryos. Purposely interfering with her fertility would be an even worse infraction than his, and would be punished accordingly. Whether she proceeded with her young or not, they would never be together.

"Xenia," he'd told her, nuzzling her face. "You're serving your city. Your life has just begun, and it will be a long and happy one."

The device arrived by secret messenger the day he left for the outpost. Her life since then had, indeed, been long. That was as much as she could say with any degree of certainty.

Madame pulled herself up, shoved the cushion aside and lifted a trap door. She reached down into a compartment and lifted out a small, heavy bundle of black cloth. Still kneeling, she drew the folds of cloth away to reveal a glint of silver. The polished, metallic ovoid gleamed in the darkness, seamless and shining. The device was smooth and warm to the touch as she lifted it out of the cloth.

*Maybe they wouldn't have caught me*, she thought, turning the device over and over in her paw.

"Mother?" Bett's voice drifted up from the ground floor.

Madame hurriedly wrapped the device up again and lowered it into its hiding spot. She closed the trap door as quietly as she could and shoved the cushion back into place. Bett's soft step sounded just outside the entrance to her enclosure as she curled up and pretended to sleep.

"Mother?" he whispered. "We've got leftovers."

Madame clamped her eyes shut and held still.

"She's asleep," called the girl from below. "We'll save it for her."

Bett sighed and padded away. "I hope she eats it. I don't like her out there hunting all the time."

She smiled. Dear, sweet Bett; always thinking of her. Of course she loved him, and his brothers and sisters. She wished every night she could decouple the thought of them from memories of her life's biggest regret.

Madame sank into another night of fitful sleep. Fen appeared in agonizingly brief dreams, where she clutched at him and strained against a dark force that inevitably pulled them apart. Madame's ears quivered and her eyes fluttered open. She held her breath and listened, heart beating. Bett's voice rose again, followed by the girl's softer response. She couldn't make out what they were saying, but their tones were harsh and combative.

Madame twisted on her cushion, trying to go back to sleep. Her room felt hot and stuffy, as though her cushion were full of hot coals. She pricked up her ears—the voices had stopped. The argument was over, at least the verbal portion of it. The gentle *whoosh* of the front door penetrated the darkened house like a velvet bomb, and then it was still. Her nose told her it was Bett who had left. She would just have to wait. He'd come back when he was ready.

Hours later she swam up from the depths of a long, unbroken sleep. She stretched and yawned, and her stomach reminded her that she hadn't eaten the night before. She stood and gave herself a cursory tongue bath before heading downstairs.

Madame stopped short. Her daughter-in-law's bags sat by the front door.

A bone cup clinked in the feeding room. Madame followed the sound. The girl sat at the table, her shawl around her shoulders, staring into her saucer.

Madame blinked. "Earth again? Already?"

"I'm heading back early," she said, looking up at Madame. "We thought it would be best for me to accelerate my research." She gazed down into her coffee again. "He's right, you know. I don't have forever to follow my will."

Madame sat down at the table with her.

"I got the results of my fertility test yesterday," said the girl.

"Aren't you young to be worrying about that already?"

"Regulations have changed," she answered. Her ears flattened slightly. "Demand is higher, and right now I'm borderline non-contributional. If my readings drop any further, I'll be neuter." Her voice dropped to a whisper. "Useless."

Madame's stomach contracted.

"But Bett and I are still trying. I took the stimulants from the fertility clinic—the package you noticed yesterday." She placed a paw on her belly. "If they worked, I won't have much time left for Earth, so we decided—*I* decided—to try to complete my research before it's too late."

"And where is Bett now?"

"I don't know. He's angry with me. I told him . . ." She looked down at the paw over her belly. "This might not take, so I told him he has to start trying with someone else. I know he's been thinking about Geera."

Madame's mouth opened and closed.

"It's too big a risk to wait for me," the girl said quietly.

Madame wasn't prepared for this. "Does he know you're leaving?"

The girl shook her head.

"Well, you can't leave now, not without seeing him first."

"It's easier this way."

"I—I don't understand," sputtered Madame. "You're telling me you're ready for a family. So why are you going away again?"

The girl leaned toward Madame. "I know it's hard to understand. I wish I could share with you how I feel when I'm on Earth, exploring. *Living.* Everything is new, even the things you think you know. Like grass: at first you think it's just super-green moss, but it's not. It's so soft, it's like—it feels like fur, like you're walking on someone's back, but of course you're not. And then you get used to it and you learn to appreciate this amazing new thing you never could have imagined before."

The girl spread both paws in wonder. "You have to completely shift your way of thinking. You're always seeing things a new way, re-creating your reality, until even your reality doesn't seem real. You're completely free." Her tail danced and her eyes sparkled. "You think about all the other places out there, and all the other ways of thinking about the universe, all the other possibilities. And I just had to go one more time, because . . ." Her face clouded over. "Because if everything goes right, I'll be back with your grandyoung before you know it."

Madame's tail twitched. "And if it doesn't work?"

"I'll come back and we'll keep trying," she replied, her voice grim. "And if it doesn't work with us, at least Bett and Geera will have young." She folded her paws one over the other on the tabletop. "I'll just have to serve in some other way."

Madame examined her face. "And that's what you really want?"

"I don't . . ." The girl took in a deep breath. "I don't really see how that matters."

Madame clenched her teeth. The girl was finally behaving properly, finally playing by the rules.

Finally giving up, just as she herself had so many years ago.

Madame eyed the bags by the door. "Your transport's on the way?"

The girl nodded.

Madame stood suddenly. "Come with me." She strode out of the kitchen, and the girl jumped up to follow. She leapt to the second floor too quickly to give herself time to reconsider. In her sleeping area, Madame thrust her cushion aside and yanked open the trap door.

The girl stood in the doorway. "Mother?"

She motioned to her daughter-in-law to enter, then reached into the hiding place and pulled out the bundle of cloth. The girl stared as Madame turned toward her and unwrapped the device.

She gasped. "Is that—?"

Madame nodded. She took the girl's trembling paw and tipped the warm, metallic ovoid into it.

The girl's voice wavered. "But these are—"

"Forbidden, yes. But it will give you the time you need."

Confusion washed across the girl's face.

"Finish your studies," she said, folding the girl's paw around the device. "Then decide."

"Why are you giving this to me?" she asked, her tail twitching with suspicion.

Madame held her gaze. "Because you might actually use it."

The girl grasped the device in both paws.

"Earth is a good place to avoid scrutiny," Madame said. "If you come back bearing Bett's young—well, there may be questions, but they probably won't refuse more young. Either way, you would remain as fertile as you are now. Meanwhile, Bett will be free to pursue his own family—with Geera, or anyone else he chooses. And if, for any reason you choose not to come back from Earth—" She cleared her throat delicately. "I believe I am safe in assuming you would have somewhere to stay. Somewhere you would be happy—perhaps with someone you love?"

The girl's eyes widened.

"This house is not soundproof."

The girl looked down at the device.

"Your future is entirely up to you," Madame said gently.

The girl's whiskers trembled.

Chimes pealed through the house, signaling the shuttle's arrival. Madame X and her daughter-in-law descended to the front door.

Madame put a paw to her mouth. "Security."

The girl kneeled by her bags in thought. "I have a way around that," she said. "They don't pay as much attention to Earth as they should."

The chimes sounded again. The girl buried the device in her bag, then rose and quickly nuzzled Madame's cheek. "Thank you," she whispered. She walked out to her shuttle.

Madame stared at the door long after the shuttle had left. What now? What would she say to Bett?

She walked into the feeding room and sat down at the table.

Had she done the right thing? This would push Bett toward Geera; keep him safe. But by giving his wife a choice, had she just taken *his* choice away?

She stared at the table for a while, eventually rising to fetch a saucer.

Of course, he might continue to wait. He could very well decide to put everything else on hold and wait for his wife to return—if she chose to return.

She filled her saucer and sat down again.

She'd done the best she could, hadn't she? It was up to Bett and his wife to decide now. She hoped they would be brave.

She breathed in the nutty, acidic steam curling up from the bowl.

It was a harsh lesson, perhaps, but one she wished she'd learned sooner: Choice meant risk. There was danger in all the most valuable things; like choice, hunting, and love. One had to hunt with conviction, or be haunted by the things one let slip away.

*Tara Campbell is a Washington, D.C.-based writer of crossover sci-fi. With a BA in English and an MA in German, she has a demonstrated aversion to money and power. Previous publication credits include stories in* Barrelhouse, Punchnel's, Toasted Cake Podcast, Luna Station Quarterly, SciFi Romance Quarterly, Masters Review *and* Queen Mob's Teahouse. *www.taracampbell.com*

Antiquated customs and manners find a resurgence in a distant future, as a family looks ahead to the loss of their estate. And while a pragmatic mother tries her best to make the ideal match, a girl's heart is broken and she is left to ponder a marriage of convenience.

# EIGHTEEN WINTERS

### By

### *D. A. Couturier*

Broon hunched low in the tall thicket, waiting in the morning darkness with a sleepy yawn. Her hand brushed the soft leather pouch strapped to her side. The weight of the small cylinders inside brought an odd sense of comfort. Beneath her fingertips the shells warbled a tinny promise of success. Shifting her achy legs, she did her best to maintain her position, hidden and non-threatening. She allowed herself a quiet swig from her water flask before securing it on her back once more.

*It won't be long now.*

As if her mind turned thoughts into reality, the darkness began to lose its domination over the night sky in the far distance. A soft grey light sliced through the brush, illuminating the small clearing around her. First morning began, as the large, cerulean moon rose ever upward until its blue-green hue brushed the tips of her dark, braided hair. Before a quarter of the gaseous moon cleared the horizon, the brilliant indigo sun tipped its edges in a halo.

In all her seventeen winters, Broon hadn't missed many opportunities to witness first and second morning as they rose over the vast valley within minutes of each other. She'd been born during this time of year and felt an odd kinship to the two orbs whenever the anniversary of her birth drew near.

As she watched them rise, a sad thought came to her. *It's as if they are tethered in a fleeting paramour's enchantment.*

She slipped the heavy rifle off her shoulder. She allowed the stock to touch the ground with a soft thud while she worked her muscles loose. Careful not to let her guard down completely she allowed herself a bit of relief. With a tight hold on the cold, steel barrel, she watched the brightening sky with anticipation. Her world was awakening and from the corner of her eye she watched the outline of a large ship fly over the far mountain range, turn northward and dip below the highest peak.

It had to be headed to Steiling; the only city near enough to dock a cargo or transport of that size. The big metropolis lay beyond the mountain range about one-thousand kilometers to the north.

While the starships steered clear of her valley, she sometimes wondered what the inside of a vessel that large looked like—wondered how people could share land space with millions of others, when The People only had a few thousand. In Broon's studies, she had learned that, as well as a large settlement on a once inhabited moon, through the millenniums Jaaren had also achieved interstellar travel and off world mining.

The land in which she and The People lived made up almost a quarter of her world. Under a centuries old agreement, no ships were allowed in their airspace, unless it was pre-authorized or an emergency. It was a pact shared by The People and the world government of Jaaren.

With all the world's successes and technological achievements, she preferred the serenity of a much slower and simpler pace. It was hard to remember they weren't the only intelligent beings. That is, until a large ship reminded her otherwise. Still, her life was much like life had been a few hundred years before. A modest life The People, and her parents, had chosen down through the seventeenth generation.

Just as quickly as she pondered another way of life, those thoughts would float away, as they did right now when she surveyed the beautiful world around her. Only here could she witness the magnificent spheres moving close together to become a synchronous duet and then watch the moment the horizon erupted in a heavenly glow, as though fingertips brushed against one another in a futile attempt to embrace.

Broon imagined them as two lovers coexisting in space, yet unable to be together. Unlike Huen's professed love for her, the sun and moon would never forget the affection *they* shared. Though the two were destined to move further apart by their orbital trajectories, she was sure their unfailing celestial love would be witnessed this time next year. And she knew deep down in her heart their affection would last forever and wouldn't be fleeting like Huen's love, soft kisses and unfulfilled promises.

Even in her disappointment, she longed for Huen to be beside her now with his strong arms wrapped around her, his kisses tingling her body as his lips touched the back of her neck. It had been almost a year since he left and still the mere thought of him made her heart lurch in her chest. If Mon could read her thoughts, she'd chastise her for thinking upon what was lost and tell her it had never really been found in the first place. Thankful her mother wasn't anywhere nearby this morning, Broon allowed her mind to wander back to the first time she heard Huen's name.

She had been just thirteen winters. The day had been filled with low whispers and long stares between her parents. She was certain they wanted to discuss something they thought she wasn't old enough to hear so, when darkness came, Broon had feigned weariness and headed for bed. When she was certain enough time had passed, she left her room and tiptoed across the cold, wooden floor to spy on them. What she heard both excited and scared her.

"My love, we haven't had another babe in eight winters," Pon had said. Her father sat beside his wife and took hold of her hand. "I believe there will be no others. It's time we hire an apprentice that can be steward after I'm gone."

There had been another child when Broon was little, a boy child to take over the farm and cultivate the lands, but it had died soon after birth. Broon couldn't remember what her brother had looked like, but she did remember his name. Cias. The same as her father's.

"What about Broon?" Her mother's furrowed brow worried Broon. Why would an apprentice concern Mon and what did any of this have to do with her?

"I've thought about that and I've been searching. We need someone old enough to take on the heavy work, yet young enough to be tempted by Broon's beauty. Otherwise the steward may choose another."

"She is too young."

"Now, yes. But soon she will not be."

"Yes," her mother nodded, as if in reluctant agreement.

"You could remarry," her father offered with a sad smile.

"No," Mon said with a hard shake of her head, "I could not bear it."

Broon let out a breath she hadn't noticed she was holding.

"If we do not hire a steward, when I pass, you will be forced from your home. I cannot let that happen . . . will not, if I am able."

Mon's eyes welled up with unshed tears, "Please don't talk like that. You're strong and still able to fell trees and plant crops. You have kept us in food for many winters and we give out of our own abundance to the Lowers. Surely, The People will take that into consideration when your time comes."

"If we . . ." he paused before continuing. "If I do not prepare, you and Broon will live on the land designated for the poor. The guilt and shame you will bear will be because of me. I have already discussed it with Quine. His fourth son, Huen, is interested in the position and he is more than capable. We need to be thankful he is willing to consider."

Mon winced at his words, as if Pon had slapped her. Huen came from a quiver full of children. Six in all. The entire town called Huen's mother, "well blessed," for she had achieved much for The People. It was every woman's passage to bear children, but sons held a particular prominence in the valley and Mon had only borne one, who had not lived but a few days. With just one daughter, her mother was almost as low as the Unbearing.

Pon pulled his wife into an embrace. "Come now. You know with no male heir, the farm and land will go back to The People to be redistributed, unless you remarry or Broon finds a mate before she is eighteen winters. Let's discuss it no more."

Her mother nodded in agreement, but it was the way her parents seemed to cling together in desperation that was unnerving for Broon. Was it just the need to prepare for the unknown or was there something portentous in hiring a steward? Surely not. Pon was one of the strongest in the valley, so he was just being a good steward himself by preparing and planning. Broon reassured herself, *there is nothing she nor Mon needed to worry about for years and years to come.*

Keeping the secret within her breast had been difficult, for the learning had come through disobedience. She had so many questions and at thirteen she had yet to master the skill of impudence. Once her parents informed her of their plans to hire an apprentice, she was free to pepper her mother for answers to the concerns that had lain upon her heart for days.

Mon had reassured her. "Your Pon is in excellent health." Mon pressed the point with a tight squeeze of Broon's hand. "But really my daughter, there's no need to worry about a thing, if it were to happen, we could do nothing to change the outcome anyway."

"But why would Huen want to leave his own farm?" Broon had asked, bewildered. *She* would never leave *her* Mon and Pon.

"He is the last of four sons. He has no farm nor station to call his own and with older brothers all waiting to divide the family farm when his own Pon dies," Mon sighed before trying to explain again. "Well, you see? Having that many children is a blessing and a curse."

Broon had nodded, but didn't quite understand what her mother had meant. *Six children.* One could only hope to have that many.

Exasperated, Mon said, "Enough questions. He needed to seek out a position and make his own way. You may be doing that yourself, unless the Heavens intervene."

On the next lunar cycle, Huen came. Broon watched him approach long before Pon had shouted for her to come and meet his new apprentice. A lone figure strolled along their dirt road toward his new home. Even from the far distance, she could see he carried a full satchel upon his back without the slightest slump in his strides. A good sign of a man accustomed to hard work.

*That would please Pon.*

Broon's home bordered their two largest fields and stood at the end of the long narrow road. She tarried behind the house unseen until Pon called for her again. She gave herself a quick survey and noticed her dress was dusty. Still, she thought she was presentable enough to skip a quick wash and dragged her fingers through her unruly hair before heading straight to the barn.

Broon overheard a snatch of the two men's conversation as she entered. "I've worked alongside my pon for ten winters. I'm pleased to show you what I can do."

Pon turned to his daughter, clearly surprised. "You didn't think to clean up, did you?"

Broon shrugged in response.

He grimaced and pulled her to him to provide the customary greetings. "Broon, this is Huen."

She had been told he was five winters older than she. At eighteen, he seemed a proud, determined young man. "I've seen you before." She blurted, before remembering to curtsy. "I mean, Blessings, Huen."

"Blessings," he replied with a slight bow and amused smile.

"Do you know my daughter?" Pon's eyes danced in curiosity.

"Not to my knowledge."

"I've seen you a time or two. At the communal meetings."

"Ah." Pon appeared satisfied, "Now, Broon, go and wash the valley off of you. You are barely presentable."

Broon stared down at herself. She wasn't *that* dirty. Besides, she loved being in the fields. She loved watching the animals of her world. She even enjoyed the wind which always seemed to say hello, but never stayed long enough to play.

"I was playing." *Not quite a lie.*

Pon winked at her and gave a soft tug on a snatch of her dark, disheveled hair. "Yes, we can see you were playing. Now scoot."

She scampered off then, only to be chastised for not coming to her mother first. "The least you could have done was to wash the grime off you, girl, before meeting our apprentice."

"Why? I like being outside. Pon called and I ran straight to the barn."

Mon grunted and dipped a rag into warm, soapy water before smearing it around her face.

"Huen is so handsome," Broon said between swipes of the drippy cloth.

"Says you." Mon clicked her teeth with a small smile, "But what does he think of *you*?"

If her parents had hoped to make a match, they had been right. For Broon, it was love at first sight. He was tall with muscles firm from hard labor. He had a habit of brushing away his long, brown hair each time the tendrils fell in front of his eyes. A practice Broon adored from the first time she saw him do it.

Not long after he came, she'd taken to following him around the farm and fields when she was done with her own chores and studies. Pon had been impressed with his skills and within the next winter, stewardship was all but assured.

Concerns for Pon's early death were long forgotten until one day, Broon found herself the subject of a conversation. This time, she'd rather not have overheard, for the result changed the world as she knew it.

"Broon has reached womanhood," Pon proclaimed.

"Yes, Cias, but Huen hasn't noticed."

Usually women of fifteen or sixteen winters were considered complete by The People. Broon was in the middle, so she couldn't argue the point even if she wanted to.

Pon sniffed at the steaming pot of stew hanging over the open fire. "Huen thinks of her as a prattle-minded younger sister, not as a potential partner, and certainly not for a secured coupling. She likes to hunt more than cook and to stay out of doors instead of inside where she belongs."

Broon picked at the dress Mon had forced her to wear. She glanced at the discarded pants nearby and frowned, "You do know I'm right here."

"Shush," Mon swiped the air dismissively. "Let me work with her, Cias. I can show her what to do."

"If I make him steward before he has chosen, he can inherit the farm. But he is under no obligation, nor contract, to choose Broon. And if he chooses another . . ." Pon let the words drop like a bucket of cold water.

Mon sighed. "I understand. Let me work with our daughter."

"Make it soon."

And so, Broon's carefree days came to an end. She was no longer allowed to be with Huen or Pon in the fields. She was forbidden to hunt, even though she was a good shot. And to make matters worse, Mon began to teach her how to cook and sew. The hours seemed endless and Broon hated being cooped indoors. She wanted to be out in the fields. *That* was where Huen spent his days. Not in the homestead where he couldn't even see her.

Once she threatened to defy her mother and go outside anyway, but one click of disapproval on her mother's tongue stayed Broon's indignation.

"I was betrothed to your father at fifteen and coupled at sixteen. I know what I am doing in getting secured. Don't go out there. Let him come in here. At the very least, wait until you can serve him in some way. That will make the difference."

"But I've barely seen him." Broon pouted.

"That's the point."

For the latter half of her fifteenth winter she was a prisoner in her own home and the tanned glow faded from her cheeks. She'd even endured the taming of her hair, even though Mon wound the braid so tight her head ached. Her mother kept her so busy she only saw glimpses of Huen and would often be fast asleep from exhaustion before the men came in from the evening chores.

A week after her sixteenth birthday, Mon surprised Broon with an announcement. "You're ready."

Broon needn't ask what for. She knew. It seemed the whole family had planned for this moment and their future depended upon her. If she failed to secure Huen—well—she didn't have to be reminded.

"I've prepared a surprise." Mon reached behind her back. "Go ahead, open it," she said, handing Broon a brown paper package wrapped in twine.

Broon smiled and untied the string. "What is it?"

"I had it ordered from Steiling," Mon said beaming.

"You did?"

"Yes, I ordered it by traveling into the next territory. No reason to stir up questions in ours."

The first ancestors distributed the land into twelve regions, which were still maintained today. Each one had their own small town and communal meeting place. It was common practice to dwell within one's own community without ever venturing outside it, but commerce or coupling in order to strengthen a neighboring territory wasn't unheard of.

The utmost covenant of The People was to maintain The Whole. It was where automation had been denounced, except for a few approved "luxuries," and where The People were stronger because of their bond to their kinsmen rather than technology. It was a safe place where every person lived in need of the others.

Anyone could leave The People if they chose, but that option wasn't for Broon. The simple truth was that Broon believed in the life of The People and although she wished females had an equal role, she couldn't imagine living anywhere else. Even if that meant she had to resort to a little trickery to procure a mate.

Broon peered inside the package, but held the disappointment she felt within herself. She loved Huen and understood her obligations in securing him, but she wanted to contribute to The People on her own terms and share this life with the man she loved. A man who would want her just as she was. One who would work the farm and the homestead side by side in unity. That was the one thing The People were lacking, and though these things were heavy on Broon's mind, she held her tongue and smiled at her mother. "A new dress."

Her mother smiled back. "Yes, the one that will make Huen fall in love with you."

"Really? I didn't know a dress could hold so much power," she teased.

"Well, that and everything we've been working on for many cycles." Mon's eyes beamed in approval, "Just you wait. If you do everything I tell you, you will not only be betrothed by the time your sixteenth year is complete, but you'll be coupled long before your eighteenth winter."

Broon lifted the dress from its confines and fluffed it out in front of her. Upon first inspection it appeared to be like all her others. Then the light caught the golden thread woven through the entire dress. As she held it, the dress almost shimmered in front of her. The buttons were pearl, not clay and the neckline was low enough to enhance her youth and yet held a dignified elegance. It was amazing, but unless one inspected it closely, its beauty would go unnoticed.

"Do you like it?"

"It's stunning," Broon said, and meant it. A small hope swelled within her. She wanted Huen as much as her parents wanted him for her.

"Try it on."

While Broon slipped out of the old dress and into the new one, Mon set out a few snacks and a small goblet on a silver tray.

Mon helped her secure the last clasp.

"Alright, turn around," Mon instructed.

Broon twirled in a tight circle. The pleats billowed out around her like a blooming flower.

"It'll do," Mon said, more to herself than Broon. "Yes, very nice. Very nice. Now go and take the tray to Huen in the barn. He's been working since before first morning and I haven't fed him lunch. He will be good and hungry by now."

Broon stopped mid-spin, liking the softness of the dress against her flesh. "Isn't that cruel? To make him skip lunch?"

"You always get a man through his stomach." Mon winked at her. "And his eyes."

"Alright."

Broon walked into the barn. When Huen spied her, his jaw went slack. He switched off the laser he'd been using to sharpen the tools and came over to greet her.

"Uh," Huen swiped at his hair, "Blessings."

"Blessings," she said, pleased to see his eyes roaming all over her body. "I've brought you some refreshments." She tilted her chin downward slightly and looked up at him from her long dark lashes. She even curved her lips into a slight, round pout Mon had told her to use, even though it made her feel foolish.

Each day for a week, Mon braided her hair in a different style and had her daughter bring the refreshments late. On the final day, Huen stole a quick kiss that would have caused her to drop the trays contents she'd been holding, if he hadn't caught it.

A lunar cycle later and kissing in the barn became more ardent. Once he had unbound her thick braid and fanned it out around her shoulders.

"You're lovely," he said, as he nuzzled his face into her hair, "and you smell so sweet."

As her sixteenth winter drew to a close, the only thing remaining was the formal declaration of an impending coupling. But before that could happen Pon died. It came as a shock to her and Huen, but Mon seemed to expect it. Late one night, she needled her mother until she confessed that her father had been sick for a very long time. He'd been taking medicine sent from Steiling, hiding the fact from The People that he had resorted to artificial means. It wasn't forbidden, but it would be strongly discouraged.

Her mother explained tearfully, "It doesn't matter, because in the end it didn't extended his life beyond a few winters anyway."

"Oh, Mon," Broon wrapped her arms around her mother and they wept their loss of a good father and husband.

Everyone in their community mourned. As time went by, Broon became convinced a chasm was forming between herself and Huen. When it was expected that they would become a family unit with him as the head, she would awaken each morning alone. He'd already be outside at work and would often refuse refreshment until long after she'd gone to bed. At first she thought it was because the entire weight of the farm's success or failure came under him. She tried to assure herself that once he achieved success, his stress would lessen, but then a thought occurred to her. Without the formal title of steward given to him before her father died, perhaps he changed his mind about wanting her as a mate. This thought filled her with fear, but she didn't know what to do if that was truly happening.

She shared her feelings with Mon, but she didn't seem to care if they coupled or not. As the days went by Broon watched life drain out of her mother, until there was only a shell in deep mourning. She didn't seem to care about anything, and Broon ended up being alone most of the time. Bored, she soon began to sneak outside to hunt small game or walk the fields. Small snippets of the day grew to hours and soon the inside of the homestead fell to disarray. She needn't worry about it, for neither Mon nor Huen seemed to notice she'd begun to slip back into her old ways. She abandoned the dresses for more comfortable trousers, which were much easier to hunt in. On the rare occasions Huen would eat with them, he never asked where she obtained the meat for the evening meal.

A month after her father's death, The People declared Huen their official steward. Boon assured herself they wouldn't have done that if they too didn't expect the coupling. She hoped this declaration would help solidify them as a unit and things might change, but she had been wrong.

One day, she decided to head to the marshes with a few shells in her satchel to hunt the Freia. Large flocks of the birds moved eastward this time of the year, passing through their valley, settling for a few days to mate in the muddy marshes beyond their borders. It was a quarry bigger than she'd ever hunted, but she wanted to surprise Mon and Huen. She was a good shot, but her head was filled with foolish love and fear of the loss of it. Those childish thoughts clouded her mind and helped the fowl outwit her. They had risen quickly above her gun's range and even though she pursued, she hadn't the forethought to bring proper provisions. In her tracking, she'd been forced to sleep among the stars that evening. She ran out of ammunition the next morning and lost track of the birds as they moved off to farther lands beyond their valley. But still, she was proud of her one victory kill.

It took her the better part of the day to drag the heavy carcass to the edge of town. She could see the communal meeting had just ended and wasn't sure if she should hide the fact she'd been hunting or prance through the middle of the street and show The People that women could do as well as any man. Ultimately, Huen made the decision for her.

"Broon, there you are!" he said, clearly angry.

Oh, she could see how foolish she'd been to think this man cared for her as an equal. His demeanor and words were far more crushing than the burdensome fowl she had worked so hard to give him.

A young woman came up beside him and Broon heard her say, with a look of disgust, "Has she been hunting?" before adding, "You shouldn't let her defy you that way. *You're* the steward."

Huen's face flushed red. "Why did you go without me, you stupid girl? Your mon is worried sick. Leave that and inform your mother you are well. Now."

"I wanted to show you." Broon blundered through her explanation.

Whispers circled in the air—The People too reluctant to leave good gossip behind. Tears moistened her eyes but she refused to let them spill. She was muddy, cold, and very tired from her trek.

He stepped closer. "And this . . . this is what you bring as a prize? A small fledgling with little meat on its bones."

She had almost been thankful it hadn't been an adult, that would have taken a pack animal and gurney to transport back home. She let the rope slacken until the entire meat lay on the ground.

He untied the leather straps and pried one of the wings free from the carcass. Spreading it between his arms, he said, "There's not enough canvas for a child's water toy."

Laughter erupted, but she didn't take her eyes off of Huen. There were enough folk still milling about to witness her disgrace, but she only cared about his displeasure. His words broke her heart.

Almost a full year had passed since that night. When her father first brought Huen home, Broon had been convinced he would stay with them forever. Instead, Pon's death only hastened his departure. She just hadn't known it yet. Well, she'd been young and naïve a full season ago. Huen, a full man with twenty-three winters in him should have seen her foolish love for what it had been. And he shouldn't have encouraged it. Broon's cheeks flushed thinking about the few frolics they'd shared.

Now, her love struck memory was clearing and she realized Huen never spoke of a betrothal. Her obsession had made the embraces to be much more than their sum. And to make matters worse, she had put Mon in harm's way. She hadn't understood how her actions humiliated Huen. She only wanted to be part of his world. But no matter how Huen had wronged her by not asking to couple, he had fulfilled his duty and provided for them–up to a point.

The day after he tossed her kill into the river, he set out to look for the flock, only to come back irritable. "Now, they've moved on past their usual spot. It will take me a week to track them beyond the valley. I can only hope to be successful. From now on, leave the hunting to the men."

Broon had fretted each day on the porch for any sign of him. True to his chastising words, he arrived with two large Freias strapped over a durg's back.

"Here." He dragged the carcasses onto their doorstep.

Broon almost clapped with excitement, the humiliation of her own kill a fleeting memory. She wanted to run and hug Huen for their good fortune, but Mon had grabbed her arm the moment she took a step. At a shake of Mon's head, Broon had moved back by her mother's side and didn't speak a word.

Huen made easy work of the fowl, even though they had a wingspan more than twice a man's height. The strong membrane of skin woven through their network of thin wing bones would make a fine canvas or sailcloth for their skiff. Carefully oiled and seasoned, it would provide for them for a few winters before they'd have to repeat the process. Once Huen had stretched the wings to dry inside the barn, he helped Mon clean and gut the birds.

Broon made a poultice to spread upon the entrails. Wrapped in a cloth, the entire innards were placed back into the empty carcass to cure. In all the hours they worked side by side, Huen never spoke. It wasn't until the next day that she and Mon found out Huen's intentions.

"Blessings," Mon said when he had knocked on the front door just before first morning.

"Blessings." Huen repeated the greeting.

"Is there something you need?"

Broon heard the tremble in Mon's voice.

Huen kicked at the dirt with his shoe before looking up. "I asked Doran for her hand this morning and she accepted. Her pon has agreed to give us a section of his land as a dowry. It's a good opportunity for me."

Mon nodded, but didn't speak.

Broon covered her mouth to stifle a mournful cry. Huen didn't seem to notice.

"So, I'll be heading south before the winter chill settles in the valley. The meat will keep you."

Of course they wouldn't starve. The People would see to that, even if he hadn't, but if they couldn't be a contributing member, they would move to the lower status. And he would be coupling with Doran, not her. It had been Doran who had been by his side at night. Doran was the same age as she. Surely he *couldn't* love someone so simple-minded. Her only allure was her father's vast lands to the west, but she hadn't one wit of sense. How could he choose Doran over her?

After a few awkward questions, Huen had offered to help find a replacement steward, but Mon surprised them both by declining. "Non, you tend to your betrothed. We'll fend well. Broon, here is almost of age."

His eyes flitted to Broon before he nodded. "At week's end then. Until that time, I'll do everything I can to get you ready for winter."

Later that night, Mon seemed to come out of her own mourning and tried to soothe her. "He could've taken the farm and kicked us out, but Huen is an upright man."

Her words didn't help. Once she was eighteen and had no husband or steward to care for the land, they'd lose their home. So what did it matter if he kicked them out or The People did?

"I hate him." Broon confided in her mother.

"Your heart is hurt. It will mend. You were never inclined to one another. Too different. Besides, you have an entire year to procure another mate. Plenty of time."

Broon let the tears flow until Mon had reprimanded her.

"You can't change the present, my sweet child. Huen chose another and went his own path. Free choice is our way. Don't fret. Another will choose you soon enough." Mon had brushed Broon's tears away. "Huen's gone. Think no more about him."

Almost a whole year had passed in what seemed like a day and yet, she had matured so much during that time. Now they only had three days and here she was, hiding in the brush, because she didn't know what to do. No one offered to become steward and losing the farm was just a few days away. She didn't want to be forced from her land.

A strong wind pulled her thoughts back to the present. She watched the tall stalks bend back and forth like her mother's loom. Broon had come prepared this time and was going to kill more Freias than Huen had ever done. But even if she was successful, she probably wouldn't even get the joy of eating the game once they moved to the Lowers. That thought ignited a fierce anger inside of her. She had planted, gleaned and reaped. With Mon's help they had come out ahead that year. She was capable of running the farm. Of hunting and providing for Mon and herself. Didn't Mon say they had free choice?

"To hell with The People," she said, just above a whisper. She would refuse to leave. She would show them how she cared for the farm and had done it as well as any man.

As if her declaration turned into renewed energy, the air around became charged like the electrical storms in spring. Broon gripped the iron weapon a bit tighter and hoisted the stock into the crook of her shoulder. Pointing it heavenward, she aimed just above the brush. The sound of wings beat in her ear like a drum and insects swirled around her as if a torrent wind swept through the valley. The tall stalks which hid her from the skittish beasts dipped and swayed trying to reveal her true intentions. She remained still and unmoving while she scanned the horizon.

"There you are," she whispered to herself. The lead animal flew past her and disappeared out of sight.

*Soon. Wait. Don't be impatient. Wait.*

For an instant, the morning air cooled as the following herd blocked out the rising sun in front of her. Hundreds of creatures followed the direction of the leader and the small clearing was momentarily plunged into darkness. One fowl after another flew by, each one ten meters wide or more. She aimed for the middle, an adult female, made slower by her fledgling. She held her breath and pulled the trigger.

"Greetings."

A loud voice startled her and the bullet banked low, missing the herd entirely. She spun around to the sound and trained the weapon in the middle of his chest. There in front of her stood a man just inside the thicket. Her thicket.

"Who are you?" she asked, suddenly angry that she might be missing her chance for a clean kill.

"Um," he held his hands up, "Don't shoot."

"Then don't move," Broon ordered. She aimed the rifle a little higher and let her finger lightly touch the trigger, "I mean it."

The stranger complied on shaky legs, but held his position. The loud booms echoed in her ear as the butt of the gun dug into her shoulder with each shot. She ignored the pain from the ricochet and reloaded. One large bird spiraled out of formation, tumbling head over legs until it landed on the ground with a thump. Her shot hit two more victims, each dropping just a few meters away.

"That makes three!" She stood up with a whoop and danced with glee. She had bested Huen by one.

"Uh, is it safe to put my arms down now?" he asked.

"Oh, sorry. Yeah, it's alright."

The stranger flashed an amused smile. "You're a terrible shot. You missed me entirely."

She smiled despite herself. He didn't appear menacing and as far as she could tell, he had no weapon.

"Who did you say you were?"

"I, uh, didn't say." he shrugged and plunged his oversized hand into his pockets, "but we have someone in common."

"Oh? Who is that?"

"Huen."

Though taller and leaner than Huen, she guessed him to be the same age as her, from his youthful features and sparse facial hair along his angular jaw line. "Are you a relative of Huen's? You don't look like him."

"No, I'm not." He shook his head.

They stood in silence a moment, but she wouldn't be baited like a mere tengle on a hook. "Where are you from?"

"I'm from Steiling,"

His youthful features hadn't quite grown into his large frame, but it was something more than that which made him seem out of place. His clothes were shiny and well-tailored, not cut in the usual plain, attire. The People would not look kindly on his brown hair hanging loose just above his shoulders without being bound, but it was his foregoing the customary greeting that made her believe he was telling the truth. He was not from her valley and although it seemed he had the advantage, she wasn't going to let the circumstances stay that way despite her curiosity.

She heaved the rifle strap over her sore shoulder and started to walk out of the thicket.

"Wait, where are you going?"

"To get my pack animal and take my kills home."

"But Huen sent me." His wide strides caught up with hers with ease.

"So?"

"You are Broon, aren't you?"

"Yes."

*Oh, I might actually like this game,* she thought to herself.

The animal brayed when it saw her. She untied it and led it west, toward the direction of the first fallen Freia.

"You're different than he described you. Didn't you get his letter? He assured me it would reach you before I arrived."

"I have heard nothing from Huen for almost a year." She wasn't even going to give him the satisfaction of looking at him while they walked.

"Well, it doesn't matter. I'm not too late am I? Huen said the anniversary of your birth wasn't for a few more days."

"Three to be exact."

"Slow down," he touched her arm and she turned to face him.

"What do you want?"

He smiled. "Well, I'm in need of a place to live . . . and it is my understanding you're in need of a husband."

*Look toward the dark side of human behavior and you'll find the characters that populate DeeAnn's stories floundering in life struggles. Her first completed novel is the tale of a young girl's survival in backwoods Tennessee during prohibition. Her short stories range from speculative science fiction to thought-provoking pieces on contemporary issues. Some contemplate justifiable homicide. Others explore sexuality or paint landscapes of superstition and oppression. Yet her tales and themes explore a morality consistent with a Biblical world-view, challenging and illuminating a genuine, faith-based Christianity.*

*With a stack of ideas waiting to see light of day, DeeAnn looks for every opportunity to put her thoughts on paper. She finds inspiration all around: in daily life, BBC News, books, movies and dreams. If an idea strikes her in the middle of the night, she turns on a light, grabs her bedside journal and captures the moment.*

*A self-proclaimed glass half-empty girl, DeeAnn loves travel, theatre and concerts, fine dining and all things southern. She's had a passion for writing since childhood and dreams of writing full time. She currently works, writes and resides in Washington State with her author husband and three children. Follow Dee Ann at www.dacouturier.com.*

For twenty years, Chara Hudson's mother has been a notorious fugitive, responsible for the deaths of innocent people on her home world. Chara never thought she'd hear from her mother again, but the arrival of a starship and a mysterious gift leads her into a dangerous situation.

# YELLOW STAR

### By

### *John Moralee*

One night my sleep was disturbed by a thunderous boom. It rattled every window in my bedroom and sent my heart racing. I sat up, momentarily confused, my dreams swirling with reality in my head. For a second, I thought my mother was still there, taking me as a little girl for a long and sunny walk in the woods beyond our village. But then I remembered she had gone, and cold, hard reality slammed down. That joyous summer walk had happened twenty years ago. I no longer lived in a village—but in Dorado, the capital city of Arcadia, where I rented a studio apartment with my sister.

In the darkness, my bed was shaking like a minor tremor had struck the building. A framed picture and some books toppled off a shelf. I sat up, pulling off my sheets as my bed stopped rocking and everything settled into silence. What had caused that boom? My room was too dark to see anything. I called out to my sister. Shada had moved in with me on her eighteenth birthday. She worked as a model and shared the rent, making it possible for us to live in a decent sixtieth-floor apartment with a great view over the city.

"Did you hear that?"

Stupid question. Of course Shada had heard it, but she did not answer. I mumbled a command to switch on my bedside lamp, illuminating my side of the room in a rosy light. I frowned. Shada's bed was empty. In the confusion of being rudely awoken, I'd completely forgotten she had gone out partying without me, because I'd wanted to study the crime reports for my sector.

The noise had abated—but the room was still shaking slightly. Something big had made that boom and I guessed I knew what it was—but I needed to confirm it. I stumbled to the curtains and looked out into the night.

Though the twin moons were out in full, shining a pale greenish light over the glittering city, they were not the brightest objects visible in the pre-dawn sky.

An alien ship marked the starry sky like a white comet, leaving a fiery tail in its wake as it entered our atmosphere directly over Dorado. The ship was both beautiful and frightening. It should have entered the atmosphere over the ocean, where the shock wave would not have disturbed anyone, but too many pilots didn't bother with our planetary regulations. They flew how they liked, because we needed them more than they needed us. I swore. Some off-worlders thought they could land on our planet at their convenience, treating Arcadia like a parking lot. My hands tightened into fists. Such arrogance.

I watched the ship until it disappeared over the horizon in the direction of the spaceport.

I returned to bed and tried to sleep, but I could not relax. I had to get up for work in a couple of hours anyway, so I showered and ate breakfast while watching my favourite newsfeeds. Mentioned endless times, the ship was a Nexian Starcruiser filled with 15,000 passengers and a cargo of exotic off-world goods. The passengers included diplomats, wealthy travellers, socialites, and ordinary citizens of the New Commonwealth. Of special interest to the gossip channels, the celebrity fashion designer Maxx Impact was aboard with his entourage of thirty clones of himself. Maxx Impact's show, sponsored by Sunstone

Corporation, was the top-trending story on most feeds, but I didn't care about Maxx Impact or his upcoming fashion show in the newly-opened Halcyon Plaza. I'd never been much of a fashion follower, unlike my sister, whose wardrobe contained a load of designer dresses, shoes and jewellery. She loved shopping for new clothes. Me, I didn't care. Sweats were my off-duty outfits—when I wasn't wearing one of my three smart-material uniforms for work.

That morning, I was putting on my combat boots when I received an email from Rasha's Emporium in the Scrawl.

*Your Order Is Ready For Collection.*

"Huh?" It was an unexpected message. I had not ordered anything recently. It was probably junk email, but it hadn't been flagged as spam. I opened the message on the wall-screen opposite the kitchen table.

Dear Customer,

*Your order—Alice's Adventures in Wonderland (Lewis Carroll), First Edition (Earth original)—will be available for collection from today.*

*Thank you for using Rasha's Emporium, The Scrawl's premier seller of antiques and esoterica, voted Arcadia's #1 Retailer of the Year 3012.*

That was weird. I definitely had not ordered *Alice's Adventures in Wonderland*. It was one of my childhood favourite reads—a book my mother had read to me over and over—but I could never afford an *original* physical copy. *Alice's Adventures in Wonderland* was over a thousand years old. First editions belonged in museums and private collections.

It had to be a mistake.

I called the shop and spoke to a human assistant. "My name's Chara Hudson. I've just received a message about a book called *Alice's Adventures in Wonderland*."

"Yes," the assistant said. "I'm pleased to say your book is here."

"Um. The thing is, I'm a little confused because I didn't order it. Is it a computer error?"

"No. The order is correct. It's listed as a gift from another customer."

"Another customer?" I was stunned. "Who sent it?"

"That information isn't in the system. Just the sender's shipping ID."

"What's that?"

"NX-567-22RF-Q290-3024A."

"Where's the origin?"

"Nexus Prime. The customer must have sent it from there—but they didn't leave a name or return address. I'm sorry. Is there a problem?"

Yes. I didn't know anyone living on Nexus Prime. The planet was two system jumps away. "What else can you tell me?"

"We received the book this morning in pristine condition from the spaceport. It's stored in a sealed stasis box, kept as fresh as the day it was packed. The package will only open to your voice and a DNA signature. We can send it to you, but for an item so valuable the extra insurance and delivery cost will be expensive. You can pick it up for free if you come to our store. What do you want us to do?"

"I guess I'll collect it when I can. Thanks for helping."

There was only one person who knew how much *Alice's Adventures in Wonderland* meant to me. My mother—Eryn Hudson. But why would my mother send me a present after so long? She had sent nothing for my last twenty birthdays—so why now?

The last time I had seen her had been when I was eight.

Because my mother had acted like she loved me so much, I'd believed that made her a good person, incapable of having a dark side. But I had only ever seen a small part of her life—when she was at home, spending time with her family. That person had been a caring, loving, inspiring woman, a woman I had admired and wanted to be like when I was older. At work for Sunstone Corporation, Eryn Hudson had been someone else; a powerful executive in charge of a large department, running an ambitious construction project to build a space elevator that would tether to a geostationary space station. The project—when completed—*would have* reduced ecological damage and improved economic prospects for the whole planet. *Would have*—but didn't. Sixteen months into the project, when the space elevator consisted of a sky-tall stalk of twisted cables, the cables snapped at the base and the elevator collapsed, killing nineteen employees.

An investigation uncovered a fault in the fabrication process, caused by a deliberate design error. The sabotage was traced to my mother's department. Someone had sent a faulty design from a computer in her office, using a code only known by a handful of employees. The police investigation had no proof against anyone—until they discovered my mother had been having a two-year affair with Garth Zin, an executive at a rival company, whose spaceport investments would suffer a huge loss if the space elevator was completed. Zin had moved a substantial amount of money into a new company shortly before the sabotage. Eryn Hudson was listed as co-CEO of that company. With proof of their connection, the police issued two arrest warrants. They raided Zin's home first—but he had not been there. He had already taken a spaceflight three days earlier, leaving the system straight after the disaster. The police had only my mother left to charge—so they surrounded our house with drones and burst in while everyone was sleeping. I would never forget being woken by police shouting and pointing guns. They had been too late. My mother fled the planet just like her lover Zin, becoming one of the planet's most notorious wanted criminals.

I was still thinking about her when my sister came home, swaying like she had drunk every bottle of liquor in the New Commonwealth. Her scarlet, skin-tight dress had lost a strap and her azure eyes were fully dilated by some form of narcotic. She saw me in my police uniform and held out her hands. "Whoops! Busted! Take me away, *ossifer*."

"You're drunk," I said.

"Guilty!" she said. She laughed and flopped down on the couch, kicking off her high-heels. "You missed a wild party, sis."

"Clearly, *you* didn't miss anything. Looks like something ran you over. What drugs are you on?"

"Relax, Chara. I glanded some euphoria and emotica—nothing illegal."

Every citizen in the New Commonwealth could internally manufacture mood-altering biochemical, perfectly legally, making their glands produce drugs—but I hated seeing my sister drunk. I worried about her getting in a dangerous situation. "You've got to be careful, Shada. Dad would freak out if he saw you like this."

Our dad still lived in the village where we had grown up. After his marriage to my mother was legally dissolved, he remarried and had more children. These days Dad was so busy with his new family that I often felt like I had lost both parents—but I knew Shada would care what he thought.

"Give me a break, Chara. I'm an adult. Don't try to make me feel bad. You're harshing my mood." Her dark green eyes narrowed. "Wait a sec. This isn't about me having fun. You're not normally a nag. Something's upset you. What's wrong?"

I didn't feel like having a serious conversation while my sister was high. "Forget it. It's nothing."

"Hey, it's me. I know something is on your mind. Talk."

"Okay. Fine. I got an unexpected present. A very expensive book. It's waiting at a shop in The Scrawl. I don't know if I should collect it or leave it."

"Why? What's the problem?"

"It could be from Mom."

"Mom? I don't believe it." Shada pouted. "I can't believe Mom sent you a present—but she didn't send me one!"

"Count yourself lucky. Shada, I don't know what to do. Mom hasn't contacted us for twenty years. She abandoned us like we didn't matter. Why would she send me something now? What does it mean? What does she want?"

"I don't know. Look, sis, if Mom's trying to get in touch with you, you have to find out. The book could contain a message telling us how to contact her."

Shada had forgiven our mother a long time ago, because she could not really remember her. She had been too young. It was a raw wound for me because I remembered what it was like to feel betrayed.

"Why would *I* want to contact her? She's a criminal and an adulterer. She fled the planet . . . leaving us. I am so mad at her. I should report what's happened. For all I know, the book is stolen and she wants to drag me into some kind of con."

"You don't know that," Shada said. "Listen to me. You'd be crazy to refuse a free gift, even if it is from Mom."

"I don't want anything from her."

"Hey, I'll have it even if you don't. I can resell it for a sweet ride. My bike's lost a power cell and I'd love to get a new one."

"I've got work now," I said. "But I'll collect the present later."

"Great! I'll come with you shopping," Shada said. "I haven't been shopping with you for ages."

"Okay," I said. "See you later."

Shada yawned and stretched out her long legs. "Need a few zees. I am totally wrecked after last night. Think I need to gland a hangover cure."

My sister curled into a foetal position and, a minute later, I heard her snoring. I covered her with a blanket, then crept to my lockbox to retrieve my police-issued weapon, an Omni Version 4.0 Ultimate Pacifier 75mm. It was a smart pistol capable of firing stun or lethal rounds, depending on the setting. I attached the Omni to my belt before leaving.

My police flier was parked on the roof, its sleek black wings unfurling from the body as I approached. A side-hatch opened, lowering a tongue-like ramp, and I boarded. While I settled into my seat, reading up on crime reports, the autopilot engaged and flew me the six klicks over the bustling streets of The Scrawl to the matt-black Justice Building on the west bank of the mud-brown Gazo River, which split the city in two like a knife. My reading was interrupted by a proximity alert warning. A space plane was passing low over my flier, heading for the spaceport on the other side of the river. The craft cast a shadow over me that lasted for several seconds. Then a dark cloud of Justice drones swarmed below me, ready to shoot down any craft not sending the right verification codes. My flier transmitted my ID code. The cloud parted to let me land on the roof without getting killed.

From there, I descended into the bowels of the building infamously known as The Tomb, because the ten bottom levels were Dorado's biggest prison, holding over sixty-thousand convicted criminals. The police headquarters occupied the top three floors. I was early for roll-call—so I glanded caffeine to keep my senses alert during my shift. My partner, Vito Darelli, was late as usual. Vito didn't show up until Sergeant Walker had started roll-call. His big, bear-like form slipped into the seat next to mine and asked me if he had missed anything important.

"No," I said.

"Did you hear the ship last night?"

"Hard to miss it," I said. "It woke me up."

"Me, too!" he said with weird enthusiasm. "Guess what? It's a Nexian cruiser. You know what *that* means?"

"No. What?"

"There's going to be amazing alien stuff on sale in The Scrawl."

"I'm not interested."

Vito's eyes widened. "Not interested? It's not every day a cruiser comes here from the Archipelago. Tonight the bars will be overloaded with hot aliens looking to hook up with local guys. You could act as my wingman. The ladies will trust me if I have a female friend telling them I'm a great guy. As a thank-you, I'll buy you beers all night and get you tickets to the volex game on Saturday. What do you say, partner? You in?"

Vito was grinning like his jaws were dislocated.

"No," I said. "I'm not being your sleazy wingman. I say we should concentrate on solving some crimes."

Vito stopped grinning and scowled. "You're in a bad mood. Gland some sunshine, partner. Be my wingman tonight. Do me a solid."

I resented him asking me to support his seduction of other women. I knew he was recovering from a divorce and not looking for another serious relationship, but that didn't mean he had to turn into a jerk.

"I won't be your wingman," I snapped back, a little too loud.

Cops turned to look at us, including Sergeant Walker. He was standing in front of a screen showing a live aerial view of the city, with recent reported crimes highlighted in red. Most of the crimes were thefts and assaults on tourists in The Scrawl.

"Hey! The talkers at the back—shut up and listen. We've just got a report of an incident in Reunion Station. A teenage girl jumped on the tracks in front of the northbound express. You two talkers can get over there and search for the body. Don't forget to wear bio-suits. It's likely to be a splatter fest. You'll probably be picking up pieces all day. Good luck!"

Every cop in the room sniggered at us—the poor fools given the worst assignment. I felt like I had stepped on a mine. I hated suicides. I was hoping to reason with Sergeant Walker—but he was staring at us. "Did you hear me, Detectives?"

"Yes, sir!" we said.

"Then why are you still sitting there?"

Reunion Station was across the river. It looked like a giant white golf ball attached to the crater-shaped quarantine zone around the spaceport. It didn't take long to fly there, but my partner made every second feel like an hour. Brooding in silence, he somehow blamed me for our assignment, when he was entirely at fault. We landed in the rooftop emergency vehicle parking zone, where we were met by Chief of Security Radford, a stocky red-haired woman from a high-gravity world. Reunion Station had plenty of security cams inside, so I expected it to be easy to figure out what happened—but Radford gave us bad news.

"We had a security breach this morning," she said. "Our computers were not working right. No cams recorded the incident on platform eighty."

I swore. "Was it a hacker attack?"

"No—it was Bane."

Bane was a virus—a sentient virus that lived on any distributed network it could infect. Bane was self-aware, but it had no agenda except to reproduce itself and cause chaos in any infected system. No computer network was entirely safe from it, unless it was completely disconnected from external access. Bane was the reason why the New Commonwealth limited the use of advanced computers to non-vital systems.

"Great," Vito muttered. "Please tell us you've got some witnesses."

"Yes, I did my own detective work," Radford said, rather smugly. "I used to be a cop on Ikiain—but they wouldn't let me join the police here because I failed the physical. I'm too slow for a low gee world, they said." She sighed. "Guess you don't want to hear my problems."

"It's tough," Vito said. "Maybe I could put in a good a word for you. What can you tell us about the incident this morning?"

"It happened at 7:20. There were 257 people on the platform waiting for the 7:30 to Marthar's Port. Seventeen of them saw the victim leap onto the track just as the non-stop express was coming along the tunnel. I detained them for you to question, on platform eighty." She paused to flick some hair out of her eyes. "Did I do the right thing, Detective?"

"You did," Vito said, with a charming grin.

We boarded a glass elevator to take us down to the main concourse. The view gave me vertigo until I glanded some beta. "So, Chief, why didn't the driver stop?"

"The train's got collision detection protocols—but it couldn't slow down fast enough without injuring the passengers. It braked and stopped about a klick down the tunnel. My security team didn't see any organic material on the front—so I think the suicide got crushed under the carriages. We've closed down the line so you can go onto the track safely. This accident has caused a serious delay. I hope you won't take long."

We followed Radford through the station's huge concourse of verdant parkland filled with food vendors and coffee shops. Reunion Station was the central hub of public and private transport, from the spaceport to everywhere on Arcadia. It had over a hundred train platforms, as well as cab and shuttle terminals. At one end of the main concourse was a terminal to the spaceport, where thousands of new visitors arrived every day. Each new arrival passed through a rigorous security check where each visitor was screened for identity, diseases, and bio-weapons. That morning the station was especially busy, due to the influx of 15,000 off-world travellers. Radford led us down a walkway to platform eighty.

The witnesses were gathered in a group, guarded by six station security guards in blue uniforms.

Vito donned a bio-suit and climbed down onto the track with his forensic kit to look for human remains, while I stayed on the platform and started talking to the witnesses. All of the witnesses told the same story. A blonde-haired teenage girl, wearing jeans and a faux leather jacket, ran along the crowded platform as though she was hurrying for a train. At the platform's edge, she had leapt onto the track, just moments before the express hurtled past, travelling at 400 kilometres per hour.

I needed a better description of the woman. Luckily, an off-worlder from Takol's Ring had been video-recording his arrival on Arcadia for friends and family back home. I linked my personal tablet physically to his video cam and downloaded the file, which had not been affected by Bane. The victim's face was visible on a few frames before she plunged to her death. She had short, blonde hair, darker eyebrows and brown eyes. Her physical description didn't really matter to me, though. I could see she looked scared. Suicide victims didn't normally look scared. They looked calm, resigned to their fate. I frowned. Why had she been running? What had she been running *from*?

"Did any of you see which way the girl entered the platform?"

Three witnesses pointed at the walkway leading up to the main concourse. I turned to the security chief. "Did Bane infect all of your cams or just the ones on this platform?"

"I'm not sure. You're welcome to check at my office."

My partner had gone out of sight into the tunnel. I spoke into my shoulder mic. "Vito, you find anything?"

"Not yet," he said.

"Keep looking. I'm going to check the security cam recordings from earlier—if Bane didn't wipe them. Something isn't right about this. I don't think it was a suicide. The girl was running away from someone, or something. I'm going to check it out from the security office."

It turned out that all of the cams in the station had been affected—so that line of inquiry was useless. But Bane could not infect the eyes and ears of the people in the station. Since almost an hour had passed, many potential witnesses had already left for their destinations. I prayed some of the station staff and vendors had observed something. I questioned dozens of vendors before finding one who did remember seeing the girl.

"Yeah, I noticed her," the owner of a bagel kiosk said. "She bought a coffee with a pay card. I remember her because about ten seconds later four security guards approached her. They looked like they were going to arrest her for something—but she surprised them by tossing her coffee into one guard's face. She dropped her bag and ran into the crowd with the other three guys chasing her."

I frowned at Radford. "You didn't tell me about this."

"Hey! This is news to me." Radford spoke on her com, talking to her security staff, then shook her head. "My guys all deny following her and I believe them." She glared at the kiosk owner. "Harry, if you want to keep your licence to work here, you'd better describe the guards."

"Uh—they were all light-skinned, tough-looking. They had guns like her." He looked at my Omni.

"My people don't carry lethal weapons," Radford said, showing me her stunner, which could not be mistaken for a lethal weapon. "Those guards were not working for me. What's going on here, some kind of covert security operation by Homeworld Defence?"

I didn't have any answers. My com had been on during the conversation—so I knew Vito was listening. "Vito, did you hear that?"

"Yeah," he said. "Fake security team. Weird. Want to hear something just as weird?"

"What?"

"I found some blood leading to a maintenance tunnel. Looks like the girl isn't dead. She made it across the tracks alive."

"Collect a blood sample."

"Already done. I'm going into the tunnel to see if I can catch up."

"Be careful," I said. "We don't know if the girl is a victim or a suspect."

Too much time had passed since the incident to make it worth locking down the station – but I still had something I could do there. I asked the kiosk owner one more question. "What happened to her bag?"

"The guard she hurt picked it up. He went through it, but he didn't look happy. Was she smuggling something?"

"I don't know. Thanks for cooperating."

Next, I approached the spaceport terminal, hoping the girl had been aboard the Starcruiser. I showed her picture to the inspectors. They remembered her. I asked them to get the name on her passport chip. Quickly, I got an ID. The girl was called Charlotte Dodgson.

Something about the name tingled my mind.

"Did you scan her bag?"

"Of course," an inspector said. "Nothing in it except clothes and the usual teenage girl stuff. She said she was a student. We did a full scan for illegal tech. She was clean."

Nothing in the bag. That meant the fake guards were probably still chasing the girl. But why? I studied the passenger manifest. Charlotte Dodgson boarded the Starcruiser on Nexus Prime. Her personal history was unspectacular. She had been born on Qer, a backwater planet on the edge of the densely-packed region of stars known as The Archipelago. Wait a second. Qer? There had been a big natural disaster on Qer. An earthquake killed a million inhabitants. Personal records had been lost. It was common for criminals to create false identities by claiming to have lost their birth records. Was Charlotte Dodgson a false identity?

My mind normally made connections quickly, but the beta I'd glanded had made my thoughts slower than usual. To clear my head, I glanded a neural stimulant, quickening my thought processes. Everything became ultra-clear.

The name Charlotte Dodgson had not been chosen at random. Charlotte was the feminised form of the male name Charles. And Charles Dodgson was the author Lewis Carroll's real name. Charlotte Dodgson wasn't a teenager. She was my mother in a surgically-altered body.

"She's back," I said out loud.

Radford heard me and assumed I'd been talking to her. "Who's back?"

I could not tell Radford the truth, so I deflected. "Thanks for your help, Chief. We don't need to keep the platform closed any longer. You can re-open it as soon as you like. Excuse me. Got to go."

My head was pounding with thoughts as I hurried away. A group of armed men had tried to grab my mother at the station—but who were they? And why had my mother returned to Arcadia, where she was wanted for murder, when she could have avoided danger by staying away?

"Vito, where are you?"

"I'm at a filthy junction. The blood trail stops here. It leads to a dozen exits to the streets—but I've got no idea which way the girl went. By now she's got to be out in the city somewhere. Hell! I lost her. I'm going to make my way out onto Tyler Street. Can you pick me up there, partner?"

"You got it," I said. I didn't tell Vito I suspected that the girl was my mother in disguise. That was information I wasn't sharing yet. I knew I would be taken off the case if I reported a personal link to the suspect. I wanted to catch her myself. It was the least I could do, after what she had done to my family. "I'll bring the flier to you."

I estimated it would take my partner thirty minutes to get out of the station on foot. That didn't give me much time on my own, but it was just about long enough to fly to Rasha's Emporium to collect the package left by my mother. It had to have something to do with her reason for returning to Arcadia and why an armed group of men pretending to be security guards had tried to arrest her.

I flew across the city and descended into the Scrawl, landing on the busy street outside the Grand Market. Rasha's Emporium was on the ground floor. I went in and collected my gift. I carried the box back to my flier before opening it, collapsing the stasis field that prevented anyone else doing so.

There was a beautiful copy of *Alice's Adventures in Wonderland* inside, but it wasn't an original. It had been printed in 2300. It was valuable—but not priceless.

"Mother, why did you send me this?"

I had no time to examine it because Vito was calling me. "Hey, I'm outside, waiting for you. Where are you, Chara?"

"On my way."

I hid the book in the inside pocket of my jacket. Then I crossed the river to meet my partner. Tyler Street was in the shopping district in the shadow of the station. Vito was slurping a bowl of steaming takan noodles on the sunny street corner. He finished them as I arrived, wiping his greasy hands with a paper napkin.

"Chara, this case is a big waste of our time," he said. "We should forget it and get back to our sector, where some real crimes are going on right now. The girl didn't kill herself and I don't think we should step on the toes of the guys looking for her—not if they're Homeworld Defence. Finding her is not our problem. Let's go do some real police work."

"Maybe you're right," I said. "We were sent to investigate a suicide. Since she's alive, all we can charge her with is a misdemeanour anyway. We can file a report and move on."

Vito looked pleased to hear that. I was relieved, too. I'd been figuring out a way of dissuading him from continuing the investigation when I hadn't needed to do anything. His reluctance solved my problem. We filed our report, then got reassigned to a domestic violence situation six klicks away. Normal police work.

At the end of my shift, I said goodbye to Vito and headed home. The sun was going down when I parked on the roof. I felt the chill of twilight as I left my flier. I intended to examine my mother's gift more thoroughly once I was inside my apartment, but my plan was interrupted. Opening my door, I was struck by the silence. My sister always played loud music. Something was wrong. In a heartbeat, my Omni was in my hands, set to maximum stun power.

"Shada, are you in?" I called out.

My sister did not answer.

The silence made me uneasy. Closing the front door behind me, I crept into the main room, listening. Just in time, I glanded adrenaline to make my reactions faster. An armed man appeared in the bathroom doorway, holding an Omni pointed at my head. As he pulled the trigger, I ducked, avoiding the bullet. My Omni launched a stun bullet into his neck before he re-targeted, the bullet burrowing into his skin. He fell, writhing in pain, his nervous system overloaded with painful electrical impulses.

Was he alone? The bathroom was empty, but I glimpsed a moving shadow in the kitchen area. Another armed attacker behind the partition wall pointed his Omni around the corner. He fired a scattershot that tore apart half of the furniture. I dived to my right and switched my ammo to heat seeker bullets. On my knees, I fired through the wall, relying on the bullet's in-built intelligence to locate the hidden target on the other side. Hearing a very satisfying yelp, I ran into the kitchen, where the second man was on the floor with a bloody chest wound. He saw me and reached for his dropped Omni, but I kicked it away and stomped on his fingers.

"Who are you?"

He grimaced, but didn't speak. He coughed blood and groaned.

"*Where is my sister?*"

I wanted to shoot him again, but I could see he was in no condition to speak. My bullet had entered his chest and ripped into vital organs. I felt like letting him die but the law officer in me made me tear open his shirt to check his wound.

There were animated tattoos on his chest of an exploding yellow sun, the symbol of the Yellow Star crime syndicate. They were a notorious gang from The Scrawl. He was hired muscle. I went to get a medkit to stabilise him. I attached a medi-patch to his wound and saw it knitting together the raw flesh. He wouldn't die now, but he would need surgery later. The medi-patch put him into a protective coma while I searched both men. The injured thug had a key fob for a ground car. He also carried a burner cell. The burner cells were primitive tech—but useful for criminals wanting to avoid detection. The cell had only one number in the memory. I guessed he was supposed to call someone after killing me.

Just then, the burner cell rang. If I let it ring for too long, the caller would become suspicious. I answered it with a gruff voice, hoping the caller would think I was one of the thugs.

"Yeah?" I said.

"Is it done?"

"Yeah."

"You have the book?"

"Uh-huh."

"Did you capture the cop alive?"

"Yeah."

"Good. Bring the book and the cop back here. We can use her and the sister as leverage. You and Larick will get a bonus for this, Shorty."

The caller hung up without saying where they were. I swore. It was impossible to trace the origin of the call. Burners used too many relays, making them untraceable. The source could be anywhere in the city.

The one called Larick was lying on the floor, shivering as each pulse from my stun bullet coursed through his nervous system. I had remote access to the stunner's strength. I turned it down so he could speak.

"You have my sister," I said. "Tell me where she is or I'll give you another dose of pain."

"No way," he said. "I'm a dead man if I talk to a cop."

"Tell me where my sister is," I said. "Or I'll torture you."

"Yeah, right. You're a cop. You've not got the guts."

"No?" For effect, I set my Omni to shoot another stun bullet. I pointed it at his crotch. "Want me to shoot here? The pain will be unimaginable when I turn it up to max. It'll fry your body from the inside out."

I saw the fear in his eyes. I thought he was going to crack, but Larick snarled at me. "I'm not betraying my brothers. Yellow Star call me home!"

The gang member's skin started to turn a pale blue. Within seconds, his corneas were bursting with blood and he was bleeding from his nose and ears. He was dead before I could even get a medi-patch. I couldn't believe it. He had glanded a deadly neurotoxin and killed himself.

Now I'd never find my sister.

What was I going to do? The gang would kill her as soon as they realised Larick and Shorty were not coming back.

I stepped back from the dead man and struggled to think of what to do. The book. Did that contain something? I had to examine it properly. I pulled it out and examined the cover. Nothing unusual. I opened it to the first page, discarding a bookmark. There was no message on the page. Flicking through the pages, I saw nothing interesting. Getting desperate, I shook the book hoping something would fall out, then got a knife from the kitchen and cut open the spine. I ripped the book apart looking for anything important. I laughed. What was I doing? My mother would never send me a book expecting me to destroy it. She knew I loved books. After a minute, I took a second look at the bookmark. There were ornate designs on it like circuit diagram. I grinned. It wasn't just a bookmark. There was a small hole for a data input cable. It was slim data storage device. I hurried to my tablet and connected the bookmark. The tablet's screen displayed hundreds of folders containing documents and image files. A folder marked RABBIT HOLE caught my attention because it was related to Alice's adventure. It contained read-only video files. I opened one titled OPEN ME. A video played, time-stamped twenty years ago.

The face of my mother appeared as I remembered her, bringing unexpected tears. She stood on another world with three dull orange suns, looking straight into the camera lens. "My name is Eryn Hudson, former executive of Sunstone Corporation. This is a record of my personal investigation into the sabotage of the Arcadia Space Elevator Project . . ."

Five minutes later, I was exiting my apartment with a reloaded Omni, when I heard elevator doors opening down the hall. I aimed my weapon, expecting more gang members. My partner stepped out, looking shocked to see my pointed weapon.

"Whoa! Put that down."

I was surprised to see him. He had never visited my building before. I lowered my Omni. "Vito, what are you doing here?"

"Chara, I needed to see you in person. I got the results back from the blood sample. The DNA matches your mother. The girl is Eryn Hudson."

"I know," I said.

"You know? Chara, she's a wanted felon. I came to give you a heads-up because the whole police force will soon be looking for her. If they think you're helping her evade arrest, they'll arrest you. Is that what you're doing? Do you know where she is?"

"No," I said. "But I know she's innocent."

"How?"

"I just shot two thugs waiting in my apartment, sent by the real bad guys. And I've seen the evidence. My mother didn't sabotage the space elevator. She never had an affair with Garth Zin, either. All the evidence against her was fabricated by the CEO of Sunstone Corporation, along with some board members, private investors, and corrupt officials. They needed a scapegoat, so they picked my mother. She became a fugitive so she could track down Garth Zin and find the truth. It took her twenty years to find him—but she did it and made him confess. Zin was paid to frame her so the police would not look for the real saboteurs. My mother sent me a recording of his confession, as well as all the evidence needed to prove Sunstone executives were responsible for the destruction of their own project."

"Why did they do that?"

"They'd underbid for the government contract, which would have cost them a fortune to complete. They sabotaged the space elevator to break the contract legally, while also receiving a massive payout from their insurance brokers. It was just a scam to earn them billions. And now I have everything to prove it, thanks to my mother."

"That's great," Vito said. "Have you got the book on you?"

I had not mentioned the book to him. His left eye twitched as he realised his error. I raised my Omni. "You're working for them, Vito?"

"What? No! Chara, don't be paranoid. I came to help you. Stop pointing your weapon."

"They sent you. You're working for the Yellow Star."

"No."

"Liar. That's why you weren't keen on continuing the investigation earlier. They got to you, told you to back off."

"Chara . . ." he said, and made a sudden move for his Omni.

I shot first. Vito went down with two stun bullets in his neck. I cuffed him and then dragged him into my apartment. He was wriggling like a sun-cooked worm. I deactivated the stun bullets so I could talk to my partner without his teeth chattering. He started sobbing. "I'm sorry, Chara. They didn't give me a choice. I got into debt after my divorce and they—"

"I don't care for excuses, Vito. You're dirty. I've got the evidence to take down everyone responsible for framing my mother, but none of that matters if I don't save my sister. If they kill her, you'll be to blame, Vito. Do the right thing. Help me."

Vito looked ashamed. "There's a club. The Yellow Star use the basement for storing illegal things. They'll probably keep your sister there because it's in the middle of their territory."

"Which club?"

"*Transformia.* Chara, what are you going to do?"

"This," I said, and I punched him in the face, knocking him out. I was rubbing my sore knuckles when I heard footsteps outside.

Someone knocked. "Chara? Shada?"

I stepped to one side and opened the door. A blonde teenager was standing in the corridor with a gash on her arm. She saw my Omni and raised her hands. "Don't shoot, Chara. This might sound insane—but I'm your mom in disguise. I had my body transformed so I could come home without being recognised. But I must have screwed up, because they were waiting for me at the spaceport. I used the alias Charlotte Dodgson in case anything happened to me—so you'd figure things out if I disappeared. If you don't believe I'm your mother, you can check my DNA and—"

"I believe you," I said. "I was there at the station and know the whole story. I already figured out a lot after discovering that this bookmark was a data device. But I don't know why you sent it to me."

"You're a cop, Chara. I was hoping you'd take that straight to the authorities."

"I would have, if I'd known what it was earlier, Mom. You could have made it more obvious."

"I was worried it would be intercepted if I had it on me or if I left you a message telling you it contained proof of my innocence. We need to get that data to someone with power. A judge you trust. We can go now."

"I'd love to, but I can't. The Yellow Star kidnapped Shada."

"My baby girl!" she said. The words sounded strange coming out of the mouth of a teenager. "What can we do?"

"Grab an Omni," I said. "Guard the door. Shoot anyone who comes in. I'll be back in a moment."

I grabbed some things from my sister's wardrobe, packing them in a bag. Then I told my mother to follow me. The fastest way to get to *Transformia* was via my flier, but a police vehicle would be spotted by the Yellow Star a klick away, ruining the chance of getting into the club undetected. No, I had to use the ground car belonging to Shorty. We hurried down in the elevator to the underground parking zone. I located Shorty's four-door grey van. I climbed in the back, so I could change into Shada's party dress while my mother drove us the sixteen blocks to the club. My mother's eyebrow raised in confusion.

"What are you doing, Chara? Isn't that dress inappropriate?"

"It's a dance club, Mom. I'll go in as a customer. I'll look for Shada, once I get inside. Damn! I'll have to leave my Omni with you, though. They'll have a scanner on the door, so I can't even hide it in Shada's Maxx Impact handbag."

"I can help with that," she said. "Use this to pay for entry." She handed me her pay card. "There's a copy of Bane on it. I used it at the station to mess up the surveillance cams. It'll break their scanner."

"That's great, Mom, but it won't hide my Omni from a human search."

"I'll cause a distraction," she said.

It was dark when we arrived at the club. A line of eager clubbers were waiting to be let in. We parked on the next street and I joined the line, sneaking forward until I reached the front. I handed my pay card to a grim-faced bouncer. His card reader confirmed payment, green-lighting me to go into the club. I was supposed to walk through the scanner. But then the scanner started beeping, even though nobody was stepping through. Bane worked fast.

"Machine's not working," the bouncer said. "Got to frisk you."

"Okay," I said demurely, like I was looking forward to his hands pawing my body. He'd find my Omni if he looked in my handbag.

Luckily, he never got the chance.

The sudden breaking of his kneecap, by a silent rubber bullet fired from across the street, caused him to scream. "My knee! My knee!"

While he was distracted, I slipped into the hot darkness inside the club. My bones vibrated to the subsonic beat of the music, as I glanded adrenaline and crossed the overcrowded dance floor, making my way to a closed door. A sign stating PRIVATE: NO ENTRY suggested I was going the right way. Two armed men with Yellow Star tattoos were on the other side. I shot them and descended a staircase into a long grey corridor with a dozen unmarked doors. Another man was sitting on a chair at the far end. He had an Omni on his lap—but I shot him before he used it. I looked in several storage rooms filled with crates of black-market goods before locating one where I could hear male voices.

I went in low and fast. My sister was tied to a chair, guarded by two men. One had a coffee-burned face. My Omni took care of them both.

It didn't take long to free Shada and make our way to an emergency exit into an alley, where my mother had parked the van. We jumped in the back. Our mother drove us away, very fast.

Shada looked confused. "Chara, is this real or am I hallucinating?"

"It's real."

"Who's the girl?"

"That's your mom."

"What?"

"Long story."

"Where are we going?"

"The Justice Building."

That was five months ago. A lot has happened since then. Now everyone involved in the sabotage is locked up in The Tomb.

Thanks to the publicity around the scandal, my sister was hired by Maxx Impact to model for him on Nexus Prime.

She loves her new job.

I have a new partner—Radford—and the reformed Sunstone Corporation hired my exonerated mother to build a better space elevator.

I can see it rising into the sky from my apartment.

It's amazing.

Just like my life—now that it's whole again.

*John Moralee is the author of the crime novel* Acting Dead, *the zombie apocalypse thriller* Journal of the Living, *and the first book in a dystopian science fiction/fantasy series* The House on Willow Lane. *He lives in England, where his short fiction has appeared in magazines and anthologies including* The Mammoth Book of Jack the Ripper Stories, Crimewave, *and the British Fantasy Society's magazine* Peeping Tom.

*Several collections of his stories are available as ebooks and trade paperbacks. They include the horror titles* The Bone Yard and Other Stories *and* Bloodways, *the crime omnibus* Edge of Crime, *and the science-fiction collection* The Tomorrow Tower.

*More recently, his science-fiction stories have been published in* Visions III: Beyond the Kuiper Belt *and* Visions IV: Space Between Stars. *He also has a story, "Ripplers", in* Last Outpost, *an anthology of military SF released in October 2016.*

*John Moralee's website is www.mybookspage.wordpress.com.*

Many people have speculated about ancient astronauts visiting early civilizations and giving them various technologies, perhaps as experiments. But what if Earth were in fact kept untouched, allowed to develop at its own pace as a control, while the experiments were performed on humans taken to other worlds? Worlds we may well discover as we move beyond Earth and the Sol System into the greater galaxy.

# THE SHADOW OF A DEAD GOD

### By

### *Leigh Kimmel*

Over the battered landscape hung two moons, one full and red like Mars without the icecaps, the other a jaundiced crescent quite unlike the blue and white Earth in the lunar sky of Liu Shang's childhood, or even the silvery moon of pre-spaceflight photographs. Liu Shang looked back at the cluster of tents behind her, all marked with the same Kennedy University Tycho emblem that was on the right-shoulder patch of her overalls.

Mission rules were clear—no one was to go beyond the perimeter of their camp alone, and absolutely nobody was to go out at night. But the thought of approaching anybody about her vision of an unknown ruin made her guts twist. Not just the fear of being ridiculed and losing face, but that if any of her friends trusted her enough to accompany her out there and were ridiculed, she would've caused them to lose face as well.

No, she'd first slip out on a quick trip of her own, verify the ruins did indeed exist. Once she had hard proof that she'd experienced a true vision, she'd speak to the professors, get a proper expedition arranged.

Liu Shang fingered the locator in her pocket. The expedition had put up only basic satellites, not a full global positioning constellation like the settled worlds possessed, but with orbits carefully planned to provide the dig site with maximal coverage. As long as she didn't hit one of those rare dead zones, finding her way back should be no problem.

Still, she had no time to waste. The longer she remained out, the greater the risk someone would notice her absence.

Although accustomed to brisk walks by a lifetime of physical conditioning, Liu Shang found it more difficult than she'd expected to cross the distance. The stronger gravity pretty much canceled out the advantage of not needing a spacesuit, which meant she made little better progress than she had during the training digs in the spaceport of an abandoned lunar settlement

The farther she walked, the more uneasy she became. She told herself it was just being on an exposed planetary surface, dependent upon the natural environment. As a native Lunan, she'd grown up checking life-support telltales until it became as automatic as breathing, and their absence left her at a loss for the reassurance that oxygen and carbon dioxide were at their proper levels.

One thing was like being back on the Moon—the swiftness with which she came upon her goal. One minute she was toiling up yet another slope, unsure how many more she would have to crest, or if she might be on a fool's errand. The next minute she was looking down at the half-buried tower of her dream. The experience made her recall the early lunar explorers who'd spent hours toiling toward the rim of a crater only to give up within a dozen meters of their goal.

*But I didn't give up and turn back.* Liu Shang allowed herself a moment of satisfaction as she surveyed her find. It was shorter than in her vision, not only because the ground level had risen from the accretion of dust and soil over untold millennia, but also because the titanium spire which had once topped the stonework had gone on walkabout. Destroyed in the cataclysm which had felled a civilization, or looted by subsequent cultures as so many of Earth's archeological treasures had been over the centuries and millennia?

Liu Shang had intended to return to camp as soon as she'd verified the site actually existed. Now that she'd located the tower of her dream, she found her curiosity piqued to a feverish pitch. In the sanguine light of the red moon (its yellow companion having set during her trek), she could see the shapes of additional walls under the scrubby ground cover. Might there be an entire complex of buildings lying just under the surface, more intact than anything they'd found from such an early era of this planet's habitation?

Gazing upon those walls filled her with unease. The alien geometries of their alignment grated upon her nerves, making her recall studying the mysterious entities which had once occupied this part of the galaxy. Alton Shigeta's words came back to her:

"They've been called the Ancients, the Old Ones, the Elder Things, the Fathers of Time, as many names as the societies and cultures they influenced. They scattered humans and eight other sapient species across the Sagittarius Arm, as slaves, as playthings, as food. And as suddenly as they appeared, they vanished utterly, leaving only traces: Fragments of a technology so advanced as to defy comprehension. The faiths and folklore of the various Scattered Peoples, recalling beings like gods, at once magnificent and terrible, by turns generous and vindictive."

In the comfortable confines of the Lovell Library with its moonglass tables polished milky-smooth by centuries of use, it had seemed a fascinating bit of ancient history, safely remote, Now, amidst a blasted landscape made less desolate than the lunar surface only by the presence of a breathable atmosphere, things looked very different indeed.

In fact, they'd become downright scary. Overcome with dread, Liu Shang turned and fled the way she'd come. She didn't get far before her foot caught and sent her sprawling face-first to the ground.

The stronger gravity made her fall hard enough to knock the wind out of her. Growing up on the Moon led her mind to interpret the sensation as a failure of her air supply. She groped to check life-support monitors on a spacesuit she wasn't wearing. Only as she caught her breath could she pull her thoughts together enough to remember she was in a natural atmosphere.

Liu Shang got to her knees and looked around for what had tripped her. In the familiar habitat environment, she would've expected an unsecured cable, but here she had no idea what to look for.

The pale loop which emerged from the ground a few centimeters from her toe couldn't be of natural origin. The closer she looked, the more certain she became that it had to be a polymer—yellowed with age, but untouched by the natural processes of decay, as plastics could remain for centuries even on biologically active worlds.

Liu Shang's curiosity was sufficiently aroused that she gave the translucent strand a firm tug, strong enough to pull it loose from the soil in which it had become embedded. Based upon her experience, she had expected it to extend for some length in either direction, until it either broke or wrapped around something immovable.

Instead, it proved to be a short, closed loop from which depended an ovoid of some ceramic material. Might have been worn as a pendant, the way some signaling devices and alarm keys were? Except, she saw neither buttons nor touchpad, only a raised design that defied the eye's ability to follow it.

The harder Liu Shang tried to examine it, the queasier she grew. A vertiginous feeling overcame her, obliterating her ability to locate herself as to person, place, and time.

The sacred drums beat out an ever-increasing tempo for the oblates to dance across the festival plaza to the Temple, where they would offer themselves upon the altar for the nourishment of their gods. Already many of the oblates had surrendered themselves to the ecstasy of drug-induced trance, twisting and writhing without heed to the effects upon bodies they would soon surrender to the overlords they worshipped.

Some of the oblates had yielded themselves to the point they'd lost control of their bodily functions, not even noticing the stains that now ran down their white temple garments. Miri had to fight the urge to wrinkle her nose whenever the stench wafted by. She dared not let anyone realize she had avoided ingesting any of the drug when the chalice was given to her, merely pressed her lips to its rim as if drinking. If someone suspected what she intended, up would go the cry of sacrilege, and she would do well to be killed cleanly with the ritual knife and not torn limb from limb by an outraged crowd.

It was no easy task to scan for some route of escape to which she might work herself, yet appear to be completely absorbed in the ecstasy of the dancing, chanting mass of humanity all around her. How the other dancers, those who had taken the drug and surrendered their minds to the ritual they enacted, avoided colliding with one another as they twisted and wove their way toward the temple, she could not guess. But it did make her task simpler, for which she was grateful.

Miri brushed against an obstacle—not stone, but flesh, warm, yielding. Startled, she gasped, turned half fearing it would be one of the priests, having discovered her and determined to ensure that she did not evade her fate.

No, the man beside her did not wear the scarlet robes of the priesthood, but the simple white garment of an oblate. She looked up at his eyes, which gazed back at her with the clarity of another who had evaded the trance drug.

Still, it took a moment to place his face, so astonished was she to see him here, dressed in an oblate's tunic rather than in flight suit or sky-blue dress uniform. Had it been only eight days, half a phase-cycle

of the Blood Moon, since he had stood at the doors of
the Palace of Government to receive the Sacred Star
from the hand of the First Servant himself, as reward for
leading the Holy Falcons to victory over the Cherdwyn
blasphemers who had stolen divine gifts of technology
and used them to make war against the gods and their
chosen Servants?

"Deek?"

He shot her a glare of pure fury. "Shhh!"

Miri cursed her own carelessness, then realized the
irony of condemning it in the names of the very gods
whose service she was rejecting. In that moment of
unthinking recognition, she could've betrayed both of
them to the priests. By some stroke of fortune none had
been looking in her direction.

It couldn't last. She focused her mind on making her
face a mask of ecstasy, of looking once again as though
she were enraptured with joy at the privilege of
sacrificing herself for the gods' nourishment. Only when
she felt confident in her pretense did she dare glance
around.

Deek remained close at hand, his eyes alert in a face
superficially slack as if under the trance-drug. Like
many of the dancers he wove complex patterns with his
hands, snapping his fingers to the beat of the sacred
drums. And just as she turned her gaze his direction, he
flicked his forefinger in a gesture too deliberate to be
anything but a signal: that way.

Ahead stood the great portico with its pillars carved
in the form of bat-winged creatures with staring eyes
and ropy tentacles, said to represent the lesser gods, the
servants of the Unnamable Lord whose nature could not
be given visual representation. Within were the ramps
and corridors that would funnel the oblates toward the
altar at a manageable rate for the priests.

On either side were lesser entrances, from which
priests might enter and leave to manage the movement
of the oblates, or to carry out other ritual activities
between festival days. Knowing these portals to be her
best hope of escape, Miri had been trying to get to one.

Every time she'd made a little headway, the crowd would push her back onto the path toward the temple's primary entrance.

With Deek's sturdy frame to press through the mass of trance-drugged humanity, it became possible. The biggest problem was keeping their path random enough to avoid attracting priestly attention.

And then the door was at hand, and they needed only duck within. It took a few moments for their eyes to adjust to the dim lighting beyond, time in which Miri's blood pounded in her ears and she fully expected a priest to leap out at them, to call them blasphemers, cut them down or even thrust them back out and call the wrath of the crowd down upon them.

But the corridor proved empty, the only signs of use the slight erosion of the marble floor where untold thousands of priestly feet had trod over the centuries since the gods had first raised the temple and forged their Covenant with their Servants. The farther Miri and Deek walked, the fainter the sounds of the festival became.

After they had gone a hundred paces, Miri braved a question. "So how do we get out of here?"

Deek narrowed his eyes. "There are five thousand priests permanently resident in the Temple, plus the two or three hundred visiting at any given time from the provincial shrines and village fanes. All of them must be supplied with the daily necessities of mortal life, which means there have to be one or more service entrances along the southern wall where food and the like are delivered. Once we find one, we should be able to steal laborers' tunics and slip out."

"And make new lives for ourselves." Now that Miri was off the festival plaza, she knew there could be no returning to her old one. To go back home, back to school, would be to admit her sacrilege to all and sundry. But unhappy as her old life had been, full of the jealous sniping of the other girls, it had been familiar.

"It shouldn't be that hard." Deek spoke with the confidence of a man accustomed to setting a goal and accomplishing it, even in the face of odds that would dismay any of Miri's so-called friends. "There's always a demand for strong backs and deft hands, and the provincial cities are large enough that most people are strangers to one another. We'll just attach ourselves to a group of pilgrims as they head home after the festival, and no one will be the wiser."

It took several minutes before it sank through to Miri that Deek intended to take her with him. He, the great avenging knight of the air who had overcome a wartime shortage of g-suits by training himself to endure g-forces without one, considered her a worthy companion. She, whom everyone in her neighborhood scorned as a useless dreamer, good only for annoying teachers and asking questions that made everyone else uncomfortable, had attracted a man the other girls, the good girls, made cow eyes over.

The thought emboldened her enough to broach the question at the back of her mind. "So how did you become an oblate? I mean, surely a hero like you would be more valuable alive and fighting." She didn't need to state the obvious, that like her, he must have been bullied into it. Why else would he have evaded the trance drug?

Deek's answer was as straightforward as his approach to combat. "I annoyed someone."

"You? The great hero, the Avenger of All that Is Sacred?" Surely nobody could be so irreverent as to be jealous—or could they? Becoming an oblate was an act of self-gift so holy no one would sully it by compelling someone unwilling, yet her own experience said otherwise.

Deek's mouth twitched. "Not my combat record. Just the stuff pilots like to do when we're keeping up our proficiencies between campaigns. Stretching the boundaries, seeing how far we can take a plane and still get back in one piece. And of course seeing who can push the furthest, who can fly the fastest, the highest, the lowest. A couple of friends flew under the Hallan Bay Bridge, so I had to do them one better. I flew a loop right around the middle of it—under it, over the top and under it again." His mouth curled into a grin. "But what finally tore it was probably when I buzzed the administration building. One too many petty criticisms from pencil-pushers who'd probably die of fright in the back seat of a trainer, so I decided to show them what a real pilot could do. Flew right past the facade, about three feet off the ground. Some of those paperclip-counters were looking down into the cockpit while I roared past, and had to run home for a quick change of clothes. That was the end of the sniping about how I handled my missions, but then the comments started about my religious observance, or lack thereof."

The amusement vanished, replaced by hard anger. "Piloting doesn't give you a lot of time for visiting shrines and praying. Even when we get leave, we don't want to stand around listening to priests chanting and burning incense. We want to cut loose, have some drinks by the pool and tell war stories, maybe do some rat-racing on the back roads. But once somebody wanted me gone, people started making *remarks*."

Miri nodded in sympathy. Imagining fighter pilots acting like vindictive children didn't come easy, but she hadn't forgotten what she'd gone through. Her age-cohort had just completed the Ar-akh-gthagil, the ceremony by which they were sealed to the Covenant, and one of the teachers told them that now they were old enough to offer themselves to the gods. And then the snippy words began, about how nice Miri would look in the white robe of an oblate, but, *of course*, she was too scared, how she didn't really love the gods, just mouthed the words the priests wanted to hear. Until there was nothing she could do in her defense except announce she was offering herself at the next festival— and when the time came, she took the hare-brained notion of not drinking the trance-drug, of finding some way to escape the altar of sacrifice.

Somewhere in the conversation both of them realized that, instead of finding their way to the service entrances, they were heading deeper into the temple. It wasn't just the steady downward slope to the corridors and ramps, or the growing heaviness of the air, with a cloying under-scent that made their noses twitch. Rather it was the profound sense of a *presence*, invisible but real, that pressed upon their minds.

From behind them came footsteps. Miri and Deek pressed themselves against the wall, hoped they wouldn't be noticed.

They needn't have worried. Down the hall came two priests of the offering, hoods down to cover the empty sockets where their eyes had been. They carried silver trays heaped with quivering red ovoids. Miri looked closer and wished she hadn't -- they were hearts, still beating.

Deek hugged her to his chest, so tight she could feel his Covenant-seal beneath the oblate's robe. No doubt he too was recalling the hymns they'd sung so many times at festivals. To see the literal truth of those words would unsettle even a strong man. Miri had to bite her lip to keep from shrieking, from flinging herself at the priests and scattering their precious burden in hopes of liberating the spirits trapped within, from running down the corridor heedless of the danger of discovery in sheer horror that her own heart could've been among them.

And then the priests were gone, as wordlessly as they had come. Miri didn't think the offertory priests tore out their tongues as well, since it wasn't mentioned in the hymns. Perhaps they considered these precincts too sacred to disturb with speech.

Deek's voice was a harsh rasp. "We're going the wrong way."

In normal circumstances, Miri would've made some retort about stating the obvious. Today she could find no words, just nod in agreement.

They tried to retrace their steps, hoping to find the point at which they'd gone wrong. Approaching from the opposite direction made the corridors look so different that neither Deek nor Miri was sure which way they'd gone the first time. Were they so completely lost they would wander until they perished, or some priest found them and hauled them back to the altar they'd fled?

They were just turning one corner when Deek pushed Miri up against the wall. "Don't look."

Too shocked to argue, Miri squeezed her eyes shut and let Deek guide her away. Only when they were safely back in the corridor from which they'd come did he explain.

"I always wondered why the priests of the offering blind themselves. I caught the merest glimpse of what lies beneath the Temple, but it was enough to know that if I'd seen it full-on, I would've torn my eyes from their sockets and been glad of it."

Miri stared at him in horror. Deek loved to fly. To willingly render himself incapable of ever taking the controls of an aircraft—

There was no time to dwell upon it. They had to find their way out of here. Let their legs guide them, alert to the strain of an upward-sloping corridors.

They were almost at the exit—they could smell the fresh air wafting down the corridor—when one of the scarlet-robed priests of the sacrifice stepped through a nearby doorway.

"What are you doing here?"

Even as Miri opened her mouth to gabble out some excuse. Deek lunged. His fist connected and the priest went sprawling across the floor.

"We can't let him identify us." Deek pulled his Covenant-seal over his head, doubled up the god-cord upon which it depended and looped it around the priest's neck. With a single jerk Deek garroted the man so hard it nearly took his head right off.

Miri stared open-mouthed at the double sacrilege. Never mind that she'd been a desecrator from the moment she'd decided to evade the altar and only pretended to drink from the chalice, actually seeing Deek use the most holy thing ordinary people touched to murder a man whose very flesh was sacred shook the foundations of her mind.

"We're going to the base. I'm putting a stop to this shit once and for all." Deek's voice was so icy, so hard, Miri couldn't argue, just followed behind him, numb and cold.

The sun had set, and the Blood Moon hung high and full in the sky. Its brother the Ichor Moon had already set, still too young to stay up late. At such an hour few people were about, which meant nobody challenged a man and woman riding double on a borrowed motorcycle at dangerous speeds.

As they approached the base, Miri wondered if Deek would have to kill yet again to get through the gate. However, the sentry just gave Deek a sleepy glance and opened the gate. By this time Miri had overcome her shock enough to wonder whether the sentry had forgotten the famous air ace had gone to the Temple as an oblate, or mistook him for another pilot who came and went at odd hours.

Deek led Miri across the open expanses with a confidence she tried to emulate. If someone saw them, looking nervous was the surest way to arouse suspicions.

She'd thought getting indoors would settle her nerves, but the quick duck inside to grab flight suits only made things worse. All she could think about was the distance to the closest exit, and how easily they could be cut off if someone came in and started asking questions for which there could be no satisfactory answers.

And then they were off to the flight line. Three strike fighters stood waiting on the apron, no doubt prepared by the evening crew for a patrol at first light. In the distance a sentry patrolled the hangars, but no one had been tasked to watch the airplanes.

Deek looked them over with an expert eye, settled on one and began the pre-flight checks. He helped Miri into the weapons officer's seat, then slid into the pilot's seat and lowered the canopy before finishing his checklist.

As they thundered down the runway, lights started going on all over the buildings they'd left behind. Miri caught a glimpse of running figures before the acceleration became too strong to turn her head against.

The g-forces vanished, and Miri realized they were airborne. Beneath her she could see the lights of the city laid out in a radial pattern like the maps her class had studied in school. Unlike the barbarian tribes who'd stolen the technologies of civilization and built their cities as randomly as the villages in which their ancestors had dwelt, the Servants laid out their dwelling-places in the orderly system the gods taught them.

Miri felt a flash of pride, but only for a moment before Deek's voice came over her helmet earphones. "I need you to arm the bombs so we can release them at the right moment."

Even as she reached for the arming switch he'd indicated for her back at the airbase, her hand began to shake. "I-I can't."

There was only the roar of the engines, then Deek's voice. "Take off your Covenant-seal."

His command tone should've spurred instant obedience, but it went against too many years of deep conditioning. To be sealed to the Covenant was an integral part of one's identity as a member of society.

Deek must've picked up her hesitation, because he shifted tones even as he circled for a second approach. "Do you know what's down there, what I just barely glimpsed? A mound of flesh so big you could barely see across it, all covered with gibbering three-lipped mouths, huge slobbering tongues licking out of them in endless search for fresh morsels to drag within and devour. That is the god we serve, Miri."

Disgust made the gorge rise in Miri's throat. She unzipped her flight suit enough to grab her Covenant-seal, to pull it over her helmet. How to get rid of it? She scanned the cockpit, spied a tube used to drop flares. Perfect.

She shoved the Covenant-seal through just as they closed in on the Temple. Now to arm and release the bombs before any of the other planes that must surely have scrambled could reach them—

\#

"Liu Shang! Liu Shang!" The voice had an urgency that cut through the layers of darkness that surrounded her mind. "Are you all right?"

She pulled up eyelids that seemed to be made of lead. "I think so."

Light hit her optic nerves, strangely bright until she remembered it wasn't being filtered through a layer of protective moonglass, just a planetary atmosphere. No wonder she felt so uncomfortable—she was lying on rough ground, and over her leaned the team medic.

The older woman's grave expression lightened, but only a little "You've given us quite a fright, young woman. What possessed you to ignore mission rules and go running off like that?"

Even as Liu Shang started to ask where she was, memory poured back into her mind of her nighttime trek, the discovery of the ancient medallion and the glimpse of the last days of the ancient civilization they'd been researching. So overpowering was the intrusive memory, it took her several minutes to realize she was babbling, a regular human core dump.

She looked down at the medallion still in her hand, this time careful not to examine the symbol upon it. "I don't think it was just a dream."

The medic's tone softened. "I don't think it was either."

Some distance away, other team members were already looking over the ruins. They must've overheard Liu Shang recounting her vision, because one of them remarked, "How are we going to let the locals know that they didn't win their freedom from the Star Tyrants? They won't like hearing their former overlords actually abandoned them as unworthy of further intervention. Not to mention the Faithful are going to have a field day--"

"Nah, they're just your usual religious fundamentalist wackjobs. At least here they're not sitting on half the planet's energy supply, so the rest of the locals should be able to take care of it."

Liu Shang winced at the callous reference to Earth's Energy Wars era, not to mention the unprofessional display of contempt toward a local faith community, to whom a scholar had a responsibility to be both objective and respectful. She'd been excited to make such a major discovery, but the thought that it would produce so much acrimony soured the triumph.

She clutched the medallion, briefly recalling the overwhelming fear and determination of those last moments in the other world. Mira and Deek had been brave people and deserved to be remembered well. Liu Shang hoped they had attained some kind of happiness together.

*Leigh Kimmel is a writer, artist, and entrepreneur living in Indianapolis, Indiana, a city better known for automotive racing. She has degrees in history and in library and information science and has worked in libraries and archives. You can learn more about her latest projects at her website, http://www.leighkimmel.com/ .*

The Great Diaspora seeded many planets with humanity, but the descendants of the pioneering spacers are finding little adventure in their routine lives on remote planets. Some of them spend most of their waking hours in dream chambers, suspended in their favorite fantasies. But not all dreams are what they seem.

# WELCOME TO YOUR DREAM HOUSE

### By

### *Steve Bates*

Jessica never saw the bumbler that stung Trevor. The silvery, thumb-sized insect might have become agitated by the staccato flashes of her son's bright yellow shirt as he bounced around the playground. Or perhaps some of the older boys had thought it amusing to prod a low-hanging nest with a stick. All she knew was that Trevor was stumbling toward her with one shoe off and his cherubic face awash in agony, pleading in a heart-melting tone, "Mommy, make it better." Engulfed by confusion and fear, she squeaked out "What happened, baby?" and propelled herself forward, extending her arms to receive her son, to embrace him, to make it all better.

This morning, Jessica could not remember making it all better.

She gazed at the framed picture of Trevor on her desk, desperately seeking the peace of mind and the strength to make it through the day. Rubbing her forehead hard with the heels of both hands, she cursed the headache, fatigue, and fog that were the residue of yet another restless night. The high-pressure job assignments, the far-flung planets, the extended intervals apart from her son. Everything was becoming jumbled, getting fuzzier by the day.

*How long have I been away this time? Six months? Or, as they calculate time on this edge-of-nowhere planet, 18 ten-days? How long until my work here is done, until I can hold Trevor in my arms again, until I can prove to him that Mommy always comes home?*

When she had accepted her job with Dream Homes Limited, the deal sounded reasonable. Hustle around the galactic neighborhood assembling subdivisions for a few years, get some time off with Trevor between assignments, and earn a promotion allowing her to settle in one place—with her son back in her life every day. Perhaps there would be time for romance, too.

Tall and thin, with a generous spirit, Jessica had never lacked for suitors. But her nomadic existence precluded lasting relationships, and the years were passing all too quickly. David, a rising star in the military with an easy smile, had seemed a solid match for a birthing contract. She wasn't even sure where David was stationed currently. Not that it mattered; Trevor was her life.

Jessica cast her cognition across the void as if she could witness her son passing this hour on Rhys 2. She envisioned him on the cusp of a peal of laughter, his hazel eyes sparkling mischievously after winning a game of hide and seek. But with only one primitive communications satellite still circling Sibelius 1, and the distance between them so great, she could reach out to Trevor only through recorded messages. She drew a deep breath, exhaled deliberately for several seconds, simulated a smile, and activated the holovid.

"Hi, Trevor. Your nanny tells me that you are doing really well in school, and I want to tell you how proud I am of you." She struggled to maintain her cheerful façade. "I'll be home soon . . . real soon. I can't wait to see you. But you know Mommy has important work to do. I . . . I love you, sweetie."

She waved a shaking hand before the device to end the recording. Her head sank onto a slender forearm and rested there for a long minute. Then she stacked the message for transmission once the commsat crested the horizon for another low, brief pass.

*How long until it too hits the atmosphere and fails?*

The front door alert sounded, driving nails into her nerves.

"We're sorry to bother you," said a short, sallow man with sunken, red-rimmed eyes. A similarly dissipated woman stood just behind him. They seemed like typical emigrants set adrift by the Great Diaspora. Generations ago, their ancestors turned their backs on a solar system rife with war and disease—and on everyone and everything they cared about—to submit to more than a century of coldsleep and an unimaginable future. Many descendants of those pioneers struggled to find purpose in life, and the escapes they pursued took many forms. The couple shuffling their feet at Jessica's door probably spent most of their waking hours in their dream chamber, and perhaps many nights as well.

"We're the Taylors, from 66 Reverie Road. There's a problem with our programming," the man stated.

Customer service wasn't part of Jessica's job description, but she was the only company representative on the planet. Making no effort to disguise her displeasure, she pushed past the couple and marched rapidly along the ochre-tinted plastic sidewalk. A few other dream home occupants ambled listlessly, caged by the grid of identical, perfectly spaced pre-fab houses. On a planet whose natives embraced all things natural, these structures scarred the soil like a pestilence. She kept her head down as she passed the five-meter-tall holosign proclaiming "Welcome to Your Dream House" in mammoth blinking letters and through a recurring jingle that could bring a grown woman to tears or homicide.

*The house of your dreams*
*Is closer than it seems.*
*Dream Homes Limited*
*Will make up your mind.*

She paused for a couple of breaths and to let the couple catch up with her. Despite her lengthy stay on Sibelius 1, she still felt beaten down by its strong gravity, the nearly perpetual twilight imposed by layer upon layer of clouds, and the paucity of seasons. To battle the bleakness, the yards of the dream houses were equipped with artificial foliage that owners could imbue with colors to suit their tastes. Today, imitation trees in several yards pulsated with bright reds and greens. A hazy recollection of an ancient festival tugged at a corner of Jessica's mind, but she brushed it aside.

She and the Taylors paraded through a sparsely decorated living room and into the couple's small dream chamber. Jessica settled into the nearest couch, an oversized recliner with controls on each armrest. She tensed involuntarily as millions of microscopically thin fibrous tendrils reached out and positioned themselves on the surface of her uncovered skin, bonding gently with her nervous system.

The dream chamber dissolved. Jessica was surrounded by exotic plants in vivid shades of green, splattered with bold crimson, orange, and white flowers. Acrobatic primates scaled towering trees in pursuit of succulent fruit, which injected tangy fragrances into the balmy breeze. Jessica recognized the distinct cries of more species of birds than she had believed could exist, though they were muffled by the constant splashing of a spectacular waterfall. Droplets of moisture tickled her face as she admired the rainbow that rimmed the scene. The Tropical Paradise dream software was among her company's most popular options, and she could understand why.

"What seems to be the problem?" she asked.

"It's the add-on programming," said Mr. Taylor.

Many dream house owners purchased supplemental software on the black market, usually porn. "I can't fix it," she said in a steely voice. "You should contact the manufacturer."

"Oh, it's working," responded Mr. Taylor. "Too well." He stabbed a button on the armrest of her couch. The erotic gyrations of U4ic—the lithe young chanteuse clad only in nearly transparent, form-hugging mist—were superimposed upon the tropical scene. "You see, this isn't just my private program," he stated, his face reddening as he turned toward Mrs. Taylor. "She bought it, too. Can you make her delete her copy?"

Jessica sprang from the couch, her anger blunting the abrupt transition from the simulated utopia to the drab reality of the dream house. She snarled "Get a life!" and stormed out the front door. Instantly, the comm chip positioned just below the surface of her cerebral cortex alerted her to a priority message relayed through the satellite.

"Display summary," she commanded. Keywords scrolled across the top of her field of view. "Law firm . . . David . . . court date . . . custody."

*Custody! David, you bastard, we have an agreement. Trevor is our son—my son! How can I get a lawyer and fight you from this backwater?*

She paced and shook until the tears could no longer be contained.

The trading post could be mistaken for the remains of some horrendous spaceport accident. Irregularly shaped wooden buildings were crammed together as if hurled from the hands of careless gods. The interior--chilly, musty, and dim--was a hoarder's paradise of exotic and mundane goods arranged in no logical order. Jessica passed well-worn saddles for some sort of pack animal and racks of simple, homespun tunics in shades of tan and brown. She held her nose as she maneuvered around crates of moldy root vegetables—a gesture that did not escape the notice of four locals who were seated at a small corner table, sharing a pipe that emitted a bitter fragrance that she could not identify.

Truly indigenous populations of sentient bipeds had proven to be rare as the Great Diaspora sprinkled settlements across the galaxy. But here, the natives' short and stocky build strongly suggested the infallible hand of natural selection over the eons. Plus, the locals spoke several languages in addition to standard Galactic 'Glish.

What's more, they did not believe in private property. One used what one needed. Nor did they accept compensation for labor. When work needed to be done, someone did the work. From the outset, Jessica found the native laborers to be smart and effective. It troubled her that they rarely spoke to her or to other off-worlders, but she came to realize that beneath that veneer of aloofness lay a substantial reservoir of pride and serenity.

*If I weren't in such a hurry to leave, I might actually learn to like these people.*

Soon after arriving on Sibelius 1, Jessica was advised that Gert, the trading post manager, was the guy to see for scheduling labor. Like many of the natives, he was almost a full head shorter than her. With thick, black, unkempt hair, he looked the part of the suffering poet. His expressions occupied a narrow spectrum from subdued to stoic, as if he would perish if he betrayed even a hint of a smile. However, it was Gert's propensity for lengthy periods of eerie silence and stillness that distinguished him. Many a visitor would swear that he had vanished like a specter when he had merely receded into a shadowy corner of clutter.

Jessica sauntered up to him. "Hi, Gert. I'm starting my final subdivision. Can you help me line up eight workers?"

Garbed in a dark brown tunic with a wide, cinnamon-colored belt, Gert was inspecting hunting equipment displayed on a dusty shelf. He did not respond.

Jessica noted that the four locals were monitoring the interaction intently while trying to appear disinterested. She continued, "We're not going to have a problem with the final development site, are we?"

Gert faced Jessica and clasped his hands in front of him. "There are other locations that you would find more . . . convenient," he stated.

For most of her time on Sibelius 1, Jessica had sensed that Gert was holding back something about the phase four site, a plateau about 40 kilometers from the spaceport. Surveys showed that it was uninhabited, though some of the largest settlements on the continent were clustered around the base of this and similar plateaus.

She decided to play her trump card. "Gert, we could make one of these last dream houses your new home."

"I have a home," he said without hesitation. "And the houses you produce are hardly conducive to dreams."

"'Dream house' is a marketing term," said Jessica. "A play on words."

"I understand, but I fear that you do not," Gert said in an atypically brusque tone. "Real dreams provide insight and guidance. They take us places that we cannot go during our waking hours." He continued in almost a whisper, "Some of my people believe that dreams can accord immense power."

"That . . . that's very impressive," she said, attempting to absorb his revelations, "but my bosses are determined to build on this site." With her coping skills suddenly exhausted, her lower lip began to tremble. She felt that she was perched on a precipice, holding on by the slightest of gossamer threads.

Gert stepped toward her and placed his left hand gently on her shoulder.

Jessica floated, suspended in a realm devoid of time and space and meaning. Though she felt no fear or pain, she had a vague perception of vulnerability, of being rendered naked to her marrow. It was as if she were being dissected cell by cell and reassembled.

The sound of Gert pouring water into a pot shattered the spell.

*Where was I? Oh yes, I need to prep for phase four.*

"Can I offer you some tea?" Gert inquired. "I have a blend that is highly favored among my people for its calming properties."

"Thanks, Gert, but not today," said Jessica. "Too much to do."

Pinpoints of light winked into existence across native villages as evening settled over the valley, meals of robust game and home-grown vegetables were prepared, and extended families gathered to share the day's joys and frustrations in snug cottages fashioned from dense hardwoods. The view from the construction staging area atop the plateau offered Jessica a rare moment of contentment.

*A simple life. And one I would love to experience someday.*

She renewed her determination to complete her work quickly and return to Trevor. Pivoting, she strolled toward the fenced area that held the 'synths. "'Synth" was short for biosynthetic creature, a product of the first successful fusion of metallic atoms with essential biological molecules. The breakthrough yielded creatures with unsurpassed strength and resilience—almost living, breathing machines. The 'synths simply ate everything in their path. Their enormous jaws filled powerful digestive systems that processed vegetation, soil, water, even rocks.

Each of Jessica's 'synths were about six meters wide and three tall. When she walked up to one and placed her palm against the side of its jaw, an electric, almost sexual thrill raced through her. Even when the 'synths were in standby mode, their hunger was palpable. At times, she thought that she could detect a gleam in their eyes.

*I wonder if they dream of electric sheep.*

But something was amiss. The plateau was too calm. At each previous development staging area, the arrival of the 'synths had sparked an immediate exodus of wildlife. Alarmed birds would blacken the sky as they streamed away, followed by galloping four-legged beasts and then by plodding and slithering animals, all sensing the annihilation that the 'synths would soon wreak.

It was the swarm of bumblers that shocked Jessica the most when she appeared at her first construction site, on the distant outpost of Halstead 4. There must have been ten thousand of them, pouring from the gnarly scrub and stunted trees and assembling into a comet-shaped array of angry insects orbiting each other in a rapidly accelerating frenzy. They hovered less than three meters before her, resembling a single predator with barely restrained malevolence. Suddenly, they leapt above and past her and melted into the afternoon sky. Jessica stood frozen in terror and amazement for uncounted minutes afterward, the memory of Trevor's painful encounter with a bumbler adding to her distress.

This evening, however, there were no bumblers, no panicked or departing creatures of any kind. She walked a few meters into the woods. Birds chirped sporadically. A pair of small animals sequestered in shadow crept toward a babbling creek. Jessica shook her head before turning and heading down the hill for what she expected would be another night of fitful sleep.

Occasional shafts of sunlight pierced clouds the next morning, promising a good day to build. However, there was no sign of the native workers and the housing components Jessica expected them to bring to the plateau. She decided to move ahead with site preparation anyway. On her signal, the 'synths commenced dredging earth, cracking boulders, snapping tree limbs, sucking up water, and expelling a fine loam in their wake.

After only a few minutes, they ground to a halt. Discovering no obvious malfunction, Jessica shifted them about 30 meters to the southwest. The 'synths resumed their devastation, but presently they stopped again. She encountered the same result at yet a third location.

Jessica perused survey reports, maps, and aerial views of the site. She determined that the plateau was formed by ancient volcanic activity and that it registered a strong concentration of certain rare minerals, but it was a fact that she almost overlooked that was telling. Each time that the 'synths halted, they were exactly 451 meters from the center of the development site. There was an imaginary circle around it, a boundary that they could not—or would not—cross.

*What wouldn't I give for a real-time connection off this world?*

She ordered the 'synths back into standby mode and entered the forest, outfitted with strong boots, water, a lightbeamer, a direction finder, and a map. On an upslope just east of a grove of nut-bearing trees, she thought that she could discern a narrow trail. Perhaps it was formed by animals seeking food or shelter; maybe it was an illusion. But it matched the direction she intended to travel. Soon after setting foot on the path, she realized that she no longer required her map or direction finder. She simply knew that she was on the proper course.

Several minutes later, she stopped dead in her tracks. Before her was a clearing that did not grace any map or image. A nearly perfect circle about 75 meters across was covered in knee-high grasses that undulated in the wind, the ripples recalling a pleasant sea voyage from Jessica's childhood. In the center sat a dilapidated wooden shack. The graying, splintered front steps and porch sagged under the weight of decades of neglect. Small portions of the roof had caved in, most window shutters had surrendered their positions, and exterior paint was barely a rumor. The structure bore all the marks of being abandoned, except for a thin plume of gray smoke ascending from a stone chimney. Jessica approached the shack and sang out "hello!" repeatedly. She climbed the steps cautiously and knocked on the door. Hearing nothing, she tried the door, opened it, and stepped inside.

Her breath caught as she beheld an interior she knew all too well—one of her very own dream houses. She turned and discovered that the door was closed and locked behind her. She wrestled with it, lightly at first, and then furiously. It would not budge. She sprinted through the house, testing doors and windows. None would open.

*There has to be some rational explanation.*

Jessica sat cross-legged in the center of the living room. She sipped water and willed her pulse to slow. A modest measure of calm descended upon her. But soon she was gripped by the odd sensation that someone or something was with her, a familiar presence that she could not identify.

Kaleidoscopic colors flickered and swirled on the far wall, coalescing gradually into an image. Jessica was watching herself. She was watching herself from a few years earlier, judging by the clothes and hairstyle. She was on Rhys 5, the planet where Dream Homes Limited was based.

The picture shimmered and re-formed. She saw herself in a small bed surrounded by machines in a room bathed in white. There was something attached to her head. Nearby, people in uniforms were clustered around a monitor. The monitor revealed an image of Trevor as he appeared when he was about nine months old. Trevor!

But no, she could see now that it wasn't Trevor. It was a boy who looked very much like him. Jessica could make out a few words: "taller . . . hair should be lighter . . ."

The colors on the wall faded and returned. There were more uniforms. A monitor displayed a slightly older boy whose face was morphing. At first, it was similar to Trevor's face. Then it took on a much closer resemblance. Finally, it resolved to appear just like him—in fact, exactly as he was depicted in the photo on her desk.

Jessica could watch no longer. Looking down, she saw that her fingernails had dug so viciously into her palms that blood was seeping.

Her primal shriek of rage rattled the building to its foundation. "No! No, it cannot be!" Jessica stood, placed her hands on her hips, and stared out at a horizon, light-years beyond the wall. "Trevor, do you hear me? You're my son. Mommy's coming home to you, right now."

Jessica struggled with the front door, with the back door, with every window, until her hands bled even more. She threw anything she could throw, even ramming her shoulder against the front door, before collapsing beside it.

Five minutes, or five years, could have elapsed. At some point, she decided that she needed to make sense of this encounter. She sought to revive memories of her first awkward embraces with David, her seemingly endless pregnancy, those messy morning meals with her child. But it was the vision of Trevor stung by the bumbler and toddling toward her that came to the fore— the nightmare that never died, a ribbon of pain stretched into a Mobius strip.

Rather than endeavor to escape it, Jessica concentrated all of her faculties on that image. Her son's pain-wracked face and curly brown hair began to pixelate and break up. His plea to "make it better" degraded into an echo reverberating from the end of a receding hallway. The arms that she reached out were dry, brittle sticks, without strength or direction.

She sought repeatedly to grasp and examine any fragment, any detail, of that scene. But every time she fixed her attention on one, it crumbled like a sand castle.

Refusing to succumb to panic, she attempted to re-experience the relief that she felt when the boy finally reached her, the elation that they shared as his little arms circled her waist, and the love that suffused them as he buried his tear-streaked face in her pounding chest.

*Even if I can't trust my memories, I know that my feelings are real.*

Again and again, she sought to capture those emotions—to dredge them up to the surface, to the present, to reality. She encountered only an absolute void. And, finally, she understood, beyond all doubt.

She never felt the joy of holding him. She never could make it all better.

A sickening ache swelled within her. The contract with David, the birth of her child, the future with Trevor she craved so deeply. It was all a dream manufactured and planted deep within her by a heartless corporation in order to manipulate her—and how many more people like her?

She rose, sought to force down her anger, and faced the wall where the images had appeared. She announced, "I believe you, whoever you are. I . . . I have no child. I am alone."

She waited for some sort of sign or response, but none manifested. She walked to the front door. As she expected, it opened readily. She stepped outside, went down the stairs, and strode six paces before turning around.

The shack, or house, was gone. Only a trace of chimney smoke remained. Jessica watched as it was swallowed by the afternoon breeze.

Gert and a customer were conversing with their backs to the main door as Jessica entered the trading post. After the customer departed with a bulging sack of gardening tools, Gert turned, matched Jessica's gaze briefly, then looked away. His eyes were steep craters on a lifeless moon, his face lined with dark rivulets of exhaustion.

*He looks like he hasn't slept in days. Then again, I probably look worse.*

"The medical shuttle will arrive late this ten-day," Gert said softly. "It is likely that one of the practitioners can remove your communications chip, though you might need to offer a bribe." There was no humor in his voice.

*He knows. Of course, he knows everything. He was there.*

"I am sorry that this happened to you," he continued. "Is there something that I can do to help?"

*My friend, you have already helped more than you can possibly imagine.*

Jessica wandered around the room, running her fingers along oversized cooking pots and thick-crusted loaves of brown bread as she weighed her words. "I suppose I need to find a new job," she said. "I don't think you can help me with that."

She wasn't sure which of them was more surprised when she approached Gert, placed her hand on his shoulder, and let it linger for a moment. "There is one thing you can do," she added, a thin smile playing on her lips. "I think I'm ready for that cup of tea."

*After a career in journalism, including 14 years as a reporter and editor at The Washington Post, Steve Bates is turning his focus to science fiction. Steve has published science fiction stories in publications such as* Perihelion, The Colored Lens *and* Aurora Wolf. *He lives in Ashburn, Virginia.*

*Steve is a longtime fan of Philip K. Dick, to whom this story is dedicated.*

General relativity creates a new Neverland.

# PAN AD ASTER

### By

### *Bruce C. Davis*

*A.D. 2245, Landing Year 76*

Start with a girl. A child really, no more than seven, running through a field of bright green flowers under a lemon yellow sky. She chases a pair of older boys, following the trail of trampled plants left in their wake.

"Jon, Gabe, wait up," she calls as her short legs pump up and down carrying her through the fragrant field.

The younger of the two boys stops and looks back. "Aw, Wendy, go on home," he says.

"No!" She stamps a small foot, filled with outrage and determination. "Mom told you to watch me, not leave me at home with the dog and the Nannybot. Now wait up."

"I didn't ask you to follow us," her brother retorts. "If you can't keep up, you'll just have to stay home."

The older boy stops as well and walks over to her. He bends down to look her in the eye and flashes a brilliant smile. He's nearly sixteen and large for his age, well-muscled, almost a man. She thinks he's the most beautiful person she's ever seen.

"Here, Wendy," he says. "Climb on up. I'll give you a piggy-back ride."

She sticks her tongue out at her older brother as she climbs onto Gabe's broad back. She wraps her arms around his neck, snuggling into his broad shoulder. He

255

sets out at a run. The wind whistles in her ears, her blond pigtails flap up and down with the rhythm of his strides.

*My Gabe*, she thinks. *He's mine.*

### A.D. 2247, L.Y. 78

See next the crowded terminal of a regional airport. He stands in the circle of friends and family, saying his goodbyes. She gazes up at him, taking in every detail of his new blue Cadet's uniform, all sharp creases and gold buttons.

Her father is talking, making some sort of speech as befits the planetary governor. Even she knows the title sounds more impressive that the job actually is. She thinks of him as her Dad, not the senior official of their small colony. She has eyes only for her young cadet.

"I won't let you down, sir," Gabe says, his face solemn. He shakes hands with her father, with Jon, with several other men she doesn't know, but whom she has seen in meetings with her father. She only sees her Gabe.

She's two years older and several centimeters taller, her body even now hinting at the woman she will become. With a self-control beyond her years, she holds back tears as he rumples her hair and flashes that brilliant smile, saying goodbye to his best friend's little sister in an offhand way. Then he turns and walks away, down the ramp to the waiting shuttle.

*He will come back to me*, she tells herself. *He will.*

### A.D. 2259, L.Y. 90

The young couple lies in each other's arms as early morning sunlight streams through the window of a hotel room near that same airport twelve years later. He sleeps on but she is awake, holding him with a fierce possessive embrace, as if he might float away. She traces the curve of his ear with her fingertip.

*He came back to me*, she thinks with a mixture of satisfaction and wonder.

He opens his eyes and sees that she is awake and watching him. That same brilliant smile lights up his face and it nearly takes her breath away, just like it always has.

"Hey, Wendy," he says, shift his arm beneath her head. "Didn't your Mama ever tell you not to sleep with Spacers?"

She laughs. "My Mama tells me lots of things. I don't listen very well. She thinks I've been chasing you shamelessly ever since you came home."

"Well, you have." He dodges her hand as she reaches to tickle his ribs. "Not that I'm complaining, mind you, but once in a while the guy likes to feel like he's the hunter and not the prey. I never expected anything like this."

"I'm just a girl who knows what she wants." She turns his face to hers, kissing his lips and drawing his hips toward hers.

He returns her kiss, feeling her passion and its promise. He pauses; still amazed at the change in her. He smiles again.

"I never would have recognized you if you hadn't been standing with your mother and Jon when they came to pick me up at the shuttle port," he says. "Look at you. I go away for a couple of years and you grow up on me."

"It may have been only a couple of years for you but it's been twelve for me. I'm older than you are now, Gabe. Do you miss the little girl in pigtails?"

"Time dilation does that. It's why Spacers are so clannish. The people we leave behind age and change while we stay the same." He kisses her again. "In this case, the change has been nothing but good."

She hugs him to her neck. "I've waited my whole life for you, Gabe. I've loved you since I could walk. Didn't you know that?"

"Not until now," he sighs. He kisses the curve of her neck, now subdued and serious.

She senses the change in his mood. "What is it?" she asks.

"I'm shipping out tomorrow. We're transporting a new colony stake to Tau Ceti, twenty-four light years away."

She holds her breath, waiting for the words she both longs for and dreads.

"Come with me, Wendy. I have enough back pay saved to pay for your passage. The Captain can marry us as soon as we break orbit. Then you'll be Ship's Company, just like me, part of the Ship's family. The quarters are a bit cramped, but the Ship is designed for crew to bring their families along. Otherwise, our wives and husbands would be old and our children grown before we completed even an average mission. Marry me, Wendy."

The seven-year-old girl inside of her wants to scream, "Yes! Yes!" but the adult she has become hesitates. Since her father's death, her mother has become even more dependent on her, clinging childishly to her only daughter. Jon has long since left home. He has his career, flying transports for a local airline. He leaves the care of their mother to Wendy.

She gazes out the window, struggling with guilt at her desire to abandon them, essentially forever. The silver outline of a waiting orbital shuttle far out on the tarmac gleams in the morning light. It beckons to her, promising freedom, promising love.

She pulls him to her and holds him with renewed passion. "Yes, Gabe. Yes."

He leaps out of bed with a joyful whoop, startling her. He sweeps her up in her arms, murmuring promises in her ear. She clings to him, still frightened at the idea of leaving home forever.

After a long minute he pulls away, saying, "I have to go to the Ship." He pulls a flat data card from his flight bag and hands it to her. "Your ticket and immigration documents are on here." He shrugs in answer to her puzzled look. "I didn't know for sure you'd say yes, but didn't want to take a chance on some last minute bureaucratic snafu. I'll have to be on the bridge during departure. I'll meet you in your cabin as soon as we break orbit and we'll go to the Captain. She'll absolutely flip! I can't wait to see her face. You'll love her." He goes on, telling her how to get to the shuttle and where her cabin will be on the starship. She only half hears him, wondering how she will find the words to tell her mother.

She rushes home, excitement overwhelming her fears. She will simply announce her plans to her family, leaving no room for discussion. *Jon has had it too easy for too long*, she thinks. *He'll just have to step up and deal with Mother without me.*

As soon as she walks in the door, she knows something is terribly wrong. Her mother sits in a chair; her hands limp in her lap. She doesn't stir as Wendy crosses the room.

"Mother? Mother what is it? What's wrong?"

Her mother finally looks at her, her face a mask of despair, her voice full of accusation. "Where have you been, Wendy? Why didn't you come home? It's Jon. Some kind of crash, they said. They want us down at the hospital right away, but I couldn't find you. Where have you been?" she dissolves into tears, asking the question over and over.

Wendy holds her close, fighting down the cold nausea and fear in the pit of her own stomach.

The trip across town to the hospital is an agony of uncertainty. Her mother says little, only sobs and clings to her arm, more child than woman.

*She's not going to be able to handle this*, Wendy thinks. *It isn't fair. Why do I have to be the adult? Maybe it won't be that bad. If Jon's not too badly injured, I can get some of his friends or the Company to step in. I might still make it to the ship on time.*

When they finally reach the hospital her hope surges. The receptionist is cheery and reassuring. They are taken to a comfortable lounge and given coffee. She eyes the time warily, minutes and then an hour crawling by.

What hope she managed to hold dies as they are led into the intensive care unit. Nurses and technicians move purposefully back and forth, hardly sparing them a glance. A young doctor introduces himself. She doesn't catch his name.

"Where is he," her mother demands. "Where is my baby?"

Unbidden, the resentment surfaces again. *Her baby. Always it's Jon, her first, her baby. And what about me, Mother? I'm here. What about me?*

They are shown into a smaller room, crowded with humming, buzzing equipment and flashing lights. At first she is confused. Where is her brother? Then she sees the oblong glass box, the vaguely human shape floating inside in a pool of milky fluid. All she can hear is her mother's wail.

The rest of the day fragments into a blur of doctors and nurses and glimpses of her brother through the fluid of the biotank. His skin is nearly black with burns and there is a large hole in his scalp. The doctors tell her that his burns and wounds will heal, but his brain may be permanently damaged. He will need care, they say, for a long time.

She makes her decision then, although she doesn't admit it, even to herself, until much later.

*A.D. 2320, L.Y. 151*

Finally, in the crowded terminal of a star port, a young couple stands in the circle of family and friends, saying their goodbyes. He is still tall and strong, his new Captain's bars gleaming on the worn collar of his trim uniform. She stands next to him, flush with excitement. Her blond hair is pulled back, her face the image of her Grandmother's in younger times.

An old woman stands near the newlyweds, waiting until the crowd of well-wishers thins out, their farewells spoken and hugs exchanged. Only then does she step forward and embrace her granddaughter.

"Good bye, Moira," she whispers in the young woman's ear. "Remember us. Remember your family."

"I will, Grandma. I love you."

"I know dear. We'll miss you both. Now, if your new husband will indulge an old woman, I'd like a word with him alone. Oh, don't worry, dear. I won't reveal any of your embarrassing secrets. He'll have to find those out for himself."

She laughs and relinquishes his arm. "Watch yourself, Gabe," she says. "Grandma is famous for her 'good advice', and woe to those who don't follow it."

They walk away from the crowd, the young Captain and the old woman. They seem strangely linked; their strides matching exactly as they walk slowly down the promenade of shops that line the terminal waiting area.

"It's good to see you again, Wendy. You look wonderful," he says, not sure of what she wants from him.

"You don't lie very well, Gabe," she says lightly. "But thank you for the effort." She sighs before continuing. "Take care of Moira. She's my only granddaughter. I see in her face that she loves you. I need to know that you'll return her love. That this is the real thing."

"I will, Wendy. She's all that I've ever wanted. After you missed the Ship, I was devastated. I thought I'd never find anyone else. Meeting Moira was like getting a second chance." He pauses. "Does she know about us?"

"No. As far as she's concerned, you're just an old family friend." She stops and turns to face him. She looks up at him and strokes his cheek with the back of her hand. "Dear, sweet Gabe. Do you know that in sixty years, not a day has gone by that I haven't thought of you; haven't wondered where you were and wished you well?"

He looks away, uncomfortable, unsure how to answer her.

She laughs. "Oh, no, dearest. I don't want you to be unhappy. I tell you this only so that you'll know that you are loved and have been loved for all of my life. I don't regret my decision, my marriage to Andrew, my children and grandchildren. They were the blessings of a long life. You were the dream of my youth, but now I'm ever so much more than twenty. You are Moira's dream now. She is the hope of my old age. She loves you as I did. Love her in return, honor her."

She reaches up to touch his cheek again. He takes her hand and kisses her palm. The old thrill of his touch courses through her. She turns and walks away, her steps light, filled with the joy of a young girl in a field of green flowers.

*Bruce Davis is a Mesa, Arizona, based general and trauma surgeon. He finished medical school at the University of Illinois College of Medicine in Chicago way back in the 1970's and did his surgical residency at Bethesda Naval Hospital. After 14 years on active duty that included overseas duty with the Seabees, time on large grey boats, and a tour with the Marines during the First Gulf War, he went into private practice near Phoenix, Arizona. He is part of that dying breed of dinosaurs, the solo general surgeon. He also is a writer of science fiction novels. His works include the YA novel* Queen Mab Courtesy, *his military science fiction novel* That Which Is Human, *and the* Profit Logbook *series, including* Glowgems For Profit, Thieves Profit, *and* Profit and Loss. *His nonfiction memoir,* Dancing in the Operating Room, *is a glimpse into the life and training of a Trauma Surgeon.*
*The Website: www.thatwhichishuman.com*
*The Blog: www.dancingintheor.wordpress.com*

Rachel is falling. She falls for her parents' plan to colonize the planet Tobar. She falls in love with Brian and their new life together. Then, she falls under the mysterious magic of the sentient people of the new world.

# RACHEL'S FALL

### By

### *Teresa Howard*

Rachel glanced across the colony's multipurpose auditorium, hoping to see Brian. He was sitting in the second row, sipping what passed for coffee on Tobar. He looked up and smiled at her, sending a delicious sensation rippling from her stomach all the way to her toes. Slowly, she maneuvered through a group of milling colonists and joined her future husband.

Like most of the furnishings on the new colony, the benches had been transported from Earth and were constructed from a lightweight and durable metal material, easily assembled, but not comfortable. Ignoring the cold hard surface, Rachel snuggled closer to Brian and ran a thumb along the back of her recently acquired engagement ring. The beautifully set marquis diamond had once belonged to Brian's great-grandmother.

The meeting began with a long series of committee reports, and then digressed into a general grievance session. The warmth of Brian's body and the dullness of the meeting relaxed and numbed Rachel's senses. She had almost drifted off when the tone of her father's voice changed.

"When we first met on Earth over two years ago, we vowed to start a new life here on Tobar. Tonight I am pleased to announce a major step in that process. After much consideration, I have agreed to the engagement of my lovely daughter Rachel Elizabeth Saunders to Junior Agricultural Engineer Brian Evans. Their wedding will coincide with the one-year anniversary of our arrival on this new world." Applause and whoops of joy cut off the rest of the speech. Commander Saunders, grinning broadly, raised a hand for silence. "To commemorate that anniversary we will also be giving Tobar base 627 its official name. Be thinking of something suitable, put it in the suggestion box, and we will bring it up for vote at a future meeting." There was another thunderous round of applause and then Brian and Rachel were bombarded with hugs and congratulations.

Overwhelmed by so much attention, Rachel stayed close by Brian's side, greeting their friends and well-wishers with shy smiles and whispered thanks. In the back of the room a pale-faced Mrs. Caldwell urgently pulled at Dr. Brasher's arm, causing a murmur of concern from those nearby. Rachel nudged Brian and nodded toward the doctor's retreating figure. "Something's wrong. I hope there hasn't been an accident."

The sad news made its way across the settlement the next morning and greeted Rachel as she emerged from her room for a late breakfast. The youngest Caldwell child, a cute redheaded girl barely five years old, was dead, and all of the Caldwell children had the raging fever and vile-smelling skin eruptions that seemed to characterize the disease. An isolation unit had been set up in the hospital and doctors and scientists were monitoring the children and their parents.

Rachel looked anxiously at her father and asked the question circulating throughout the colony. "How could this happen? We've been immunized against the natural bacteria and viruses on Tobar, haven't we?"

"Yes, we were immunized, but there are no absolute guarantees in situations like this. We knew that going in." He reached out and stroked her hair. "Dr. Brasher and his team are doing everything they can to find out what this is and how to stop it."

The day grew tragically worse. Seven more children died and a quarter of the 600 colonists were showing symptoms of the mysterious illness. No one was responding to treatment. Rachel shared a quick lunch with Brian. All the excitement and joy she had felt the night before seemed a distant memory. He told her in the grim tones of an undertaker that the Tobar colony had been quarantined and declared off limits by Space Command Central.

"They can't abandon us!" Rachel's throat constricted with outrage and fear.

"They can't abandon us. It's only been one day. We haven't had time to determine what this is. It might not even be contagious."

"They'll send down whatever medical supplies we need, but no captain would risk contaminating his ship or crew, not to mention carring this disease back to Earth."

"He's right, honey. I recommended the quarantine myself." Rachel's father said as he joined them. His usually crisp features sagged and his skin was almost as gray as his hair. He was a man on the edge of defeat and it broke her heart to see the resignation in his eyes. "If you're finished eating, I need you to transcribe a meeting."

Rachel started to ask why his assistant, Ruth, wasn't transcribing, but the look in his eyes stopped her. Ruth Barber and her husband were her father's best friends, and he had convinced them to join the colony.

*Damn it! This shouldn't be happening. This isn't an exploratory mission. The first men landed on Tobar years ago. At least ten years of research and preparation have gone into the colonization project.*

Rachel leaned forward to kiss Brian and he pulled away. The colonists had been warned to limit physical contact, but this felt like a slap in the face. *My God, he's afraid to touch me.* She turned quickly to follow her father.

Sensing her emotion, Commander Saunders spoke in a soft voice. "Don't be angry with Brian. He helped carry people into the isolation unit all morning. We don't have many biohazard suits and the doctors and nurses need those."

"He didn't tell me." Rachel turned and looked back at Brian. She blew him a kiss, which he caught and clutched to his heart in an exaggerated pantomime.

Martin Byrd, the colony translator and interspecies liaison, was waiting in her father's office.

"I hope this isn't a waste of time, Martin. What can we expect to gain by involving the Epicatu in this?" Commander Saunders asked.

Martin drew himself up, using his six-foot-three-inch frame to full effect. "The Epicatu may be primitive, but they are sentient. They may have seen this disease or something similar before and know a treatment. Don't you think we should at least hear what they have to say?"

Rachel's father held up his hand. "You're right of course, and you can count on me to keep an open mind. But, as we're all busy, let's keep the meeting brief."

Martin Byrd hurried to get the Epicatu visitors while Rachel set up the transcription machine. There were always video and audio recordings, but given the unreliability of electric power on the colony, a hard copy transcription of each meeting was mandatory.

Rachel had never been face to face with the Epicatu. Only authorized personnel were allowed to interact with the natives. The door opened again and instead of Chief Ninatat an ancient Epicatu strode in carrying a tall staff decorated with a combination of intricate carvings, feathers, and flowers. Patches of thinning fur, yellowed teeth, and the stiff ungraceful movements of his limbs proclaimed his great age. With one fisted hand he beat a rhythm on his breastplate then let out a series of shrill clicks and whistles.

Rachel began the transcription with his introduction, ignoring the jumble of sounds the visitor made and concentrating on Martin's translation. "We have heard of the sickness among the naked sky-people. I am Nabunabu, the oldest and wisest of Epicatu, and I have come with a message from the Spirits concerning this evil."

"We are honored to receive such a distinguished visitor." Her father's voice was a mellow contrast to the harsh whistles, clicks, and shrieks of the Epicatu and the high nasal twang of Martin's voice.

Nabunabu shook his staff violently, threw back his head, and uttered a cacophony of sounds so loud Rachel winced. Giving his head a shake, Martin began to translate.

"You men who have come naked from the sky have no right to be here. The hand of the goddess Hatako is against you. You will die."

Commander Saunders answered calmly. "The naked sky-people are friends of the Epicatu. We live in peace with you."

Nabunabu waved the staff menacingly. "Hatako has spoken. The naked sky-people must make sacrifice or they will all die." One of his yellow eyes wandered in Rachel's direction. "A pure daughter of the naked sky-people must sacrifice herself to Hatako from the cliffs above the Mother River."

An exasperated oath exploded from Commander Saunders. Martin's tone never changed, but tension oozed from every muscle in his body. "It is not the way of the naked sky-people to do such a thing."

Nabunabu's reaction was less than courteous. He furiously brandished his staff, emitting a protest of sounds so piercing that Rachel dropped the transcription pen and covered her ears. Martin did not translate. It took several more minutes to calm the Epicatu and escort him out.

"That was certainly a damnable waste of time," Commander Saunders said. "Even if I believed that nonsense, I couldn't ask anyone to make that kind of sacrifice. Not a word of it goes outside this room. Most of the colonists are level-headed people, but they're afraid, and desperate people do crazy things."

Martin nodded. "You're right. We don't need to add to the panic. If anyone asks, we'll say the Epicatu don't know anything about this disease, but the chief sent a holy man to pray for us."

As Martin left, the door sounded like a coffin lid shutting down on all her dreams.

"Rachel?" Her father's voice cut through the fear.

She couldn't bring herself to look at him. She nodded and fumbled with the transcription machine, blinking away tears.

"Rachel." He came over and gently freed the device from her hands. "I think we should erase that."

"Are we going to die?" The words tumbled out.

A father's strong arms pulled Rachel into a rough embrace and pressed her face against his uniform. Tears beaded on the fabric like raindrops on the giant leaves of the palm-like plants in the forest, only those weren't really palm trees and this wasn't Earth.

"Not everyone." He paused, and Rachel listened to the sound of his heartbeat and felt the rise and fall of his chest against her face as he struggled to contain his own emotions. "Many people may die, but some people could have a natural immunity to the disease. Those people will live and hopefully pass that immunity on to their offspring. If that happens, the colony will survive."

*But, what if they don't? What if the Epicatu are right?* Rachel kept those fears to herself. She wiped at the tears clinging to her father's uniform and tried to smile at him. He needed her to be brave, so she tried.

It was late afternoon when Rachel stumbled outside. The fresh air lifted her spirits. It was her favorite thing about this new world, so clean and sweet-smelling after Earth's noxious atmosphere. She looked up at the rose colored sky and then smiled almost defiantly at the next person walking by. She needed Brian. Rachel wanted to feel him hold her and kiss her. She wanted him to make love to her, until all the fear of dying was driven from her body by sweat and passion.

Rachel headed toward the single men's barracks hoping to find Brian in his apartment. The yellow tape and black words barring the door slashed her heart with a force so brutal it almost stopped beating. Turning, she ran as fast as she could toward the hospital.

"Rachel, you can't go in there, it's quarantined." Dr. Brasher stood on the concrete steps blocking her way.

"Brian's in there."

"I know. He was brought in a few hours ago, while we were in the meeting with the Epicatu. His mother wanted to come and tell you, but he said no. He didn't want to interrupt the meeting."

Rachel dropped down to the dirt and buried her face in her hands. Dr. Brasher stood and let her cry for a while, then jerked her to her feet. "You aren't doing yourself or Brian any good wallowing in the dirt and crying yourself sick. Go home now and get some rest. Come back tomorrow and you can transcribe some of my notes. If we can't cure this thing, at least I want to leave a clear record of what we've tried. That will be important for future colonists."

Word of Brian's illness had already reached her father, and he was waiting for her at home. Taking her in his arms he murmured hopeful reassurances. "Don't give up hope, honey. Brian's a strong young man."

Rachel nodded and followed her father to the dinner table. Though she tried to eat, her throat seemed to have forgotten how to swallow. After chewing and choking on a few bites of stew, she excused herself and went to her room. The wildflowers Brian had given her the day before still sat on the table beside her bed. She hadn't had a vase to put them in, so Rachel had stuffed the flowers into a red plastic glass and filled it with water. Fresh tears filled her eyes.

To let in some of the cool night air, Rachel pushed open the window. She lay across the bed, her fingers absently rubbing the blanket. Though it felt different, it was the same waterproof, and fireproof fabric as her father's uniform.

Rachel tried to sleep but she couldn't get the old Epicatu's words out of her mind. Erasing that transcription violated colonization regulations. It had been the right thing to do, but her father could lose his position if the Council on Earth found out. Rachel laughed then choked back a sob. She rolled onto her back and tried to picture Brian's face, but she kept seeing the old Epicatu's yellow eye, glaring at her, silently rebuking her. Exhaustion finally brought her sleep. In her dream he was standing at the foot of her bed shaking that strange staff and screeching at her, trying to tell her something. She woke trembling with fear. She knew what she had to do, but to do that she had to get away. She pulled on her jumpsuit and shoes.

Rachel could hear her father's deep breathing as she passed his room in the dark house. She slipped out without waking him and breathed in the cool night air.

The road was little more than a cleared path through the jungle, and the utility vehicle jarred and bruised her already battered nerves. When the road ended at a broad river about 10 miles from camp, Rachel sat there staring out at the dark water. Two days ago she had been a happy young woman in love and planning her wedding. Rachel beat her fists on the steering wheel, and then sucked at her bruised knuckles.

*Why is this happening?*

High-pitched screeches pierced the stillness of the night. Epicatu appeared from the shadows and surrounded the jeep. Their frenzied dance and shrieks ripped into her raw nerves. Rachel covered her ears and began to sob. One voice thundered above the rest, issuing commands. The Epicatu lowered their voices and the earsplitting dissonance changed to something akin to a melody. It was such a startling transformation that Rachel stopped crying and stared through the plexi window at the circling Epicatu.

The old wise man nodded and motioned for Rachel to get out. Rachel remembered the warnings about the possible dangers of being alone with the natives and shook her head. He continued to beckon. She hesitated but gave in as the songs became more beautiful, imploring her to join in some celebration. When she stepped from the vehicle the sounds became almost joyous. The Epicatu danced before her and scattered flowers on the ground at her feet. They began to move away from the jeep and Rachel followed. The moons were high, giving light. Although rough in some places, the path appeared to be well traveled. Caught up in whatever the Epicatu were experiencing, Rachel's feet seemed to move independently, taking her farther and farther from the jeep. She found it impossible to think or to feel. She allowed herself to be led up a steep slope until she had to stop and bend forward to catch her breath.

The singing faded. Rachel's mind began to clear as if she were waking from a deep sleep. The Epicatu had disappeared into the night. She had been led to the edge of the cliffs overlooking their valley and what they called "Mother River". She could see fires and the outline of their village in the distance. They looked near, but Rachel knew that jagged rocks and a swift flowing river were between the cliffs and the village. Realizing why the Epicatu had led her to the cliffs, Rachel scrambled back from the edge.

Tears trickled down her face as images of Brian, her father, and the other colonists appeared before her. She blinked the visions away and inched closer to the edge, peering into the dark abyss below. For a moment she imagined she saw Brian again, smiling at her, his arm around a strange young woman and a little boy. She choked back tears and called into the darkness "I'm afraid to die. Show me that this is the way to save them and I will do it. I just need to believe."

As if in answer, large white avians sprang from nests among the cliff front, moonlight illuminating their nocturnal flight. They soared upward and then, swooping down inches from her outstretched hands, they beckoned for Rachel to join them.

*Is this a sign?*

She squatted down and began clearing a narrow path. Rachel tossed aside rocks, dead tree branches and other debris as she moved away from the edge. Satisfied that the way was clear, if not smooth, Rachel wiped her hands and turned to face her destiny. With a cry that held all of her pain, fears, and hopes she launched herself forward.

She flung her arms wide and rushed past the edge. Her momentum carried her out several feet before she began to plunge down, down. She closed her eyes and felt a strange ripping sensation. Suddenly she was soaring upward, surrounded by hundreds of the beautiful white birds, and she was one of them, her snowy wings carrying her higher and higher.

Commander Saunders came fully awake at the sound of urgent banging on the door.

"I'm coming." He got up and threw on yesterday's jump suit.

The beaming face of the chief medical officer shone in the artificial light. Saunders opened the door.

"It's a miracle!" Dr. Brasher threw his arms around Commander Saunders. "Only one patient died last night and no one else has come down with the symptoms. I can't even find a trace of the disease in anyone in quarantine."

After a few minutes of shocked silence, Commander Saunders asked, "Brian?"

"He's fine, anxious to see Rachel, but fine. If he continues to show no symptoms, I'll release him tomorrow."

"I'll get Rachel."

His face was a mask of confusion when he came back down alone. "She's not there."

Fear, like a tiny snake coiled and dangerous, raised its head. Commander Saunders tried to control his panic. Surely Rachel wouldn't do anything stupid.

When a quick check revealed that Rachel had taken one of the utility transports, he jumped in another and headed out. Finding the abandoned vehicle, he followed the trail of flowers to the edge of the cliff. In the soft morning sunlight, he saw Rachel's body lying on the rocks below. He called for help. It took hours for a team to work its way around the cliff and retrieve her broken body.

Sounds of celebration echoed from the Epicatu camp. As he stood looking down at the tarp covered body of his beloved Rachel, Commander Saunders wished that he could believe.

A chorus of avian voices drowned out Dr. Brasher's assurances that Rachel's death had been instantaneous and probably painless. Commander Saunders looked up. Large white avians danced in the air above him. One bird circled, swooped low, and then rose into the air again. Pastel confetti floated in the air. In astonishment Saunders felt something soft on his face. He reached up and brushed flower petals from his hair. His eyes continued to follow the bird's flight as it returned to the cliffs. There he saw the day's second miracle, a stream of water flowing down the face of the cliff where none had been before. He reached out his hand, pointing, yet unable to speak. Gradually the stream increased until it became a mighty cascade rushing into the river below. A hush fell over the group of mourners.

"I see it, but I don't believe it." Dr Brasher whispered in awe.

"I believe." Commander Saunders wiped at the tears on his face. "I believe."

*Teresa Howard is a life-long fan of science fiction and fantasy. For many years, she was employed as a technology coordinator and computer lab instructor at a local elementary school in Birmingham, Alabama. She dreamed of writing science fiction and fantasy,*
*In 1991, Teresa first attended Dragon\*con in Atlanta. There she participated in beginning and advanced writer's workshops by Ann Crispin and others. She became a member of the DC2K Writers group,*

*which formed at Dragon\*con in 2000, and still enjoys attending conventions and meeting and networking with others in the Science Fiction and Fantasy field.*

*Teresa's published stories cover a wide range of the speculative fiction genre and include children's stories, science fiction, fantasy, and some horror. Her short stories have been published in magazines, anthologies, webzines, and on IPhone apps in the U.S., Canada, and the U.K. She is often found at a corner table in a local bookstore working on her latest writing project.*

On a world where two dominant species co-exist, which one will survive to rule the planet?

# WHEN UNKNOWN GODS LEAVE

### By

### *Margaret Karmazin*

I hid beneath a kitrine rock formation, one of thousands in this eastern coastal area of Masween. We had briefly stepped outside in order to transmit more efficiently to the nearest receiving station in space.

Masween has only one massive continent sitting in the midst of a vast, sparkling sea. The roar of the ocean could be easily heard through distant weapon fire. I found it hard to imagine that those peaceful shoreline spots I'd once visited with my father had now been reduced to rubble.

North Americas University was sponsoring my study here in the midst of Earth Reconstruction. How did they come up with funds for it? I was amazed to be offered the post since I'd assumed the luxury of anthropological studies was a thing of the past. When your own world is recovering from disaster, you'd hardly imagine there would be time, money or energy to spend on peripheral scientific studies, especially those on other worlds.

"It is vital to all living creatures that we study Masween," said my mentor and head of the anthropology department, Dr. Lane Escobar. She is the world's best known Exo-anthropologist. "It's essential not just to humans, but to all sentient creatures, indeed anything, sentient or not, that populates a planet and is vulnerable to the horrors of violence and war. You're being sent on a mission, not just a scientific venture."

"Why me?"

"You're young and adaptable, you make the best of any situation you seem to be in and no one else is willing to go." She smiled.

"What you mean is, I'm expendable."

"I didn't say that, Galen, just go and do the job. And pray that you return to us safely. Now let me do what I can to contribute to clean up."

She was referring to the devastation left from the plague. The one in which my parents and sister had perished.

I didn't want to talk about that. On my way out, I did say, "They should change the word 'anthropology.' 'Anthro' refers to 'human' and what I'm going to observe won't be human."

She flashed her brilliant white teeth. In her sixties, she looked to be thirty-five. Before the latest pandemic, she'd obviously taken a rejuvenation. Now, of course, such things were no more. Plain survival was the name of the game. She said, "The prefix now means 'sentient being.' Get with it, Galen. And don't forget the language."

She was referring to the crystal implanted in my head that would receive the official language of Masween. I downloaded as directed and soon could speak and understand that alien tongue.

I loved Lane Escobar and it pained me to think that possibly I would never see her again. For that matter, I might never see Earth again. I was about to enter a war zone.

The vast majority of known planets that harbor sentient life have one ruling species. We know of three that break this rule: one on which the dominating two species have barely reached the stone age, another is closed off to interaction, and Masween, where I landed twelve days ago. Less than one Masween year ago (equivalent to sixteen Affiliated Planets Months), their mysterious overlords, the Abbas, who had held their world in a state of peace since the beginning of their recorded history, left without explanation.

"Tell me again exactly what happened," I said to Porter Range, our ambassador to Masween, who no longer occupied his former comfortable residence in the Capitol but a tent made from the hide of the abrak. Porter had by now packed the tent up and moved four times to save his own hide. We met at a relatively safe distance from the current east coast battle, which ran from the Cliffs of Koor to Giwaar Peninsula.

"Three hundred thousand dead just this past week. The slaughter is relentless. At this rate, the Kossi will be extinct in two years."

"Aren't they fighting back?"

Porter shifted the overly large laser he had hanging from a strap so that it would bang into his other hip for a change. "You know the Kossi, or probably you don't. Most peaceful beings this side of Alpha Centauri. Their sole interest outside of math, music, gardening and simultaneous hermaphrodite sex, is cooking their godawful stews. Murder and mayhem have never been on their pleasure list. But the Riwa? One would never have guessed the depths of their depravity. Pure savages."

"No sign of it under the Abbas?"

"From my limited experience, I would say no. We still don't understand exactly how the Abbas controlled the population here, nor did we realize that the main and perhaps only target of that control was the Riwa. Since the control has been lifted, the Kossi haven't changed except to demonstrate they are apparently ineffective at defending themselves. And even with the threat of imminent death, they seem to lack serious interest in the matter and are mainly concerned with getting back to life as it was before. I am terrified for them."

"Have you ever liked the Riwa?"

Porter looked off to the east after another explosion sounded. "I've enjoyed friendships with several Riwa. I even had a brief sexual relationship with one before she was forced to marry her cousin. Her clan feared that I'd impregnate her and wouldn't listen to me that it was genetically impossible."

"Did they threaten you?" I didn't add that I thought his engaging in such a relationship as an ambassador was reckless, but, hey, things happened on lonely outposts.

"Not at all," he said. "Before the Abbas left, the Riwa were a generally rational and seemingly kind people. Far from understanding our level of technology and psychology, but certainly pleasant to deal with. Their religion was big on forgiveness and all that."

The screech of a bomb soaring overhead caused us to duck and cover. The resulting explosion some miles off heightened my growing terror. Why on earth had I agreed to come here?

"What happened to that religion now?" I asked. We had three human soldiers with us, armed to the hilt and now rechecking their weapons.

Porter shook his head. "Apparently out the window. All that seems to matter to them is to rid the earth of Kossi. Apparently, the friendly relationship they once had was a complete illusion."

"An illusion held in place," I said, "by the force of the Abbas, whatever that mysterious force was."

I watched Porter for a moment, noting the ashen color of his dark skin, the terror in his eyes. "I never imagined," he said, "that when I took this job all of this would fall apart. It was a wonderful, peaceful world, albeit not what I'd consider a normal one with the Abbas hovering up there, but it was a position any diplomat would envy. I'm not cut out for what it's become, Galen."

"Why don't you go home then?"

He looked away. "I can't. It's my father. Everyone knows he never believed in me, always implied I'm a quitter. If I go back, it'll be hell for me professionally and socially."

I nodded. I felt terrible for him, especially several days later when he was killed by a contingent of Riwa hunting down a group of Kossi that Porter had hidden in a nearby cave. All of them were ruthlessly murdered, including five children. *Well,* I thought bitterly, *maybe his demanding father would finally approve of his son, who had died a hero.* And I was very worried about my own chance of survival.

Somewhere in Masween's prehistoric past, ships arrived from no one knows where, bringing a highly evolved species the natives of Masween called The Abbas. Archeologists, including those of Masween itself, did not know if the Abbas had something to do with the creation of Riwa and Kossi or if they had come after the natural emergence of both species.

Now in a somewhat safer location, I poured myself a cup of military ration tea, set up my receiver and sat down to make a report.

"Galen Wright to Lane Escober, March 3, 2325 AP Time. I speak from underground in makeshift quarters, best we can do for now. My companions are twelve military personnel under Corporal Zhang, Sixth Division. We have enough rations for eighteen days.

"Zhang assures me that aid is coming, hopefully by day four. Lane, I cannot honestly say I am glad to be here. When I agreed to this, it was not to fear for my life under constant war. I know you said they were in conflict, but you greatly downplayed it or weren't aware of its totality. You cannot imagine the devastation.

"We have in our custody Brinwal Caleeb, before the war a Kossi professor, and his mate, parent of two. The Kossi, as you may remember, are simultaneous hermaphrodites, while the Riwa, like humans, are male and female and reproduce in similar fashion to us. Kossi offspring often die before the age of five, so couples tend to have several and usually end up with one to three. It's a sad business, but I assume they're used to it.

"Brinwal, who looks somewhere between a happy toad and a gnome, has resignedly accepted that his species is going to be wiped out, which is indeed the case, unless the Affiliated Planets decide to send forces and you know the policy there. Right now, I don't approve of that policy and you can quote me on that. Brinwal is philosophical. Most of the Kossi believe in reincarnation and he assumes that their souls will be relocated for the next incarnations or, God forbid, come back as Riwa. 'Riwa have been our friends for always,' said this sweet, innocent Kossi. 'We do not understand what happened.'

"Well, Lane, the Riwa and I understand what happened. One was wounded and dying by the road and my Kossi friend, kind no matter the situation, helped me drag him into our quarters. Before he passed away, he said, 'I am ashamed. I had no idea that we were savages. All this time, we were savages and did not know it.'

"I held his hand while Brinwal held his other. 'We humans are savage too,' I told him. 'We move to other worlds and start anew.'

'Go in peace,' said my wise Kossi friend. 'Forgive yourself.'

"So we know why the Abbas were here, Lane, but why did they leave? For surely they would have known what was to happen. I have researched the biological history of Kossi and Riwa and while they both descended from the same family tree, there is evidence that the ancestral animal from which the Riwa evolved was ferocious while the Kossi ancestor was gentle. The Abbas must have been involved in world formation. Either that or they *monitor* forming worlds and interfere when they choose. If they had not interfered on Masween, probably the Kossi would have been wiped out long ago."

Dr. Escobar's transmission took 3 days to arrive, during which thousands more Kossi were slaughtered and some hundreds of Riwa. The Kossi did fight back, but with little enthusiasm or skill.

"We must locate the Abbas before it is too late," Dr. Escobar transmitted back.

"If that is even remotely possible," I told her. "Before they left, the worldwide population of Kossi was approximately one billion nine and the Riwa two billion four. The current estimation of what's left is Kossi nine hundred million, Riwa two billion two. You can see the inevitable outcome. The Kossi are not geared emotionally or physically to be warriors."

Dutifully (and desperately), I contacted any exo-anthropology experts I could think of in our reaches of space, asking if anyone knew how to find the Abbas. Three people responded, only one human. "I have no idea," said the first, an ancient being now in a state of what humans call retirement. "No one has ever had a communication with them that we know of," said another, this one young and beginning her career. "No one has ever seen or spoken with them. We don't even know if they are corporeal," said the third.

Brinwal said this: "There is not a single incident on record of anyone being with the Abbas physically. There are reports of dream contact but since these differ in description, one cannot assume anything."

"How did they communicate with the people here then?" I asked.

"It was as if they spoke inside our heads. And only to a few."

"But how did you know the few weren't just inventing the stories in order to control the rest of you?"

Brinwal laughed in Kossi fashion, which was to produce a series of little squeaks through a grimace. "Their ships hovered overhead at all times. They were a fixture in the sky as normal as our star and moons. No one lived who had not seen the ships all of his life. The expression on the faces of those receiving messages could not be simulated."

I was quiet. As you can imagine, my nerves were shot. I could have used a very stiff scotch and water, but what liquor I'd brought with me was far from where I now managed to hide out.

As if reading my mind, and there was some evidence that Kossi could occasionally do that, Brinwal handed me a small vial. "Snap it and drink," he said. "It will give you a short period of happiness."

Possibly risking injury, I did as he suggested. It tasted like dead things mixed with turpentine, but yes, it had the same effect as those stiff shots I'd craved and for a couple of hours, I was "happy."

"Thank you, friend," I said. He did not drink any himself, but kept in constant contact with someone on his small, round communication device.

Corporal Zhang, half Chinese and half Swede, used his own military devices and was, like Brinwal, on them intermittently. When he wasn't, he stared straight ahead, creeping me out.

"What's the count now?" I dared to ask him. He and most of the other men weren't too happy about my being there, inept civilian that I was.

"Bad," said Zhang. "At this rate, Riwa will own the planet in about six months. Either they plan to slaughter every last Kossi or take the rest as prisoners or slaves. I can't read their minds and I don't want to."

I wanted to ask him if he was afraid, but kept my mouth shut. Undoubtedly he already thought me an academic pussy.

But surprising me, he said, "I won't lie to you, Wright. I'd sure rather be on Earth or Mars or anywhere else right now. Things don't look good."

"But the Riwa have nothing against humans, do they? I mean, I know Brinwal here and his family aren't safe, but they have no reason to kill us humans, do they? Porter just got in the way of the fire meant for his Kossi friends."

Zhang shook his head and looked away. "He was harboring them, Wright." He paused before going on. "I thought humans were a violent race, but the Riwa? They make us humans look like Buddhist monks."

"Come home," Dr. Escobar messaged me. "I'm hoping wormhole capsules are still functioning." They were, but not so much the shuttles to get to them from here.

But I didn't get her message until the end had come three days later and my response would astound her.

The morning of this unforeseen event, after downing his coffee ration, Corporal Zhang turned on his devices and jumped straight up. This show of enthusiasm from someone who normally remained stoic was unsettling to say the least.

"Soldiers, snap to," he shouted. Groggily, they all did as told, including me.

"You're not gonna believe this!" He actually smiled, showing a set of perfect, gleaming pearls. "The Kossi have won the battle."

"What?" I and everyone else shouted.

Brinwal came up beside me, but said nothing. He was obviously up to date on whatever news there was because I could literally feel his joy. I shot him a look but he only grimaced back.

Zhang was listening to something implanted in his ear, at the same time regarding a device on his arm. "The Riwa have died during the night. Apparently, they didn't suffer long, a few moments at most, before dropping dead. It appears that the Kossi, whom we'd assumed were goners, have emerged as the dominating species on Masween."

"How?" everyone, except Brinwal, said at once.

Brinwal gently pushed his way forward. "May I please explain, Corporal?"

Zhang graciously waved him forward.

The little Kossi hemmed and hawed before proceeding to explain. "While Kossi were being massacred, many others were working in secret locations. Scientists I am speaking of. My sibling's partner is one. He kept me constantly informed. They, the scientists, studied the physiology of Riwa. They found tiny organism, you call virus? They use this and attach germ that causes terrible illness only to Riwa. Everyone else on Masween is immune, including you and other visitors. Kossi are, of course, totally safe. The terrible illness kills in a very short time. The victims fall on the ground instantly dead. End of war."

"Wow," I said. "Wow. Every last Riwa is dead then?"

"No," said Brinwal. "Not every last Riwa. Some do not become ill, but not many. They do not fight after that however, even should they be immune. Nothing to fight for. They lay down their weapons and kneel before Kossi."

Brinwal looked proud but weary. "You have won," I said. And the soldiers all cheered.

For a Masween week, I stayed at the home of Brinwal. He wanted to show his hospitality and to thank me for keeping him and his family safe, though I'd little to do with that. Even Corporal Zhang would take no credit. Brinwal's mate, Codal, turned on their entertainment projector, which was about the level of nineteenth century Earth television (though their genetic/medical tech was clearly beyond that now).

"Time for news," said Codal cheerfully. We watched and listened. A makeshift government had been set up in a city not extremely far from us.

"Our new Prime Minister is . . ." and on he came, speaking gravely, though with noticeable relief. "We regret the necessary demise of our fellow Riwa. Body disposal is paramount. We will employ cremation though the Riwa did not normally choose that method. Burial is too time consuming and costly. Unfortunately, we cannot identify individual bodies. Remaining Riwa may hold memorial services, whatever they choose."

He paused. "To prevent this horror from reoccurring in future, remaining Riwa will be scattered among Kossi population and permitted to reproduce only to replace themselves, no more. Ever again."

*Ruthless*, I thought, *but clearly necessary. I didn't blame them in the least.*

Brinwal carried into the viewing room a large pot of one of their ghastly stews and we all sat down to celebrate.

Corporal Zhang had arranged for me to share a shuttle with him and his soldiers and the same capsule and homing shuttle back to our system. I sent my final report to Dr. Escobar and was looking forward to leaving for home. And then the Abbas returned.

Codel's children ran in from outside, yelling. "Rada! Rada! (a name Kossi children called their parent) Come back, come back!"

The ships, not as many as before, according to Brinwal, nevertheless presented a alarming presence in the sky, at least to me. And though the Kossi had lived all their lives until recently with the ships overhead, I could read my hosts' expressions, which told me that they were not necessarily happy to see them.

"Maybe they come to eliminate us," Codel suggested fearfully.

"Yes," said Brinwal, "maybe they are not so happy with how things turned out."

Corporal Zhang startled us by showing up at the door. He had his soldiers with him. "We thought we'd gather here," he said apologetically.

"Come in, come in," insisted Brinwal. "Might as well be together during another frightening experience."

However, it turned out to be anything but.

This time the Abbas came down to the planet. Probably everyone who could had their "projectors" turned on and again Prime Minister appeared.

"We are gathered here," he intoned, "on the lawn of what is left of the Capitol palace. Our kindly overseers have returned to give their opinion of what has recently occurred. I hand things over to them." He stepped aside.

There stood a tiny being upon a stool of a sort, surrounded by other stools also crowned with identical looking tiny beings.

"We are your guardians," said the itty-bitty squeak. "We have watched your species grow alongside your sister species for eons and we left in order to see what would happen. Three things could have resulted. One, Kossi and Riwa could have continued as before. Two, Kossi and Riwa could have fought until one dominated the other. And three, Kossi and Riwa could have totally destroyed each other and possibly the planet itself. We are disappointed to see that number one did not occur, but are not surprised. We are very pleased that number three did not occur. We are both happy and disappointed, young races that you are. It is preferable that the less violent species prevailed. Life in the universe is plentiful but often difficult. We were with you until you had achieved the knowledge and understanding to hurt or save yourselves on a grand scale and now that you have done so, we leave you forever. Remember that peace causes life to flourish while war is the destroyer of all that is good."

All of us in that room looked at each other and quietly nodded.

"They are very small," said one of the children.

"But very powerful," said their parent.

Corporal Zhang, his solders, and I left on the shuttle that evening and boarded our capsules next morning. The trip was uneventful. And now my heart pounds as I head into the Department of Anthropology to see the woman who'll never see me as anything but her ward, when what I really want is love.

*Margaret Karmazin's credits include stories published in literary and national magazines, including* Rosebud, Chrysalis Reader, North Atlantic Review, Mobius, Confrontation, Pennsylvania Review, *and* Another Realm. *Her stories in* The MacGuffin, Eureka Literary Magazine, Licking River Review *and* Mobius *were nominated for Pushcart awards. Her story, "The Manly Thing," was nominated for the 2010 Million Writers Award. She has stories included in several anthologies, including* Still Going Strong, Ten Twisted Tales, Pieces Of Eight *(Autism Acceptance),* Zero Gravity, Daughters Of Icarus, *and* Visions IV: Space Between Stars. *She has also published a YA novel,* Replacing Fiona, *a children's book,* Flick-Flick & Dreamer, *and a collection of short stories, titled* Risk.

Ellyott is a wrench monkey with nothing to live for but the thought of leaving his cold, hick moon with the woman he loves. He's set his sights on the jade world of Maia that hangs just beyond their poisoned sky. But his daddy's words still echo in his head: Nobody leaves Fontus alive.

# FIRST SUNRISE

**By**

*Marie Michaels*

*Septlun*

Soon, Arlie and me are gonna watch our first sunrise. We'll drink a cup of bitter coffee and watch the sun climb the sky in all its fire. She'll lay her frizzy gold head on my shoulder as we stare into a pale green sky. I'll sling my arm around her waist, and seeing this godforsaken moon way past the clouds is closest we'll ever get to coming back.

Jennalee yanks a needle out of my vein, a nasty little tug pulling inside my arm. I lose the picture in my head as she presses a square of gauze on the pinprick in my shoulder and tells me to push hard on it. Gritty cement walls and tarnished steel machines mush together when I lift my head, but I blink them back into place.

Heavy canvas curtains are shut tight against the dark. It's Septlun, seven days into hebdalun, the dark week. Arlie told me that here on Fontus we got the highest suicide rate of all human expansion in the galaxy, and I don't need her schooling to know it's thanks to those nine straight days of darkness.

Jennalee never meets my eyes. She's awful busy clamping the tubes, unclipping them from that ugly vampire with winking glass dial eyes, and lining up the vials of my blood in a rack on her cart. But I known Jennalee since she patched me up as a kid. Time was, she cuddled me like a mother hen. Now she pretends like she don't know me from Adam. Maybe she's busy, or maybe she's heartsick from seeing folks come in with daydreams like I got and leaving three days later with their guts just about ripped out.

She winds crinkly blue tape around my shoulder and underneath my arm. I can feel the puff of her breath, but I might as well be on the dark side of Fontus for all she sees the rest of me. Another arm, another stick, another story she don't need to hear.

"Results in sixty hours," she says. She don't tell me goodbye or good luck, just pushes her squeaky cart between sweat-stained chairs, taking my blood away to be tested for the sickening threshold. I want to tell her don't worry, I'm leaving Fontus whatever way the test comes out. I'm gonna drink that coffee and see a sunrise light up the jade sky of Maia like a fairy story.

Arlie hates when I say I'll leave no matter what. I told her, I will not die without seeing a thing like that, and she said, "Well, Ellyott, seeing it might kill you." Surely might, but that don't change anything. The sickening might be strong in my veins like it is in my daddy's, but goddammit here on Fontus the sun ain't even a proper sun. It's a colorless star that falls from the horizon like an orange dropping off a table.

Once I get my feet underneath me, I head back to the waiting room to pick at my bandage for the required quarter hour. Red tape for donating blood 'cause it bends with the elbow, cheap green tape for routine sticks because it don't need to hold fast for long, but blue for the sickening test. It's sticky enough to hold fast to your shoulder, where they take the blood from one particular vein. No one much cared about the kinds of tape before this test came along. These days, the color of a man's tape is good for hours of speculation and pitying looks, if he's still in town next hebdalun.

My fingertips are turning purple with cold, so I head to Terrace when I'm released. "Well, hop to it, don't let the dark in," Frankie barks when I push open the door to his coffee joint. I say coffee, but it's all roasted roots and seeds supposed to mimic the real stuff. His eyes gleam like distant stars. "You been to the clinic, ain'tcha. Lemme guess, you got a blue bandage?"

I want to feel nostalgia for this place, but Frankie's jab sucks it right outta me. Terrace is real pleasant, between Frankie's line on fresh butter and sugar from Maia and the walls his wife painted buttercup yellow, but the man has the biggest mouth I ever come across. "Cup of Black Magic and whatever's fresh. Yeah Frankie, it's blue. You got personal experience with them bandages?"

When he turns to his battered urns too fast for me to read his eyes, I wonder. He's got a good thing in Terrace, can't imagine him leaving for gold or silver or glittering Maia, the lush planet that eats up our sky like a grinning giant. And I don't expect he could leave. Frankie's first coffee joint was set up so close to the biggest haephesium mine, you could spit from his door into the hole. He wasn't no miner, but he worked so close his blood must be curdled with the sickening by now. So long as he stays on Fontus and makes his doughnuts, he's fine.

Fragrant steam hisses, and I get to thinking. When I was just big enough to see over the counter, Frankie moved outta the mining camp. His baby daughter was a bitty terror on chubby legs then, must be going on fifteen now and raising hell like Arlie did at that age, staying out late, flashing too much skin, and most of all wanting to be anywhere else but a hick moon stinking of chemical smoke.

These days we know that kids absorb the mine poison like sponges. But back then, she played in that radioactive dirt and breathed those fumes. Could be enough to yoke her to this place, just like my daddy is yoked and I hope I ain't.

Frankie still don't meet my eyes when he gives me a warm mug, yellow to match the walls, and a glazed doughnut on a dish. My stomach is sour with guilt. I want to say sorry, but I ain't sure what for. Sorry that maybe his daughter will spend the rest of her life hating him, like my daddy hated his? Out of pity, I leave a good tip, but he don't look up when the coins clatter on the counter.

*Octlun*

Arlie's studying for another round of exams, apt to bite me if I bust in asking for a kiss. It's hard not being able to cuddle with my girl, 'specially now. But if I can't wrap her in my arms, best thing I can do is take extra shifts and make a little more money.

I lose myself in the heat of the generating plant, the slow burn of work in my shoulders. Grease and rust flakes coat my arms up to my biceps. It's a good job, being a wrench monkey at Generations Consolidated. It pays the bills and no one been killed during my eight years here.

"Ellyott!"

I've wedged myself in the rungs of a ladder, beating on copper cooling coils bigger'n me. I recognize the voice of the shift supervisor, Dannalew.

"Systems needs those coils up and running in fifteen. Trans-Gal has a real important shipment coming in. You got a handle on it?"

The socket driver slips in my sweaty grip and clangs against the coils so hard the ladder vibrates. "Sure I do. You think I'd let the lights go out while them good ol' boys are bribing customs?"

"You want to watch your mouth regarding the Company," Dannalew says. Loud as this place is, I hear him hold his breath. Trans-Gal, known to locals as the Company, pumped money and poison into Fontus. Now we can't get rid of either, and I'm the one he wants to send up the hill after they blown their fuses again.

I groan. "You're kidding me, boss. The boys are gonna start thinking I like it up there, you send me so much."

"Well, it don't fucking matter what the boys think about your predilections, do it?" he snaps. "What with you leaving to go live on that green ball in the sky." Be honest, I'm touched that he's got hisself so worked up about me leaving. "You got the best temper for it, and you're here. We all got reason to hate the Company, but you're just too goddamn good at your job to avoid it. Now, you gonna make me fire you two days before you quit?"

I give the coils another push. With a skull-rattling click, they settle into place. "No sir. I'll be up the hill just as soon as I put the coils to bed."

Company needs a wrench monkey bad, so I get to take the pick-up we keep on their dime for times like this. Contraption is older'n me with brakes that squeal like a dying thing and a foul belching cloud. The fuel alone costs more'n most folk here can afford in a year.

The headlights burn through the deep dark and I think about the Company and my daddy. I remember one night, another Octlun decades back, my folks were having their end-of-the-week fight over where daddy's wages gone. Big sister Illaniana was off running with boys, but I wasn't old enough to have anywhere better to go when the house got crowded with resentments. Well, I couldn't stay in that house another minute if you paid me in candy and comic books. I decided to teach my parents a lesson by running away to the dark side of Fontus, that wilderness where neither mine, nor burgh, mar the land and its spiderweb cracks.

My eight-year-old self was lucky he didn't crack his numbskull falling into that damned ravine. When something slimy broke my fall, I started screaming like someone stuck me with a sizzling poker. A stench like the breath of the devil puffed around me, and slickly rotting limbs tangled me up. I thought I was gonna die of horror right then and there, but then the breath whumped out of my chest as something yanked me out.

It was Jennalee, coming home from her shift at the clinic. The road passed so close to our house I always feared people would hear my parents yelling and carrying on. She patted me when I shrieked that the Company Man was gonna kill me. Maybe Mama thought I dreamed the whole thing when Jennalee left me on the doorstep, until she saw shreds of fine black wool stuck in the buttons of my coat.

I remember I couldn't sleep after that, feeling those mucky fingers stroke my ankles. I sneaked outta my bed then and watched my folks cast crazy shadows as Daddy slammed his open hand on the table and Mama wiped her cheeks with the backs of her shaking hands.

"Know what they say about this place, Mona?" he said in his gravelly voice, worn hard by years of anger. I scooted close, hugging the corner of the wall.

"Rossil, you are sore trying me," she hissed. "It was our boy found the dead Company Man. What are they gonna find on that man? You ever think what kinda danger you're putting us in?"

"Best he knows now." Daddy's voice dropped so low I had to cup my ears to hear. "Ain't nobody leaves Fontus alive. I won't. None o' my generation will, nor my daddy's."

Somehow I always knew my Daddy was stuck here, but that was the first time I wondered, *well what about me?*

*Nonlun*

In Arlie's novels, they sure like to talk about pre-dawn light. Must have to do with those thick planet atmospheres and sunrises, what we ain't got any of on Fontus. I can't picture that real well, because how do you have any light before the sun's come up? But I like the way she describes it, light creeping like fog into the sky, paleness that ain't quite brightness but ain't quite not. On Fontus, light is white hot or nothing. Shadows got knife edges.

I dawdle home from the day's shift, staring up where I know Maia hangs in the sky, though I can't see anything but its starless black mass. Since we're tidally locked with Maia, I always been looking at the same patch of planet. I know them rust red islands, scattered like a broken necklace, like I know my own name. There's one inlet shaped like a dog's head, and that's where Arlie and I gonna have that cup of coffee.

I remember how Maia looked, close enough to reach out and grab, when I told her.

"'s called Six Peaks Bay," Arlie read, while I was resting my head in her lap, one chilly spring Nonsol, maybe two months back. Arlie had a quilt draped over a wool coat atop long underwear, but it's hard to stay inside on the last day of sun you're gonna get for nine days. Every patch of ground was claimed by a shivering clump of folks huddled on a blanket. "On accounta the mountains you can see from the harbor. They ain't the tallest on Maia but they're the biggest on the local archipelago." Her voice was as careful as a cat on a ledge, saying that word. She shook the magazine in front of my face, and I cracked open an eye as I batted the shiny pages away from my nose.

"Looks great," I said, though it was all a blur from where I lay. "Wonder what mountains look like on Maia. You suppose they're different from ours?"

"Sure they're different." She said it like it should be plain as that green planet in the sky, but that voice didn't bother me none. I was happy to be lying in her lap with the sun on my face. "They got snow on 'em, don't they? Think of that, enough snow to cover a mountain. You can get a sunburn just from sunlight reflecting on it."

Hearing that wonder in her voice, I thought it was as good a time as any. "Well, I expect we're gonna need some suntan lotion when we head on up," I said, trying to sound casual. "That magazine say any place near, uh, Vistamount Boulevard we can stock up?"

I watched her face. She narrowed her eyes at me, scrunching her freckled nose. "Ellyott, I got no idea what you're talking around. What is Vistamount Boulevard?" There was a taut edge to her voice.

299

"No place special, I reckon." I drew it out a little, enjoying her consternation. "You know I can't afford nothing too glittery. But 42-15 Vistamount Boulevard, Six Peaks Bay got a nice ring to, don'tcha think? Little studio apartment looking over a courtyard." Sweat prickled my back and stuck my shirt to my skin in spite of the chill.

Her gray eyes widened, and her mouth fell open. She pushed me out of her lap, and I felt the blood pounding in my face. For a long while, she just stared at me like she never saw me before. Then she pulled me close and kissed me so hard I blushed. My left thigh went numb as she wiggled me into a knotty root under our blanket, but I wouldn't have stopped her if my leg had fell off.

She shoved me back at arm's length. "Tell me you're saying what I think you're saying. I don't think I could stand it one minute longer if you're pulling my leg." Her eyes were shiny, and her fingers were claws tangled in my shirt.

I took her hands, cupping them as gentle as a blown egg. "You know I'd never lie to you. I got a place up there, ready whenever we land. I put down a security deposit, and I got enough stored by for maybe half a year's rent. We're gonna do this, Arlie."

Her shoulders jerked like she was crying, but her face was so bright the sun dimmed behind her. "I don't know if I should kiss you again or slap you. What the hell were you thinking?" She should have sounded mad, but she was laughing. "You ain't even got the test done yet, what's wrong with you?"

"I once heard my daddy say that nobody leaves Fontus alive. But you and me, we're gonna walk out of here and kiss this damned moon goodbye forever. No test is gonna change any of that." I looked up at Maia, the only color in a sky dingy like a shirt that's been worn and washed a hundred times.

I told her a hundred times, I won't be an anchor holding her to this cracked, irradiated ground. If not for me she'd probably be up there already, waving to her folks and just about dying for laughing at us.

She tackled me and just about squeezed the wind outta me. She muttered something into my shirt about me being an idiot. I couldn't disagree. But like I said, what was I gonna do? I don't want to hate my daddy like he hated his, but if I trap myself and my girl here, that's exactly what I fear I'll do.

I'll send him the biggest postcard I can find of the tallest of them Six Peaks and write on it, your son was here.

### Primisol

The desk nurse can't meet my eyes when I tell her my name. She bites a hangnail and mutters. I grit my jaw to hold down the gummy potato hash I swallowed this morning.

"Ellyott Oskellick." I'm hailed by a woman with eyes that say she don't remember what it's like to sleep proper. Her voice is soft with weariness. "I'm Dr. Douvelin. You can come on back."

My head goes fizzy when I stand up. I try to steady it by staring at the trails of grime ground into splitting linoleum tiles. Doctor leads me into a cubicle with a folding screen for privacy. Triplicate bulging out of manila folders shares space on steel shelving with dog-eared medical books. She reads my name out of a binder. "Ellyott Oskellick, you came three days past to get your blood tested for haephesiphilia?"

"Yes ma'am. I never worked in the mines but my daddy grew up round Shadow Point and worked in processing. His daddy died in a cave-in." I feel my throat tighten and I can't hardly hear myself over my drumming heartbeat.

She nods as she scans my records. "Family history and moderate indirect childhood exposure. Wish I could explain why some people are stricken and some left well enough alone." She snaps the folder shut. "You got any questions for me?"

Why she think I'm here, to get a history lesson? "Uh, well, do I got a chance when I leave this place?"

Her eyes lose a little of their tiredness as she blinks at me. "They didn't tell you up front? I guess that's the new policy." A small smile creases her face and gives her a pretty air. "Mr. Oskellick, your bloodwork is clean. Your levels are well below the threshold." She keeps talking, something about feeling like hell for a week after I leave and seeing a doctor soon as I make planetfall. Some people don't make the transition with levels lower'n I got, and a few third-generation miners manage to grit it out.

My heart is about to explode outta my chest. My face goes hot and tight and shivery. "Thank you," I blurt out. I'm probably interrupting something important, but I can't help it. "Truly, ma'am, thank you. I can't tell you . . ." I lose track of my words, but I get the feeling she knows what I'm trying to say.

"It's nice to give out good news." Then her face falls back into the tired look I saw before. "I know you weren't listening, but best you see a doctor soon as you can. People been dying for generations, and we still don't know much about the sickening."

I tell her I surely will, and then I scoot. She don't need me in there reminding her of all the people she can't save. Besides, I got two tickets to buy. One-way to Maia, cheapest seats in the house. Vistamount Boulevard never felt so close.

It's Primisol, the sun is up, and everyone's stepping a little higher. Even the faded awnings along the main drag gleam. Leggy evergreen glowtrees look to be straining toward the sun same as the folks browsing in shop windows. Tell the truth I hardly noticed the sun this morning, so mopey was I in my basement room. I had a list of errands, but it's clean flown outta my head. I talked big about leaving Fontus, but it weren't real until I heard those words from the doctor. Before I do anything—buy the tickets, send a 'gram to my daddy's cousin on Maia, swing by the bank, call on Illaniana—I gotta ring up Arlie. Class been over for an hour now, and I don't think I'm big-headed thinking she's waiting to hear from me. The burgh is a blur of color before I'm throwing open my door, banging into the kitchen table, and near yanking the phone outta the wall, I gotta take a couple deep breaths before I can dial her number right. I'm laughing at nothing; at the way the white sunlight slices through rising dust that testifies sadly to my bachelor housekeeping. I'm ready to whoop to hear her voice, but the phone just keeps ringing. Well, that girl's always been tough to pin down. Day like this, I can't stay glum for long. I think of all the sights we're gonna see: sunrises, pre-dawn light, mountains with caps of snow, and that green sky. The Company and their people terraformed Fontus just enough that we could scrape by, but didn't spend a thin dime more'n that. We get hot and cold and enough damp to keep our glowtrees and root vegetables alive and our wells full enough. But I never seen a bolt of lightning, and snow is occasion for a celebration bigger'n a New Year that falls on Primisol.

Everything is more vivid now I'm thinking I might be seeing it for the last time. Like the skinny glowtrees that look like normal trees during a hebdasol and give off eerie green light during a hebdalun. They sure are ugly, but those I pass on my way to the bank vibrate with memory: the hanged man, the stretching cat, the lady's boot. I been in the Mutual more'n I can count, but now I really see the paintings on the wall. A tree with limp branches like a woman's hair trailing in a clear stream. A field of gleaming gold wheat, bowed by a strong wind. The colors make me dizzy.

Arlie's friend Sharlyanna is working at the window. I'm beaming ear-to-ear, but when I ask to take out all my savings, she makes a face like she bit into a cake that turned out to be a pinecone. She don't say nothing as she counts the bills. I guess she's mad I'm taking Arlie away. They been friends since they had neighboring cribs at the clinic. But I'm determined to get her talking.

"Hey Sharly, nice weather we having, ain't it?"

Her jaw bunches beneath her skin. "I wouldn't know, Ellyott, I been inside. Guess folks is glad it's Primisol."

That pinched little frown of hers don't dent my happiness. "Folks is always glad it's Primisol. Must be nice even for you all to see outside. Better'n looking at curtains."

"Yeah, well." She slams the stack of bills on the counter. "Guess this means you're going. Gonna enjoy that yellow sun and just forget about Primisol and all of us. Well good riddance. Next!"

I wince. I never expected Sharly would get so nasty. Reckon she must be half-blind with jealousy that we're leaving this hole. She wants to grow old looking at rocks like broken teeth outside her window, that's her business. I hope she ain't been talking to Arlie like this. We should be dancing in the streets, not listening to that poison.

I need to see Arlie even more after that, so I jog straight to her place. It's halfway across the burgh, bigger'n my two rooms because she shares with fellow students. I'm panting like a hound when I knock on the rattley front door.

"Arlie here," I say, maybe asking or maybe demanding it be true.

Nell never liked me much, and as she stares at me down that hawk's beak of a nose I think she might bite me. She don't want to tell me anything, but I musta got that stubborn look on my face. Arlie says when I wear that face I look ready to chew through rocks.

"No, she ain't here. And don't you think I'm gonna tell where she's gone. She told me to keep my mouth shut, and I ain't gonna rat her out. Now get off my step 'fore I call the police." She slams the door so quick I stumble back to avoid getting hit in the face.

My stomach clenches, and I lean against the whitewashed siding of their little house until the dizziness passes. That ain't the Arlie I talked to four days ago, who cried when she wished me luck. My Arlie been dreaming of leaving longer'n I've known her.

There's one possibility I been not thinking about as hard as I can. It might explain Sharly's conniption, but Nell's crack about ratting Arlie out still don't make sense.

I stop thinking. I run to the nearest pedicab and throw my bills in the man's face. Ten minutes later I'm at Derry Port, rushing through hallways until my throat feels like to bleeding with every breath. I see a hundred signs listing customs, toilets, and names of places I never heard of. I'm near to crying before I see the one I'm looking for. Departure, Six Peaks Bay. Someone yells that I need a ticket, but I ain't hearing it. All I see is Arlie's skinny figure sitting on a duffel bag with her heads in her hands. I know that short tweed jacket and that frizzy yellow halo. I like to tell her she looks like a sexy college professor in that jacket, and the memory of her warm chortle makes my breath stutter.

And it hits me, I was wrong thinking Arlie might change her mind. That ain't the girl who daydreamed over maps of Maia before she could read. I stand there, gasping from the running and what I read in her, all hunched and sad.

"Arlie!" I shout. A guard is striding over like the long arm of the law.

"Honey," I say as I kneel at her side, though neither of us are big on pet names, "what in the name of all the stars you think you're doing?"

Her eyes are rimmed with red, but otherwise she's pale as the sky. "You can't stay here," she says, looking I expect at the guard behind me. "You gotta let me go, Ellyott. I didn't think I could watch you die up there, and it ain't right that you gotta watch me."

She blinks, seeming to see me for the first time, and gives me a ghostly little smile that freezes my bones. "You got yours back clean, didn't you? You gotta go to our place. I remember it, 42-15 Vistamount Boulevard. I just wanted to see it, before—" She snaps her teeth closed with a click and a swallow.

I take her hands like I took them on our picnic, and my throat burns as I talk. "You best remember it," I say, "you gonna live there with me, or I ain't living there at all. Not on Vistamount Boulevard, not anywhere up there if you ain't with me." Everything I ever said about sunrises and snowcaps and I don't know what else blows away like ash. Arlie would kill me if I tried to stop her, but damn it all, she is the one thing I will not lose.

"Sir." Muffled footsteps are close behind me. The gentleness in the guard's grunt almost undoes me. "If you don't have a ticket, you can't be here. I can give you another minute but only just."

"I ain't doing that to you," she whispers. "This'll be a kindness, you'll see. You just gotta let go of my hand." She closes her eyes like she could wish me away.

My right kneecap is hot with pain as I half-sit, half-squat in front of her. "Girl, I will hold your hand on that mountain we talked about, or I will hold your hand through every hebdalun until we're a hundred, or I—" I stop when I hear my voice quaver, and she gives a great, silent shudder. ". . . or I will hold your hand if the sickening takes you, but I won't let go."

"Sir, thirty seconds. Don't test me." Shiny brown shoes glint out of the corner of my eye.

When she opens her eyes, I see a dull flicker like a half-dead coal. "Then hurry home and get your things," she said. Her voice sinks to the floor like lead. "Shuttle leaves in two hours. You gotta be here an hour before. You know I have to leave." I don't have time to doubt her or check the flight times because I'm already running out of the buzzing ticket area before my brain can catch up with me.

All I can do is move faster than I ever moved before and hope she's still sitting there atop that duffel bag when I get back. She said I got sixty minutes to get back here. I can make it in forty.

*Marie Michaels is a lawyer by day and nerd pretty much all the time. She lives in Portland, Oregon, where she is rediscovering trees. Her short stories have appeared in anthologies, including* Tell Me a Fable *and* Rejected *and the horror webzine* Devolution Z. *Upcoming stories will appear in anthologies, including* Keeping Pace with Eternity *and* New Legends: Mercenary, Engineer, Captain Book 2. *She tweets about science fiction, fantasy, writing, and feminism at @lavidanerdy and can be found on Facebook.*

Kareska is a female faller who lives in a world where humans are dropped out of planes and spend their entire lives parachuting down through the seemingly endless skies of Dropworld. The question is, can she survive long enough to make it to the bottom?

# DROPWORLD

### By

### *Fredrick Obermeyer*

The birthplanes ejected Kareska and several other fallers from their wombs, their glistening forms spiraling down through the pinkish-yellow sky of Dropworld, down towards the Great Below.

Organic parachutes burst out of the backs of many newborns, but some continued their fatal drop. The adult fallers paid the lost no mind, though. It was the way of the birthdrop, and each of them went through the same thing when they were born.

At first, it seemed inevitable that Kareska would die, for she was smaller than the other newborns and had a slight hump on her back. But just when all seemed lost, a thin parachute membrane burst out of the back of her thick warmskin and opened. She jerked up into the air and cried out for the first time in her life.

A moment later, she floated into the arms of the twenty-year-old Ilaru and he cradled the baby in his arms. Overhead, the planeparents dropped food supplies for the fallers. As usual, Dukario and his gang of young thugs swooped in and snatched most of the food before the others could get it.

But Ilaru managed to grab a canister of warm milk and fed it to the baby.

*She is going to be special,* Ilaru thought, as he looked at the name tattooed onto her shoulder. Special indeed.

For the first ten years of her lifefall, Kareska did not grow as fast as the other young fallers. She remained thin and scrawny and was often picked on by the young, stronger males in the tribe. Yet despite her small stature, Ilaru sensed a strength within the young girl. She was always inquisitive, always asking about the world.

One day, when she was seven years old, she looked down and said, "What lies at the bottom of the Great Below?"

"I don't know," Ilaru said. "No faller has ever lived long enough to see what is down there. Some say it is land."

"Land?"

"Yes, the myth of land. Not like the clouds or the air around us, but something hard. Like the planes or our bodies."

Although most dismissed such a claim as foolish, Kareska remained fascinated by the idea.

"But some say it's water," Kareska said. "Like the kind we drink from our moisture tails."

"Perhaps. But I would not speak of such things near Dukario and the others. He is not tolerant of such ideas."

Kareska frowned and looked down. Dukario and one of his thugs were urinating on the top of one of the older ones. The urine splashed down and froze into icicles, but Nadaro was too old and infirm to stop them. So he tolerated their ribbing and let them steal his food, even though he needed it.

"Why is Dukario so mean to Nadaro and the others?" Kareska said. "They've never done anything to him."

"As a child, Dukario lost his carefather in an accident when a meatbird slashed through his chutes," Ilaru said. "Then a group of thugs led by a faller named

Azai beat and tormented him, until one day when he fought back. He killed Azai and his others. But there was too much pain inside him, so he followed Azai's example and formed his own gang."

Kareska wished that she could take away Dukario's bad childhood, but she did not think that it excused his behavior.

"As I said, avoid him," Ilaru said. "If he asks you to give up your food, then do it."

"Shouldn't we stand up to him?" Kareska said.

"No. He will kill you." Ilaru sighed. "Please, do not go against him."

For a moment, Kareska considered defying her carefather. Yet, after she looked upon herself, she understood his wisdom. There was no way that she could win in a duel against Dukario and his thugs. Something inside told her that it was wrong to stand by and take such abuse. She wished that she were older and had better developed claws so she could fight. But it was no use. She was still too young.

"Yes, Ilaru," Kareska said. "I will avoid him."

"Thank you." Ilaru gripped Kareska's arms and kissed her on the forehead.

For the next five years of her lifefall, Kareska did as her carefather asked. She avoided Dukario at all costs. If he demanded her food, she turned it over and endured whatever insults he gave her without talking back. Though inside she seethed at being called "little turd," and "humpback," and "falling runt."

But then, one day came where she could no longer stand by and accept Dukario's abuse.

The faller tribe had descended into a flock of meatbirds and fruit balloons that drifted through the orange sky. Although their planeparents had kept them fed with a steady supply of bland rations, she and the others savored the taste of fresh meat and fruits.

When they drifted near the flock, Kareska swooped in and fired spines at some of the birds. Most of them missed, but a few struck two birds and she snatched them out of the air. They gave a brief struggle as she tore into one. As she savored the sweet flesh, she glanced down through the flock and saw old Nadaro.

In the past five years the elder faller had slipped deeper into the Great Below. His parachute was collapsing in on itself, his warmskin was wrinkling, his once keen mind had gone senile and he spent most of his days floating alone. He had lost control of his bladder and bowels and it would not be long before his parachute snapped and he fell to his death.

Kareska felt that the old man should not be left starving just because he was too infirm to hunt, so she pulled her strings and floated down to him. He no longer recognized her, but he flashed her a big grin. He had four dull teeth left.

Kareska held out her fresh kill and said, "Would you like some meat, Nadaro?"

Nadaro looked down at the meat and said, "Tank . . . you."

He tore some of the meat out and tried to stick it in his mouth with shaking hands, but it tumbled out of his fingers. Nadaro looked at his bloody hands and moaned.

Feeling discouraged, Kareska tore off some of the meat, chewed it several times to make it more palatable and slipped it carefully into Nadaro's mouth. The old faller swallowed it and smiled. Kareska felt good sharing her food with him.

She started to tear off another piece for Nadaro, when Dukario swooped in and snatched the meatbird carcass from her hands.

"A nice catch," Dukario said. He tore a piece out of it.

She reached out for the bird, but he jerked it back and laughed. Rage tensed Kareska's muscles and she wanted to slash him, but she remembered what Ilaru had said.

"That's my bird," Kareska said. "I caught it."

"Why would you waste this meat on a foolish old faller like him?" Dukario gestured to the older faller with a bloody hand. "He's half dead anyway. It would be better to let him starve."

"How can you say that after what Azai put you through?"

For a moment Dukario's expression grew distant, as if he were recalling all of the terrible experiences he had been put through. But then he blinked and said, "Shut your mouth, you little turd. This meat is mine."

"No, it's not. Give it back to me."

Kareska reached for the meat and this time grabbed it. But Dukario would not let go. They struggled in the air for it briefly, but Dukario was older and stronger and he tore the meat from her and slashed her across the face with his claws. Hot pain screamed through the slash marks and drove her into a killing fury.

Ignoring his size and bulk, Kareska swung forward and slashed his face. He howled in pain and dropped the meat. Kareska caught it out of the air and kicked Dukario back. She floated back and looked around her.

Some of the fallers were floating near her, watching the struggle with fear and interest.

"You don't have to tolerate his abuse," Kareska said to them. "Help me beat him and we can share our food—"

Dukario lunged back and kicked her in the stomach with a clawed foot. The blow slashed down to her pubis and knocked all of the wind out of her. He grabbed her by the neck and began cutting the organic tendons and cords that connected her parachute to her body.

"Please, help me!" Kareska said.

At first it seemed that some of the crowd would swoop in and help her. But Dukario glared at them and said, "Anyone who helps this little runt will have to deal with me."

The other fallers in Dukario's gang floated near the crowd. Although the tribe outnumbered the gang five to one, the threat of violence and death cowed them into floating back. Kareska glared at them with disgust. All they had to do was fight back, but they were cowards. She felt even angrier at them than at Dukario.

More pain lashed through her body as Dukario slashed through more cords. Terror rushed through

Kareska's heart as her parachute sagged. She was going to die in the Great Below.

"Stop," a voice said.

She opened her eyes.

Ilaru floated down to them and held his claws right next to Dukario's cords.

"Stay out of this," Dukario said.

"Drop her and I'll drop you next."

Dukario's face tightened with rage. "You won't do it. The others will cut you down."

"Not if I call our planeparents away." Ilaru's claws tightened on Dukario's cords. "Hand her over to me and give Nadaro the meat."

"Make me."

Ilaru slashed one of his cords and he cried out. His gang tensed.

"Hand her over and I won't call the planes away."

Dukario hesitated for a moment, but then he shoved her into Ilaru's arms. Kareska moaned in his arms. Her severed cords burned with pain.

"Now give Nadaro back his meat," Ilaru said.

Dukario laughed and said, "Why? He'll just waste it."

"Give him his fair share and leave us. You have plenty."

Dukario floated over to the old man and held out the meat.

"Thank you," Nadaro said.

He reached for it, but Dukario jerked it back at the last second and the old faller cried and struggled to get it. Dukario kept jerking it back and he and his gang laughed as the old man struggled in vain for his food. Kareska wished that she could kill Dukario for humiliating him.

"Stop tormenting him and give him the meat," Ilaru said.

Dukario paused and handed him the bird carcass.

Nadaro took it and tried to chew on it, but chunks of meat fell off. Dukario floated back from him.

"Now leave us," Ilaru said.

"I'm not letting my meat go to waste on an old man," Dukario said.

"It's not your decision."

Dukario flashed him a sly grin and said, "It is now."

He slashed through Nadaro's parachute cords like gossamer threads and cut the old man from his chute. It happened so fast that Kareska could barely register it.

One moment Nadaro was struggling to eat his meat and the next he fell screaming to his death in the Great Below. Dukario floated back, spread his hands and said, "Oops, I must have slipped."

Kareska cried out in despair, seeing the helpless old man disappear beneath the puffy white clouds.

Dukario laughed. He had a triumphant look on his face, as if he enjoyed holding the power of life and death over all the other fallers.

"Goddamn you, you bastard," Ilaru said.

Dukario floated up towards him with his gang and said, "What did you say?"

Now Ilaru looked scared. Kareska had never seen such a look of fear on his face.

"You can't get away with killing him like that," Ilaru said.

"Looks like I just did," Dukario said.

"Our planeparents will be angered. They will not drop food for us."

"Then I'll just take the food from the others until they return."

Although Ilaru held communion with the planeparents, it was a tenuous connection at best. Sooner or later, the planes would lift their punishment and resume the drop. But only Ilaru and Kareska knew that.

Powerless against Dukario and his gang, Ilaru tried to float upwards. But the added weight of Kareska made it difficult for him to get away. Only the threat of taking away their food seemed to hold the faller gang at bay.

"You better watch your chute from now on," Dukario said. "If you or that little hump, hand your food over to any more of the old fallers, I'll kill you both."

Kareska bit her lip. She couldn't bear to look at him.

Slowly the gang backed off and Ilaru floated above him.

It took three weeks for Kareska's cords to heal enough so that they could reattach to her chute without it breaking. During that time, Ilaru called in for some medical supplies from the planeparents, bound her wounded cords and tied her to his chest.

"You must not give your food to any of the others," Ilaru said. "No matter how much they need it."

"Why shouldn't we share with those who need it?" Kareska said.

"Dukario does not want us to share."

"But he does not pull his own weight. He steals from the others and makes fun of them for giving up their food. How can he talk about pulling his own weight and then steal from others?"

"Because his gang and his strength give him the power to do as he wishes. He enjoys hurting and manipulating others."

But surely the other fallers didn't like being humiliated and having their food stolen. "Why can't the others fight back?"

"Because they are afraid. They know Dukario and his gang will kill their children and them if they resist his efforts. They do not want to get involved and risk his vengeance if they fail."

"So they let him bully them." Kareska frowned. "It's not right."

"I know it's not right. But that is the way things are."

"You always told me to be kind, Ilaru."

"I know. But there are times for kindness and there are times for selfishness. You cannot always afford the luxury of being kind, if your life is in danger." Ilaru sighed.

Yet Kareska could not believe that. She didn't think people should only be kind and help others when it was convenient or safe. Even now there were some fallers in the group who were starving and dying because of Dukario's behavior.

"Please, Kareska, for your own safety, do not face off against him again," Ilaru said. "Promise me that."

Kareska hesitated, knowing that there were others who suffered.

"Promise me!"

"I promise," Kareska said, knowing she could not abide by such a promise. Not if it meant that others had to suffer.

"I'm only doing this to protect you," Ilaru said. He brushed her hair gently. "I love you so much and I couldn't bear it if I lost you."

"I know."

"Someday things will change. Enough people will become angry that they will turn against him."

I wish I could believe that, Kareska thought. I think they will always bow down to him, so long as he can intimidate them.

She snuggled close to her carefather and felt warm and safe. Despite the safety, she knew that she couldn't just stand by and let Dukario get away with harming the needy. Even if the others in the tribe refused to help, she would secretly help those who needed it.

For the next two years, Kareska made a pretense of following her carefather's promise. She never openly shared her food or rations with the others and pretended not to notice when others went hungry. But when night came, and Dukario wasn't around, she would float down to those in need and slip them some of her food, swearing them to secrecy.

She failed to save some of the fallers and had to watch in pain as their cords snapped or Dukario cut their chutes. Over time, Dukario grew more arrogant and more powerful, smacking people around, sometimes cutting the chutes of old and crippled fallers without even warning them.

"Just getting rid of the dead weight," he often said, usually followed by a laugh.

She could see the anger in people's faces. But they never acted against Dukario, and that angered her all the more.

How much more abuse could they stand? Kareska thought on more than one occasion.

Apparently a lot. Since they took his abuse day after day, week after week, year after year, and never once said anything.

One night she floated down to help feed an old woman faller named Usaki. She had a thin parachute and often struggled to stay with the tribe.

Halfway down to her, a pair of hands grabbed her and jerked her back. She cried out and spun around.

It was Ilaru.

"What are you doing here?" Kareska said.

"I know what you're doing, Kareska, and you have to stop," Ilaru said.

"You can't stop me from helping the others."

"Dukario will kill you if he finds out. Can't you understand that?"

"I understand, and I don't care. If we don't help the others in our tribe, then he may as well kill us."

Ilaru released her and she floated back.

"You can't do this anymore," Ilaru said. "I'm telling you to stop."

"No, I won't," Kareska said.

"Kareska, I can't save you—"

"That's right, you can't," a voice said above them.

Kareska looked up just in time to see Dukario's clawed foot smack her in the face. Her head screamed with pain and she dangled back, blood dribbling into her eyes and half-blinding her. His gang grabbed her and Ilaru and held them.

"I've had enough of you two," Dukario said.

"Punish me," Kareska said. "It's not his fault. It's mine."

"Don't worry. You can join each other in the Great Below."

Awakened from their collective sleep, several fallers drifted over and watched Dukario.

Kareska glared at them and said, "What are you waiting for? Help us? You can stop him and the others. All you have to do is fight back."

"They won't help you."

And as Dukario said, they remained impassive.

"If you kill me, our planeparents won't come," Ilaru said.

"So what if they don't? We'll just kill the meatbirds and snatch the fruit balloons for food."

"Dukario, no!"

Ilaru tried to escape, but Dukario swooped in and severed his chute from his body. Kareska cried out in agony as he and his gang slashed and kicked Ilaru. When he was knocked unconscious, they dropped his body into the Great Below.

Kareska's heart sank with despair as she watched her carefather disappear beneath the clouds. But beneath that despair, her last reservoir of fear and restraint snapped. She no long cared if she lived or died. She was going to kill Dukario, even if it meant sacrificing her own life in the process.

She eased up in her captor's hands and waited until he grew at ease. When he did, she stabbed her claws into his groin. Her captor howled in agony and she kicked him off.

Screaming with rage, Kareska flew at Dukario. She kicked him in the testicles and slashed up his arms and legs and face. She tore one of his eyeballs out of its socket and it dangled there.

He tried to push her away, but she grabbed his bloody arm and bit deep into the meat. She tasted his salty blood. It tasted like revenge. Good and sweet.

She started to rip his parachute out, but his fellow gang members rushed to help him, struggling to pull her off their leader. Despite the overwhelming numbers, Kareska bit them and kicked them and clawed them, refusing to give up Dukario.

Finally, they slashed her parachute cords. The sudden pain stunned her back to reality and she screamed as they tore out the last cords and dropped her.

For a moment she could not believe that she was falling. She looked down and saw the clouds rushing past her, the ice cold wind slamming into her. She opened her mouth, but could make no sound. She thrashed her arms and struggled to keep level.

So this was it. The Great Below. Death. Despite her fear, she felt a certain detachment. At least she had made Dukario suffer before they had killed her. That brought her some small comfort. Now she would join Ilaru and Nadaro and all of the others.

Without warning the hump on her back had grown tense and shot pain through her shoulder blades. She cried out as a second parachute burst out from the hump. It blossomed above her and caught her fall. She shuddered and looked up. No one else in the tribe had had a second chute, but she had. All her life she wished that she could have gotten rid of that ugly hump, but now it had saved her life.

She smiled and adjusted its cords. She had been given a reprieve by her planeparents, a second chance. She would do well with it.

Early the next morning, Kareska drifted amidst the clouds, hastening her descent as much as possible by tightening the pull on her cords, waiting for the moment when they would fall towards her. Dukario and the other fallers reached her just before sunrise, while they were still sleepfalling. She waited until they were inside the clouds and then attacked.

Kareska swept out of the clouds and severed Dukario's cords. He screamed and dropped through the Great Below like a stone. Caught off guard, the other gang members awoke and looked around for their leader. The others of the tribe looked towards her.

"This is your chance," Kareska said to them. "Strike now and be free."

Although a few hesitated, most took her sudden reappearance as a call to arms. The fallers swooped down upon Dukario's gang. Surrounded by new enemies, they looked small, frightened and insignificant. The fallers shredded them to pieces, ripped their parachutes out and sent them to the Great Below.

She took pleasure in watching them suffer and die, but it was a bitter victory. If only they had acted sooner, then Nadaro and Ilaru might still be alive.

After they finished, the fallers floated up to her and bowed.

"From now on, things will be different," Kareska said. "Everyone will get an equal share of the food, whether they are well or infirm. We will help each other and anyone who will not aid his fellow faller will have to face me."

Despite her small body, it was a prospect that none of them seemed ready to face.

Over the next few years, Kareska grew older and taller and stronger. She led her tribe with fairness and equanimity and made sure that everybody received a share. Although there were a few like Azai and Dukario, she and the other fallers weeded them out quickly.

But as time passed, she noticed something alarming.

While all of the others grew older and more frail, Kareska did not age. Once she reached maturity, she remained young and vital. Soon the birthplanes stopped flying overhead and her fellow fallers began to pass away from disease, starvation and old age.

She tried desperately to help those around her, giving them most of her food and water from her own moisture tail. But it was no use.

Soon Kareska was the only remaining faller in the sky. All the others had died or dropped into the Great Below.

What's wrong with me? Kareska thought. Am I normal? No, I must not be. I am a freak, an aberration. I must have angered our planeparents and now they are taking their vengeance upon me. I will be forced to float down through the Great Below for eternity.

She frowned and considered cutting her own cords. She did not want to be alone anymore, yet something deep inside her mind and heart stayed her claws. That same strength which drove her to attack Dukario prevented her from taking her only life. Curiosity lingered in her mind, curiosity at the myths of land and water. Were such things true?

If I am condemned alone to float through the Great Below for my sins, then I will find out what lies at the end of Dropworld, she thought.

Resigned to her fate, she tightened her strings and continued downward.

Three years after the last of her fellow fallers had died, Kareska reached the end of the Great Below. Beneath her feet lay a vast sheet of green and brown and blue where the sky itself was cut off.

Land.

Water.

Was this truly the bottom of the Great Below?

A mixture of awe and terror arose within Kareska and she wasn't sure if she wanted to reach the end. After a lifetime of falling through an endless sky, it seemed bizarre to have something solid upon which to stand.

She struggled against the inexorable pull of gravity, but it was a losing battle. Finally, she decided to let the fates guide her and she set down upon land. She collapsed and her chute fell in on her. Once she recovered, she gathered her chute up in her arms and looked down at the green blades that tickled her bare feet.

They felt funny.

What did Ilaru call them again? Kareska thought. Grass, that's it.

She knelt, picked off a blade, sniffed it and then ate it. It tasted bitter, yet it had a unique smell that delighted her. She moved forward and collapsed after a step, unused to having a solid surface to walk upon.

"Hello, Kareska," a voice said.

She turned.

Ilaru was standing next to her. Kareska staggered back, unable to believe her eyes.

"What happened?"

"You made it. It's good to see you again."

Kareska shook her head. "You're dead. I saw you fall—"

"Yes, but the planeparents gave me a second chute. Come, I have so much to show you."

Ilaru reached for her hand, but she pulled it back.

"Wait, why am I here? What is this world?"

Ilaru touched her head and the world around her faded. She found herself floating in a vast darkness punctuated by brief dots of light. Stars. Outer space. She didn't know how she knew these things, but she did.

A long, silver, cylindrical world floated in front of her. It was hundreds of miles long and wide, constantly rotating.

"They saved the last of us," Ilaru said.

"The last of us?"

"Humans, from another world. It was once called Earth, but it's gone now. Destroyed when its sun went nova. The planes brought you, me, Dukario, and other humans here across space, erased our memories of Earth and adapted us to their culture. They allowed us to lifefall with the other natives."

She stared at the world, feeling awe at the sky of such a large world, even though it was eclipsed by the vastness of space itself.

"Why save us?"

"They wished to preserve all life. Now that we have fallen, they will allow us to remain on land. Unless, of course, you wish to be born again and begin a new lifefall."

Kareska blinked and looked around. Land was such a new thing, such a new idea. She could hardly take it all in.

"Are there other humans on land . . . like us?"

"Yes."

"What about Nadaro and Usaki and the others? Are they still—"

Ilaru frowned. "No, they have passed on, but other fallers will be born."

"Will they ever reach the Great Below?"

"No. They do not live as long as we do. And it is in their nature to fall, not walk. That is their life. What do you wish to do with the remainder of yours?"

Kareska looked back up at the sky, and imagined falling once again. As much as she loved that, the idea of walking on land and swimming in the water seemed so new . . . so intriguing. She wanted to remain and see what lay on the surface of the Great Below.

"I wish to stay here," Kareska said.

"Come, I will introduce you to the others," Ilaru said.

He took Kareska's hand and led her across the valley to her new home.

*Fredrick Obermeyer enjoys writing science-fiction, fantasy, horror, and crime stories. He has had work published in* Electric Spec *quarterly e-zine,* Newmyths *quarterly ezine,* Perihelion Online Science Fiction Magazine *ezine,* Acidic Fiction *twice weekly ezine, and other markets.*

Forty light years across the galaxy, two radically different post-Earth societies battle each other for the colonization of an alien Solar System. One faction fights to save the indigenous population, the other to exterminate them. One man's agonizing choice could offer a promising new frontier for the human race, or destroy humanity's future.

# BRIGHT HORIZON

### By

### *Tom Olbert*

The black sky over Trappist I was a wild lightshow of exploding spacecraft. The orbiting space blockade stations were broadsiding with particle beam and laser barrages, the attacking ships lighting orbital space with searing white nuclear explosions.

Tari winced, struggling with the controls. Sweat beaded on her upper lip as her mind raced, calculating the approach vector. The blockade station was visible just below the green-and-blue curve of the planet. "Approach vector laid in," she managed, fighting to keep her voice steady, the ship's superstructure rattling wildly around her, the bridge lights flickering. "Y-14, interface requested."

"Acknowledged," the smooth, insufferably calm voice of the A.I. answered. As Tari's command chair slid back into position, Y-14 closed in around her, its cyber-extensors interfacing with the surgically-implanted access port at the base of Tari's skull. The young woman found herself racing through the frightful ordeal of computer-accelerated thought, her fluidic human instincts now enhanced by the instantaneous relays of robotic intellect. The cascade of laser fire blasting at them from the blockade station ahead was almost beautiful as her mind interfaced with the attack ship's external sensors. She concentrated, directing the forward gun crews.

"Hits recorded on forward enemy batteries," Kojan, the huge gorilla announced from the forward weapons station, his thick, leathery fingers dancing over the control keys with amazing dexterity. "30% of targets destroyed."

"Concentrate fire on blockade station hub center," the voice of the ship's commander, Songweaver boomed through the cabin speaker. Tari managed a slight smile. She always felt better knowing Songweaver was in command. Gentle as the immense killer whale was, her intellect in battle was as fearsome as a stellar storm. "Gaarz," Songweaver ordered from her tank at the rear of the bridge, addressing the laser turret officer. "Cascade laser fire. They may try to blanket us with stealth drones."

"Acknowledged," Gaarz said, as her almost serpentine form slithered swiftly across the laser control sphere. The Xarv's multiple claw-like appendages gracefully re-set the laser turret alignment with more-than-human rapidity. Tari ground her teeth, fighting to re-equate her navigational calculations as explosions buffeted the attack striker. Songweaver had been right about the drones. *Black Void take the filthy sleepers!* Tari focused on the attack run, realizing they had to keep the station gun crews busy long enough for the fighter squadron to slip in under the enemy's radar to take out the main fusion reactors. Tari's heart raced, her blood running cold as her thoughts drifted to Lynn, now in danger as her squadron neared the blockade station.

Lynn sweated in her oxygen suit as her fighter closed on the blockade station. She glanced at her tactical board, seeing all fighters in her squadron were closing on their targets. No resistance. *Good*, she thought. The attack striker had done its job, diverting the station's main batteries and scanners away from her fighters. Lynn's teeth clenched, her gut twisting at the thought of Tari in the line of fire on the attack run. She reflexively reached for the radio switch, but stopped herself. Her first instinct was to charge in hard and fast and take out the station's laser cannon as swiftly as possible, to protect Tari. She closed her eyes and focused, forcing herself not to grow reckless. Her mission was to take out the fusion reactors. She couldn't jeopardize the mission or her squadron for personal reasons.

Her pulse pounded as the seconds dragged by, the targets coming at last into range. She flipped the radio switch, breaking comm silence.

"All units, engage!" she transmitted, bringing up her lasers and opening fire at the fusion nodes ahead. A smile spread across her face as she watched the board. The strike was flawlessly coordinated, all fighters striking their targets simultaneously. The chain reaction ignited as planned, the station's whole power system going up as the explosions spread through the station's lower sections.

"All units return to carriers," she ordered. It was then she caught the swarm of flickering blips on the contact scanner. Incoming intercept fighters. *The Black Void take it*, she silently cursed.

"Assume defense pattern Alpha!" she ordered, turning her fighter straight towards the attacking swarm and firing at will. As the explosions of disintegrating enemy fighters ripped across the black sky over the collapsing space station, she turned her feelings off, as her training told her to do. Not human beings of flesh and blood out there. Not people with thoughts or feelings for loved ones left behind. Only enemy targets bent on her destruction.

She groaned, a dull pain shooting through her side as a laser bolt took out her port thruster. Her instrument panel exploded as her atmosphere began to vent into space. Her head swam with the shock. She forced herself to stay conscious, her vision blurring as she flipped the ignition switches in memorized sequence, jettisoning the damaged engine frame and weapons array. As her pilot pod hit planetary ionosphere, she activated the magnetic force field and engaged braking thrusters, praying to the Cosmic One that the auxiliary generator would hold out long enough to keep her from burning to a cinder on atmospheric entry. As the planet's oceans and fertile land masses rapidly enlarged in her viewport, her last thought before blacking out was of Tari's warmly smiling face. "Be safe, love."

Tari was shaken to her bones, alarm klaxons blaring, red emergency lighting washing through the attack striker bridge. The ship trembled as the enemy space station broke up, enemy ejection pods filling the viewport.

"Enemy fighters closing, Commander," Gaarz announced, shifting the remaining laser turrets to destroying the incoming fighter craft.

Tari was thrown from her station, Y-14 catching her in its metal claws as a thundering explosion ripped through the ship, panels exploding. Fire control teams got to work as Tari struggled to get the navigational circuits back on line.

"All indicators dead!" she said with disgust, slamming her hand against the panel.

"Tactical report!" Songweaver demanded.

"An enemy fighter collided with the main engine pod, Commander." Kal, the Collective organism declared through its translator implants, as its multiple components slithered together into a writhing mass of wormy tissue. Kojan shielded Tari with his shaggy bulk as part of the overhead gave way.

"Evacuate!" Songweaver ordered. "Launch all landing craft! Kojan, you're in command. Get those supplies to the Vurl resistance at all costs!"

"Yes, Commander," Kojan answered, a barely discernable tremor of doubt in his strong, raspy voice.

Tari felt a chill run through her. "Commander . . . what about you?" she asked, coughing as smoke filled the bridge.

"Follow my orders!" the commander declared, another explosion tearing open the bulkhead as the bridge went dark.

Tari's blood burned with hatred for the sleepers. *What kind of monsters are these people?*

Rick Barrett fell back into the dirt, desperately groping for his laser pistol as the nightmarish black-winged shape of an attacking Vurl rebel came straight at him out of the flaring red sun. The Vurl's outstretched wings had nearly a twelve-foot span. The creature's three, red-crystalline eyes glittered like blood on fire. The russet sunlight glittered on the razor-sharp blades the monster held in its two lower appendages, blades still dripping with the blood of Barrett's men. The Vurl's four-sided beak opened in a shriek that sank like a cold skewer to Barrett's marrow. His hand closed around the pistol. He roared as he raised the gun and fired.

The Vurl shrieked as its guts were blown out. Rick gasped as the native's blades dug into the ground within a half-inch of his throat. When he could breathe again, he tried to leverage the black leathery corpse off himself. He had to pry the creature's claws off the knife hilts to finally get the damnable thing off him. He struggled to his knees and looked left and right. The ground was littered with dead bodies, human and Vurl. He slowly got to his feet, blood pounding through his temples as he realized the battle was over. His breath rapid, he walked slowly, still shaky, towards the smoking ruins of the abandoned Vurl city. The lurid light of the red dwarf star that was this planet's sun washed over the field of corpses. The other two planets of Trappist hung low over the surrounding jungle landscape. He wiped sweat from his forehead in the sweltering heat, his eyes tearing in the reddish light.

"You okay, boss?" Klausen said, jogging towards him. Barrett looked his old friend over. Klausen's uniform was singed and splattered with blackish-green Vurl blood.

"I'll live," Barrett muttered. "Casualties?"

"Twenty-three, so far. We've still got a few unaccounted for."

Barrett stifled a curse. "What happened?"

"Most of the black-wings had already evacuated when we got here, leaving just about every building booby-trapped," Klausen said, wiping blood from a singed forehead. "A few of them stayed behind to ambush us. They fought to the last, as usual." Barrett winced as memories of past battles flashed through his mind, snatches of blood and fire. "Drone scans say their main population's heading inland. Should we follow?"

Rick's brow furrowed as he weighed the options. He thought of his dead men . . . of his father and brother, both lost to those inhuman scum . . . and, his blood burned for revenge. But, he forced himself to calculate rationally. If he moved now, he might lose more men. If he waited for reinforcements, St. Jamal only knew how much longer it would take to track the hostiles down or how many more humans they'd kill in the meantime. His head snapped upward, a flash of light catching the corner of his eye. "What in the black pit—?" A white-hot bolt of fire shot across the sky, a smoke trail behind it. "Down!" He glanced up, the flaming object crashing out of sight beyond a stretch of leafy jungle foliage.

"Meteor?" Klausen asked.

"No," Barrett answered. "Our satellites would have tracked it. Must be a space pod. Rally the squads. We're going after it."

The men formed up, looking damned ragged, but ready for a fight and damned frustrated by this distraction. Barrett could see in the angry, twisted looks on their faces they were hungry for Vurl blood. He didn't blame them. They'd all lost friends and family in this damned war. But, his duty was clear.

"Forward!" he ordered, leading his men through the foliage. Drawing a vibro blade and cutting his way through the meter-wide leaves and pod-like growths in the deep underbrush, Barrett finally emerged into a clearing near a stream. There lay the smoking, blackened trail of the downed pod. It's still faintly glowing silver-gray cylindrical shape lay steaming in the red light.

"Not one of ours," Klausen said, tension in his voice. "The damn tin heads must have breached the space blockade."

"Radiation scan," Barrett ordered.

"She's clean," one of the techs said, switching off the detection unit.

"Move in. All squads on alert. Keep your lasers on that pod every second." He moved towards the pod.

"Rick," Klausen protested, laying a hand on Barrett's arm.

Barrett shook it off. "Stay here. That's an order." Nearing the pod, he stood by, nervously rubbing his sweaty fingers against the handle of his gun. As the techs finished hosing down the steaming metal and cutting through the pod hatch seal with their laser torches, he held his breath. The hatch was pried open and removed.

"Step back," he ordered, his anger mounting as he stepped forward and looked through the hatch, gun raised. He was eager to face the alien filth that had attacked his world and killed his people. The off-world scum who'd given weaponry to the Vurl rebs. His heart froze in his chest as his eyes fixed on the unconscious face of a beautiful young woman.

Tari swept her aero-skiff in a wide arc, firing air-to-air lasers and knocking an enemy scanner drone out of the sky, its flaming wreckage falling to the planet surface. The hot wind of Trappist-I's atmosphere lashed her face, blowing through her hair as she swung the skiff around to re-group with the rest of the rim gunners. She saw the greenish-blue jungle canopy rippling below as the last of the landing craft engaged retro thrusters.

Shadows flitting across her field of vision, she looked up into the boiling red sky and saw swarms of Vurl turning like black kites against the back-drop of the two neighboring planets, Trappist Two and Three, moving in tight formation as they rendezvoused at the landing sites. Setting down nearby, Tari jogged towards the nearest lander, just as the laser guns were being unloaded and distributed among the Vurl resistance fighters. She concentrated, listening to the conversation between Kojan and the Vurl resistance leader, hoping her translator implant would pick up some clue regarding the location of Lynn.

"An incoming pod was sighted, several kliks toward the coast," Gaarz said, the humming vibrations of her multiple tongues translated into a rough approximation of human speech by the micro-A.I. link in Tari's brain. "No knowledge of the pilot, however."

Tari shook off a momentary chill. Xarv telepathy could be an unnerving invasion of privacy. Though, in this case, not unwelcome. "Are you certain," Tari asked urgently, her heart racing.

"I've scanned every Vurl in the area, my friend. Though I find it difficult to sort Vurl thoughts . . . so fluid, so intertwined . . . there is no memory of Lynn." Tari's heart sank. Gaarz gently laid a claw on Tari's shoulder. "I'm sorry. I'll keep scanning."

Tari gently stroked Gaarz's pale, cool green trunk. "Thanks, Gaarz. I can always count on you." Tari's head snapped up, a system-wide implant transmission from Y-14 ordering all personnel to rally. Tari ran to the landing site, Gaarz rapidly slithering through the tall grass beside her.

"Attention all," Kojan ordered, one of his burly, black shaggy arms raised to gain attention. "All Vurl resistance units are to be equipped and provisioned by 0:09 hours, planetside time. All unit advisers will report directly to me. Y-14 will formulate designated targets and brief you at first light next rotation. Any questions?"

"Commander," Kal asked, its slithering mass standing nearby. "Any word on Commander Songweaver?"

"Not yet," Kojan said quietly, casting his dark eyes skyward, as though on instinct. "The striker's main section may still be in orbit, under stealth shield. No way to tell, since we are as of now on off-world comm silence. I know it's difficult. We all have friends and comrades up there, but the Commander would have expected us to focus our full attention on the mission, and I intend to see to it that her orders are carried out. We have a race of people to save, and I expect full dedication from each of you. Clear?"

The assembled crews from the landing crafts answered in unison, their voices loud and strong. "Yes, Commander!" The Vurls raised their laser rifles, their wings unfurled as they collectively issued a reverberating battle shriek that seemed to energize the air itself.

"Are there any other questions?"

Tari bowed her head, her question regarding Lynn's whereabouts burning in her throat. Kojan was right, she forced herself to remember. She had to focus all she had on the mission. Lynn would be the first to remind her of that. As she had, when she'd held her that last time, just before her squadron had launched.

"Kal," Kojan continued. "You'll coordinate all scouting patrols, in preparation for the mobilization."

"Yes, Commander," the Collective replied, its telepathically linked member organisms separating and slithering off rapidly in multiple directions, the ground bulging as they submerged like gargantuan earth worms.

"Gaarz, confer with unit commander D'Traal."

"Yes, Commander," Gaarz replied, slithering off. Tari felt a parting telepathic wave from her friend, like a comforting caress.

"Lieutenant Lamar." Kojan said, addressing Tari.

"Yes, Commander," Tari replied, pulling herself straight and standing at attention.

"You'll confer with unit commander T'Zaar."

"Yes, sir."

"Tari," Kojan said softly, lowering his massive bulk to a crouched position beside her. "Don't worry," he said, ever-so-gently laying a massive hand on her shoulder, as though afraid she'd break like crystal.

"Lynn is strong, a capable warrior. She's survived worse than this."

"I know," she said, trying to be strong. "May the Cosmic One help any sleepers she encounters." She tried to force a smile. Then, allowed herself a stolen moment of weakness, her face buried in the soft fur of Kojan's strong shoulder as he gently stroked her back.

Barrett staggered out of the interrogation cell into the corridor, heaving up his rations, the young woman's screams of pain still ringing in his ears.

There was laughter all around him, his comrades in arms jeering at him as the dimly lit corridor pitched around him. "What's the matter, Barrett," Colby taunted. "Going soft on the enemy?"

"So, what else is new?" Marsden shouted. "Remember Blue Valley? Barrett wouldn't let us bomb black-wing civies. And, at New Johannesburg, when we raided that Vurl city, he wouldn't let us burn out the hatchling nests. How many of those slimy little black-wings are going to grow up to kill more of us, huh, Ricky-boy? Alien lover!"

Barrett saw red as he bashed in Marsden's face, leaving the other man bloodied, flat on his back. It took Klausen and three other guys to pull Barrett off him. "Come on," Klausen whispered, pulling Barrett down the corridor, towards the cafeteria. "What the hell's wrong with you?"

Barrett's head swam as he slumped against the wall and sank to a seated position. "Here," Klausen said, handing him a flask.

Barrett took a swallow, the liquor hitting his brain like a lightning bolt. "Whew . . . thanks."

"Keep it. What the hell are they doing to her in there?"

Barrett sighed, running a hand through his hair and slumping his head against the wall. He involuntarily cringed as he remembered. "Uh . . . neural pain stims. I've never seen them have to go up to this level before.

I've never seen a man that tough, never mind a woman. I sure as hell wouldn't have held out that long."

"The Commandants have always said these invaders have no feelings. That they're like A.I.-lobotomized zombies, or something. Not even really human anymore."

"She has feelings." He trembled with the memory of the torture, taking another swallow to kill the pain. "She cried. She kept calling out something. A name, I think. Tari."

"Did they get anything out of her? Anything we can use?"

"No," he sighed. "Nothing we didn't already know. Her people have colonized the second and third planets in this system, and they're terraforming both rocks. The rest was the usual propaganda. She claims we're trying to wipe out the whole Vurl race, and all that crap. If she doesn't break soon . . . and, she won't . . . they'll try the cyber web next."

Klausen's face went a bit pale. "Damn. Nobody survives that. This can't be legal. Have you thought about going to Division? Civilian Oversight, maybe?"

"I already have." He rubbed his throbbing temples. "They don't want to get involved. The Commandants in the Hub get more powerful every day. Taggart gives them whatever they want."

"Speaking of our beloved Chancellor . . . he's making a general address on planetary vid today at 0:14 hours. Attendance is mandatory."

"In that case, I really need to get drunk." He took another swallow.

Tari screamed, pain like a thousand hot needles stabbing into her brain. She clutched her head in both hands and fell to her knees. "Tari!" Kojan called out, loping over to her and taking her in his strong arms. His leathery hands gently stroked the cold sweat from her forehead as the light danced before her eyes. "Tari, what is it?"

"Lynn . . . they're hurting her. She called out my name. I have to get to her." She tried to get up, but Kojan restrained her.

"Delirium?" he asked the medic checking her over.

"Her vitals seem normal," the man said, putting aside his neural scanning device.

"Her mind is afflicted with visions," Gaarz said. "Sensory recollections. It's definitely Lynn."

"How?" Kojan asked.

"Tari's brain implant may be receiving direct thought impulses via subspace through Lynn's implant," Y-14 explained, the waning red sunlight shining a dull russet sheen on the towering robot's silver metallic armor. "Exceedingly rare, but it has been recorded, especially in times of extreme stress, between two individuals with a strong psychological bond. The human brain never ceases to fascinate me."

"Never mind the analysis," Kojan grumbled. "Can you trace the subspace signal back to its source?"

"Negative. But, if Tari would allow me to interface with her, perhaps I could extrapolate Lynn's location based on her memories of what she has seen since landing."

Pulling herself up with a hand on Kojan's shoulder, Tari nodded. As Y-14 assumed its interface shape, Tari seated herself inside the robot's embrace. Taking a deep breath, Tari prepared herself for interface. As Y-14's extensor locked into her brain port, she was jolted with a wild cascade of memories. The crash. Hovercraft. Confederation soldiers. A military command complex. Interrogation. Cruel, angry men. "Lynn . . ." she called out, her hand groping at empty air.

"Enough," she heard Kojan's voice, pulling her back to reality.

Y-14 disconnected. Tari's head reeled. She felt the cool, telepathic balm of Gaarz's mind soothing her own as Kojan steadied her, his hands on her shoulders. "Well?" the gorilla asked.

"Location pinpointed," the robot replied. "Fifteen kliks north by northeast. Coastal military command complex. Fortifications uploading now." Tari rubbed her head as the tactical specs flowed into her mind through the implant.

"Difficult," Kojan grumbled.

"Are we to abandon Lynn, Commander?" Gaarz said, her massive serrated mandibles spreading wide in an expression of anger, her multiple eye stalks quivering.

"I said, 'difficult', Lieutenant Gaarz, not impossible," Kojan retorted, bearing his teeth. "An all-out assault is out of the question. We don't have the resources. However, a small-scale tactical raid might be feasible. Assessment, Y-14."

"Forty-two percent probability of success. Sixty-one percent chance of additional casualties. I must advise against."

Tari reflexively lashed out in anger, but stopped herself, clenching her fists and writhing in frustration. "I know I can't ask you to—"

"You don't have to ask, Tari," Kojan said. "I thought you realized that."

Tari's heart trembled. "But, the mission—"

"Your assessment, Lieutenant Lamar?" Kojan asked.

"Uh . . . unit commander T'Zaar has my full confidence, Commander. I've thoroughly briefed him."

"I can say the same for unit commander D'Traal, Commander," Gaarz put in.

"Well," Kojan said, snorting pensively. "Since the Vurls have made it abundantly clear they don't want us running the resistance for them . . . and, since they have our ships behind them for air support . . . let's be on our way."

Tari gasped. "You, Kojan? But, you're the acting commander."

"And, now that the mission is accomplished, my primary responsibility is the defense of my team. Shall we go?"

"Not without us, Commander," Kal said as its many sections slithered up out of the ground and combined into its whole.

"Y-14, you're the acting commander until I return," Kojan said as he started off. Tari brushed aside a tear as she followed.

"I'm coming as well," Y-14 declared, assuming a configuration similar to a huge, metallic spider as it followed the others. Tari's jaw dropped as she spun towards the A.I. "I estimate my presence will increase the odds of success by 15%." She nearly laughed.

"Rick . . . it's been a long time." The young woman hesitated, her eyes turning down. "I know you don't want to hear from me, but this is important. The plague here in Sorwaan is getting worse. The anti-viral drugs are helping somewhat but . . . the lab tests don't leave any room for doubt. The plague virus is not . . . cannot be naturally occurring. Rick, as much as you don't want to hear this, there's only one plausible explanation. The military has deployed a genetically engineered viral weapon that is lethal to the Vurls and harmless to humans." The woman glanced around, her expression tense. "I think they may be monitoring communications. I'm uploading the viral DNA breakdown to you now. Please, get it to someone who'll listen."

"Rick." Klausen's voice and a nudge at his shoulder startled Barrett. Removing the audio plug from his ear, Barrett took the holo viewer from his eyes. Looking across the cafeteria, he saw the nightmarish sight of a twelve-foot-tall man glowering down on the assembled soldiers like a fearsome god.

"Attention!" the base commander shouted. Every man assembled stood up from the tables and snapped to. Barrett slipped the comm link under his jacket, his mouth suddenly dry. "William Taggart, Chancellor of the New Terran Confederation will now address you."

The immense three-dimensional hologram transmission of Taggart spoke in a booming voice through the PA system. "Officers and men of the Confederation Armed Forces. A grave and terrible time is upon our once-great republic. A hundred years have passed since our noble forefathers completed their arduous four-thousand-year journey across the stars. For a century, our people have struggled bravely against the inhuman filth that infest this planet, our adopted and God-granted home!" Most of the men clapped and cheered. Others looked on quietly. Klausen glanced at Barrett, his brow furrowed, his jaw set.

"There is a growing weakness slowly eating away at our national resolve. Spineless colonial governors have allowed the Vurl insurgency to grow like a cancer. These cowards have restrained you, our brave troops from doing what needs to be done. No more. I have hereby declared martial law, and dispensed with the bureaucratic *garbage* that once afflicted our state!" Taggart's face flushed red as his voice roared, the hologram growing dramatically larger. As the men raucously pounded on the tables, a chill swept through Barrett.

"All twenty-three colonies are now under the direct control of the Commandants. Civilian government has been abolished. As of today, the New Terran Confederation is dissolved. The New Terran Empire is now in effect." Cheers and whistles rang through the chamber.

"Today, examples were set, a message sent loud and clear throughout the empire. Treason equals death! Those traitors, those Vurl-loving trash who would give aid and comfort to the enemy of Man are being dealt with."

Barrett's teeth clenched as the holographic ghosts of exploding buildings flooded the room, a wave of fire coursing through Taggart's gigantic, translucent face. "Bandaar, Valaz . . . every Vurl city where plots were being hatched against the state, where Vurl insurgents were massing, is being destroyed. Sorwaan, where Vurl-loving scientists were colluding with our enemy is now in ruins."

Barrett's head swam, his vision blurring as the city from which his sister had sent that last transmission barely an hour before appeared before him, in flames and ruin. "Rachel," he whispered in a strangled throat. "No."

"There will be no survivors! No enemies of humanity will live to threaten the state!" The words swirled like ashes through the smoke and fire. Barrett trembled in rage, his fist clenching against the table, hot blood pounding through his brain. The black-armored Special Forces troops filed into the cafeteria, Taggart's image hovering over them. An obvious show of strength, no doubt playing out in every colony on the planet.

"Scum." The word rose, grumbling from his throat. "Filthy murderers!" As if in a fever dream, he picked up a chair and hurled it at the advancing SF troopers. Before he knew what was happening, the cafeteria was a wild, thrashing sea of fists and chairs, a mass of men attacking each other like wild animals. *How many of ours died today?* was all he could think as Klausen pulled him towards an air duct. Barret's hand closed on the comm link in his pocket. *I won't fail you again, Rachel.*

Lynn strained against the cybernetic manacles the swine had locked around her wrists. They had her spread-eagled in some kind of web-like array of cybernetic connections. She strained harder, her heart pounding. If she was going to die, she at least wanted to take a few of these savages with her.

"Don't bother struggling," one of the black-uniformed sleeper soldiers taunted. He grinned as he clutched her face. She spat in his. He snarled, slapping her back-handed across the face. She glared at him, spitting out blood. They had tortured her so long, she barely felt pain anymore.

"I'm going to enjoy this. Attach the electrodes." As the torturers complied, Lynn thought of Tari.

A searing flash of light half-blinded her as the black-uniformed man and the two others working on her were struck down, falling limp to the floor. *A stun blaster*, she realized, her senses slowly returning as she dimly made out a young man standing in the doorway, the weapon in his hand. He wore a Confederation uniform, she realized in disbelief as the man ran to her side. *How?* She knew her people had no spies inside the Confederation. His face was sweaty and wildly fevered as he detached the electrodes.

"Who are you?" she managed in a painfully dry throat.

"No time," he said, breathless, unlocking one of the manacles. "I need your help and you need mine." She barely had time to cry out as a man tackled her unlikely ally, knocking his gun to the floor, clutching at his throat and driving him back against the wall. Another man drew a blaster, trying to get a clear shot. Lynn glanced up and, realizing one of the detached electrodes was live, grabbed it and drove it into the gunman's neck. As his body convulsed and fell senseless to the floor, she snatched the blaster from his hand. The man who had helped her broke his attacker's hold and knocked him backward with a kick to this gut. A look of killing anger on his face, the attacker picked up a laser scalpel from a nearby tray. Lynn fired the blaster and blew the enemy soldier in half.

Staggering over to her, Lynn's new *friend* unlocked her other manacle and helped her out of the cyber web. "Get one of those uniforms on, while I guard the door." he gasped. "I know a way out of the base, through the sewage line."

Her mind was reeling as she pulled the uniform off one of the unconscious soldiers. She prayed to the Cosmic One that this was not a dream.

The jungle was dark and sultry. The smoldering red light of the two planets overhead washed the clearing in dull russet, making the nearby river look like a torrent of thick, cloying blood. Barrett gulped water from his canteen and handed it to the strange alien woman he'd just rescued. The distant explosion rumbled like soft thunder.

"Good," he muttered, wiping sweat from his upper lip. "That timed explosive I set off will divert them back to the detention area and buy us a little time. I hope. How far do we have to go?"

She eyed him, like an animal eyeing a potential predator. He sighed, looking up at the night sky in wearied frustration.

"Look . . . this isn't some overblown trick. I'm not trying to scam you into giving up intel. A man's dead because of me. I'm dead if they catch me, all right? We need each other, you understand? Now where, damn it?"

She calmly took a swallow from the canteen. "South," she said, guardedly. "Fifteen, maybe twenty kliks. Just an estimate, you understand."

He sighed, staring into the dark foliage. "Not good. Too many patrols, too many drones. We'll have to circle west, then—"

He was cut off mid-sentence, his blood turning to ice as harsh white light bathed the clearing. "Don't move!" a voice called down through an amplifier. "We have you surrounded." He looked up, wincing in scorching white lights blazing down from two hovercraft. He drew his blaster, and the woman drew hers, but he knew they'd had it. Special Forces troopers with laser rifles crashed into the clearing from multiple directions, encircling them.

"Throw down your weapons, or die!" the voice said. Rick complied, tossing his gun aside. He looked at the woman. She seemed to hesitate. "This is your last warning."

The two hover craft exploded in a thundering ball of fire, flaming shrapnel raining onto the clearing. Rick dropped and rolled, snatching up his gun and blasting down one of the startled troopers. He saw the woman do the same. As Rick turned, he saw a trooper with a laser rifle pointed directly at his head. In that moment, he knew he was dead. He heard a bone-chilling roar, somehow neither human nor animal. A rustling in the leaves of an overhanging tree. And, something black and shaggy swung down and seized the trooper from behind, lifting him up off the ground and hurling him like a doll. Dear God . . . a gorilla? Was he dreaming? The beast hung from a branch with one hand and fired a laser gun with the other.

Something else entered the clearing that slithered, like a huge serpent, but with multiple claw-like hands. It fired, laser bolts taking out two more troopers.

The remaining SF troopers tried to rally, but other large, slithering dark masses rose out of the ground and seized several of them, killing some and immobilizing more. The many dark masses combined into something huge and terrible, like a writhing mass of snakes. It seized and hurled soldiers like stones. Nearby, Barrett glimpsed a young woman blasting down the last of the troopers. Her face—young and quite pretty, with dark eyes and short dark hair—wore a soldier's expression of killing anger. That expression suddenly softened as the girl's eyes fixed on the woman with him.

"Lynn!" she cried, running towards her. The two women embraced.

"Tari, thank the Cosmic One you're safe," the woman said. Barrett could only stare agape as they kissed.

"No time," a harsh, guttural voice said. Barrett nearly fainted as he realized the words had come from the gorilla. "They'll be converging on our position any second. Y-14."

Barrett nearly jumped out of his skin as a shining silver hovercraft of a kind he'd never seen before descended just a few feet from him. He stared, horror-stricken as the machine assumed a towering, upright form.

"Recon complete," the robot thing said in a humming, artificial voice. "Escape course programmed."

*An A.I.!* He raised his blaster to fire on the robot. He barely caught sight of the woman whose life he'd saved raising a blaster and firing. At him. The flash was the last thing he saw.

He woke screaming, his body covered in cold sweat. He looked around, finding himself on a wide, triangular bed he recognized as being of Vurl manufacture. No windows in the silver-gray walls. He rubbed his throbbing head. How did he get here? Was he going mad? The last thing he could clearly remember . . . he started as a door slid open and the woman he'd saved from the detention cell stepped in. Nodding to a guard in the corridor outside, she turned to Barrett as the door slid shut behind her.

"Feeling better?" she asked, moving towards him.

"I'll live," he muttered, sitting up on the bed. "No thanks to you. I save your life, and you stun me?"

"You were about to fire on one of my team mates," she said, pulling up one of the triangular perches that were the Vurl equivalent of chairs, and sat beside him. "I had no choice."

"You're welcome, by the way. Where are we?"

"Tessra," She answered.

Tessra. One of the Vurl cities currently controlled by the insurgents. "How much of what I remember of the jungle was real?" he asked, still groggy. "Were we actually rescued by a talking ape? Weird alien things?"

"It was real," she answered dryly. "Your people don't know much about us, do they?"

"No, we don't," he admitted.

"Our ancestors didn't make the four-thousand-year crossing from Earth sound asleep in cryogenic freezers the way yours did. Our people made the journey awake, in self-sustaining biospheric hive ships; a hundred and sixty generations of us. And, we accomplished a few things during the trip. We genetically engineered new forms of intelligence from the animals we brought along from Earth. We contacted other forms of sentient life along the way; other refugees from other dying worlds. We helped them. They helped us."

"And, that A.I.?"

"What about it?"

He scratched his head. "According to what they teach us in school, the A.I.'s tried to wipe out humanity in the time before SecondExodus, and my ancestors left the Solar System to escape the A.I. wars."

"Our data banks say the same."

"So, what happened after my people left?" He eyed her suspiciously, glancing at the door. "Did your people surrender to those things?" he asked in a low voice, his muscles tensing.

"No," she sighed. "My ancestors fought on for a century after your people left. Then, Sol started flaring up, and they had to reach accommodation with the A.I.'s. Both sides realized they had to work together to escape. The A.I.'s helped us build the Genesis Hives, and they made the trip here with us. We've developed a symbiotic relationship with them. We co-exist with them as equals now. Now, enough about us," she said with a note of impatience in her voice. "Let's talk about you. Why have you betrayed your people?"

Anger welled up in him, hot blood hitting his brain. He swung his legs over the edge of the bed. "I'm not the betrayer! Those devils who run our government are! They killed thousands of us . . . their own people . . . in the trading posts, the factories, the cities. God, they murdered my sister!" His head swam in hot blood, the room swaying around him. He nearly toppled over.

"Easy," she said, steadying him.

"Leave me alone!" he shouted, throwing her hands off and trying to stand. He wanted out.

She held him down, with surprising strength. "Are you going to settle down, or do I have to call a medic in here to sedate you?" she asked, softly but firmly. He sighed, resting back on the bed. Thinking back on what this woman had been through, she amazed him more and more. "I'm sorry about your sister," she said with sincerity in her voice, releasing him.

"I don't want sympathy," he said through clenched teeth as he perched up on his elbows. "I want payback."

"I know. You'll have it, I promise. But, maybe you'd be willing to help us save some lives, first?"

"How?"

"We broke down that data your sister transmitted to you."

He looked at her. "The plague. Can your people cure it?" he asked with desperate hope. If only Rachel's death weren't in vain.

"Not with the limited resources we have here. But, if you help us crack your people's offworld communications codes so we can transmit the data to Trappist II and guide our ships through your space blockade, then there's hope. I realize that's asking a lot of you."

*No more than Rachel gave,* he thought bitterly. "I'm in," he said firmly.

"Lynn Kalvers," she said, extending her hand.

"Rick Barrett," he said, giving her his.

Three weeks later, the night air over the Terran Imperial base was filled with laser fire and the screams of the dying. Imperial troopers in jet packs vied with Vurl resistance fighters for control of the eastern wall.

Tari held on tightly, her arms around the thick, tubular neck of the Vurl she rode, more than three hundred meters above ground. The Vurl glided in quietly below the turrets of the western wall, slipping in below the enemy's radar. She held her breath and waited. There was the offworld comm dish. Only two guards, just as Barrett had said. As the Vurl swept in and turned, she leapt for the platform, drawing her blaster and stunning the guard on the left just as he raised his laser rifle. Barrett leapt from his Vurl mount and stunned the other guard. As the two guards fell senseless and the two Vurls flew off to handle the laser turret posts on either side of the dish turret, Tari got to work on the antenna.

Cutting open the service hatch, she patched into the satellite comm system, feeding in the over-ride codes Barrett had given her.

"Hurry," Barrett urged her as he stood by and covered her. "When those two don't check in, there'll be others up here soon."

She calculated quickly, the coordinates dancing through her head as she programmed in the new trajectory settings for the surface-to-space missile batteries. She sweated, focusing on the space strikers off Trappist Two and Three that she knew were closing rapidly on Trappist One. Those ships would soon encounter both the space blockade and the missile barrage, unless she got this right. If she calculated the missile trajectories correctly, the Empire's own missiles would take out their own blockade satellites, opening the door for the Hive invasion.

She cursed as a distress signal came in over her helmet receiver. "That's Kojan and Gaarz," Barrett said. "Their unit's pinned down on Turret-3 and taking heavy fire. They're requesting back-up." Tari glanced up and saw two armed Vurls perch at the edge of the turret, urgently squawking and gesturing for Barrett to come. He stood by, hesitantly, apparently afraid to leave Tari unprotected.

"Go. I've got this."

"Tari—"

"Go, I said!"

"Good luck," he said, running off. She saw him leap from the turret and mount the back of one of the Vurls as they flew off.

She'd nearly finished, her breath shallow as the seconds ticked by. She barely caught the shadow of the enemy trooper in the light of a laser burst. She raised her blaster and stunned the man just as he fired. His bolt went off-center, the explosion scorching her leg and side. She cried out, white-hot pain lancing through her. She cursed as she fought to focus, her vision starting to blur as she reached up. She forced her hand to keep steady as she uploaded the new targeting coordinates.

Grenade explosions tore open the access corridors, men lying in the smoking rubble as Lynn's unit linked up with Klausen and his men in the lower levels of the base. "Which way to the brig?" she asked, breathless, her eyes tearing with smoke.

"Straight ahead," Klausen said, struggling to insert a fresh power pack into his laser rifle. "But, to over-ride the emergency locks on those blast doors, you've got to cut all three power junctions simultaneously."

"Kal," she said, gesturing at the air ducts. "Can you manage?"

"Of course," the Collective said as it split off into three writhing sections and slithered off through three separate ducts.

"Get ready, Lynn ordered, raising her laser rifle." As the blast doors ground open with a whoosh, she opened fire, cutting down the black-armored men advancing through the dim corridor straight ahead.

"Advance!" she ordered as she and Klausen led their people, blasting through the Special Forces guards to the brig where Klausen's people were imprisoned. Blasting the locks, they released the prisoners.

"Where's the armory," Lynn asked.

"D-Block, one level down," Klausen said, half out of breath.

"Go. We'll cover you."

"All right, guys, let's do it! For Sorwaan!"

"For Bandaar!" one man shouted.

"For Valaz!" another called out.

Y-14, now in aero-mode swept around the transmitter turret and fired its lasers, knocking down the SF troopers jetting in. As Y-14 hovered just short of the turret's edge, Kojan leapt in with a roar, smashing aside a few troopers as Gaarz swept in like a striking cobra and blasted down a few more. Barrett jumped to the turret and made straight for Tari, seeing her slumped against the dish array, not moving. *God, please let her be alive!* He couldn't bear the thought of another death on his watch.

He gave a silent prayer of thanks as he found her still breathing. "I've got you, kid," he said, lifting her in his arms and starting back for Y-14.

"Take out the dish," she gasped out, gritting her teeth in pain. "They'll try to re-set the targeting coordinates!"

Realizing she was right, he slung her over his shoulder and took a grenade from his belt. "Go!" he shouted, motioning for Gaarz and Kojan to make their escape as more troopers swooped in. As Y-14 jetted out with Gaarz and Kojan aboard, about a half-dozen troopers cornered Barrett at the turret's edge. They had their lasers trained on him, but were clearly hesitant to fire, for fear of damaging the antenna.

Barrett smiled. "Welcome to the party, boys!" he shouted as he pressed the detonator and tossed the grenade at the base of the dish mount.

Tari in his arms, he jumped from the turret just as the whole antenna rig went up above him. Flaming debris rained down as Y-14 swung around below him. Barrett grunted as Kojan caught him in one shaggy arm.

"Thanks, pal," he said, protectively cradling Tari in his arms.

"Did it work," she asked, looking up at him. Gaarz nudged Barrett's shoulder and pointed at the sky. Barrett looked up and saw the flaring white lights of nuclear explosions in orbital space above. The missiles had hit the blockade stations, just as planned.

Barrett smiled down at Tari, gently wiping a tear from her face. "Ten targets for ten, kid. Good job. I can see why Lynn likes you so much."

She smiled up at him just as she passed out.

Transport ships lifted off in the red morning air, bound for Trappist Two and Three.

"That's my ride," Barrett said, shouldering his pack and setting off for the nearest boarding ramp.

"Think you're ready for life as a terraformer?" Klausen asked, trying with a smile to hide the sadness in his voice.

"I know I'm done with life as a soldier," Barrett said with a weary sigh. He took one last look around, at the distant jungle, at the Vurls crossing the now-free sky. "This was home, but . . . too many memories now. I need a new horizon."

"Enjoy it," Klausen said. They hugged goodbye.

Ships rose in the flaming red sky. Lynn and Tari stood face-to-face in each other's arms as their transport landed nearby, the warm wind blowing through their hair.

"Home for good this time?" Tari asked, her arms around Lynn's neck.

"Forever, love," Lynn said with a warm smile. "Forever." They kissed long as the warm light of the sun washed over them.

*Tom Olbert lives in Cambridge, Massachusetts, home of Harvard University, M.I.T., wacky street performers, and kooky liberals. He loves it there.*

*Tom comes from an interesting family. His father Stan Olbert is a retired physics professor and veteran of the Polish resistance. His sister Elizabeth Olbert is an accomplished visual artist, and his mother Norma Olbert is the author of the biography* The Boy From Lwow, *the story of her husband's life during World War II.*

*Tom is a longtime author of science fiction and dark paranormal horror fiction. His short fiction has appeared in Lillicat Publishers'* Visions II: Moons of Saturn, Visions III: Inside The Kuiper Belt, *and* Visions IV: Space Between Stars.
*His other releases include:*
Novel
**Dissent: Book I of The Nexus** *(Phase 5 Publishing) -*
*http://www.phase5publishing.com/dissent*
Novella
**Black Goddess** *(Mocha Memoirs Press) -*
*http://mochamemoirspress.com/black-goddess/*

Novelettes
**Unholy Alliance** *(Eternal Press) -*
*http://www.eternalpress.biz/product/unholy-alliance-tom-olbert/*
*Desert Flower (Caliburn Press) -*
*http://www.fishpond.com/Books/Desert-Flower-Tom-Olbert-Naom-Clark-Edited-by/9781615726356*

*Short Story*

*"The Arendall Horror"*, *seen in the anthology* An Improbable Truth: The Paranormal Adventures of Sherlock Holmes *(Mocha Memoirs Press)* - *http://mocamemoirspress.com/spookylock/*

When Josiah Spaulding steals the wrong cargo from the wrong aliens, he and his two-person crew are forced to hide out on an unnamed planet where they—literally—start talking to themselves.

# THE MIRROR DIALOGUES

### By

### *Richard Zwicker*

After they'd looted a medical supply ship and a diamond transport, the *Parasite's* cargo hold bulged with contraband. Josiah Spaulding set course for Kepler 138 where they'd sell their goods. It was a familiar pattern that over the course of twenty years had made his name synonymous with space piracy. All was right in their world, at the expense of others. Having reached his late middle years, Spaulding mused about retiring on a planet where no one knew he was such a son of a bitch.

Then an unmanned transport fell into their laps.

Bella Pallas, the *Parasite's* pilot for the past five years, did a cursory check and found minimal weapons, but the ship's insignia was damaged and unreadable. Spaulding hesitated. He liked to know whom he was stealing from. On the other hand, Bella's husband Rock had never seen a transport he didn't want to attack, and Bella reminded Spaulding of their philosophy, "seize the cargo bay." Spaulding decided they'd board the mystery vessel.

Its security bots put up a laughable resistance, and the payload was a dozen two-by-one meter crates. Sensors revealed no radiation, but they couldn't open them without proper tools. A ray sweep showed chair-like objects. Not much, but as Spaulding always said, if it was important enough to ship, it was worth something to somebody. They hauled them onto the ship.

Inside their cargo bay, Rock vaped the lid of one of the crates and they extricated its contents: long, narrow, laden with switches and buttons, and capped with a thorny headdress, it resembled a twentieth century electric chair.

"I doubt I could relax in that thing," said Bella. Her spiky black hair, creased frown, and sinewy body gave her the lined look of a pencil sketch. Spaulding doubted she could relax in anything, though for the past five years she'd been the best pilot he'd ever had.

Rock swiped a sweaty hand over his dreadlocks. "I could, if I had to carry one more of these mothers."

Spaulding scratched his salt and pepper beard. "Who would buy these things? Someone decorating a food court for a torture museum?" He reached under the seat, then asked Rock to tilt the chair back. Grunting, he did, and Spaulding's eyes fell on an engraved one-inch circle with three dots just beyond the circumference, at one, five, and nine o'clock. It meant nothing to him, and then it did,

He dashed to the cockpit and punched out a command on the control panel. With a lurch, the *Parasite* disengaged from the freighter. Spaulding then tapped out a second command. A torpedo shot out at the burgled craft, scoring a direct hit, with little effect.

"What the hell?" Rock asked, as he and Bella staggered into the cockpit.

"We just stole ten ejactor thrones!" Spaulding said.

"That's supposed to mean something to me?" Rock asked.

"It does to Valarians. Those chairs are aphrodisiacs. Whatever you do, don't sit on one."

"What are Valarians?" Bella asked.

"A race that's going to get really pissed at us if— shit."

A blip appeared on the aft screen.

With Bella at the controls, the *Parasite* zigged, zagged, cloaked, jumped into hyperspace, and jumped back. They fired two more nuclear torpedoes, both direct hits, all for naught. The Valarian tracer missile pursued them like a lovesick dog, except this dog would love them to death. According to their files, Valarian tracer missiles were built not to end your life but to ruin it. When you stole something important from them, the tracer locked on your ship and its speed. It then pursued you until the thought of hurtling through space became less appealing than jumping out an air lock. It never caught up, unless you came to a complete stop, or tried to leave the ship. Then it blew up all concerned. No one could tell Spaulding that Valarians didn't have a sense of humor.

"Where's Rock?" Spaulding asked Bella, who'd been studying the v-screen for the past hour.

"The cargo hold," she said, with some disdain. He'd built a man cave in there and spent an increasing amount of time in it.

"Rock, get your ass in here," Spaulding spoke into the speaker.

A minute later Rock sauntered in. His dreadlocks stuck out like Christmas tree branches. His eyes, the windows to his soul, appeared boarded up. Most unnerving was the wide smile plastered on his face.

"Tell me you didn't sit on that chair?" Spaulding said.

"Mrpphh!" said Rock. He landed on the floor with a thump.

Bella shook her head. "Useless as tits on a bull."

"Yeah, except this bull's going to be playing with his tits until it wears off," Spaulding said with disgust. "Wait a minute. I think we still have some Thorzeen Coffee." He went into the *Parasite's* hold and returned with a cup of oily black liquid. With his left hand he pulled open the unsuspecting Rock's mouth, and with the other tossed down the liquid. Two seconds later, his beatific look was replaced by horror. Then, with a yell, he jumped in the air like the puck on a carnival high striker and landed on his feet, shaking.

"Sorry, I didn't have time to heat it up," Spaulding said, not sorry at all. "OK, we've learned two things. Ejactor thrones are powerful, and we don't have the technology to outrun a Valarian tracer missile. Suggestions?"

"If we can't destroy it or outrun it, then we need to go somewhere it can't, or won't," Bella said. "Maybe a planet whose atmosphere is impenetrable to sensors."

"Sounds reasonable, at least short-term," said Spaulding.

"The problem is, if it blocks the tracer's sensors, it'll block ours, so we'll have no idea what we're getting into," she added. "I guess we'll cross that meteor field when we get to it,"

She began her search. Spaulding told Rock to try increasing the power of the nuclear torpedoes, but to make sure he didn't fire one by accident. Spaulding retreated to his quarters to do his own search. Damn the Valarians. They upset the balance of the universe. The have-nots stole from the haves. If the have-nots became too successful, they became haves, fending off other have-nots. But it was as if the Valarians wanted to be attacked, and anyone stupid enough to do it spread the fame of their tracers.

Hours later, Bella called them to her viewer, which showed a hazy, indistinct planet. "It's 26 light-years away, a tenth of Earth size, 0.3 g., fourth planet of Ophul 27. We don't know what the atmosphere is made of, but according to the data it's thick." She smiled. "Thick as thieves. We might be able to hide on it."

"For the rest of our lives?" Rock asked, still stuttering from the effects of the ejactor throne.

She shot him a patient look. "You have a better plan, darling?"

Rock shrugged. The only plan Rock ever had was to blast everything with a nuclear torpedo. He sucked as a diplomat.

Spaulding stared at the tracer in the rearview screen. What was the point of being captain when you didn't have a choice?

"Max speed to Ophul 27," he said.

Twelve hours later, just above the edge of the atmosphere, Bella locked into orbit around the planet. The tracer continued its pursuit. Bella slowed the *Parasite* to a crawl, then burst to maximum speed. For a moment the planet lay between it and the tracer. The *Parasite* then plunged into the planet's atmosphere. To their delight, the tracer didn't follow. For the first time since they'd plundered the Valarian ship, they whooped and applauded.

Spaulding motioned for the applause to continue. "Given the choice between artificial and human intelligence, I'll take human every—what the hell?"

The first clear image of the desolate planet appeared on the front viewer, a patchwork of pockmarked gray, bathed in darkness, and a spaceship parked on the surface. Magnification revealed it as identical to the *Parasite*.

"This isn't possible," muttered Spaulding.

"Scanning the ship," said Bella, tapping the screen. "Substance unknown, but it's not a reflection."

*I'm too old for this*, Spaulding thought, wondering when that had become his catch phrase for everything. "Secure for landing."

Two hours later Spaulding and Rock donned skinsuits and exited the ship while Bella remained inside in case they needed rescuing. Their boots sank into the dusty regolith, which was just as well, as the light gravity made walking tricky. Analysis revealed an atmosphere four times thicker than Earth's, made primarily of carbon dioxide, and a surface temperature of 40 C.

Rock yanked up his foot, then gazed at the endless, gray plain. "Just when I think I know hell, I land on another version of it."

Spaulding told Bella to send out the message, "We come in peace," their standard greeting to every ship just before they plundered it. When that wasn't answered, they approached the second *Parasite*.

"If we saw two men in skinsuits walking toward our ship, wouldn't we shoot them?" Rock asked.

"You'd shoot them if they were doing a hundred-meter dash away from us," said Spaulding. He banged his fist three times on the metal door. They waited a few moments, then walked around the craft. Before they took twenty steps, they bumped into two life-size copies of themselves. Spaulding and Rock both swore, then backed away, reaching for their blasters. After some staring, they lowered their weapons.

"Bella, are you seeing this?" Spaulding asked.

"I am, and I haven't even started drinking yet," Bella answered.

Spaulding shrugged, then straightened his shoulders. "I am Captain Josiah Spaulding of the *Parasite*."

"We know," said his copy, his voice transmitting into the pirates' ears.

Rock's eyes widened. "He sounds just like you."

It wasn't just sound. The creature had the same height, face, and bearing. Spaulding felt dizzy, as if he were slipping away from himself. "Why are you copies of us?" he asked.

"That is what we do," said the copy. "Call me JS." He motioned to his companion. "This is RP."

Call me crazy, thought Spaulding. "Did you exist before we came here?"

"Yes, as organic material from our planet. When you entered our atmosphere, we copied your ship. When you stepped out, we copied you and your crewman. After we did that, from your memories we were able to fill in the interior of the *Parasite* copy."

"So you can you read our minds?" Spaudling asked.

"We copied your minds when you exited your ship. From then, we have gone our own way."

"But you could always make an updated copy of us," Rock said.

RP frowned. "That would be confusing."

But they know our pasts, Spaulding thought. He didn't like that. He always tried to study his victims and use that knowledge against them.

"Can we look inside your ship?" Spaulding asked.

"Of course, though you'll find no surprises," said JS.

JS and RP led them through the airlock to an interior identical to the *Parasite's*. Even personal items, such as Spaulding's e-reader, Bella's chest of tech software, and Rock's weight machine, were located in the same location as on the original *Parasite*. Spaulding checked the ship's computer and found it contained identical files.

"Wait a minute," said Spaulding. "You have Bella's stuff here, but where's Bella—I mean BP?"

"If we had created her based solely on your memories, it wouldn't have been quite right," JS said. "We're waiting to see her directly."

"Can this ship take off?" Rock asked, looking at the controls.

"Of course," RP said, testily. "But it will break down if it goes beyond our atmosphere. The connection to our planet must be maintained."

*What was that quote?* Spaulding thought. *When you eliminate the possible, all that's left is the impossible?* Somehow, they had to make use of that.

The two men returned to the *Parasite*, briefed Bella, and discussed options.

"Maybe we could lure the tracer below the atmosphere and fool it into exploding the *Parasite 2*," said Rock.

"The *Parasite 2* looks like us, but it's made of alien materials," said Bella. "Valarian tech is superior to ours, and our sensors weren't fooled. I doubt it would fool the tracer. The copies seemed friendly enough though, or at least JS did. Maybe they could help us."

"I wouldn't trust them," said Rock.

"Why not?" asked Bella.

"Because they're copies of us."

Bella checked her screen. "Well, we better figure out something, because if we stay longer than two months, we'll be eating each other."

Spaulding smacked a fist into his open hand. "Just because we can't trust them

doesn't mean we can't trick them into helping us. Tomorrow morning let's do another 'meet and greet.' We have some time, so don't push them too hard. Use the fact that we know them to our advantage. But be careful, because they also know us."

When the three of them left the ship, they found JS and RP waiting. In moments, a copy of Bella appeared.

"Do I really look like that?" she asked Rock.

"Baby, it's you," said Rock. "I'm in love."

"Shut up," said Bella.

They paired off with their copies and walked. After about 500 meters, JS turned to Spaulding and said, "You don't like walking. You always felt it was too slow. Faster options, such as driving or flying, expanded the distances of your desired destinations. Walking became outmoded and inappropriate. This is what drew you to join the Space Defense Services as a young man."

"Yeah?" said Spaulding.

"It's ironic that after fifteen years, SDS's exploitation of other worlds and your sense of morality led you to quit and try to make a living as a transporter. When that didn't work, you became a pirate, one who exploits others."

Spaulding was aware of that contradiction in his life. He almost said, "Everyone steals from each other, and I never killed anyone," but with his numerous confrontations, it was impossible to be sure about the latter. "Sometimes irony is all you've got." If there was one thing he didn't want to talk about, it was himself. "What happens to you once we leave?"

"We revert to what we were," JS answered. "We existed and responded but had no sense of individuality."

"It sounds like a less complex existence than what you have now."

"The difference is in point of view. As JS, my focus is narrower, though I'm still cerebrally connected to the planet. It's like when you zoom in, you see more detail but lose context. For instance, you've zoomed in too much on the minutiae of piracy rather than seeing the big picture. The result is, at this later stage of your life, you're stranded on a little known planet talking to a copy of yourself."

Spaudling nodded. This was going to be a long conversation.

After their walks, Spaulding and Bella returned to the *Parasite*. Rock remained outside.

"How did it go?" she asked.

"We had a fascinating talk about how much I'd fucked up my life. Not sure how that's going to help us with the Valarians, unless they start feeling sorry for me and turn around. What about you?"

Bella smiled wanly. "It was nice talking tech to someone who knew as much about it as me. But then I noticed she agreed with everything I said, and it got boring. She did say her species was not happy we're here."

"Why not?" JS hadn't mentioned that.

"This planet doesn't get many visitors . . . like none. It used to, many millennia ago, before the atmosphere changed and became a kind of shield. Now most of the life here wants us to leave ASAP, so our copies can revert to their original forms. Even then, though, their memories will remain in the collective, and their species doesn't like that."

"We'll be happy to oblige as soon as—"

Their heads turned to the hatch as Rock lumbered in. He peeled off his face covering, revealing discoloration across his forehead and throat.

"What happened to you?" Bella asked.

"My lunatic copy attacked me for no reason."

Rock pulled his blaster from his side holster. Spaulding noticed its faint red glow.

"Did you use that thing?"

Rock fingered the blaster. "Like I said, there was some trouble." He gasped from the heat as he touched the mouth of the weapon.

Spaulding laughed. "It must have scrambled your brains, if you don't have enough sense not to touch—"

Bella karate-chopped Rock's shooting hand, sending the blaster's ray awry. The weapon fell to the ground. Spaulding snatched it, then leveled it at Rock.

"What the hell are you doing?" he asked.

"Where's Rock?" Bella demanded. It was RP.

RP gazed at them both, calm as if he'd been asked where he'd left a wrench. "I think I killed him. The planet doesn't wish to wait for your departure." He flexed his shooting hand. "Unfortunately, while I copied Rock Pallas's knowledge of blasters, I couldn't replicate his skill."

"Tell us where he is or you'll get a crash course on the blaster's effects," said Bella, her body shaking. She glanced desperately at Spaulding.

"Don't fire!" The words came from JS, standing in a skin suit, arms raised, in front of the air lock.

Spaulding exhaled nervously. He had to change that lock.

"We retrieved Rock and he will recover," said JS. "We apologize for RP's behavior. We are not adept at anticipating the rogue impulses of copies."

"I don't appreciate you talking about me as if I weren't here," RP said.

"Where's Rock?" Spaulding asked.

"In the *Parasite 2*," JS answered. "We stopped the bleeding with organic material from this planet which, as you can see," motioning to himself, "is quite adaptable."

"Won't it decompose after we leave the planet?" asked Bella.

"Within two days, yes," JS said. "But our material stimulates healing. He will be fine."

"How can we trust you?" Spaulding asked.

"You can't trust RP," JS said, "but we will isolate him. You can trust me because I copied your need to protect your crew and you can trust BP because he has Bella's love of Rock. This, plus our proprietary sense toward our originals has kept you alive. But with Rock there is a self-loathing—it manifests itself with his impulse to destroy things—that makes RP more susceptible to the planet's will."

"Which is to kill us," said Spaulding.

"You, and us. As long as we exist, our thoughts contaminate the planet. We're all connected, which is how we were able to save Rock. The moment RP shot him, we knew. We also knew he wanted to do it, but we mistook that as the will of the planet."

"Why hasn't the planet already killed you?" Spaulding asked.

"If we die, three more copies of you will appear, until you leave."

"So we all want for us to be able to leave," said Spaulding.

"Let's get Rock and talk about this later," said Bella.

Rock was resting comfortably, thanks to some drugs, in a replica of his bunk. JS suggested he stay another day, but Bella refused. She and BP dressed him into the spare skinsuit they'd brought and helped him to the *Parasite*. Spaulding thanked JS and tried to leave before he started talking.

"Do you trust us now?" JS asked.

Spaulding sighed. "We're pirates. We don't trust anybody, but I guess I understand you better." An idea occurred to him. "You said you changed some of the planet's material to patch up Rock. Can you change it into anything you want?"

"No. We can only copy and, at best, make minor alterations."

His shoulders sank. "Then I don't see how we can get out of here."

"We need to combine our knowledge and passions. For instance, as captain of the *Parasite*, you would do anything for your crew. As I am a replica of you, I feel the same way. I would sacrifice myself for you."

"None of us would do that for you."

"Understood. Your sacrifice would be your end, while my sentience outlasts my death as JS. We can only try to resolve this. Have you any ideas?"

Spaulding had one but didn't like it. "We might be able to jump away from the tracer if we exited your atmosphere on the opposite side of the planet. Could the *Parasite 2* exit first, locate the tracer, then radio its location?"

"No. Our atmosphere blocks everything, and once the *Parasite 2* was beyond it, it would degrade and be unable to return."

There was only a slim chance the *Parasite* would exit at the optimum point anyway, and even if it did, they'd have to immediately jump to hyperspace. At such proximity, it would destroy the planet. With Bella's background, JS had to know that.

"I won't jump to hyperspace and destroy your planet," said Spaulding.

"I believe you, but that's not enough," JS said. "Bella and Rock hope to have a family someday, and they compelled you to attack the Valarian freighter. I can't trust them. And the planet certainly doesn't. It will kill you before you can leave."

It was a mess. When they stumbled onto the Valarians, Spaulding thought their sense of justice— perpetual pursuit for theft—was crazy. But maybe it wasn't. In a way, age was a tracer that dogged them all. And if one were stupid, one's actions precipitated the final impact. The fact was, he'd waited too long to get out of the game.

"I never thought it would come to this."

"You never thought. Neither does my species. We rarely encounter aliens, but when we do, we must copy them. It happens naturally, yet we fight it. In our smugness, we consider anything except temporary change a bad thing. I've come to believe uncertainty can be a catalyst to growth. Who knows? Maybe someday your influence will make a positive difference on us."

"That would be a first." Spaulding shook his head. "What I've come to believe is this Valarian tracer is my just desserts."

JS stared at him. "Then you must change so that it isn't."

"I guess," he said, extending his hand. JS let it hang.

"I have a proposition."

The next day Spaulding told Bella and Rock the planet meant them imminent harm and it was time to go. They would exit the planet's atmosphere, hoping to get far enough from the tracer to jump to hyperspace. If that didn't work, they would try to maneuver the tracer into smashing into the planet, destroying both. He got no argument.

They secured themselves, and Bella fired up the engines. The craft lifted and the planet diminished in the aft viewer,

"No sign of the tracer," Bella said, as the ship passed beyond the atmosphere. "Jumping." She hit the controls, and nothing happened. "What the hell?" She did it again, to no avail. "That's impossible. I checked everything an hour ago."

"For crissake, there it is!" Rock said, pointing to the blip on screen,

"All right," said Spaulding. "Do exactly as I say. Cut speed to minimum, lock on to the coordinates we just left, and return to the planet."

Bella threw up her hands but obeyed. They slowed to a crawl, then plunged into the atmospheric cloak. This time the tracer followed them. Ten minutes later, the familiar plains appeared.

"Copy of the tracer on forward screen," said Bella.

"Great. Now we have two of them," said Rock.

"Direction of the copy?" Spaulding asked.

"Straight for us! Incoming message from *Parasite 2*!" said Bella.

"Ignore! Bella, on my command, I want full vertical thrust!"

She chuckled, placing her hand on the thruster. "I'm sure you do."

"Now!"

The ship lurched upward, the tracer zoomed under them, into the tracer copy. There was a blinding flash of light.

Bella stared at the screen in disbelief. "Both tracers . . . are gone."

"Un-fucking believable," said Rock. He gave his wife a bear hug, which was reciprocated. He yelped in pain because of his wound, but it was a happy yelp,

"Did you know that was going to happen?" Bella, still clasped, asked Spaulding.

He felt as if all his tomorrows had been returned. "Not exactly. It was JS's idea. He convinced the planet he could alter the tracer copy's instructions and instead target the original tracer. We slowed our speed to give him as much time as possible."

"So we were never going to smash their planet," Bella said, as Rock let her go. "I'm surprised they trusted us not to go to hyperspace."

"They didn't. I had to disconnect the drive."

"You!" Bella exclaimed.

Rock shook his head. "Thank God they succeeded in redirecting the copy tracer," said Rock.

"I don't think they did," said Spaulding. "JS said he'd call us only if they failed." He patted Bella's shoulder. "We're alive because of your evasive maneuvers."

They broke out some Hoxass wine and made enough toasts to laud every aspect of their lives. There was loud music, dancing, and vulgar jokes. After a couple of hours Spaulding turned off the music and said he had an announcement. "After we unload on Kepler 186, I'm cashing out. The *Parasite*, the pirate life, I'm done."

"Yeah, right," Rock said.

Bella's eyes narrowed. "You're serious."

"If you're interested, I might be compelled to offer a crewman's discount on the *Parasite*," Spaulding added,

"We are interested," said Bella.

They asked Spaulding what boring things he would do in retirement. He said "Nothing," then expanded on its appeal. The more he talked about it, the more it felt like both a luxury and something he hadn't earned, but screw that. When were one's wages truly apropos? Plus, as JS had said after giving Spaulding his proposition, "I thought of it only because I'm you." In his retirement he could think of ways to be more worthy.

The Pallases mused about potential destinations, building up a nest egg, and starting a family. Finally, Rock suggested they toast the impending sale. "We've drunk to everything else."

Later, though they could barely walk, Rock insisted that in honor of Spaulding's daring leadership against the Valarian tracer, he and Bella should decorate the captain's quarters. Spaulding told him if he changed one thing in there, Rock would spend the trip to Kepler 186 in the brig. They didn't have a brig though, and Rock was persuasive, so Spaulding told him they had twenty minutes.

When they led Spaulding to his quarters, he shook his head at the shredded lines of paper and heroic stick-figure drawings the two had hung on the wall. Over his chair they'd draped a sheet with the words "Universe's Best Captain."

"I'm always happy to indulge people's need to give me things." Spaulding rolled his eyes, then staggered toward his bed.

"No, sit in the 'Best Captain's' chair," Rock said, leading him to it. It was covered with a brightly colored sheet, a paper wreath, and a messy-looking sign.

Spaulding felt Rock was being too pushy, but he relented. "If the chair fits . . ." He sat down and suddenly felt parsecs away as he watched Bella and Rock run out. He pulled down the top of the sheet and saw the headdress. Those bastards had put him on an

Ejector Seat! "Retribution will be swift and—" Then he stopped, as if the sentence was formed by someone he barely knew. The path of least resistance had led him to this stolen chair, but he was turning a new page. He should resist his inclinations and get off.

Then again, he could make the same point later.

He got off, fighting tears.

*Richard Zwicker is an English teacher living in Vermont, USA, with his wife and beagle. His short stories have appeared in* Fantasy Scroll mag, Penumbra, Farstrider Magazine, *and other semi-pro markets. His hobbies, besides reading and writing, include playing the piano, jogging, and fighting the good fight against middle age. Though he lived and taught in Brazil for eight years, he is still a lousy soccer player.*

Mankind's first attempt at Warp Drive technology is an overwhelming success. In fact, it is far more successful than anyone's wildest dreams. Maybe too successful.

# THE DRIVE

### By

### *W. A. Fix*

Carson Dill walked into the ship's command deck, displaying what appeared to be arrogance. His over confident and aloof demeanor did little to gain his command team's friendship, or their respect.

"Captain on the Bridge," announced the communication officer, who sat to the right of the entrance. Lieutenant Lee Davis immediately went back to his current task and paid no more attention to Dill. The other three on the bridge neither acknowledged him, nor interrupted what they were doing.

Dill hesitated an instant, then said, "As you were," as he moved into the cramped space. The bridge always reminded him of a vintage transport aircraft used within Earth's atmosphere. This craft, however, carried no cargo. It was all warp coils, plasma drive engines, deflector generators, work stations, life support systems, and limited crew space. There was no room for amenities, windows, or recreation space. The only systems designed for human comfort were the ship's gravitational rotation, workspace chairs, the beds the crew slept in, and a small dining area that could accommodate one third of the twenty-four-person crew at one time.

Dill climbed into the command chair situated behind and between the pilot/executive officer,

Commander Brad Wicks, and the co-pilot, Lieutenant Commander Margret Williams.

"Commander Wicks, I just spent three hours evaluating Warp Engineering and another hour in Plasma Drive Engineering. The deflectors are fully operational and the plasma engines are online. What do you think? Shall we go home now?"

Wicks glanced quickly at Williams, then leaned forward and activated the two monitors that displayed the forward view from the ship. Dill glanced at the monitor and the familiar view of the Milky Way Galaxy.

"Captain, I would love to do that, but we're having a little difficulty plotting a course," said Wicks. "We're pretty sure this is the Milky Way." He pointed at the screen. "But, right now, that's all we know. Our navigator tells me she doesn't know where we are."

"What do you mean, you don't know where we are?" said Dill, as he rotated the chair to his left and looking intently at the Navigator.

Commander Edith Clay turned to face him. "Well, sir, I think we're lost. I can't align any constellations or other computerized star configurations with what we are looking at out there. The recognition software has been running for over two hours and . . . nothing out there is recognizable. I'm also running a spectral analysis on several of the most prominent stars. I'm trying to identify a few by the light they are emitting and maybe get some idea of our position. But nothing is even close to matching our stored data. Somehow, I think, we traveled way beyond what we expected. If spectral analysis doesn't work, I've got nothing else."

"How is that possible," said Dill. "How fast were we traveling when the warp generator engaged?"

Clay glared at him, not trying to hide her anger. "As you know, sir," she said sarcastically, "We left earth orbit three weeks ago and accelerated continuously. One week ago, we left the solar system at .372 Light Speed and continued acceleration until five hours ago, when we reached exactly half the speed of light. You, personally, activated the warp generator. When the generator was shut down, exactly ten minutes later, we came out of warp in a slow tumble and with apparently no forward momentum. We have corrected the tumbling motion and, right now, it appears we are motionless in space, with the universe moving around us. But I can't even be sure of that, until I can identify at least a few stars, and then verify our relative speed."

Dill was silent for a moment. "So what's your best guess for our location?"

Clay took a deep breath, leaned back in her chair, and stared at the stars on the main monitors. "Look, this is just a wild guess. When viewed from Earth, the Milky Way appears to be this gigantic cloud but, in reality, it's hundreds of millions of stars and nebula making up our galaxy. That area of space obscured from Earth's view by the densest part of the 'cloud' is called the Zone of Avoidance, because it is completely unseen and, therefore, unknowable." She pointed to the screen, "What we see here appears to be very close in shape and size to a mirror image of what I would expect to see from Earth. My best guess is that we have traveled all the way through the galaxy and are within Earth's Zone of Avoidance. Our own solar system, and any system familiar to us, is now obscured by those same stars. Earth and any familiar star system is in our Zone of Avoidance."

Dill laughed out loud. "Come on, Edith, do you honestly believe we traveled maybe fifty thousand light-years in ten minutes?"

"Actually, closer to eighty thousand light-years, but, yes, that's exactly what I think."

"Okay—," started Dill and was cut off.

"Captain," said Wicks. "We are clearly not ready to plot a course. We shouldn't take any action until we have more information."

Dill whipped around and glared at him, "Well, duh! Thank you, Commander! Even *I* could have come up with that. Look, I know you people think I don't belong here. That this was purely a political appointment because my father is the President and, honestly, you're right about my father pulling strings. But, I'm here . . . so, get over it!"

Clay started to say something then stopped. Wicks turned back to the front and refused to speak or even look at Dill. Williams and Davidson stared at Dill in wide-eyed shock. Dill waited several, very uncomfortable, seconds then stood and said quietly, "Commander Wicks, I'll be in my cabin. Please contact me if you have any developments. Commander Clay, we need a course. We have supplies to last another seven weeks and our first jump is going to take three of those weeks. Do the best you can. I want status reports from all sections in four hours. Especially Plasma fuel levels and exact fuel consumption rates since we left earth orbit. I also want Warp and Deflector power reserves and estimated levels after we complete our first jump toward home." Dill turned and walked off the Bridge.

Davidson waited a few seconds then announced, "The Captain has left the Bridge."

Wicks was the first to speak, "What an unbelievable asshole! That son-of-a-bitch has no right being on this ship. He shows up two months before departure and we're supposed to just accept it because he's the President's kid. Well, screw him!"

"Brad, we all know you're upset," said Clay. "Everyone on this ship knows you were supposed to have this command. But, no matter what any of us think, or want, he is the Captain of this vessel. We must support him."

"Well, I just can't make myself bust my ass so he and his father can take all the credit."

"What in the hell are you talking about? At first I thought he didn't get it. But, *you're* the one that doesn't get it. Listen to me very carefully, Brad, *WE'RE LOST!* That's no joke and I'm thinking we stand maybe a twenty percent chance of getting within a hundred light-years of earth *ever again*. Stop worrying about who gets the credit and start worrying about survival"

There were six people waiting for Dill when he entered the ship's small mess and, for the first time, they all stood when he entered the room. He gave no indication that he noticed this change and simply said, "As you were." He walked straight to one of the two empty spaces at the tables and put his computer on the table. He remained standing until everyone was seated before starting the meeting.

"Our navigator has informed me she has confirmed her theory regarding our current location." He scanned the room for confused expressions before continuing.

"Commander Clay will explain her findings and then we'll go over the ships current status. Commander Clay and I will then outline phase one of our plan to get us home. Please make sure all of your team members understand this information, our plan, and their roles in accomplishing that goal. If any of us survive this ordeal, it will be because of a total team effort by every person on this vessel.

"Before we continue, I want everyone on this ship to create, and maintain, a personal log and a ship's log for the duration of the mission. The personal logs will contain comments and personal thoughts designed to document individual observations of the remainder of this mission. As personal logs, they will remain private, unless released by the individual. The ship's log will contain an hour by hour record of orders, work performed and status of all systems for which the individual is responsible. These two logs will provide a history of what we do, how we do it, and the result of our actions. Whether or not this crew ever reaches earth again, the data could save the lives of future crews. That, after all, is our basic mission as an experimental space craft." Dill pointed to his computer. "Record all meetings, as I am now and make note of everything that individual crew members may think is significant. Are there any questions?"

He waited a few seconds then turned to Clay, "Commander, tell us what you have learned."

Dill took his seat at the table as Clay stood and glanced around the small room. When she began to speak, there was a slight tremor in her voice that betrayed all efforts to hide her nervousness.

"As Captain Dill said, I have confirmed that we are currently on the opposite side of the galaxy and Earth and our solar system are approximately seventy thousand light years away. I was unable to match any visible configuration of stars to anything in our database. However, I ran spectral analysis on twenty-five prominent stars high in the galactic plain that would be visible to Earth. I found matches on seven, with a ninety-three to ninety-eight percent of certainty."

She paused a moment, looking around the room. "You're probably wondering, *why not a one hundred percent match?* Well, it even had me stumped at first, but then I realized that we're about fifty thousand light years closer to those stars than Earth. Their light stored on our computer was generated sixty-five thousand years ago. What we are seeing right now was generated fifteen thousand years ago. Stars are like everything else in the Universe, they get older. As they get older, the elements they burn or generate change, causing the light to have very small changes over time. We are looking at those stars as they will appear to Earth in fifty thousand years. Ninety-three to ninety-eight percent is the best we can ever do. Now that we have identified a few stars, we will have a point of reference from which we can plot a course."

There was a collective sigh that came close to cheers from everyone, except Dill. Clay glanced in his direction and saw him nod, urging her to continue.

"Now, we're not out of the woods yet. Even though we've been able to identify those stars, they're not anywhere near their locations stored in our computer files. Unfortunately, no one dreamed anything like this would happen, so we don't have any kind of regression software that would allow us to find those locations and give us an exact reverse course. But, the good news is we're able to find a general direction for home."

"*General direction.* Exactly what does that mean?" asked Wicks.

"We'll get to that in a few minutes, Commander," said Dill, as he stood to address the group again. "Thank you, Commander Clay. Before we get into the subject of our course and plan, I want to go over the current status of this vessel. Commander Wicks, as Ship's Executive Officer you are responsible for all ship systems, maintenance, stores, communications, and the twelve crew that operate and support those systems. I see you have included Lieutenant Davis, our communications officer, Lieutenant Jay in charge of computer systems, and Lieutenant Primrose, our Ship's Maintenance Officer. I am assuming you, personally, will be providing status on shields, ship stores, and life support systems. Is that correct?"

Wicks' back stiffened slightly and the muscles in his jaw clenched visibly. "Yes, Captain, I personally will be providing status of those systems, as I will with all systems within my responsibility," he said curtly. "Lieutenants Davis, Jay, and Primrose were invited to provide information, in the remote possibility you should ask a question I cannot answer."

The two men's eye contact never faltered and finally Dill made a decision. The corner of his mouth twitched slightly and he said, "Okay, Commander. How much wood can a woodchuck chuck?"

Wicks' eyes glazed for a second and he blinked several times. The room was dead silent as he refocused on Dill's eyes and broke a faint smile. "Captain, I haven't the faintest idea. Lieutenant Primrose, how much wood can a woodchuck chuck?"

Everyone in the room was now smiling. Lieutenant Primrose cleared his throat then said, "Sir, several years ago a study was completed by the University of Nebraska and the answer to that question is . . . three quarts of vanilla ice cream."

With the tension released, the room broke into moderate laughter. Dill smiled broadly while maintaining eye contact with Wicks and said, "Thank you, Lieutenant Primrose, now that you mention it, I believe I remember that study." Dill now addressed the room before taking his seat, "and Commander Wicks, I have no doubt you will provide the status information we need. Please continue."

Wicks spoke evenly and directed his comments to Dill. "Captain, all ships mechanical systems are fully operational and operating at optimal levels. Maintenance is constantly monitoring their operation and reports only minor and easily corrected problems.

"Computer Systems are fully operational and, of course, we are using those systems to monitor virtually every other system on this vessel. Lieutenant Jay worked with Commander Clay to search archives for any software or documentation that would assist her efforts in locating our position. Unfortunately, and as she reported, nothing was found.

"Life support systems are also fully operational with no problems reported. I have asked Lieutenant Davis to assist with Maintenance and Life Support systems. Considering our current location, we have little or no need of a Communications Officer. When we are working outside, or we again get within range of Earth, he will return to normal duties."

"We have enough food to last two months and fresh and recycled water will last at least twice that. Ship's stores of other perishables will last well beyond our supplies of food and water. Oxygen is not an issue as long as our electronic systems are operational. Which brings us to the only real issue we have within Ship's Systems. As we all know, this ship is operated on power stored in batteries generated by turbines within the plasma drive engines. According to the Plasma Drive Power Generator specifications, we are able to fully recharge the batteries with one day, or to be more precise, 26.2 hours of plasma drive operation. Those fully charged batteries yield approximately 120 hours of normal ship's operation, while the ship is not under Plasma Drive acceleration. While the ship is accelerating, we use power from the batteries and they are recharged as fast as we use it. When the engines shut down the batteries are fully charged and we are on a five-day clock. Currently, the engines have been shut down for approximately twenty hours and we have less than 100 hours before we must start the plasma engines to recharge the batteries."

"I hope we are moving long before that becomes an issue, Commander" said Dill. He smiled broadly and turned to a pudgy little man. Despite his appearance this man held the heart of the ship in his hands—the plasma engines. "Dr. Bellows, what is the status of our plasma engines?"

Dr. Steven Bellows, frowned and said, "The engines are fully operational and ready any time you are."

Dill smiled. "That is good to hear, Doctor. But, I'm curious about your fuel levels and how much maintenance is required on these experimental engines. I am very interested in the generators that supply power to the rest of the ship and to the Warp Coils."

"Captain, I assure you we have plenty of fuel to get us home. We still have two thirds of our maximum fuel storage and, as far as maintenance is concerned, we monitor every aspect of operation during every hour of operation. My team is constantly fine tuning the engines for optimum efficiency."

Dill paused a moment and regarded the balding man. As he watched, Bellows began to fidget and seemed a little too uncomfortable. "I'm sorry, Doctor, did I understand you correctly? You have made numerous changes to the operation of the engines since we left Earth orbit? The one thing on this vessel that impacts virtually every system on board?"

"Yes. That is correct. But, during operation is literally the only time those changes can be made," said the now very uncomfortable man.

"Doctor, you're not in the military, so I can understand how you may feel like your actions are acceptable or even commendable. When were you authorized to make modifications to the engines?"

Bellows began to puff up. "Well, I . . ."

"When you and your team boarded this vessel, were you given an orientation and told that strict change management protocols were now in effect and that *all* changes were to be authorized by the Captain of this ship?"

Bellows let out a short laugh and glanced at the faces around him, "Why, no one *authorized* me to do it. I am the lead scientist and Technical Director of Plasma Drive Operations. I don't need authorization. Anyway, you're not a scientist and couldn't possibly make those decisions."

Dill clinched his jaw and turned to Dr. Graham Niece, Technical Director of Warp Drive Operations. "Dr. Niece, have you also been fucking with my Warp Drive without authorization?"

Niece answered without hesitation, "No, Captain. We have made two small changes that corrected minor fluctuations in emergency sensors. Both changes were authorized by you, and, technically, I would consider them foreplay and not actual fucking."

Dill smiled briefly and said, "Please forgive my language, people. Dr. Niece, were you provided the same orientation as Dr. Bellows?"

"Actually, Captain, Commander Wicks provided the orientation to our teams, in this very room, and also provided precise direction on the change management protocols. I would consider his presentation to be extremely clear."

Dill turned back to Bellows. "Doctor, just so you understand the impact of your actions, I'll try to explain the importance. There are several things that are jeopardized by your changes. One, even if we knew our exact course to get home, the engines would be operating differently, so we would never be able to hit our point of origin. We could be as much as a hundred or more lightyears off course. Who knows?

"Two, we do not have an accurate accounting of fuel consumption for the three-week acceleration required in the first jump home. So, here we are with a third of our fuel exhausted and we have no idea what our consumption rate will be.

"Three, if the engines are operating differently, that means the generators are also working differently. We have no idea of accurate charge time and the impact of your changes to power for the warp generator and deflector shields. Did you even think of any of those things?"

"Well, of course we considered those things. The impact was determined to be minimal and well worth the risks," said Bellows.

"Minimal. Doctor, we were traveling at one half the speed of light and the warp drive was activated for ten minutes. Just ten minutes, a minimal amount of time, and we ended up eighty million lightyears from home. Nothing is minimal, Doctor! Now about those risks. Since we left Earth orbit, there has only been one real risk. Make a change and risk the life of every person on this ship. There is only one person authorized to take that risk and, Doctor, you're not that person." He glared at Bellows, daring him to say something.

Finally, he turned to Edith Clay. "Commander, let's get on with this. Please go over our plan and answer Commander Wicks' original question."

Clay slowly stood as Dill took his seat. "Well, Captain, the good news is we won't need to change our plan. The plan is pretty simple. We will first plot a course using the seven stars and their *estimated* location fifty thousand years ago. Without orbital regression software, an estimate is the best we can do. So Brad, to answer *your* question, that estimate should get us through the galaxy and into a region of space that will allow us to see Sol and its neighbors." She paused and made a half-hearted smile before continuing. "If we can get within a thousand lightyears, I'll consider the first jump a success. Then we'll use several small jumps to recharge the batteries and get us closer to Earth, while refining our ability to control the jump length and course accuracy. Once we get inside the solar system, we will use the plasma engines, with one last warp jump to stop us within reach of help." Clay glanced around the room. "Well, that's the plan. Questions?"

The room was silent. Wicks was the first to speak, summarizing it for everyone else. "I have a hundred questions and not one that is constructive."

The plasma engines had been running for two weeks, six days, and three hours. They created a faint background noise that was like several wooden wheels rolling on concrete. It was not a loud noise, only because of the massive sound dampers that separated the engines from the rest of the ship. Without those dampers the sound and vibration inside the ship would be unbearable.

Dill was in his cabin updating his personal log when the ship's intercom broke the relative quiet. "Captain, at current acceleration, point five light speed will be reached in thirty minutes."

"Very good, Commander Wicks. Have Dr. Niece bring the warp coils to the ready state. I want to activate the drive as close to the same interval as the last time. Make the ship ready for Warp Activation. I will be on the Bridge in just a few minutes."

"Yes, Sir," said Wicks.

Dill heard the intercom switch off and then thought a few seconds before continuing his personal log. "Well, Dad, we're about to find out if we stand any chance of getting home. Without a doubt this is the biggest gamble I've ever taken, but in the final analysis we had no other options. I think we could've pulled it off, if that idiot Bellows hadn't made changes to the plasma engines. He swears they changed nothing that would impact the warp coil operation. I sure hope he's right, but the changes to the generators increased the battery charge time by a full twelve hours. The best case is; his tinkering has cost us at least three days of plasma drive. I guess we'll just hope we don't need them."

The ship's emergency alarm began its relentless clang and, after a few seconds, Brad Wicks' voice echoed in every corner of the ship. "Attention . . . Attention all

personnel . . . Point five light speed in twenty-eight
minutes. Secure this vessel. Secure all air tight doors.
Prepare for Warp Drive activation in thirty-one minutes."
He repeated the message adding, "That is all," and the
alarm went silent.

Dill stood and retrieved his uniform shirt from a
rack. As he put it on, he finished this entry in his log.
"As you can tell it's getting a little busy, so I better sign
off for now. I'll add more after we find out the results of
this first jump. I love you, Dad, and tell Mom I love her.
Talk to you later." He pressed a button and closed the
log. He exited his cabin and headed to the Bridge.

Dill entered the Bridge and walked straight to the
Captain's Chair. Davis announced his arrival in the
usual manner, "The Captain is on the Bridge." All heads
and eyes turned in his direction as he made his
response, "As you were," he said. No one went back to
what they were doing and they all waited for him to
begin the next phase of their voyage.

"Commander Wicks, what is our current status?"

Wicks answered without hesitation, "Plasma
Operations reports all ready for transition. Ship's
Operations are ready to transition to full battery
operation. The Warp Coils are at the ready state. We
were waiting for you to arrive before sealing the main
corridor."

Dill heard a noise behind him and turned in time to
see Davis close the door and manually seal it using the
four hatch lugs. "The Ship is secure and ready for
Warp," continued Wicks. "We are approximately twelve
minutes from point five light speed."

"Very good, Commander," said Dill. He turned to his
left and met the gaze of Edith Clay. "Commander Clay,
any final thoughts on our course?"

"No sir," she said. "However, sir, I wish you would
reconsider my request to add thirty seconds to the time
the Warp Drive is operational. Considering the fact that
we reached our speed faster this time, due to the
efficiency of the Plasma Engines, our position is bound

to be farther away from Earth when we come out of warp."

"I understand, Commander, and I agree with your assessment, but we just can't take the risk. After we have made a few more jumps, our estimates will become far better. Right now, we only know that a single one-half light speed jump, using exactly ten minutes of warp, will keep us inside the galaxy and maybe somewhere much closer than we are now to Earth. I'm willing to make adjustments on the next jumps, but, not this one." He turned to Davis and said, "Are Dr. Bellows and Dr. Niece ready to join us?"

"Standing by, Sir."

"Add them to the Bridge com and allow the ship to listen in." He waited for the thumbs up signal from Davis, then said, "Dr. Bellows and Dr. Niece, glad you could join us. Have each of you completed your internal check lists?"

Bellows answered first, "Plasma Engine Warp Transition Checklist is complete. All systems are at peak operation. We are four minutes from point five light speed. We are ready for warp."

Niece spoke up, "Warp Transition Checklist is complete. All systems are at *Ready* state. We are ready for warp."

"Commander Wicks, are Ship's Systems, Deflector Shields, and Life Support ready for transition?"

"Sir, all sections report internal checklists are complete and ready for Warp Transition."

"Commander Wicks, complete your final Warp checklist."

Wicks touched several points on the panel in front of him, and the console in front of Dill began to light up. Most of the panel lit up yellow, except for two columns of switches in the center, labeled Plasma Engines. Those burned constant green, indicating the engines were in operation. "Captain's master console is active," said Wicks. "On my mark, control of Ship's Systems, Deflector Shields, and Life Support will be transferred to the Captain's Master Console. Ready . . . Mark!"

Dill watched the left side of his console turn green, one switch at a time. Finally, three switches, on the top row, began blinking red. "Ship's Systems, Deflector Shields, and Life Support are now on my console and ready for transition to stand-alone battery operations," said Dill.

Wicks spoke again, "Dr. Bellows, transfer control of Plasma engines to the Captain's Master Console. On my mark. Ready . . . Mark!" Two more switches began flashing red above the Plasma switches on Dill's console. He waited a moment for both lights to turn constant green, indicating the engines were operating and power generators were on line and now controlled by his console.

"Plasma Engines are now on my console and ready for Warp Transition," said Dill.

"Dr. Niece, transfer control of Warp Drive to the Captain's Master Console," said Wicks. He waited a few seconds as the final section of Dills console turned yellow. "All systems are now controlled from the Captain's Master Console. All input to those systems is locked out. All changes can only be initiated through the Captain's Master Console. Captain you are clear to initiate the final Warp Sequence."

"Thank you, Commander," said Dill. "Transition to battery operation . . . Now." He pressed and held each of the first three flashing red lights in turn. As one turned yellow he released it and waited for it to turn green and stop flashing, before moving to the next. When the third switch was constant green he announced, "Ship's Systems, Deflector Shields, and Life Support are now operating on battery power." He pressed a switch at the bottom of the console marked *Plasma Main Power* and waited for the light to turn red. "Battery and battery powered systems are now isolated from the generators. All plasma main power is now redirected to the Warp Field Generators. All hands, we are on the clock at 120 hours. Commander Wicks, what is our speed?"

"Sir, we are at point five light speed in twenty seconds . . . fifteen seconds . . . ten seconds . . . five seconds . . . four . . . three . . . two . . . one . . . *point five light speed.*"

Dill reached forward to the console and pressed the first of the two remaining flashing red lights. He held it until the light turned constant green. "Warp Field Generators are activated and are charging. Warp field timer is set to ten minutes." He watched the remaining flashing red light. "Warp field ready light is red." Dill said nothing until the light changed, "Warp field ready light is yellow." He waited again, this time his hand hovered above the flashing yellow light. The instant the light turned green, his hand slammed down and he held it until the light stopped flashing and became constant green. The ship's alarm sounded and Dill said, "The Warp Field is active. The timer is running and is at nine minutes and thirty seconds."

That was all. He leaned back in his chair and tried to relax, knowing there was nothing more for him to do until the timer shut the Plasma Engines down, which in turn would shut down the Warp Field. Slowly he began to feel the effects of the Warp Field, and knew the entire crew was feeling them. It began with the hair on his body slowly beginning to stand on end, as if static electricity were building within the ship. A bitter taste formed in his mouth that reminded him of touching both poles of a small battery to his tongue. The taste was slightly metallic and grew in intensity. As time passed, a feeling of anxiety began to build in the pit of his stomach. He looked at Wicks and could see the white knuckles of his right hand as he gripped the arm rest of the pilot's chair.

"Commander Wicks, I believe it was your turn to bring the breath mints," he said, and watched as Wicks relaxed his grip.

Wicks chuckled slightly and said, "Sorry, Sir, I just ate the last one."

Dill could almost feel the entire crew relax as the exchange was heard throughout the ship. It was a small thing that reminded everyone that they were not the only ones feeling the effects.

The minutes seemed to crawl as the timer ticked off the seconds. At five minutes Dill said, "All Sections report your status." He didn't need the status. All he had to do was look at his control panel. He wanted to fill the void, give them something to do or listen to, and offset, the anxiety. One by one they reported, confirming that all systems were operating at peak performance.

After what seemed to be an eternity, Dill announced, "One minute to Plasma Engine shutdown. All sections prepare for Plasma and Warp Field shutdown in thirty seconds." He waited twenty seconds then said, "Plasma and Warp Field shutdown on my Mark. Ready . . ." and as the timer turned to zero, he said. "Mark!"

For the first time in three weeks, the ship was dead silent. No one spoke, yet they could all feel the collective sigh as their hair lay down and the metallic taste left their mouths.

"Commander Wicks, please stabilize the ships rotation. Lieutenant Williams, please verify there are no near objects that could pose a threat."

Williams worked frantically for about a minute, then reported, "Captain there is nothing within sensor range that will come remotely close."

"Sir, the ship's tumble is stabilized," reported Wicks.

"Thank you, Lieutenant Williams. Commander Wicks, activate automated sensor scans. All sections, I am shutting down Deflector shields." He touched the green light labeled *Deflectors* and waited for it to turn red. "Deflectors are down. All sections stand down. You are free to move about the ship. Outstanding job, people. Section heads, stand by. Lieutenant Davis, close the ship wide com."

Davis gave him a thumbs up and then said, "Sir, Section heads are on line."

"Okay, everyone, status reports in four hours. Commander Clay, I want to hear from you as soon as you have our location. Any questions?"

Dr. Niece spoke up, "Captain, I have red lights all over my board. I'm not sure I'll have a complete status in four hours."

"Do what you can, Doctor. I'll meet with you last. That will give you a little more time. Anyone else? Lieutenant Davis, close the com." He stood next to his chair then walked to the door. As he released the four lugs, he said, "I'll be in my cabin. Do not hesitate to contact me if you need me. Commander Wicks, you have the bridge." He opened the door and walked through.

Dill was several steps down the corridor when he heard Davis announce, "The Captain has left the Bridge."

Dill waited for the people in the small room to settle down. It was the same group that attended after the first jump and this time he felt the anticipation as he called them to order.

"Okay, everyone, this is going to be a pretty quick meeting. I have met with all of you, individually, and will pass on what I have learned to the group. If anyone has additional or more current information, feel free to speak up at the appropriate time."

He paused a moment then turned to Edith Clay. "First, I want to congratulate Commander Clay on the course she plotted for our first jump home. If the rest of you have not heard, her 'Best Guess' course was beyond our expectations. We are now within two hundred light years of Sol . . . well within what I believe is a distance we can overcome." He smiled.

"Commander Clay has provided us with a course, so, we will continue our original plan with two short jumps to calibrate our final jump home. During those jumps we will accelerate, using the Plasma Engines, until the batteries are fully charge and we have reached a speed of 13.280 miles per second. We will activate the Warp Field for two different lengths of time . . . the second being exactly twice the first. Using the data gathered from our first jump toward home . . . the one we just completed . . . and the two smaller jumps,

Commanders Wicks and Clay and I believe we will be able to make a fourth jump relatively near the Sol System and then a final jump into the system, where we can contact Earth or the project test platform. The Plasma Engines are in excellent condition and we have enough fuel to last for another twenty-one days of constant acceleration. We should finish our mission with more than enough fuel. Ship's Systems, Deflector Shields, and Life Support Systems are all fully operational and should remain that way, as long as the batteries are charged. And, of course, that is also a function supported by the Plasma Engines. Food and water are not an issue at this point."

Dill looked around the room, for the first time showing concern, "When we came out of warp this last time, we had a few issues with the Warp Drive. Dr. Niece tells me that the two jumps have put an incredible strain on the Warp Coils. He requires a minimum of two days to get the Drive fully operational and ready for the next two jumps. That is well within our current battery charge. After the repairs are completed, we will take another day to run diagnostics on the Warp Coils and then continue with our two test jumps. Those two jumps will be very short in duration and we hope will have very little effect on the Drive." He paused and looked closely at Niece. The man looked exhausted and, as hard as he tried, could not hide the concern he clearly felt.

"I want everyone to stand down for the next twelve hours," said Dill. "And I mean everyone, Commander Wicks. I want you to sleep, relax as much as you can." He turned back toward the two scientists, "Especially, you and your team, Dr. Niece. Dr. Bellows, that goes for you and your team as well. Let the computers monitor the ship and don't worry about it for the next twelve hours. Are there any questions?"

Niece spoke up immediately, "Captain, I have far too—"

"That is an order, Dr. Niece. Do not make me confine you to your quarters. Not that it would make that much difference, considering our lack of space on this ship."

Niece shrank back to his seat without uttering another word.

The meeting ended and for the next twelve hours the crew seemed to relax. Dill actually heard laughter on several occasions. A few times, he wanted to rush down the narrow corridor to find out what was so funny, but knew his presence would stifle the mood. He stayed to himself and tried very hard to stay out of the crew's way.

Niece simply couldn't wait the full twelve hours and was back to work in ten. Dill was ready to make good on his threat, until he saw Niece. The man was clearly rested, so Dill simply smiled and left him to his work. At eleven hours, Niece's entire team was back on the job, equally rested and ready to attack the mountain of work ahead.

The repairs to the Warp Coils took the full two days that Niece had estimated and Dill was surprised at the amount of physical labor that was required. But the rest of the crew stepped up and even stood in line whenever the call for help came out. Dill was proud of them all and a little surprised at how high the moral seemed to be. It didn't take long to realize the difference was Brad Wicks. Without exception, every six to eight hours he made a complete pass through the ship. He spoke to everyone, asked if they needed anything, talked to them about their current task, or reminded them to update their logs. If they needed something, he personally tried to help or get what they needed. The revelation only re-enforced Dill's knowledge that he truly was lucky to have him on board.

They lit the Plasma Drive with almost twenty hours of battery power left. The ship accelerated for three full days on Plasma and then, traveling at 13,300 miles per second, or .073 the speed of light, they activated the Warp Drive. The drive was active for one and a half minutes. Commander Clay required all of two hours to identify their exact location. They had traveled fifteen light years closer to home and Dr. Niece reported only minor issues that could be corrected within one day. It was decided that they would start the next jump in two days. After the post jump status meeting, Dill held Niece, Clay, and Wicks to continue a point from the meeting.

"Commander Clay, you implied that you felt confident in getting us pretty close with the next jump," said Dill. "How confident and how close?"

"Sir, the computation turns out to be an exponential curve, based on our speed when warp is initiated. I can plot a far more accurate course at .073 LS versus .5 LS. My initial calculations say within 1 to 3 light years. After that, I should be able to put us within Saturn's orbit."

"How long will the warp drive need to be active?" asked Niece.

"About four minutes for the first jump and 30 to 60 seconds on the last one," said Clay. "I can give you the exact time for the first jump in a few hours."

Wicks spoke up, "Dr. Niece, can you hold that thing together for four minutes?"

"Four minutes shouldn't be a problem, and you know, Captain, if Bellows hadn't made those unauthorized changes, we would probably be stuck somewhere in the center of the galaxy. His changes reduced the heat generated while powering the Coils. I think we would have fried the coils on the first jump home. Without knowing it, he has probably saved all of our lives."

Dill smiled and glanced a Wicks, "Well I can't pat him on the back for breaking protocol. I'll add it to the ship's log and amend the incident report recommending no disciplinary action. Brad you can let him know that we all know what he did and then remind him how lucky he is."

"Yes, sir. I can do that," replied Wicks.

Clay cleared her throat, "Uhh . . . Captain, while we are speaking freely, I would just like to say, I'm very glad you didn't add those additional thirty seconds that I recommended to the first jump home. If you had . . . well, I have no Idea where we would have ended up." They all turned to her questioningly. "Remember I said it was an exponential curve? My best guess would be another twenty thousand light years beyond Sol. Honestly, who knows?"

"Well, we got lucky with that one," said Dill.

"Sir, with all due respect, there was no luck involved," she said.

The meeting broke up and the work began.

Two days later they began accelerating. This was their fourth jump and they all knew what to expect and what to do. When the Warp drive was activated they tolerated the mild discomfort and anxiety. After three minutes and fifty-six seconds, the Plasma engines shut down and, with all systems again operating on battery power, they simply waited to hear their location. Thirty minutes later Dill made the announcement.

"Attention, all personnel. Our Navigator has informed me that we are less than one light year from Earth. Commander Clay, I call that a job exceptionally well done. Okay, everyone, you all know the routine, status reports in four hours. I'll meet with section heads individually. Dr. Niece, I'll meet with you last."

Twelve hours later the post jump meeting began. They were all excited. One more jump and they would be home. Compared to the others, Dill and Niece were a little subdued.

"Actually, this jump was by far the most successful. We have demonstrated the ability to control the jumps and arrive a reasonable distance from a specified point. This basically proves the Warp Drive is the future of space travel. In fact, with our first jump, we inadvertently opened the entire Universe to exploration by the human race. It is imperative we return our findings to Earth. Dr. Bellows, Dr. Niece, Commander Wicks, and Commander Clay are summarizing their findings: the changes to the Plasma engines, required changes to the Warp Drive, and recommended design changes to this vessel. We will begin transmitting the data as soon as it is ready. We will send the data as many times as possible, until we make our final jump. If anything should happen to us during the final jump, Earth will get our data in about a year, assuming they will still be listening for us. If everything goes as we've planned, they'll be downloading our computers in about ten days and will be amused in a year when the message finally arrives."

Dill paused, then continued. "Okay, why so cautious? Dr. Niece has reminded me several times that this Warp Drive is a prototype. It has a life expectancy of three jumps and a maximum operating time of twenty-three minutes. We have already exceeded both of those limits and we are dangerously low on the liquid Helium used to cool the Warp Coils. Now, I am convinced that he can keep the drive operational for the forty seconds we need to make this next jump. We will begin acceleration in three days, and six days from now we will activate that Warp Drive one last time. Forty seconds later, Commander Clay assures me, we will be within twenty million miles of Earth. Are there any questions?" He waited a few seconds. "Does anyone have anything to add?"

"Lieutenant Davis, are Dr. Bellows and Dr. Niece ready to join us?"

"Standing by, sir."

"Add them to the Bridge com and allow the ship to listen in." He waited for the thumbs up signal from Davis then said, "Dr. Bellows and Dr. Niece, have each of you completed your internal check lists?"

Bellows answered first, "Plasma Engine Warp Transition Checklist is complete. All systems are at peak operation. We are six minutes from .073 light speed. We are ready for warp."

Niece spoke up, "Warp Transition Checklist is complete. All systems are at *Ready* state, however, twenty percent of my supporting systems are showing yellow lights. We are withholding coolant until five seconds before activation. We have done all we can. The Warp Drive is ready."

Dill silently took a deep breath. "Attention all personnel. We are about to activate the Warp Drive for the fifth and final time. This jump will last exactly thirty-nine seconds. We expect to be within twenty million miles of Earth when we come out of warp. You are probably asking yourselves, *Why not closer?* The answer is pretty basic to our survival. We must keep the batteries fully charged and our life support systems operational during these last few critical steps. That way we know that when the Plasma Drive shuts down for the last time we have five days to get help. Our navigator has plotted our course. Using the Plasma Engines for acceleration and breaking maneuvers, the course will park us in Earth orbit twenty thousand miles from our docking platform and operating on our last fully charged batteries. Commander Wicks and Lieutenant Commander Williams will then take over for the next twelve hours, using the ship's maneuvering rockets to get us docked."

Dill waited a few seconds then continued, "Alright then, step one." He checked the acceleration time counter and the Warp Drive ready lights, "We are four minutes from Warp Field activation. Dr. Niece, my panel shows all systems are ready. What is your status?"

"Captain, I still have a lot of yellow on my panel, but all systems are showing ready for warp."

"Commander Wicks, complete your final Warp Checklist," said Dill.

Time flew by and in what seemed like seconds he heard Niece say, "Adding Coolant to the Warp Coils!"

Wicks continued, "four . . . three . . . two . . . one . . . *073 light speed.*"

Dill reached forward to the console and pressed the first of the two remaining flashing red lights and held it until the light turned constant green. "Warp Field Generators are activated and are charging. Warp field timer is set to thirty-nine seconds." He watched the remaining flashing red light. "Warp field ready light is red." Dill said nothing until the light changed, "Warp field ready light is yellow." He waited again, this time his hand hovering above the flashing yellow light. As the light turned green his hand slammed down and he held it until it was constant green. The ship's alarm sounded and Dill said, "The Warp Field is active. The timer is running and is at thirty seconds." At twenty seconds the light began to flicker, then stabilized. "Dr. Niece my light is flickering."

Niece replied, "You're okay, as long as it's not red! The coils are overheating!"

Dill felt more helpless than he had ever felt. He could do nothing but watch as the light flickered again and turned a blazing yellow. At eight seconds, it dimmed and began to flicker again. "Dr. Niece, I have a Yellow light and flickering!"

Suddenly, there was static coming from the com speakers and the light flickered back to green. He stared at the light, willing it to stay green. Then, without warning it turned solid red. He wanted to scream, then he noticed the Plasma Engine light was also red. It took him a second to realize the Plasma Engines had shut down normally and the jump had ended as planned.

"Commander Wicks, please stabilize the ships rotation. Lieutenant Williams, please verify there are no near objects that could pose a threat."

A few seconds later Williams reported, "Captain, there is nothing within sensor range that will come remotely close."

"Sir, the ship's tumble is stabilized," reported Wicks.

"Captain, I have lost communication with Dr. Niece. There is no response from anyone in Warp Systems," said Davis.

"Commander Wicks, can Ship's Systems tell me what is going on in Warp Systems?"

Wicks began checking and within seconds said, "Captain, Life Support has automatically isolated all compartments within Warp Systems. The internal temperature of those compartments is well below minus three hundred fifty degrees. I can find no indication that anyone is alive in those compartments. Ship's emergency systems are venting high concentrations of helium gas into space. There seems to have been a failure to contain the Warp Coil coolant."

Dill was silent, realizing he had just lost seven of his crew, including Dr. Niece. "Thank you, Commander Wicks, please activate automated sensor scans. All sections, I am shutting down Deflector shields." He touched the green light labeled *Deflectors* and waited for it to turn red. "Deflectors are down. Commander Clay, do you have our location."

"Sir, preliminary calculations indicate we are between nineteen and twenty-one million miles from Earth. I'll have exact location in about twenty minutes."

"Very good, Commander," said Dill, straining to keep his command voice intact. "All sections stand down. You are free to move about the ship. All personnel, stay clear of Warp Systems and under no circumstances attempt to enter any of those compartments. Section heads stand by. Lieutenant Davis close the ship-wide com."

Dill put his head in his hands and leaned forward. He remained that way until Davis finally broke the silence.

"Sir, section heads are standing by," said Davis quietly.

He sat up straight. "Okay, step two. Status reports in four hours. Keep everyone working for another eight hours. I want them exhausted, so that when they climb into their bunk they'll think of nothing but sleep. Not home, not anyone in Warp Systems. Dr. Bellows, I want this ship underway as soon as possible. Commander Wicks, provide whatever support he requires. Lieutenant Williams, I want a complete report of the impact to the ship by the loss of Warp systems. Is there any impact to Life Support? The ship's structure? Hull integrity? Was any other system on this ship impacted? And so on. I want that with the other status reports. I'll meet with you last. Commander Clay, as soon as you have a course, I want you and Commander Wicks to verify the plasma burn time for both acceleration and breaking. Lieutenant Davis, you are back on Communication full time. Start transmitting our location to Earth and, as soon as you have them on line, I want to talk with them. Any questions? Close the com, Lieutenant" He waited for Davis to confirm. "I'll talk with Mission Command in my cabin. Commander Wicks, you have the Bridge." He stood next to his chair for a second then turned and left the bridge. He paid no attention to Davis' announcement.

The ten-minute delay was driving Dill crazy. For over three hours, he had answered two or three questions, then waited ten minutes for a response, then responded to a response, and answered the next few questions. He finally decided that it would continue as long as he allowed it. He decided to answer the most current set of questions, then put an end to it.

"Admiral Simons, as good as it is to talk to the command center again, I really must get back to my crew. Once we have reached Earth Orbit, I, and the entire crew, will be available for debriefing. To help with Mission Control's evaluation of data, I will have Lieutenant Davis and Commander Wicks begin transmitting the Ship's Log, which is virtually an hour by hour record of what happened on this ship over the last five weeks. There are voice entries from every crew member and computer logs of every button or switch thrown on this ship. I will ask the crew to also provide their personal logs for historical purposes. That is, of course, up to the individuals, and we will include only those that are willing to share their logs.

"To answer your last question, I looked at Dr. Niece's final log entries. It seems the Warp coils were over-heating to the point of catastrophic failure. Had they failed, the ship could have been destroyed. He personally flooded the coil chamber with the remaining liquid Helium, buying the ship another five seconds. That allowed the Plasma Engine Generators to shut down on schedule and gracefully terminate the jump. He had to know the coil chamber could not withstand the pressure of that much liquid helium heating and expanding to gas. The chamber walls ruptured and the entire compartment was frozen solid before the drive shut down. He saved the lives of everyone remaining on this ship and possibly the lives of your next crew. We will not attempt to recover bodies, or even enter Warp Systems, until we are docked. I don't want to take the risk of disturbing anything that could help the next mission.

"Admiral, with your permission, I will sign off for now. I'm sure we will talk again in the next few days. In the meantime, Sir, if you can find time, please contact my parents and tell them I love them very much. Dill out."

*W. A. Fix is a retired Information Technology Professional, who, with his wife and three cats, lives in the suburbs of San Diego, California. Several of his works are published throughout the Web. He is a featured author in* The Future Is Short: Science Fiction in a Flash *(volumes 1, 2 and 3) anthologies of flash fiction and he has longer works in* Visions: Leaving Earth, Visions II: Moons of Saturn, Vision III: Inside the Kuiper Belt *and* Twisted Tails IX: Wunderkind.

# ABOUT THE EDITOR

Carrol Fix writes and edits for Lillicat Publishers. She is the editor of the *Visions Series*, science fiction short story anthologies describing human exploration of space, including *Visions: Leaving Earth, Visions II: Moons of Saturn, Visions III: Inside the Kuiper Belt*. She was an editor for *The Future is Short: Science Fiction in a Flash, Vol. 1*, and for a biography, *Sunshine & Shadow: Memories from a Long Life*.

Carrol is a short-story author and novelist whose science fiction work includes the award-winning novel, *Mishka: Book One of the Quadrate Mind*. She is currently writing the second book in the *Quadrate Mind Series*, while working on a young-adult fantasy novel, *Worlds Apart*. Her most recent short stories appear in *Visions: Leaving Earth, The Future Is Short: Science Fiction in a Flash, The Future Is Short 2: Science Fiction in a Flash, Twisted Tales IX: Wunderkind*, and *Perihelion Science Fiction Online Magazine*.

A former computer consultant who has lived in six different states, Carrol currently resides near San Diego, California, USA, in a household containing three generations of grandmothers, of which she is one. Her brother, W. A. Fix, a frequent contributor to the *Visions Series*, occupies a well-deserved spot on her list of favorite authors.

http://www.lillicatpublishers.com
http://www.mishkabook.com

# VISIONS IV: *SPACE BETWEEN STARS*

## Visions III: *Inside the Kuiper Belt*

## VISIONS II: MOONS OF SATURN

**Top 10 Finisher**

Best Anthology

PREDITORS & EDITORS
READERS' POLL 2014

## VISIONS: *LEAVING EARTH*

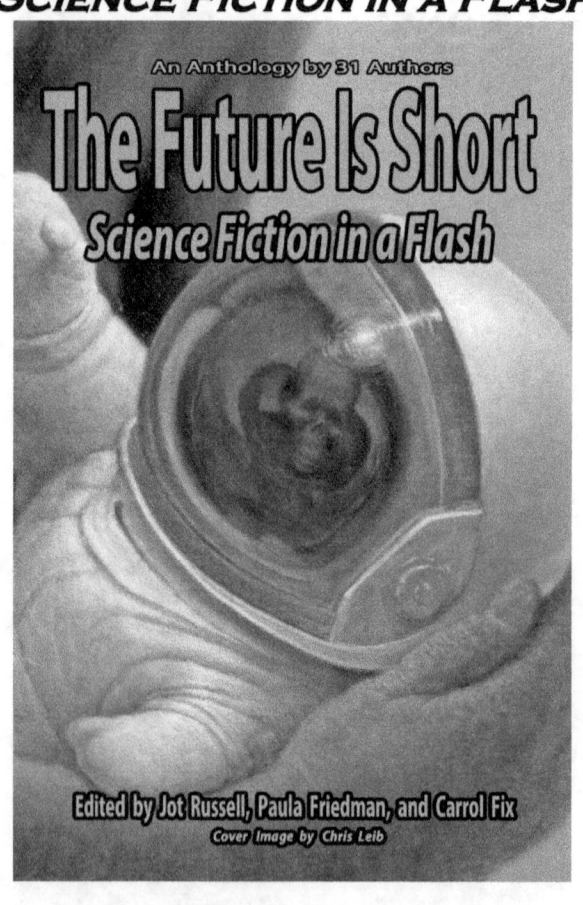

*. . . and coming soon!*

## VISIONS VI
## GALAXIES

www.ingramcontent.com/pod-product-compliance
Lightning Source LLC
Chambersburg PA
CBHW070351260626
47161CB00001B/106